fork this life

Volume One

An Internet revolution tech tribute
by: ryan rutan

https://www.forkthislife.com

This is a work of fiction. Names, characters, places and incidents either are the product of the author's imagination or are used fictitiously. Any resemblance to actual persons, living or dead, events, or locales is entirely coincidental.

Copyright © 2020 by PolarPort Interactive, LLC
All rights reserved.

All product names, logos, and brands mentioned therein are property of their respective owners. All company, product and service names referenced are for identification purposes only. Use of these names, logos, and brands does not imply endorsement.

Other trademarks and trade names may be used in this work to refer to either the entities claiming the marks and/or names or their products and are the property of their respective owner.

Published in the United States by PolarPort Interactive, LLC

ISBN 979-8-6497-5426-2

For more details, questions, or feedback, please visit:
https://www.forkthislife.com

Luke,

Don't ever let the world dim your shine ♥.

Stay awesome :)

This novel pays tribute to all those who lived at the bleeding edge of technology during the mid-late 1990's. This pivotal era of technical innovation ushered humanity from the digital dark ages and into a more open, connected and informed world.

Life is a marathon with unexpected twists and turns. When things don't go as planned, you can lay down and get steamrolled, or say, "fork this life" and make a new plan.

DEDICATED TO

To my loving, intelligent and supportive wife, *Michelle*, and our insanely wonderful daughters, *Maddi* and *Abby*.
Life is so much sweeter with your crazy in it.

To my tribe of friends that radiate nothing but support, positivity and, above all else, constructive feedback to continue to strive for excellence no matter how long it takes.

*Mel/Adam/J/A, Travis/Steph/AB, Colleen/Susan/M/B,
Megan/Brian/C, Deirdre/Em, Kimbo,
Mom/Dad/B/H/T/C*

And, last but not least, to a group of individuals, often faceless, that made some eternal memories growing up!

*Ian C, Multi, Kas, spiffy, Peter/Curtis/Ryan, Stephen S, Jessica V,
ElCooCooi, KingTut, Capper, Jaden, SpinCycle, AceX,
Jester, Spectre, Jigga, Fool, Kodiak, Maverick*

This book is also dedicated to anyone who has ever dared to try something new, or reached for something bolder, in the hopes of finding happiness, meaning or fulfillment in this crazy thing we call life.

FEATURED TRACK

Sonic Youth - Bull In The Heather

1

Oh, What A Night

There I was, standing buck naked at the base of the clock tower, and somehow, I knew that compared to recent days, today wasn't so bad. Judging by the complete absence of my shadow, it must have been near high noon. I could feel sunbeams splitting the puffy clouds hanging across the beautiful blue sky and searing the crown of my head. All signs pointed to the makings of a typical central Texas summer afternoon. I heard a collective murmur in the distance and turned to face it. To my surprise, I was center stage at a graduation ceremony in The Quad at The University of Texas at Austin. A sea of faculty and students adorned in black robes, burnt orange stoles and caps hanging from their necks perplexedly watched as I instinctively stumbled back toward the podium.

Something wasn't right. Foregoing my obvious lack of clothing, something was definitely off. Thoughts raced in rapid succession through my head: *What's the topic? Why am I speaking? Valedictorian? Public flogging?* I placed my hands on the podium rails, taking full advantage of my newly found forward facing cover, and tried to focus on the task at hand. The only problem, I didn't know what it was.

My cerebral cortex was flooded with incoherent thoughts, but one stood out more than the others: *I dropped out of college?* Compelled to say something to diffuse the gurgling tension in my bowels, I leaned forward to the microphone and said the first thing that came to mind. "Texas …?"

As if by twisted Pavlovian conditioning, the chorus yelled back in unison, "Fight!" With an accomplished smile, I turned to the faculty seated behind me to celebrate. I wasn't sure if it was my exposed pasty buttocks, my recent demonstration of high-quality oratory skills or possibly a combination thereof, but every one of them shook their heads in abject disapproval. One of the observers at the end stood up and began to walk in my direction. I started to feel warm. Not that good pit-of-the-stomach warm feeling you get when things are going right. This was the *shit is hitting the fan and you're standing bare-assed center stage in front of a bunch of strangers,* kind of warm. Panic sweats ensued as she walked closer, I assume she because of the massive red hair updo that levitated her ceremonial cap, I could only focus on the blood-stained golf club she held tightly in her hands. The last coherent thought I remembered passing through my mind was: *I wonder if Tom was watching.*

*** FLASH ***

Concussions can make for a nasty injury. Symptoms include grogginess, memory loss and a sensitivity to light and sound. That crazy lady must have given me a good one too, because I felt like I had every one of those symptoms dialed up to eleven. I instinctively reached for my head to check for a bump or some sort of medical grade dressing, but all I felt was the familiar feeling of disheveled hair, glasses and patchy facial scruff. Savoring this reassuring sense of normal, my hands raced to inspect the rest of my body. I was pleasantly surprised to find myself fully clothed, but I was lying on the ground with a bright light shining in my face. I peeled myself away from what felt like a cocktail soaked adhesive strip when an outstretched hand cut through the blinding light with a washed-out voice that said, "Get on up here, buddy." With a jerk, I felt my entire body rip from the floor, and I was standing in the middle of the

TapHouse stage holding Patty's meaty hand. I took a few moments to collect my thoughts and make sense of my new, yet familiar, surroundings. It was Trivia Night, and from the looks of things we were in the middle of a sudden death finals match. Standing next to Patty was Anto and Morgan, but where was Angie?

I surveilled the room hoping to find her somewhere in the wings. I checked the bar near her favorite beer tap, the one that looked like a stoned Big Mouth Billy Bass, and the jukebox where we always fought over which song to play with our last quarters. No dice. As I spun back around to the group, I noticed our team was squaring off on stage against our arch-rivals, the J4ck4l5. On any given day, these guys were annoying douchebags of the highest order, but when it came to trivia nights at the TapHouse, they were annoying douchebags who were infuriatingly good at pub trivia. Something felt different about tonight. They seemed smaller than normal; weaker even. Perhaps this was the night we finally had a chance to break their streak, but I couldn't stop wondering: *Where was Angie?*

A familiar anxious feeling crept into my stomach. I frantically cataloged every facial feature in the bar. Not once did I spot her oh-so skeptical furrowed brow or her distinctive smirk amongst the crowd. I looked left, then right and behind me, still no Angie. Anto is now telling me it's my turn for the face-off. Without thinking, I walked towards center stage and placed my hand on the table next to the buzzer. Keith and his aromatic Axe alpha-male aggression were waiting for me. The moderator reads the question aloud, but his voice is incoherently muffled, like listening to someone yell through four feet of water. I see Keith raise his hand for the buzzer. I don't want him to win. *He can't!* Not tonight, not this time! My hand exploded into the air like a cargo net shot from a cannon to envelop the buzzer. *What was the question?* I may not know, but I'll be damned if I don't at least try. As my hand closes in on the buzzer, the room stretches, and the button begins to bob and weave in circular patterns that invoke nausea and dizziness.

I can feel my consciousness fading, but I need to press the buzzer before it's too late. As soon as my hand makes contact with the sweaty plastic bevel, my eyes close and I hear a loud obnoxious buzzing sound erupt in my ear drum.

****** FLASH *****

A cold splash of water hits my face, and then another. I'm standing in a bathroom hunched over an exceedingly short sink cabinet with the faucet ricocheting pails of water off the counter edge. The sporadic splashing of the water on my face feels cathartic and calming, despite the accompanying wet shirt and pants, but leaves me with a familiar question. *Where the hell am I?* While I could assume it was a bathroom of sorts, I could tell right away this was not one of the bathrooms at TapHouse. For one, the floors were not covered in rubber tiles but rather a short shag carpet that tickled the stretched skin between my toes. Water dripped down my face, while I blindly searched for a hand towel to dry my face. *Found it.* Just to the left of the sink, affixed to what felt like a carpeted wall was the unmistaken texture and feel of a hand towel hanging from a towel loop. I threw caution to the wind and pulled the towel off the hanger and blindly dabbed my face and lips dry. *I smell flowers??*

My reflection in the mirror looked like hell, to put it mildly, almost as if I didn't recognize myself. *Bathroom, confirmed.* The shag carpet was a tacky shade of mint green, and the upper half of the walls were covered in an obnoxiously busy floral wallpaper that Martha Stewart would have gladly exchanged five more years in jail to never see again. Despite the nauseating color palette, textures and overall feeling of vertigo, I did notice one thing behind me that stood out. It was a tall dirty almond colored tub with jacuzzi jets and controls mounted along the back wall. That in and of itself wasn't special, but rather it was the only thing under four feet that wasn't covered in that god-awful green shag. I stared at the tub questioningly and heard a rhythmic sifting sound coming from within, like one of those "sounds just like rain" sticks filled with little high-pitched Nerd candies. I turned slowly, so as to not disturb the rotation of the earth, to further investigate the noise; placing one foot in front of the other veering towards the tub. I had never taken a field sobriety test in my life, but part of me felt like my improving coordination warranted me touching my nose with my finger or reciting the ABC's backwards. The ever-changing laws of physics quickly cured me of my modest humor, and I focused on tight roping my increasingly clumsy ass to the tub.

As I got closer, I could make out a dark brown hue around the inside of the tub. It wasn't water, or even liquid. It looked like a pool filled with tons of tiny brown beads. With each step closer the pool seemed to double in size, making it the largest bowl of cocoa pebbles I had ever seen. *Why am I not hungry?* When I reached the edge, I saw a very disturbing visual. It was Wade. He appeared to be buck naked and was playfully backstroking half submerged in what was now clearly a large vat of coffee beans. In retrospect, I wish my brain would have registered the sight earlier and protected my innocence, but the presence of this *memory?* proved I had already suffered substantial traumatic damage. I distinctly remember seeing him flipping over to deep dive into the mound of coffee beans and seeing an ass-crack full of coffee beans smiling back at me like chocolate chips on a lopsided stack of pancakes. At this point, I couldn't tell what made me sicker: the bathroom decor or naked Wade flopping around in his pool of coffee beans. Before I had a chance to deliberate the question, an answer was forced upon me. The divot in the pit where Wade went under began to undulate and shift in place like an earthquake about to erupt. Wade exploded to the surface with a steaming cup of coffee in his hand. He looked me directly in the eyes with his innocent Cheshire smile, and asked me the same question he has asked me every day since the first day we met. *Coffee?*

That's it. I'm going to hurl. Committed to action, I turned around and lunged for the crusty shag covered toilet seat. *If I miss the toilet, people may not even notice!* With that in mind, and who knows what in my stomach, I prepared to release reparations to the porcelain gods with any grace and humility I might have left. My forehead was sweating, and my heart raced. I couldn't keep my eyes open, and I knew this wasn't going to be pretty.

*** *FLASH* ***

My torso shot forward like a catapult, with my hands extending out to catch what would most surely have been the Mary-est of Hails in the history of projectile vomiting. Alas, this immaculate reception was interrupted by a series of violent dry heaves, and the realization that I must have been dreaming the whole thing. I placed my hands on the surface below me to steady myself and collect my thoughts. A sense of calm, tainted with the hallmarks of an early onset hangover, washed over me. For even though my eyes were crusted shut, forehead sweating, stomach churning and head pounding, I could smell the familiar surroundings of home and my own bed. *And grease?*

My hands felt my ninety percent off, bargain bin, Egyptian cotton three hundred thread count bed sheets as the deafening sounds of modems handshaking in the server room below echoed in my head. Even though at this very moment it felt like the slightest pin drop of noise could split my cranium in two, those screeching sounds were inexplicably soothing tones for my soul. I wiped the crust from my eyes to see a white-hot supernova exploding just outside my window. *Damn it, Ben! Shut the blinds next time.* With eyes closed and my hand shielding my face from the morning sun, I haphazardly scrambled for the blind cord across the room using a blend of drunken parkour, Riverdance and the occasional desperation induced Jedi Force reach. *Jackie Chan wishes he was this smooth.* Fifteen adventurous seconds and six profanities later, I managed to find myself sitting upright back against the wall, with the blinds shut and only one shin throbbing as much as my head. Let's hope this wouldn't be my highest achievement of the day.

The room was now pitch black, but I could finally see. *I am Riddick.* I observed the wake of destruction left by my blind closing gymnastics maneuver, and I felt a distorted sense of accomplishment. *At least the window didn't break this time.* My toppled clothes hamper had regurgitated two weeks of well-worn t-shirts and shorts across the floor covering the remnants of my personal collection of failed DVD-R burns strung together on a bungee cord. There was a shimmering blue shiny mound of something hanging off the edge of my high-quality full-size futon. It looked like one of those party bright colored wigs that people wear at crazy new years parties. I immediately turned my attention to the other side of the bed, which, given the clear impression in the pillow and comforter, looked as though someone had slept there, and it wasn't me. *I'm a right side of the bed type of guy.* My attempts to recall any memories of the previous night, and who might have been in my bed, were thwarted by a hammer crushing pain behind my right eye socket. It was time to start the morning pilgrimage to the bathroom. I grabbed the blue wig from the foot of the bed, hoping the tactile texture would spur some sort of lucid recollection. Sadly, the only thing I could think about while staggering towards the door were the imminent perils that awaited my feet on my long quest to find the toilet.

I consider myself to be a *typical* introverted nerd bachelor minimalist, which means my paychecks are spent on rent, internet, electronics, food, comic book sci-fi toys and then everything else. Actually, my rent is dirt cheap and internet is free, *thanks Tom*, so I guess that means it's just electronics, food and toys, which sounds about right. Every day I open my bedroom door to face my impressive all-in-one kitchen/dining room/living room micro-apartment and I'm reminded just how set in stone those priorities have become. Specifically, the optimal placement of my computer desk in the living room and then everything else. My workstation is a thing of beauty and is by far the most expensive, ornate and well-planned area in my apartment. I could go into excruciating detail about every last rig customization, or the strategic placement of my Todd McFarlane Spawn collectible in relation to all the other figurines, but there are hardly enough seconds in a decade to do it proper justice. It's easier to focus on the hodgepodge shit-show of furniture and half-assed decor that comprises the rest of my humble abode.

In the near corner of the living room, I have a bamboo papasan held together by crumbling reed straps and duct tape with an *authentic* Hawaiian themed cushion. My TV is connected to my computer and centered in front of a large black *faux* leather couch located in the middle of the room. *Peeling the backs of your legs, arms and ass from it on hot summer days was especially pleasant.* The coffee table in front of the sofa is covered with a lineage of gaming consoles that included an NES, SNES, N64, DreamCast, PlayStation and PS2. Every connected cable and controller were meticulously tucked away and stored to reduce unnecessary tangles, and each console was connected into a series of interconnected 4-port AV switch boxes. Playing any game in this setup was a bit like cracking a safe combination to get started, which I thought gave the experience a bit more "je ne sais quoi". Next to the TV, as it should be, I have my floor to ceiling media case filled to the brim with CDs, DVDs and various gaming media. *Yes, they are all sorted and alphabetized.* Finally, encapsulating this space are perfectly positioned speakers and a massive subwoofer to immerse myself into the full Dolby 6.1 experience. *It pays to not have neighbors!*

The dining room and kitchen are practically one in the same, as there is little space between them and they each receive the same level of detailed decorative attention. *None.* The dining room table is small, round and wedged into the far corner with two mismatched, *but comfortable*, padded chairs. The kitchen counter, *if you can call it that,* has a simple sink, a microwave and an electric hot plate with very little room for anything else on the counter, except the toaster which rests on an ever-present counter-height stack of pizza boxes. The remaining kitchen is mostly occupied by an oversized refrigerator heavily stocked with half empty random condiments, two percent milk, Mountain Dew and a six-year-old five-pack of Jolt that never seems to disappear. On the random occasion I want to channel my inner Emeril, I'd whip up a box of Hamburger Helper in one of my overly abused and misused pans and settle in for a night of fine dining. *BAM!*

Practically every furnishing in my apartment, sans my bed and toothbrush, were acquired through people's discarded moving day bargains, including my collection of broken lava lamps sitting atop my kitchen cabinets and a spinning disco light ball I got for a dollar at Spencer's on clearance. I didn't take pride in the state of this eclectic collection, or how I acquired it, but I also didn't care. All these items had one thing in common. They worked and that meant I could focus my investments on things that mattered most, and while I don't care too much about my general furnishings and non-digital creature comforts, I do take pride in making my apartment feel like home.

When it comes to decorations, I've never considered myself a throw pillow or tapestry kind of guy. Wall posters have always been my go-to medium for accentuating a living space because they serve three critical functions: 1) their uniform size makes them easily replaceable, 2) they can easily cover large patches of imperfect wall and *most important* ... 3) they are relatively inexpensive if you know where to look. Don't get me wrong, I'm not some knuckle dragging heathen who will slap just any notion onto his walls. I have standards. There is a method to survey the field of available options and a process to properly select and place every poster that goes in my apartment. The easiest, *and cheapest,* way I've found to get posters is to contact our local Blockbuster, Hastings or movie theater and request them after they are done using them in the store. Hell, sometimes they have boxes of extras they'll gladly let you comb through just to get the clutter out of their stock rooms. This is the main reason that most of my posters are for movie or music promotions, but there is one wall in my bedroom that is reserved for the crème de la crème in poster decor.

Possibly the most perfect form of artistic expression to adorn the walls in my inner sanctum, Demotivators and their cynical wit inspire me daily to face the world's challenges head-on with the appropriate levels of snark and skepticism. Every New Year's Day, *for as long as I care to remember*, I make a point to add a new Demotivator to my bedroom exhibit. An investment in my growing emotional maturity, if you will.
While it may seem benign to others, the words **Procrastination, Ambition, Indifference, Potential, Stupidity, Idiocy, Irresponsibility** and **Cluelessness** have helped me through some pretty difficult times, and yet I can't help but wonder when I'll finally get around to buying this year's poster to kick-off my next block of eight.

I stood in the doorway with the blue wig in hand and took stock of the war-torn dystopian party central that laid before me. *What. The. Hell!?!? Ow ow ow oooowwww!?!?* I held my breath for what felt like an eternity letting the migraine radiating behind my eyes subside and, if I was lucky, I would wake up again to a world that was a little less broken. I could feel yet another series of daisy-chained head throbs slowly creeping their way from behind my right ear, and it was abundantly clear that this was the real world's mess laid out in front of me in all its glory. Somewhere in all this chaos were clues that would help me figure out what happened to my apartment and suddenly all those years of finding Waldo didn't seem like such a waste.

The first thing I noticed was Anto in her usual spot, curled up in a ball inside the divot of the rickety bamboo papasan. It may not have been strange for her to have crashed there, but the fact that she was covered with beach towels, Cheerios and Trivial Pursuit question cards piqued my curiosity. Patrick's long hairy legs were hanging in a contorted position off the back of the sofa. Judging by his body position and the Crash Bandicoot screensaver on the TV, it looks like he passed out trying to win another upside-down challenge. It's not the first time he's tried this feat, and the blinking retry screen suggests victory eluded him yet again. In the far corner of the apartment, Morgan is sitting with her back to me at the dining table and is fiercely typing on her laptop while listening to her music. Morgan rarely came to the apartment, but it wasn't a surprise to see her working, even this early. *What time is it?* She was always creating algorithmic masterpieces constructed of the cleanest source code of any developer I had seen. Like me, she rarely slept when she felt inspired or was in the middle of a problem. It was quiet given the aftermath, except for the distinct whirring of the oscillating fans running in all corners of the apartment. Piecing together this story was going to take time, but first, I had the sudden unmistakable urge to take a leak. I cautiously shuffled through scattered piles of crushed Solo cups and grease soaked What-A-Burger wrappers on my way to the bathroom, and that is when I saw the whiteboard on the wall near my computer desk.

8̶ 7 Days Left

The number eight was crossed out and the number seven was printed in large bold red letters, circled and underlined, twice. Even in my impaired intellectual state I was able to fully grasp the impetus of the message, and that's when it all came rushing back to me. Thirteen years of memories, emotions and decisions flooded my every available neuron. Synapses relentlessly fired, triggering immense waves of emotion and conflict as I contemplated alternate realities that could have been had I just made some different decisions. My body, let alone my mind, was not in the proper state to handle this fervent trip into my past. My pulse raced. My heart pounded in my rib cage as my forehead sweat bullets. I reached for a chair back to steady the spinning room but grabbed nothing but air. I fell to my knees physically and mentally overwhelmed with my eyes transfixed on the whiteboard as the colored words burned themselves into my brain. Throughout this mental maelstrom there was one name, one face, that seemed to remain clear and constant. An anchor that made sense of all the concurrent emotion, panic and doubt I was feeling. It was Tom.

I deeply inhaled and exhaled to try and salvage what was left of my vertical conscious self, but to no avail I couldn't escape his stare, *his disappointment.* I was overcome with a cruel medley of love, sadness, bitterness and anger all at once. *What would he say, if he could see me now!? Why did you have to go and mess things up? It was all his fault.* I felt cheated and abandoned so much worse than ever before, but more so, I felt the need to prove to Tom that what he did was selfish and wrong. I felt ... I felt ... I felt like I was going to puke. I stumbled to the bathroom, pushed aside Nerm the mannequin, *don't ask,* on my way to the toilet. I lifted the toilet seat and knelt on the fuzzy u-shaped toilet mat under my knees. *At least it isn't green shag.* I firmly seized the sides of the bowl and felt my stomach contents reach escape velocity and achieve exodus into an exciting new world of pipes, sewers and hopefully mutant turtles. My head throbbed like a banging aluminum trash can and my breath fumed concentrated hot garbage. As the water and vacated chum swirled, I could only think about the team and how we got here, but it was clear that neither Angie, Patty, Anto, Wade or Morgan were my immediate concern. The universe wanted my mind focused on Tom. *What did he get me into?*

FEATURED TRACK

R.E.M - What's the Frequency, Kenneth?

2
Thomas Joseph Andersson

Thomas Joseph Andersson was an extraordinary man, and the most influential person I have ever known. While we met each other later in his life, he shared so many stories about his early years that I felt I had lived two lifetimes with him, one as a friend and another as family. He was born in Jollyville, Texas to two relatively young parents, Mark Andersson and Lois Smith. Mark was drafted into World War II in 1942 at the age of 23 and was trained as a field radio operator. His unit took part in Operation Overlord in Normandy in 1944 where he took shrapnel to his right leg from an exploding land mine. He was medically discharged from service and returned home to Jollyville where he met Lois who was a rehabilitation nurse and local women's rights rabble-rouser. They married in 1945, and Tom was born shortly after in 1946. He was notably a mischievous child spending most of his early childhood tinkering with toys and gadgetry, *just like me*, under his father's tutelage. According to him, he deconstructed his first radio at the early age of seven; however, to his family's dismay, he didn't successfully put one back together until he was nine. If you replaced the word "radio" with the words "computer", "Stereo", or "VCR" you could describe me, as well.

The lingering effects of the shrapnel took a toll on Mark's mobility and health over the years. By the time Tom was fourteen years old, his father suffered from frequent bouts of pain and depression and took his own life. Tom believed that his mother was never the same after that day, almost as if she had been broken beyond repair. To help support his family, Tom filled his father's shoes after school at their family's bathroom fixture shop, Andersson's Bath & Bidet. His mother left her regular job and tended to the accounting books for them, while Tom and his grandfather were the primary sales and support staff. Even though he had zero passion for selling bathroom fixtures, he quickly found a rhythm and the sales started to thrive again on multiple fronts. Tom always discounted his role in the business' success, jokingly saying, "Success was practically guaranteed because everybody poops", but it's what he did on the side that was most intriguing to me. When he wasn't selling toilets or faucet fixtures, Tom earned a solid reputation in town for his ability to fix almost any kind of electronic equipment. Customers would bring him their broken electronics, and, if Tom could fix it, they would compensate him by buying a low-cost drain valve for ten to twenty dollars more than the sales price allowing him to pocket the difference. In most cases, when these customers did need bathroom fixtures, Andersson Bath & Bidet was their first choice. Tom always said it was this side business that kept his sanity throughout those early years.

This newfound cadence; however, was short-lived. About two years after Mark passed, Lois died unexpectedly. It was clear that Tom didn't like to talk about this period in his life, so I never pressed him on it. *He only ever mentioned it once.* All I know is that he moved in with his grandparents and continued to work there until his grandfather retired in the late 1970s. By 1981 both his grandparents had passed, and he was the sole owner of the store and the land it was built on. Tom's passion for electronics continued to grow as his tolerance for bathroom fixtures faded. In 1983, he got his first computer, an IBM PC Jr, and from that point on, Tom was hooked. *That man really had a thing for that clunky wireless infrared keyboard.* He decided to sell-off the bathroom fixture business, while keeping the shop, warehouse and land. He used the money to remodel the building, adding a small studio apartment on the second story of the warehouse for him to live in, and by the middle of 1983, Andersson Electronics was selling and repairing all sorts of electronics, with a heavy focus bringing personal computing to the city of Jollyville.

Andersson Electronics quickly became a staple in the community and Tom was rewarded for his hard work with abundant customer loyalty and respect in the community. Like many people his age, with minimal expenses and a surplus of excess cash, Tom acquired a few habits, smoking pot, and *unhealthy* hobbies, like antique collecting. Making matters worse, he also had a newly cleaned warehouse with ample storage to spare, and he was on a mission to fill every last square inch. Old gasoline pumps, glass Lance cracker jars and all sorts of random Americana memorabilia quickly filled the shelves and storage bays in the warehouse, even though Tom rarely interacted with any of it beyond longing glances as if standing on the precipice of a time machine. The thrill of the hunt grabbed a hold of Tom all too often, and rarely let him go too long without an acquisition. His most prized possession by far, even though it didn't run, was a 1967 Sunfire Yellow Stingray convertible. Despite the car being a solid collector's item for any classic or muscle car enthusiast, he was most proud about how he got it. Sometime in the late eighties, one of his regular customers from the bathroom fixture days would always drive it to the shop to show off and inevitably complain about having spent a ton of money fixing something else he broke because he didn't know how to drive it properly. Tom would always respond by asking him, "When are you gonna sell me that Corvette?" One day, the customer showed up and Tom jokingly offered him the best computer in the shop in a straight-up trade for the car. That afternoon, Tom had one less computer and a travel trailer delivered to his warehouse with the non-running yellow Corvette and many of its parts boxed and scattered across the seats and floorboards, as the owner had been looking to try and sell it off piece by piece. Even though it didn't run, and he didn't know a damn thing about cars to properly fix it, he loved this vehicle mightily. He would "work" on it in his spare time to clear his mind, which mainly meant sitting behind the steering wheel, top down and smoking a fat doobie listening to music after hours. The only thing that could make this time more complete was if some classic Willie played on the radio; a request he frequently made to any radio station that would listen. It was his sanctuary and most prized possession.

During the early-to-mid 1980s, Tom continued to sell a variety of electronics, but as the personal computing industry surged, Andersson Electronics quickly evolved into the town's dedicated computer shop. During this time, the Commodore 64 popularity slowly gave way to the Amiga 500 and Apple Macintosh which led shop sales until the nineties. They practically sold themselves on name recognition alone, which gave Tom plenty of time to read up on the ever-changing computer industry through his plethora of magazine subscriptions. Shortly after 1990, a flurry of IBM PC compatible clones from Acer, Compaq and Packard Bell running Windows 3.1 dominated shop sales, with each company relentlessly releasing faster models to jockey for lead position. Tom claimed this chaotic period caused him to go bald. I told him that he was wrong. I didn't believe he ever had hair!

In 1992 Tom bought his first computer modem, a blazing 9600 bps phone cradled haus that would open the doors of Andersson Electronics' future wide open. He found a list of bulletin board systems (BBS) in one of his Byte magazines and wanted to give them a try. The allure of a BBS to allow multiple computers to connect to a central location via modems over the phone line to read news, send mail, play games and exchange various information was quite compelling to him. Tom liked the utility apps like FidoNet, email and multi-user chat (MUC) a lot, but he absolutely loved to play the games. Among his favorites were TradeWars *Awesome*, PimpWars *Awesome-r* and Freshwater Fishing Simulator. *We gave him so much shit for that one!* In less than a month Tom committed to figuring out how to launch his own BBS to bring people together and curb his rapidly growing long-distance bill. By early 1993, Tom-NET was born with an impressive twenty local phone line bank running on MajorBBS. Most of his paying members came from advertising on other popular BBSs, but he wasn't quite sure how to promote Tom-NET locally since most of the city's population was mentally and financially tapped out by just owning a computer. This ultimately led him to create the Community Corner where anyone in town could demo new computers or kick the tires on Tom-NET. It was a great idea, which took a while to catch on, but if it hadn't been for the Community Corner, I may have never met Tom *or Angie.*

My name is Benjamin Michael Wilson, but most people call me Ben. Unlike Tom, I was born in Danbury, Connecticut in

1979, *just in time for Carter.* My mother, Elaine, is a registered nurse and tended to work lots of odd hours at the hospital, which gave me more time for mischief than recommended by the surgeon general. We moved to Jollyville in December 1993 after my "father" got caught in flagrante delicto with his "temp secretary" and decided to leave us high and dry so he could "get some perspective" and "find himself". *Asshole!* He wasn't around much when I was younger, and even less when we were eighteen hundred miles apart, which was fine by me. As long as his alimony checks kept my mom from having to pick up even more shifts, he met my minimum paternal expectations. I rarely think of him anymore, but I guess it's important to clarify that when I say father, he ain't it. I never forgave him for what he did to my mother, but I also hated him for what he did to me. Moving sucks but moving over Christmas break to a new state and new school because your degenerate paternal guardian gets caught in an adulterous affair at a Motel 6 by the chatterbox wife of a resident priest, really sucks. When asked if we were moving to distance ourselves from him, or the onslaught of door leaflets and flyers offering to save our souls, my mom simply replied, "Does it matter?" It was a shotgun relocation, the moment my mom got the approved transfer. We packed in four days, found a house to rent in three, travelled for two and unpacked in one. Everything was moving a mile a minute, and I didn't even realize that school started the next morning. *Crap!*

When it came to school, people would probably say that I was an academic slacker. I was in all honors classes, but rarely put forth any effort to surpass my personal minimal academic standards, which was an A-. Every now and then I'd get sloppy and get the occasional B/B+, but I didn't sweat it. It was nothing against Jollyville High School, in particular, I just felt school was a colossal waste of time and that I could learn more on my own if I just had the right books. Those feelings aside, my favorite classes at "JollyHigh", *strangely I was the first to come up with this nickname*, were definitely Computer Science and Math. Both of them came naturally and the teachers could smell it on me like a cheap cologne. From the moment I arrived they tried to recruit the new kid to their various UIL teams. Number Sense. Mathematics. Calculators. Even Computer Science. They had UIL events from them all, but the thought of spending my weekends studying and taking more tests really wasn't my cup of tea. Once I made that crystal clear, they all reluctantly let me be. My Computer Science class gave me a chance to learn a new language, Turbo Pascal 7.0, which was a refreshing upgrade from a less than basic QBasic primer last semester. *PRINT "QBasic sux"* Math was a different story. The Algebra II class was a bit behind my old one back in Connecticut, so I mainly spent the class time writing programs on my TI-82. In a way, that's how I met my best friend, Wade.

It was a Friday about three weeks into the semester, during Algebra II, which was my last period of the day. We were studying matrix multiplication that week and the teacher was a real hard ass on showing your work. I felt it was tedious *and redundant* to show all the intermediate steps when I could do most of the math in my head. So, I decided to make a program that would display all the intermediate steps for me, so all I had to do was copy it down. Some might consider this cheating, but I didn't. It takes a lot to fully understand a skill to write a proper program, and I felt that the effort to master the subject should warrant some residual benefits. Thanks to my program, I finished that Friday's quiz thirty minutes ahead of the next person, a fact I noted as I pretended to double check my work until said person turned in their quiz to not draw attention. After class, Wade tracked me down in the hall.

"Hey man, you're Ben. Right?" he asked pausing only long enough to take a quick sip from his coffee cup.

"My name's Wade. You like coffee?" Before I could respond, another one of his half-life pauses expired. "It looked like you blazed through that quiz pretty quick. I've never had a problem with math before, but all these matrix rules, or how she makes us do it ... *head exploding motion* You must be pretty meticulous about checking your work though. I could have sworn I saw you finish way earlier."

At this moment, I had the sneaking suspicion I was about to be blackmailed, but to my surprise he finished his rambling comments asking for help.

"Any chance you'd be interested in helping me get the hang of this matrix multiplication stuff? I'm free now, if you are? We can go to FlowJoe's." Before I could even think to respond, he blurted out. "I'll drive." I'm not sure if it was my unconscious altruistic nature, or merely the fact that he had a car and I was already tired of riding my damn bicycle, but I agreed. I tossed my bicycle in the back of his beat up 1985 Chevy step side, and we were off to FlowJoe's Coffee House. *Wherever that was?*

After about an hour of tutoring I realized he understood the basic concepts just fine, but he was making way too many nonsensical arithmetic errors along the way that compounded his problem given the way the teacher graded. I showed him the program that I wrote and offered to put it on his calculator so he could check his work after the fact. I also told him that he should put a few errors here and there and slowly improve rather than being better overnight. Even though I believed that I was in the right, I was nothing, if not overly paranoid about getting caught and having to explain my actions.

"This program is wicked! How long did it take you to make that?" Wade was ecstatic, but not exactly talking to me, from what I could tell. It was like he was having an outer-inner dialogue with himself while maintaining eye contact with me, but not waiting for my response. *This guy was weird, but funny.* "This calls for a celebration!"

He surged from the table and rushed to the counter to order a Cappuccino and a double slice of banana bread. When he returned to the table, there was an odd silence that fell on our conversation. He slid me the banana bread, but he was preoccupied counting the number of times he stirred his coffee. 9 ... 10 ... 11 ... I knew absolutely nothing about this guy, so I just picked up the conversation where he left it.

"About a day," I blurted out, awkwardly poking at the walnut chunks in the bread through the cellophane.

"Really? That's it. Damn, you must be smart!" he replied.

"Yeah," *I can't believe that worked*, "The base program was pretty straight forward, but I had to spend a lot of time tweaking the output format to make it easier to copy down the steps." I proceeded talking about the program's technical merits, but Wade's eyes still focused on his stirring until they glazed over completely and became unresponsive. For a second, I thought his heart literally exploded from a caffeine overdose. I had first-hand accounts of three cups of caffeinated beverages in the past three hours, but based on his rapid speech, I suspected he had to be pushing at least seven or eight for the day at this point. *How does this guy even sleep?* He eventually blinked, shook his head a bit and snapped back into the conversation as if nothing happened and took another refreshing sip of his go juice.

"Man. You must really be good at computers." he joked. "Have you ever been to Andersson Electronics?" He pointed across the street. *How had I been in town this long and not known about a computer store? WTF?!?!* "It's a pretty cool place. He's got some interesting techie magazines to look at and you can mess around with the computers if you are interested. I sometimes challenge Tom to a game of Minesweeper. That guy is really ... really good!" *Minesweeper ... great! =*

The rest of Wade's commentary fell on deaf ears as I stared at the large neon sign on the roof and craned my neck to attempt to see through the window glare across the street. I wanted to go check it out right now, but it was getting late and my mom was coming off her shift in a few hours. This was definitely the high point of my day! Wade and I left FlowJoe's a few minutes later and he dropped me off at my house.

As I unloaded my bike, Wade had an epiphany, "You know, I have to drive by here to get to school anyways. If you'd like, you can ride with me. Meet you here around 7:35 on Monday?"

My mind was still riding a high from discovering the computer store, and I immediately agreed. Not riding my bike to school was definitely a bonus, and while Wade seemed a bit crazy, our eccentricities seemed to balance out. Besides, I was not a morning person, or an exercise person and definitely not a morning exercise person. *It's worth a shot.*

I saw Wade's smile grow ear to ear like the cat from Alice in Wonderland, as he yelled, "Later, Homey!" and gunned the accelerator.

I remember the next morning like it was yesterday. It was a Saturday, January 22, 1994, and I had just gotten my shareware copy of Doom in the mail the week prior. According to the instructions, my home machine met the *minimum* system requirements, but after installing it I was rudely introduced to the world of *recommended* system requirements. The menus were sluggish, the sound was choppy, and the weapon-toting marine crawled like he was Virgil in an assisted walker traversing the bolgias of Hell. There went my Saturday, best laid plans ruined because of my dad's slow ass computer. *Damn you, marketers!* I was about to spend another day playing a copy of Lands of Lore, when I thought about what Wade said about the

Community Corner at Andersson Electronics. Without hesitation, I threw the floppy disk in my bag, grabbed some snacks, Discman and headphones and jumped on my bike to go see if this supposed computer place lived up to the hype.

When I pulled up to the shop, I parked my bike under the "Help Wanted" sign in the window and walked inside. A loud set of door chimes struck against the top of the door and announced my arrival to the room. There was a distinct welcoming smell of fresh electronics and static, freshly vacuumed carpet and Nacho Cheese Doritos. *My favorite.* To my immediate right were four long, high tables with two computers on each of them powered by an impressive daisy-chained array of power strips. It was ordered chaos in its purest form. Towards the back on the right, a bald guy, *Tom,* was talking with an older guy at a glass sales counter filled with various modems. Behind them was a large glass window with opened blinds that appeared to be the manager's office. On my left towards the back, near the side parking lot entrance, there was the magazine rack with a couple of comfy chairs in front. It wasn't the largest selection I had seen, but it had the usual suspects: Byte, DOS Resource Guide, Wired and Popular Mechanics. To my immediate left were two long tables, with two computers each, nuzzled in the corner of the room underneath a "Community Corner" sign and centered between two large pane windows located on the front and side of the building. *Score!* There was an open bag of Doritos and a backpack at one of the tables, so I chose the other one and got to work.

I reached around the back of the computer and plugged my headphones directly into the sound card and tried playing one of the embedded Windows test sounds. *Nothing. I guess the sound card isn't properly configured.* I reached into my bag and pulled out my handy MS-DOS boot floppy that got me out of or into plenty of trouble back east, *depending on your perspective*, and pressed Ctrl+Alt+Del. Once the computer rebooted, I started slowly tapping the Del key to engage the BIOS setup. This rig was a screaming 486DX-66/8MB, at least six to eight times faster than my wimpy 386DX2-40/4MB at home. *This is going to be fun!* I ensured the boot disk order included the 3.5" floppy first, saved changes, and then restarted the computer using my boot disk to a familiar flashing **A:\>** cursor. I first opened **C:\CONFIG.SYS** and moved some devices to high memory to free up conventional memory. *OCD Habit*

#178. Despite the quick tune-up, the file didn't have any noticeable errors related to the sound card. Then, I checked **C:\AUTOEXEC.BAT** and found the root problem. The included sound card utilities were properly initialized, but the root directory was missing from the system path. *SoundBlaster 16. Nice.* I confirmed the directory and appended a quick **;C:\SB16** to **PATH**, saved changes, removed my boot disk and waited for the computer to restart. The Windows startup sound exploded from my headphones and I was now cooking with gas.

    I inserted the Doom disk into the floppy drive and ran **A:\>install.bat** as it was written on the label. All that mattered in life right now was the slowly moving progress indicator. The next three minutes dragged on as I listened to the computer grunt and snort lines of data from the floppy disk to the hard drive. *Installation complete.* Woohoo! **C:\DOOM\DOOM.EXE** <ENTER> The game loaded insanely fast and I remember thinking the glowing red eyed skull menu cursor was a nice touch, a detail lost on my piddly home computer. New Game <ENTER> Knee Deep in the Dead <ENTER> Hurt Me Plenty, Ultra-Violence or Nightmare? *Pace yourself.* Ultra-Violence <ENTER> The game loaded and in no time, I was shot gunning zombies and monsters in a 3D-like hell covered in blood. *This was awesome!* The next two hours were a bit of a blur, but I do recall craving some of those unguarded Doritos behind me. I made it to Mission 8 and was squaring off against the Barons of Hell, and I had just landed a shotgun blast center mass on one of the Goatman twins. I circle strafed around a pillar for cover and quickly switched to the BFG to unload in his general direction. *Damn it, I missed!* Before I could reload, I got nailed by a plasma ball from his twin brother and died. That is when Tom tapped me on the shoulder with that iconic smile on his face, and we talked for the first time.

    "I see you got the sound card working. I was just about to throw it away and buy a new one. What did you do, if you don't mind me asking?" he asked in a joking manner. *I think he was joking, right?*

    "Mainly just fixed some typo's in your system path in the AUTOEXEC." *Damn it!*

    I just admitted to tampering with the computer. My brain was still focused on the game.

    "It was missing the SoundBlaster utility folder. That's all." I finished begrudgingly.

In an effort to try and not get kicked out of the first cool place I had found in town, I offered up more details.

"I also cleaned up some of the CONFIG.SYS as well to free up some more conventional memory, but nothing else really. I promise." I was doing my best to hide the fear from my face. If this were my computer, I would go ballistic if someone installed something on it without my permission *which they would never get.* I was already typing **DELTREE C:\DOOM <ENTER>** in my head and rehearsing a fake apology in preparation for the impending ass chewing. *It was worth it!*

"What game is that?" Tom asked.

What? I was shocked. I blinked like twelve hundred times and then blurted out, "uh, Doom ...?"

"Doom, huh? Mind if I give it a whirl?" Tom slid right in and loaded my last save game. I tried to show him the keyboard and mouse controls really quick, but he insisted on getting right in there. On his first attempt he lasted maybe ten seconds, fifteen tops. He tried a few more times, and then just laughed a bit.

"It's no Minesweeper, that's for sure! I guess this just isn't my game. You seem to have a good handle on it, though. I've been watching you on and off for the past few hours. You really gave that keyboard and mouse a beating." he laughed.

"Sorry about that," I used my sleeve to wipe the sweat off the palm rest, "sometimes I just lose track of time when I'm playing games. ... ... Also ... sorry about installing the game without asking, I just really wanted to play it, but my home computer wasn't quite up to snuff."

"Oh, don't worry about that. You fixed the sound card, so we'll just call it even. OK?" I think I smiled my first sincere adolescent smile.

"I've never seen you around here before. New to town?" inquired Tom.

I instantly became self-conscious about my accent. I didn't have a stereotypical New England Boston accent, it was a more subtle southern New Englander, but perhaps it was the absence of the Texas twang, *like Wade,* that gave me away.

"Yeah. My mom and I moved here about a month ago. I just learned about this place yesterday." I replied.

"Well then, allow me to Welcome you to Jollyville, and to Andersson Electronics. I'm Tom Andersson. The owner." Tom extended his hand. "What's your name?"

"Ben ... Ben Wilson." I replied, reaching out to shake.

"Well then, Ben Wilson. Did you happen to see my Help Wanted sign out front. *I had.* You seem to be pretty handy with computers. Any chance you'd be interested in some part time work? After school, weekends and such?"

Let me get this straight. I mess with your computer without your permission and you offer me a job? It was too good to be true. It seemed like a trap. Good things never happened to me without the other shoe dropping in quick succession, but truth be told it had been a long time since I had seen even one good thing, so I might have just been overdue. My mind immediately went dark. *This guy's a pedophile. Run!* I took a moment to let saner thoughts prevail, and then asked for clarification, "What would I be doing?"

"Pretty much whatever is needed in the shop. Help fix computers. Computer sales, if you are up for it. Helping people on Tom-NET, or in the Community Corner. You know, figuring out computer stuff with me ... and the occasional window washing and vacuuming of course," he chuckled. "Stuff like that."

It sounded perfect, and I could definitely use the money. Besides, there was something genuine about Tom that just made it feel like the right thing to do. "Sounds great," I replied, "when would you like me to start?"

"How about next Sunday? I've got some things going on tomorrow, but I'll show you the ropes then and we can go from there. $10/hr. sound fair?"

My jaw nearly hit the floor. If I were a cartoon character, my eyes would have popped out of my head like a cash register with dollar sign pupils. Kids my age typically got minimum wage, which was less than $4.25/hr. This was more than double, and I got to work in the town's ONLY computer shop. *Calm down.* I swallowed my excitement and eked out a tempered, "Sure. I guess"

We shook hands for the second time that day and sealed the deal. "Sounds great. Will see you 8AM next Sunday," Tom said. He gave me a quick pat on the upper back and went to talk to a new customer that just walked in. I stared at my hand in disbelief. *Did that just happen?* As far as I was concerned, Mission 8 could wait for another day. I closed out Doom, re-opened Windows to how I found it and re-packed my bag. I turned to head out, and that was the first time I saw Angie.

She was well into A Tale of Two Cities and crunching on what were probably the most delicious Doritos ever made. I think my face was stuck between expressions; part smiling about my new job and awestruck by her deep brown eyes and black hair, because she laughed with her quintessential smirk when she saw me over the top of her book. *Wow!* Like a smiling drunken T-Rex, I did a quick short hip-locked elbow wave in her general direction and bumbled my way out the front door. *Smooth, Ben! Real Smooth!* I wanted to tell someone about my awesome day. My mom was unfortunately still at work, but I saw Wade's truck at FlowJoe's. He'd surely get a kick out of me working here. I saw Wade sitting at a corner table flicking sugar packets against the wall like paper footballs. *This guy is strange.* I wasn't sure where I was going to begin. Would I talk about fixing the computer? Finding the BFG? Getting the job? Whatever it was, there was a more pressing matter I needed to attend to first. I went to the front counter and said, "I'll have your biggest bag of Doritos. And a glass of water."

FEATURED TRACK

Green Day - She

3

Today Was A Good Day

There is so much that can be said about Angie, it's hard to know where to begin. Angela Marie Swanson was born in Jollyville, TX in 1980. She was almost one year younger than me by age, but always four to eight years more mature. Unlike most kids her age, and even some older ones, there was no question on what she wanted from life. She grew up as an only child in a small trailer park about four blocks from Andersson Electronics and tucked behind the library. Her father was an auto mechanic who owned a small shop a few miles away, and her mother was a career waitress juggling two or three restaurants at any given time. Both of them, more or less, were absentee parents for her young adult life, but it wasn't always that way. She wasn't a fan of talking about her family, but over the years she slipped up a few times and made brief mentions of wildly planned birthday parties or fond family Christmas memories. Something along the way changed, and it forced Angie to become more independent. *Something we both understood.* Her parents gave her a meager allowance for food, clothes and general spending, but she earned extra money tutoring kids after school and on the weekends. For all her intelligence and *uh-mazing* looks, it was her sharp wit and kindness that I always found most attractive. Little did I know that this simple job offer from Tom would intertwine our worlds in the most spectacular ways.

Mom came home extra late that Saturday, so I had to wait until Sunday morning to share the news with her about the job and carpooling with Wade to school. After she shared her textbook cautionary tales of doom and gloom, "What does this old man really want?" or "Does his car have passenger-side airbags?", we eventually agreed to give it a try as long as I didn't suffer academically or physically. Next weekend could not come fast enough. I spent the rest of that Sunday compiling index cards of helpful DOS commands and Windows hacks I'd learned over the years and kept them in my backpack. It was busywork of the highest order because I knew practically every character by heart, but patience was not my strong suit.

I stood outside my house Monday morning waiting for Wade. Part of me wondered if he would even remember that he offered to pick me up, or if he was so caffeinated that he attributed our conversation to a tree. I really didn't care if I was late to school today or *missed it all together*. My mind kept skipping forward to the weekend leaving the weekday obstacles obliterated in a wake of collateral damage. About two minutes before I called "no joy" and began pedaling my bike, I saw Wade's truck barrel around the far street corner like the bus from Speed blaring loud music. His factory speakers crackled under the strain of Dexter's shrill voice as they played Bad Habit by The Offspring. Wade was impassionately yelling along to the song, treating the coffee cup in his hand as a makeshift microphone.

Drivers are rude ... Such attitudes... ♪ I knew what lyrics came next, and I didn't want my mom, who I knew was listening from her bedroom, to freak out about Wade's behavior behind the wheel. I quickly tossed my bike in the back, hopped in the passenger seat and slammed the door.

"Gotta keep this bus above 50, Annie!" I joked. "Let's go!" My hands drummed a rapid beat on the dashboard. Wade got the reference and replied, "Let's get this big Pinto on the road! Ha haaaa"

He punched the gas with a crazed look in his eyes and we were off just in time to not sully my mom's prying ears. I can't say the same for other houses on our street. *You stupid dumb sh...* ♪

We got to school with plenty of time to spare, which was a new experience for me. I had grown accustomed to hog-tying my bike to the rack and slipping into class right as the bell's final echoes finished ringing. Wade parked in the student on-campus parking lot and I thanked him for the ride as I muscled my bike out of the truck bed so I could go lock it up. He threw me a nonchalant wave of acknowledgement with a thumbs up gesture but didn't let the comment break his concentration on a magazine he started skimming the moment we parked. *OK Then. Moving on.* I walked by the main office and caught a glance of that unmistakable black hair through the window. *Doritos girl.* She was talking to some athletic football guy towering over her. Her patchwork blue jean jacket looked great from the ... *clank* My bike pedal clipped the metal flagpole and I fell over the top of my bike trying to catch my backpack and seek cover. *Smooth, Ben. Real smooth.* I dusted myself off and turned to see if she was still at the counter. *Did she see me fall?* She was gone. Thankful, and yet annoyed, I locked my bike chain, dropped my books off at my locker and went on to my favorite first period class, English. *NOT!*

That was the longest school week in known student history. It was like the Earth changed orbits and created five additional leap year catch up days all crammed into a single week. Every day felt like some drawn out Breakfast Club purgatory, passing the time by counting the clock seconds and shoving pencils in my nose. *Ok, maybe not that bad.* There was a saving grace to all this boredom and that was plenty of time for people watching. I had been in school nearly three weeks and could tell you how many floor tiles there were from my locker to the cafeteria, but I had not paid much attention to any of the faces in the crowd, except for Wade and *maybe* my teachers. I discovered that we had quite a few goofy looking people at our school, but strangely her face seemed to keep popping up everywhere I went. It felt like every twentieth person I noticed, turned out to be her. Regardless if I was walking in the hallways between classes, or waiting in the Hot Pocket line at lunch, I could always pick it out of the crowd, and once I noticed it, I couldn't look away. Hell, I even started seeing her mesmerizing smirk on clock faces and poster boards throughout the day. Fate was either inundating me with signals, or I was going certifiably nuts! *Possible Doritos overdose?*

It also didn't help that I was on edge about starting a job. I had never really had a real job before, unless you call my mom negotiating a "character building" rate with our HOA in Connecticut to push mow a two-acre entryway during the peak months of summer humidity, a "real job". *Thanks Mom!* Anxiety permeated my every thought and action, so I sought distractions where I could find them. I debated many times over whether to visit the shop early and get a leg up on my first day, or just play it cool. *What should I bring? I never asked about a dress code!?!* No decision that week went unscrutinized. I obsessively packed and repacked a separate backpack full of cables, boot disks and snacks for the first day. Every time I caved and jumped on my bike; I would swing back around by the time I reached the end of the block. I was effectively paralyzed in a never-ending flux of indecision, and all I could do was wait. *Argh!?!!*

  The week wasn't a complete waste though. Wade got an "A" on his next quiz and just like that we were done with matrix math. It was smooth sailing for him from then on out. Apparently, this was an odd rough patch for him, as he had the reputation of blowing the curve on most of his classes. Including this one. *Why did he need my help?* On the surface he was a model student with his perfect attendance record, *since Kindergarten,* but deep down I knew the signs of someone who didn't want to fully apply themselves to school. He had a few honors classes, but he wasn't your typical grade grubbing maniacal honors student. He applied himself just enough to keep his pride intact, but not enough to stand out in the crowd. The more we talked, the more I realized that even though we were born a few thousand miles away we were inexplicably similar at our cores. *Except his core ran on unfiltered caffeine.* Every morning, I drafted off Wade's impeccable attendance record and slowly kissed my bicycle riding to school days goodbye. His nine cup-a-day habit quickly became routine for me as well, and by Saturday evening, I stopped the hypocrisy and accepted Wade's coffee choices and quirks and focused on my own dietary issues which now consisted of downing four to five snack bags of Doritos a day. I licked the savory remnants of the Cooler Ranch powder from my fingertips, tossed the bag to the floor and vowed to swear them off for good. *Until the next day.*

  My alarm rang promptly at 7:15 AM, and one minute later I was dressed and ready to go. *Sleeping in your clothes has its advantages.* I slipped on my shoes and scurried to the kitchen to wolf down a bowl of Honey Nut Cheerios. Teeth brushed? *Check.* Deodorant? *Check.* I grabbed a granola bar for the road and locked the door behind me at 7:30 sharp. *A new record.* It felt weird jumping on my bike. It was only a week, but it was as if my ass had already rejected the trusty saddle contorts in favor of Wade's worn in truck seat. I alternated standing and sitting to avoid the uncomfortable bruised wedgie feeling that was creeping up my ass. The crisp morning air and warm rising sun made for pleasant eye candy as I zigged through sidewalks, zagged through driveways and jumped the occasional curb. I rolled up to the bike rack at the shop at 7:50 AM and noticed the "Help Wanted" had been taken down. Tom was straightening things by the door and waived me in.

"Good morning, Ben. How was your week?" he said.

"Good enough," I said awkwardly shrugging, "it was a bit crazy though, otherwise I would have been in here more often." I was hoping this would best explain my absence without opening the door for further questions. "What can I do to help?"

"Sure, but before we get started, I've got something for you." He grabbed something from the counter and polished it on his shirt. "I figured you could use this now that you are officially an employee." He handed me my Andersson Electronics name badge with "Ben" already printed on it. I pinned it on my shirt while Tom started his rundown of daily tasks and general work.

I was responsible for keeping all the computers on the floor functional, fast and updated for customers to try. When I was comfortable, I could help sell new equipment and help answer questions and troubleshoot issues over the phone. I'll never forget his next words for the rest of my life.

"Look, nobody's perfect. As long as you keep trying your best and learn from your mistakes, that's all that matters to me." Despite his reassuring tone and supportive words, visions of me accidentally exploding the entire shop in an epic Nakatomi fireball kept popping in my mind. *Keep your shoes on, Ben.* So far, this job seemed too perfect to be true, and I was convinced I was destined to screw it up one way or another.

"Ben?" Tom asked, nudging my shoulder and waking me from my mini-fugue state. "Any questions?"

"Uhhh, don't think so." I looked around at the shop figuring out what to do first. "How about I start over there in the Community Corner?"

"Sounds great! I'll leave you to it," he replied and flipped the switch on the neon "Open" sign in the front window before walking back to his office behind the counter. *Deep Breath!*

I was on a mission to check every floor computer before too many customers arrived that morning and make sure they were all set up the same, including my improvements from last weekend. I pulled my Discman and headphones from my bag and flipped through my CD organizer. Get a Grip. Dirt. Licensed to Ill. Mellow Gold. Gonna Make You Sweat. *Don't Judge.* August and Everything After. Dookie. KoRn. Nevermind. Ten. Pork Soda. Core. Superunknown. Undertow. Blue Album. This morning felt like it needed an extra oomph to get off the ground. *KoRn. Track 05. ▶||. Divine.* With the "computer fixing" mood in full effect, I set out to tackle each computer striking the keyboard to the killer beat. Computer files changed in a flurry as I alternated between computers to save time between reboots. At this pace, I would be done in no time. It wasn't until I completed my first circuit around the table that I realized the first on screen error message, and then another. Two of the four computers I started working on had crashed with large "Application Error" dialogs covering the screen. *Shit!* Perhaps, a bit too much oomph? I promptly swapped CDs and popped in the Counting Crows. I took a deep breath and pressed Shuffle. Starting over one at a time, I fixed my stupid typos and returned each computer to faster working order. By 9:30 AM I rebooted my last computer. That is when she walked in the front door and headed straight for the Community Corner.

She was wearing a pair of well worn-in jeans, a tattered cream-colored Veruca Salt t-shirt and a green plaid overshirt flapping in her wake as she walked to the tables. Her loosely tied black Doc Marten boot laces skipped the ground with every step. She was definitely dressed differently than at school, except the boots. She seemed to wear them every day! Everything about her outfit screamed "Back the hell up!" but nonetheless, I was drawn in like a paper clip to a magnet. Her flowing black hair was pulled back into a disheveled ponytail and her bangs hanging around her blue-tinted circle-lens sunglasses. I was standing across the room in the Sales area, where the grunting noises from the rebooting computers were masking the sounds of my churning stomach. She unloaded her backpack and acknowledged my existence with a tilted head nod and slight smile. I attempted to say "Hello", but my lips, mouth and throat were not in-sync after ninety minutes of solo computer repair and singing under my breath. All that surfaced was a scruffy "heh..." sound. *Weak!* I quickly returned focus to the nearby computer trying to pretend that did not just happen, but I couldn't help stealing opportunistic glances of her reading <u>A Tale of Two Cities</u> around the corners of the view obstructing seventeen-inch monitors. She looked as though she was nearly done with it. I think I zoned out for a few minutes, I don't really remember, because out of nowhere I felt a tapping on my right shoulder that made me jump out of my skin. *Holy Shit!* Before my feet hit the ground, *shortly after my Discman and headphones*, I violently snapped back into consciousness and collected most of my mental faculties. *Some of the physical ones were still rebooting.* I turned expecting to see Tom, or maybe a customer, but instead it was her, standing right behind me full on laughing at my spectacular spazzing Kramer impression.

"Um.... Hi" I said in a confused tone. *How long had she been standing there?*

"He speaks!", she said boisterously as she continued to laugh at my expense. "So, you're Tom's new helper, huh?"

"Uhhh yeah ... I guess. It's my first day." My responses were on an impaired autopilot, meeting the minimal qualifications for an active conversation but dancing ever so close to a fatal crash and burn landing.

"Apparently. I've been in here at-least five minutes, and you haven't even welcomed me. Tom's a bit of a stickler on customer service." she chuckled. *Stupid. Stupid. Stupid.* I felt like a command prompt waiting for a super user to press the <ENTER> key so I could regurgitate some canned responses.

"So, my name is Angie. **BLINKING CURSOR** You must be Ben? **BLINKING CURSOR**" she said pointing towards my name tag. "You're new in town? **BLINKING CURSOR** or just a humble hermit who likes computers? *<ENTER>*"

Something finally switched on in my head. *HCF complete. All systems, operational.* I could sense words and original thoughts, even humor, proof that the neurons in my brain were back in action. I was a fully functioning teenager again. *Relatively speaking.*

"Yeah, my mom and I moved here about a month ago. So, 'No' on the hermit front, but 'Yes' to 'likes computers.'" I slowly tallied each answer off like a five-year-old first learning to count, but my humor finally made a debut. "And the name's, Benjamin Wilson, but you can call me Ben. I've seen you at school, I think?" I reached out to shake her hand.

"Oh yeah, where?" she asked inquisitively as we shook hands.

EVERYWHERE! "Around. Hallways and stuff like that. I mean, I saw you here last Saturday, too. Right?"

"So, you were looking at me?" she laughed. "I couldn't tell if you were making those faces at me or that crazy game you were playing."

"Yeah, sometimes I get kinda lost in the moment." I scratched the back of my head, trying to think of a way to change the subject. All my Doom related material went out the window when she called it crazy! "So, you know Tom pretty well, huh?"

"Yeah I come here a lot," she replied, scoping the room with an air of familiarity, "for over a year now. That corner is the quietest and has the best natural light for reading if you care about those sorts of things."

"I'm a bit of a dark room and loud music kind of guy." *Why did you say that?!*

"That explains the pasty complexion and being hard of hearing, I guess."

I scratched the back of my head, not quite sure how to respond, but maintained a hearty smile. *Ouch!* It's no surprise that the conversation took a determinate pause. I was ill-equipped to carry on extended conversations with members of the opposite sex, but in this case, her banter was intense. I believe she sensed the awkwardness and kick started the conversation with a new topic.

"Tom lets me use the computers for school. He says that I'm here so much, he should just rename the Community Corner to Angie's Corner." There was a hint of sadness in her face as she feigned her chuckle. Perhaps she struggled at the small talk as much as me? "Tom's a really nice guy. He really cares about people. I used to use the library computers, but they are crazy slow and always broken, which is weird because no one ever uses them. Tom keeps these computers up to date, and he even installed Microsoft Office so I could do my schoolwork."

"That does sound pretty cool of him." I replied passively. This was the moment where I first realized that I had stumbled onto something very special here at Andersson Electronics.

"You play board games, by any chance?" she asked.

"Every now and then, but I'm more of a Nintendo or PC game kind of guy."

"Well, Tom and I sometimes play them when things are slow. Are you any good at Trivial Pursuit?"

"I'm OK, the topics are usually a bit dated for me, but I'm not a complete moron." I replied.

"Great, we could use another player to help with the tie-breakers! Anything is better than him wasting away in his office playing Minesweeper. Am I right?" She laughed, placing her hand on my arm and looking me straight in the eyes. A tingling sensation shot through my body, as if Blanka was channeling all ten thousand volts through my body. *Block. Block. Block.* My knees nearly melted on the spot, and unbeknownst to me, my ears started to turn a bright shade of crimson. She bit her lip with a light laugh, and said "I'd better let you get back to work … But … if you ever need anything you know where I'll be … most of the time," she motioned her head towards the corner. "It was nice chatting with you, Ben."

Her final words echoed inside my head as she walked back to her corner. Before she sat down, I had already come to the conclusion: I was hooked. *First Doritos, and now Street Fighter II.* I had talked to a few girls in my short existence, but none before today had ever rendered me completely speechless. As the warm tingling sensations from our conversation dissipated, I could feel the anxiety's cruel grip already starting to squeeze my chest as I worried about possible future talks. I picked up my Discman and turned my music back on and tried to focus on finishing the computers and tackling the rest of the task list. This at-least kept me quasi-normal, while my brain tried to unravel a never-ending deadlock of attraction, angst and hormones.

I made it ten minutes before I stole another peek to see what she was doing, and when I did, I noticed she was making a hilarious pirate face at me. *Or maybe it was Popeye?* I followed suit and shot back my best Ace Ventura smile and mouthed the words "Allllll … righty then". *Sense of humor, check.* We spent the remainder of the day exchanging goofy looks and randomly tossing paper balls across the room at each other, but I was still tongue-tied on how to start an actual conversation. Every time I mustered enough courage, a customer came in, or Tom needed help in the back room. It was extremely frustrating, but on the bright side, I sold four modems on my own that day. When I returned from the backroom, I noticed all her stuff was gone, except her book. I looked up in time to see her walk passed the corner window towards FlowJoe's. *It was now or never!* I ran to the table and grabbed her book. The Mission Impossible music playing in my head was underscored by me also humming the tune under my breath. I hurdled a chair, spun away from the table and took off running out the front door. Just as I turned the corner outside the door, but after no more than three to four steps into my scamper, I noticed she was already heading back to the shop. We met midway at the bike stand. She was obviously amused at my natural running form.

Like a monosyllabic caveman offering a busted bouquet of dandelions, I extended my hand to her and said, "Book?"

"My Hero!" she exclaimed in over dramatic fashion. "What would have I ever done without it?" Her whimsical reaction to the encounter set my mind at ease, and I tried again with a few more syllables.

"That's a really good question, given that I'm not sure what you're even doing with it. I don't think it's on any of the reading lists." I said.

"I take it you are not an avid reader of fine classical literature?" she responded in an apparent displeased tone.

Damnit! "Well ... I like to read, sorta, but I'm not big into all the classics and stuff. I guess you could say I'm more into the ... modern....s?"

"Moderns, huh? What kind of moderns are we talking about?" she knew I was bullshitting her hard. It was time to come clean.

"DOS for Dummies," I replied, trying to frame it as a joke, and not condemn me to the ranks of uncultured swine. She immediately slapped my arm with her book.

"A real page turner, I take it?" *She got the joke.* "I'm just messing with you. I like to read, but it's not always this stuff. This one is for Academic Decathlon, but the story's not that bad." She seemed a bit embarrassed admitting she liked it, and quickly changed the subject. "So ... is this your bike?"

"Yeah, it's my trusted steed. At least on the weekends, I catch a ride with Wade on school days."

"Oh yeah, I heard you two were hanging out."

"Yeah? Is there something I don't know?" At this point I felt like I was being judged. I knew Wade had a few social quirks, but so far, he seemed to be on the level and up front about just about anything, which is something I really respected.

"He's a bit ... odd, shall we say. Good ... but odd." It was obvious she was choosing her next words more carefully. "He definitely gets a bad rap. Ever since middle school, when his dad died, his personality completely changed. He became more agitated, distant ... and jumpy. Maybe it's just all the coffee he drinks, but he's definitely a good guy at heart, I guess. I'm sure he enjoys having someone look at him with fresh eyes."

I had no idea about Wade's father. All this time, I hadn't given two cares about my father not being around, but that was his choice. I started to realize that I didn't know much of anything about Wade beyond school and coffee. Come to think of it, he was always much more interested in me talking about myself than telling me anything about him.

"Thanks for letting me know that. He really is a nice guy, and definitely adds a lot of excitement to the day." I laughed. "Getting back to this marvelous piece of machinery." I patted my bike seat and ran my hands over the handlebar brakes. "Do you have one? Perhaps we can go for a ride sometime?" *Did I just ask her out for a bike ride?* The words escaped my mouth bypassing any quality control filter, as if my heart and hormones were at odds with my brain. I was now in unfamiliar territory and feeling way too comfortable.

"I don't." My stomach dropped. "But ... let's not let that stop us. I'm sure we can figure it out!" She said, patting the front crossbar." She pulled a paper strip from her bag and quickly scribbled something before handing it to me and continuing her walk back towards FlowJoe's. I looked down in confusion to read the message.

Let's Talk Tomorrow at Lunch =) ... Angie

I watched the shoelaces from her boots bounce in rhythmic stride as she crossed the street to the coffee shop in utter disbelief. *Umm ... what just happened?* My hand clinched the note tightly as I walked back with my heart beating out of chest and head spinning. An unmistakable smile was on my face as I leaned against a Community Corner table re-reading the note when a chuckling Tom's voice snapped me out of my trance.

"Pretty good first day, I take it?" he asked. "Looks like you sold a few modems, and the customers said you did a great job answering their questions. You should be proud." He then tossed a paper ball at me nailing me square in the face. "I also see you met Angie. That's something to be proud of too!"

Even in the little time I had officially known her, I knew he was right. I knew she was something special. How often do you meet someone in a small town like Jollyville that is that pretty, smart and likes to hang out around computers? On any given day the chain of today's events could have gone drastically different. I savored the thought of all that had transpired in my first day and simply replied, "Yep, Tom. You're right. Today was a good day!"

FEATURED TRACK

Smashing Pumpkins - Tonight, Tonight

4

Kicking Tires & Lighting Fires

From that day forward, school was never the same. Lunch quickly became my second favorite part of the academic grind, beating out Math but still behind Computer Science, but not by much. Truth be told, I was still getting used to the concept of a social lunch hour. Back in Connecticut, before my world went to shit, lunch equated to snarfing down preservative ridden snacks and playing hack until the bell rang. I can't say I had any deep personal relationships with any of these people, but we all implicitly understood the "no talk, just hack" mantra. The first few weeks of school, I had little to no lunchtime interaction with anyone. The most riveting "conversation" I can remember from that era was a heated discussion from some guys around me in line about which was the better flavor Hot Pocket: Ham & Cheese or Pepperoni Pizza. They looked to me for a tie-breaker vote, but all I said was, "as long as it's not Lunchables, I'm fine." *It's Ham & Cheese, though. Come on!* Beyond that exhilarating Jack Handy deep thoughts moment, lunchtime was spent avoiding the crowds and dodging the standard new kid inquisition. I sought refuge in one of the few places on campus I could eat in peace, avoid the Texas heat with air conditioning and antisocialism was the norm: Chess Club.

On my first day of school, I noticed a sign in the Math hall on Mr. Dan's door about the club's lunchtime ritual: "Bring Your Lunch and Your A Game." To this day, I'm not sure if the school granted this respite indoor dispensation for academic purposes, or if they simply felt sorry for those who chose It willingly. Either way, I didn't mind. Like it or not, many of the kids were just like me. No one had to teach them the mantra because they inherently understood the painful annoyance of unnecessary blather.

I knew how to play Chess, and even enjoyed it on occasion, but no one in the room loved Chess more than Mr. Dan. He arranged weekly brackets populated with random number draws from a hat and kept track of points throughout the year in an official chess binder. One of the few rules in Chess Club was that you had to play at least one game every day to stay in the room. Nearly half of us were using this opportunity as a social escape and we had a not-so-secret silent competition to see who could get eliminated first each day. If we were lucky, we'd get paired up with one of the Bobby Fischer wannabes and deliverance was achieved with a self-inflicted Fool's Mate. *Oh no, Checkmate? Again!?* The remaining players were typically indecisive paste-eating lemmings that were incapable of compiling even a basic strategy to win or *lose*. When paired up with one of these blockheads, it was tempting to swallow your pride and lay your own king out flat just to end the suffering. On the other hand, when two tank masters faced off it was like watching high quality performance art. Each player went to extensive lengths to avoid any resemblance of a winning strategy. It was quite entertaining to watch. When the tanking act was complete, we retreated into different corners of the room to spend the remaining time doing various activities by ourselves. One of the sub-groups in the room was addicted to playing Magic the Gathering and were always getting in trouble for talking too loudly. *Fireball this. Tap that. Assassin lotus thingy. Illegal phase. Blah blah. You're dead.* As for me, I preferred silence, so I hung out in the far corner writing programs on my calculator.

Everything I knew about lunch changed that Monday. Angie and I met outside the cafeteria after collecting our respective foods of choice. I'd be lying if I said I wasn't self-conscious of my Hot Pocket + Gatorade combo next to her salad and Clearly Canadian medley, but she didn't seem to care. We walked around the end of the Science building towards an oddly pear-shaped cedar tree. She slung her backpack in stride onto a small peg from a branch above and took a seat on one of the many bare and weathered low hanging branches. The branch lightly bounced beneath her giving an illusion of comfort. I fought a lesser trafficked branch for a similar relaxed position with less elegance. If you ignored the occasional cedar sap and random twigs poking you in the ass, this place was practically perfect. It was shaded, blocked most of the wind and dust and once you get situated, pretty comfortable. Above all I got to spend more time with Angie, which is all that mattered to me at this point.

      A few days into our new lunchtime ritual, Wade stumbled across us in our hideout after serving a partial lunchtime detention for arguing with the Chemistry teacher about covalent bonds and their relevance in explaining shitty-tasting coffee. *His words, not mine!* Wade normally spent his lunch off campus because it allowed him to listen to music and swing by FlowJoe's to reload his caffeine coffers, but he started joining us for lunch more and more. At first it was just the last half after his refill run, but eventually he started bringing a larger Thermos and our official lunch trio was born. Angie and Wade only casually knew each other in middle school, but they bonded quickly when it came to rehashing the past six to eight years of juicy dirt and school gossip for the entire school. The anonymous people in the halls soon became named faces with backstories and quirks, just like me, and my island of one flourished into a bountiful peninsula of three. It wasn't long until lunch wasn't enough, and I had to see Angie more each day. We passed notes in the hallway and worked out a system to briefly see each other during mutually predefined water and/or restroom breaks. *I had it bad.* I even asked Wade to scrape his brain for anything he could remember about Angie's past on our rides to and from school. Anyone she's ever dated? *Trey Davis. 7th Grade. One week. I hate him.* Rumors? *None on record.* Scandals? *Only one. It involved the school's live mascot named Hambone, a chaotic homecoming football halftime show and an animal's right to freedom. Go Hogs!*

      That's not all we talked about though. I stuck by my intentions to learn more about Wade and try to be a better friend. After a dismally failed direct attempt to ask him about his dad, I shared some insights into my own misgivings about my absentee father figure. The following day, he drove a different route home from school and stopped by the lake overlook parking lot. We sat in silence for nearly five minutes in the truck. No talking. No music. Just the sounds of a light breeze and birds rustling in the surrounding trees. Wade abruptly broke the silence, "My dad died in a car accident in Colorado when I was twelve." He closed his eyes and rested his head on the top of the steering wheel as if he was physically exhausted by his admission. Eventually he picked his head back up, and we had a much-needed discussion.

His dad was on a business trip in Colorado, sometime in January, and he was driving to the airport in heavy snow when he was struck by an oncoming eighteen-wheeler that drifted from its lane. Wade comes to this spot often as it is the closest place he's found that reminds him of the last trip he took with his father to the Grand Tetons. He went to counselling for depression and nightmares for nearly two years before things started getting remotely better. The dad's life insurance coupled with the proceeds from the lawsuit against the trucker's company was enough that Wade's mom paid off their house and she never had to work again. Instead of a job, she used the opportunity to follow one of her passions of becoming an author. Unfortunately, after three years, according to Wade all she had amassed were a collection of disconnected chapters best suited for one of those trashy romance novels. Wade didn't go into further detail and I didn't ask.

Many things made more sense about Wade that afternoon. First off, Wade's nearly endless funds for coffee despite not having a job? His family wasn't rich, but they rarely worried about money, and given how frugal he was, it left him with an unusual amount of discretionary spending money for the small indulgences he enjoyed. Second, Wade's intense infatuation for coffee? This one connects back to mornings with his dad before work. His father would always brew a pot of coffee, and Wade loved the smell of it, but hated the taste. After his father passed, Wade kept brewing the coffee in the mornings, but poured it down the sink. When his mom told him it was wasteful, he started drinking the coffee rather than give up his regimen and quickly acquired a taste for it. Lastly, his beat-up truck and why Wade spent so much time in it? It was his dad's truck, plain and simple, and he was committed to squeeze every last mile out of it. It's also the reason why he didn't follow the typical Texas teenager path and drop a new stereo and subwoofers into his ride. Wade and his dad would go on long drives just to talk and listen to country music and the way the speakers still crackled on certain songs was far too sentimental to warrant replacement. These were some of Wade's fondest memories with his dad that he wanted to hold onto as long as possible. Pushing all that macho crap to the side, I really felt for the guy and the raw hand he had been dealt and from that day forward, I knew our friendship was truly something special.

  Our carpooling escapades would continue to become even crazier and memorable through the years, but not without one small improvement to kick start the fun. Practically every car driven by a teenager in Jollyville was defined by its car stereo, or lack thereof. Wade's stereo was pretty old, but sounded good enough, but it only played cassettes, which put a damper on me contributing tunes to our drive with my CD collection. Since he wasn't keen to upgrade his stereo, I did him one better. With one of my first pay checks from the shop, I bought Wade a small appreciation present: a CD-to-Cassette adapter and DC power kit for my Discman. It felt a bit like when Homer gave Marge that birthday bowling ball with his name already engraved into it, but now we could finally have some musical variety besides Wade's six rotating cassettes. This option added a whole new level to our carpool shenanigans. My Discman was a few years old and didn't have the fancy anti-skip protection of the newer models, so every time Wade jumped a speed bump or cornered hard, the music would stop while it rescanned the CD. It became a game for us to see just how much we could get away with before the Discman cried "Uncle". Our biggest claim to fame was catching at-least two feet of air exiting a deep intersection dip going twenty-five miles an hour and successfully cradling the Discman through the bumpy landing and we didn't miss a beat! *Suck My Kiss!* ♪

  By the time Spring Break rolled around, I was on autopilot. My only variance was whether or not school was in session. When I wasn't in school, I was pretty much working, or hanging out with Angie and Wade. When I was in school, I was wishing I was working, or hanging out with Angie and Wade. This well-oiled machine was able to sustain itself, despite the weekday academic interference, but there were now so many more parts of the day to look forward to that I carried considerably less contempt for school than normal. Every weekday started out with a nourishing bowl of Honey Nut Cheerios, or the occasional Captain Crunch, and a Pop Tart for the road. *No sprinkles. Gotta keep it healthy.* Wade and I would rock-paper-scissors for DJ and blast music all the way to school. Our musical tastes were pretty compatible; however, every now and then Wade would throw a curveball and play some ICP or Ace of Base just to mess with me. *Admittedly, it wasn't all THAT bad.* Angie was usually already at school studying in the library. *She was relentless!* She wasn't in any of my classes because she was a sophomore, but between our various water fountain rendezvouses and lunch, I got just enough of her to make it to the end of school without twitching from withdrawal. Thankfully, she hitched a ride in our after-school carpool to the shop. By this time, I started to work every day from four to seven in the evening and six-hour shifts on the weekends. We usually had thirty minutes or so once school let out to make the five-minute trip, so we'd routinely take more scenic routes if there was a good conversation going, or we just wanted to listen to music. When Angie was with us, there was no contest for musical control because she volunteered to ride bitch in front of the stereo. Besides, she had great taste in music and was always full of musical trivia nuggets relevant to the song. This is how I got into Veruca Salt and 4 Non-Blondes and entered my tangential alternative chick rock phase. Wade was the epitome of punctuality, and always made sure we arrived on time. Not so much so that I wouldn't be late, but because he really didn't want to miss the end of FlowJoe's afternoon prices. Angie and I typically carried the conversation into the shop while he ducked off for a fresh cup, and that's just how things went. After work, Wade's reliable taxi service would drop her off, then me and we would repeat it all over again, every weekday.

  Saturdays and Sundays were a bit more open, since I didn't have to be at work until noon, which was great because I loved to sleep in! Mom was usually at work, or sleeping in herself from a long night shift, so there wasn't a lot of time for face-to-face interaction. Our main source of contact was a notepad on the kitchen stove. Each morning, I would stumble out of bed and pedal to the shop to meet up with Angie by ten o'clock. Wade was always sitting in his favorite corner at FlowJoe's usually on his second cup by the time I rolled up and would come and join the party in the Community Corner. My shift each day was fairly fluid, since I hung around off the clock often. Working at the shop was the best job in the world because it never felt like work. I literally got paid good money to be around friends and computers, every single day, and that describes pretty much every week through the rest of the school year. *What could be better?*

Wade started spending more time at the shop that summer, and our JollyHigh trio stayed intact. When Tom and I worked with customers, both of them would hover in the Community Corner doing their thing. Angie split her time studying for the SAT and preparing her paper ball arsenal for the next invasion. Wade was less motivated and usually played Solitaire while nursing his coffee. When things weren't busy, we'd all circle up around the service table and play board games to pass the time. *Tom's idea.* Tom's favorite was Trivial Pursuit, by far. Angie's was Scrabble. I preferred 1313 Dead End Drive, but it was harder to set up and play in small intervals, whereas it wasn't uncommon for us to have a background Scrabble game ongoing for weeks at a time. Wade didn't really have a favorite game until we discovered Hot Shot Trivia.

Hot Shot Trivia was a homegrown game that Wade accidentally created when he surprised all of us by reading a stray Trivial Pursuit card he found on the floor aloud, "Pop quiz, hot shot. Who was elected Senator for Tennessee in 1985?"

Angie chimed in the fastest, "Al Gore!"

"One point to Angie!" Wade exclaimed, confirming her answer was correct. He was pleased someone joined him in his revelry experiment, so he continued down the card. "Pop quiz, hot shot. Who attempted to assassinate Ronald Reagan in 1981?"

Picking up on what was now going on, Tom came out of his office with a heightened state of intrigue and responded, "John Hinckley."

"You are correct. Point, Tom!" Wade said in his best game show announcer voice.

Random free minutes accumulated over hours, days and weeks until we finished all the questions in the game. We stored the question cards in an old tin metal tray he repurposed from the backroom, which Tom labelled "Hot Shot Trivia." He mounted it to the wall below a new corkboard we used for scoring, and a larger bin below it where we tossed all the used cards. It was a great way to pass the time, and we all took turns reading the questions in our best famous celebrity voices. Thankfully, the Trivial Pursuit franchise was on a tear, releasing Master and Year in Review Editions, which made for a perfect never-ending game, much like the Sandlot. It also made it extremely easy to buy gifts for Tom, since he loved the new trivia game format. He'd overtly feign surprise at yet another Trivial Pursuit edition, tear into the box, find the cards and then chuck the board and game pieces into the trash. Upon gently cradling the new cards into the tin wall hopper, he would draw a card at random and invoke a six-question lightning round to christen the deck.

Tom was an exceptionally smart guy, not just trivia-smart, but resourceful-smart, too. He was more or less a self-taught electronics handyman and could usually figure things out with little or imperfect information, which led to some interesting problem-solving sessions with our customers. Some people have childhood memories of changing the oil on the family car with their dad. I had troubleshooting customer computers with Tom. Customers would lug their desktops into the shop, and Tom and I would hook it up at the service table, which had a spare monitor, power cord and a bevy of random PS/2 keyboards and mice to help troubleshoot. When it was a mechanical or hardware issue, Tom was like an engineering psychic communing with the analog spirits telepathically to diagnose the problem. When it was software related, I stepped up to the plate with a pretty good success record, but sometimes we were both stumped and that's when the real problem-solving fun started. Tom and I would make a relatively blind guess on what the problem might be and see who had the better instincts. Tom won most of these contests because he knew the customers better and was accustomed to the many technical *and non-technical* problems they presented.

One time we had this older Compaq computer come in since "it keeps locking up when I get online" My theory was that it was an IRQ conflict with his modem and possibly the sound card. Tom chuckled under his breath and wrote his idea on a piece of paper. When I flipped the computer around to plug in the monitor, I noticed that it had two sets of modem jacks on the back. Apparently, this guy recently upgraded to a 28.8k modem, but his computer had an embedded 9600bps modem on the motherboard. My theory was showing promise. *I bet he forgot to disable the onboard modem.* Once the computer was started, I quickly jumped into the BIOS > Advanced > Onboard Modem. *Score! It was still enabled!* I changed the setting to Disabled and confidently restarted the computer. The Windows start-up screen took a bit longer than normal to load, but I figured it was just a slower computer, and then the familiar churns and hums of the computer stopped, and the screen was obviously frozen. *Damn!* Tom said, "Let me have a crack at it." He flipped his screwdriver in the air and caught it by the handle. He opened the computer casing, and the problem was clear as day. Judging by the multitude of colours, hair types and shear volume, our customer had at-least three cats, or a large Mogwai with a shedding disorder. I gagged a bit at the disgusting sight while Tom took the computer outside for a good dusting. While he was gone, I looked at his slip of paper. He nailed it. "overheating power supply caused by cat hair". He brought the computer back holding a freshly frosted bottle of canned air and it booted up like a champ. The customer mindlessly nodded his head as Tom explained how cat hair and dander get sucked into the computer by the power supply fan, and that he should consider opening the case up and blowing it out every month or so. The customer happily replied, "I'll bring it back next month", paid Tom and took his expensive heated cat bed home.

   Tom inverted the canned air and sprayed a cold splash of air on the back of my neck jokingly mouthing the words "King of the Shop" as he did his goofy backwards cha-cha shimmy back towards his office. Some might think that was antagonistic, but this was just Tom being Tom. He savored the taste of victory, but was equally respectful in defeat, and was always on the lookout for the next challenge. *What doesn't kill me, makes me stronger, right?* Tom upped the ante by creating a promotion that if we couldn't diagnose a computer problem in forty-eight hours, he would waive the diagnostic fees. *The computer stores back in Connecticut would go broke if they tried something like that.* Most of our customers enjoyed this competitive atmosphere, and in some cases, they even took a sense of pride thinking they had the next big unique computer stumping problem. Our customers were cool like that, and definitely unique to the shop, as Tom was extremely customer focused. Little did we know that one of our lesser known customers would come in and change the trajectory of Andersson Electronics and Tom-NET forever.

It was a warm July morning in 1995 and Angie and I were having an oh-so enlightened discussion, *a.k.a. argument*, about the musical merits of Hootie and the Blowfish's new single. *What kind of name is Hootie? Seriously!?!?* Tom was in his office attempting to conquer seventy-five mines in Minesweeper, and Wade was madly sipping and clicking away at his latest computer game addiction: Taipei. One of our nerdier customers, Graham, came in to pick up the latest copy of Wired. He would normally stick around the shop scanning the pages and talking random tech with us, but on this particular day, he flipped straight to the back of the magazine and pulled a floppy disk out from inside the cover and passionately flung it into the trash like a frisbee.

"Piece of garbage!" he said, packing his things to leave.

"It's just a disk. What gives?" I asked.

"America Online is such a scam. Forty free hours they say. Horse-shit!!" He took a beat. This wasn't some run of the mill rant. He was legitimately agitated to the degree he was trying to crack the disk open and shake out the bits. "They pass out these disks like candy, and neglect to tell you about all the long-distance fees. Two hundred and ten dollars later, it would have been more cost effective to just mail my computer to Colorado."

"You paid two hundred dollars to use America Online in one month?" I asked.

"No. I paid two hundred and ten dollars to SBC, just for long distance. Then, I paid forty bucks to A-O-Hell for a fifteen-hour overage!" he replied.

I had used AOL back in Connecticut on a friend's computer, but it was just once using the same type of AOL free hours. With all the craziness at school and the shop, I guess I never gave it a second thought about the Internet, since I had a crappy modem on my computer.

Graham started back on his tirade, "AOL. Prodigy. CompuServe. They are all the same. All offering free hours, or unlimited hours, but don't say a damn thing about long distance. If Tom-NET let me connect to the Internet without paying long distance, I'd gladly pay …" He pondered the thought and then blurted out, "… sixty bucks a month. Maybe even a hundred. The savings would be a steal for anyone in Jollyville or the surrounding area."

Tom's ears must have started to burn because he dropped his MineSweeper game midway and came out to listen to the conversation. The remaining few minutes Graham hung around were filled with him firing off profanities at the ISP conglomerates and railing on the goofy picture of Richard Dawkins on his magazine cover. *It was admittedly weird!*

After the door closed, Tom said, "That's not a bad idea. Why couldn't Tom-NET help get people on the Internet?" He reached down below the counter and pulled out a brochure he received from MajorBBS a few weeks prior. On the front, it advertised in big bold letters an upgrade to MajorBBS and a new Galacticomm module that supported TCP/IP for the I-N-T-E-R-N-E-T. I could see ideas rapidly forming and pinging around behind his eyes. He was going to turn Tom-NET into its own ISP.

"Angie." Tom prompted. "Quick math check, please. I have twenty phone lines. Each cost about $5 per line to maintain. Assuming I could charge at-least $50 per month for Internet access, I should be able to get about $900 profit per month once everything is in place. Right?"

"That sounds like an overly simplistic way to look at the business problem, don't you think?" She cautiously replied, "but yes, your math is correct."

"Hold on, I'll be right back." Tom dashed into his office and closed the door. He jumped on his computer and we could hear his modem chattering in the background. Through the window, we could see his colorfully ANSI-decorated terminal scroll as he logged onto Tom-NET. He started chatting with someone online and after the brief exchange he disconnected and picked up the phone to make a call. Tom sat up straight in his chair, puffed out his chest, and spoke firmly with his elbow resting on his desk as if exerting physical dominance through the receiver.

"Woohoo!!!!!," erupted Wade from the Community Corner. "I am the Taipei masteeeeeeeerrrrrr!" By his reaction, you'd think he had cracked the human genome in ten minutes by hand. Wade had finally beaten the game and read his fortune aloud, "Carelessness does more harm than a want of knowledge." He took a moment to let this profound wisdom soak in and then responded to the computer, "Wise you are. Domo arigato, Mr. Taipei" and bowed out as he stepped away from the computer. Angie and I were cracking up, and he even started laughing. The one thing I valued most about our group is that we could always be ourselves around each other. No false pretences. No facade. What you saw is what you got, and we liked it that way!

A few minutes later the battle was settled, and it was official by a vote of two to one, Hootie sucked. Angie argued the jury was tainted by adolescent testosterone, but she realized it was pointless to try and convince two guys who still pissed their pants laughing while listening to Weird Al. *Who doesn't!? I filled that kitty cat so full of lead... hehe!* We may have differences in music taste, but Jagged Little Pill was an album that united us all. Each of us could belt out the lyrics to any one of the songs at the drop of a hat. We were midway into smoothing things out with a chorus of "Head Over Feet" when Tom flung his office door open with the bravado of a man who had conquered the world.

"We have forty-five days." he stated proudly.

"Ummm ... OK, to what?" I replied.

"To figure out how to become an ISP," he replied. The awkward silence was coupled with equally whiplashed blank stares of confusion. "I talked to one of my friends on Purple Ocean who knows a lot of this stuff, and he gave me the number for UUNet in Dallas. I just leased a full T1 line for the next three years at an awesome rate, and I called MajorBBS to have them send me everything we needed to get started. Everything should be here in a few weeks, and the new line should be installed by mid-August. So .... by my calculations, that gives us two weeks to try and figure out how this is all going to work."

He clapped his hands and rubbed them together looking to each of us with an excited look. My first impression was that he was nuts, but to be honest, I didn't really know what to think. We were just talking about this thirty minutes ago, and now it's becoming real. That is how it was with Tom: one hundred miles a minute, downhill and eyes wide open screaming the entire way. Angie and I simply gave a pair of timid thumbs up, but Wade had the more appropriate reaction, when he said, "What's a T1?"

The next few weeks, I spent my free time at Hastings across town skimming the technical books on hand for any tips and tricks I could find on how to connect computers to the internet for basic web browsing and email. One of the books came with a floppy disk of helpful utilities in a plastic zipped pouch inside the front cover. From the looks of the seal, I was not the first person to have this idea. *Unzip.* I made a copy at the shop and returned the disk the next day. *Zip.* Trumpet Winsock dialler and Netscape Navigator 1.0 were included on the disk, and the book referenced how to obtain a copy of the Eudora Mail client. By the time the T1 line was installed in mid-August, I had already cross referenced the TCP/IP SLIP configuration provided by UUNet and MajorBBS, and I was ready to kick the tires.

Tom, Angie, Wade and I watched intently as Tom's modem chirped, squealed, squawked and ultimately connected for the first time. *Connection Established.*

"Now what?" I said, as the connection timer incremented.

"Try this." Angie slapped down a Popular Science magazine with an article about the Internet. I opened Netscape Navigator and typed http://www.shakespeare.com in the Location bar: <ENTER>. The large grey pane wiped clear and slowly rendered a classical picture of ole' Billy Shakes with the phrase, "**W**elcome to the **S**hakespeare **W**eb" in big letters across the top of the page. *We were online!*

Angie spent the following week working with Tom on sales projections and price points. Little did Tom know that his small investment in Microsoft Office would pay dividends via a self-taught in-house Excel grand master. Based on her charts regarding depicted capital investments, expenses and income, it was her idea to create two types of accounts: an unlimited account for $50 per month and a $20 per month option limited to 10 hours a month with overage fees similar to the national competition. This helped get more revenue out of the existing phone lines we had and made the price point more attractive to try. She projected the venture would be on the road to profitability in less than 4 months, if we could get 50 unlimited and 30 limited subscribers by the end of year. With sales planning in good hands, I used this time to make an instructions document outlining the Windows 3.1 installation steps such that we could easily repeat our setups. I even convinced Tom to recruit Wade to help set up new computers part time. After spending so much time at the shop, he was destined to pick up a thing or two about computers between his caffeine injections, and he could easily follow the instructions. My favorite idea throughout this new enterprise came from Tom though, who had a knack for killing flocks of birds with one stone. He drove out to Austin and snatched up all the free AOL disks he could find squirrelled away in magazines and give-away displays. Next he disabled their write protection tab with a piece of electrical tape and converted them into free Tom-NET setup disks with our software pre-configured and ready to go. It was his way of saying "Thank You" while gracefully bowing with a mighty middle finger salute to the big bad national ISP. *I loved how Tom thought!*

August 1st, 1995 was our inaugural launch for the Tom-NET Internet Service. We went all out by paying for advertisements in the local paper and radio spots, as well as working a promotional deal out with Hastings. This made our first week that much more disappointing. We sold only two accounts that week, and the rest of the business was basically the same. Customers came in to get their computers serviced but didn't understand enough about the Internet to try or purchase it onsite. The next few weeks continued in similar dismal fashion and felt like a wet diaper hanging around our ankles. Every positive accomplishment was weighed down with the glaring under performance of Tom-NET's Internet access, but Tom didn't seem to be worried. He was confident things would turn around; it just needed some time. He was right, and he didn't have to wait very long because everything changed when Microsoft released Windows 95.

Everyone knew it was coming, and everyone wanted it, but no one would fully grasp the full impact Windows 95 would have on the computing world. It was more than just new software with a sexy new interface and extra eye candy. It was a fundamental shift from 16-bit to 32-bit software that fuelled an unprecedented surge in demand for new compatible hardware. *In short, just about everyone needed, or wanted, a new computer.* Tom built his first lot of eight Win95 compatible computers on a Friday afternoon in mid-August, and they were ALL sold out in less than an hour. We couldn't build them fast enough, let alone keep them on the shelves. Tom even worked a deal with Ingram Distribution to start carrying copies of Windows 95 upgrade packs, both floppy disk and CD-ROM versions, because they too were hard to come by in our small town. With all this extra business, we started getting more interest in Tom-NET. This was a problem because my setup instructions weren't Windows 95 compatible. *Ah Crap!*

All the software was different, and even if the application name was the same, it had different screen icons altogether in different locations. Few customers actually read the convenient text below the icon. I spent more time during support walk throughs describing what the icon looked like, rather than just say the word listed below it. *Click on My Computer ... the icon that looks like a computer! *smh** By using a combination of the limited Internet resources I found on WebCrawler, and my go to Hastings library, I manufactured a new set of instructions using Dial-Up Networking instead of Trumpet Winsock and downloaded a 32-bit version of Netscape Navigator. *Damnit Microsoft! Why didn't you just install TCP/IP by default!?* Thankfully, by losing the Trumpet Dialer, the larger 32-bit Netscape installation still fit on a single Tom-NET floppy disk. After a few runs to procure some more "Tom-NET Setup disks" and some snazzy new labels, we were up and running and well on our way to reaching our end of year goal.

Summer was coming to an end, and Angie and Wade were no longer passive bystanders, but rather permanent additions to the Andersson Electronics team. Wade setup computers using the playbook I designed for him, while Angie became the grand poohbah of all things money, organization and planning. Even with their help, we were all swamped beyond measure. Thirty-hour weeks weren't going to cut it during school, and Tom was going to be stuck by himself during most of the day. We were victims of our own success, and we needed to find some help, and fast! It was the last Sunday before school started, and we were closing up the shop after another ruckus day of selling and troubleshooting computers for the Tom-NET faithful. Tom wiped his forehead with a weathered sigh as he turned off the neon "Open" light and placed the "Help Wanted" sign back into its familiar position in the window. It was hard to believe it hadn't even been a year since I first joined, and we were already looking to add more people to the team. Thoughts of guilt and fear fluttered through my mind. As much as I hated school, I welcomed the break from the flurry of crazy computer folk and their litany of self-induced problems, but I knew it was the right move for the shop and Tom. I only hoped that whoever joined our team wouldn't disrupt the vibe I had going with my newfound family.

FEATURED TRACK

Jamiroquai - Virtual Insanity

5

Big Fish, Bigger Pond

Customers continued to pile into the shop. Wade and I were so busy doing setups we forgot to pick up our class schedules during early admissions, but Angie pulled some strings for us when she went. I found a free five minutes to review mine after helping an infuriatingly nice, yet doltish, senior citizen setup a dial up networking connection for twenty ... straight ... minutes! *sigh* *What teachers was I saddled with this year?* Pre-Cal-Massey. *Piece of cake.* Physics-Loop. *Could be fun.* Theater Arts-Attaway. *Never talk to random teachers in the hall, at least it fulfills my required fine arts credit.* English-Eisaman. *This could be a problem.* Computer Science II-Floyd. *Winner!* Student Service-Library. *Woohoo!* Wade and I had two classes together, but beyond that it was the typical scholastic gauntlet designed to test my patience. This year was special though. Wade and I were seniors! I had waited three long years for this moment starting back in Connecticut and couldn't wait to be done with school all together and just spend time doing what I wanted to do. *What did I want to do?*

Angie was a little more optimistic about her classes; however, she resented needing one more semester of athletic credit. After last year's infamous mascot fiasco at the football season opener, she was blacklisted from the band. It looked like she was going to have to suffer through a semester of P.E. when she found a loophole and auditioned for the flag team. She was a natural at slinging those decorated sticks of destruction. It paired well with her chick rock persona and proved to be too good an opportunity to pass up. The flag coach struck a deal with the band director that she was under strict instructions to stay out of trouble and keep a wide berth from Hambone and his 4H handlers. *Nevertheless, they relocated his pen to the other side of the field that season.* After school and the shop, there was only one other thing on her mind, the SAT. She had been studying for more than a year and was determined to score a perfect 1600. Others in her class were focused on the PSAT, but she felt it was a waste of time. Her first shot at the test was coming in just a few weeks, and every free waking moment had been spent preparing, which was something we reminded her of every day during summer.

All I can remember about that first week of school is that I was constantly distracted and pissed off. It all started when Wade won the Monday morning music duel and opted to blast his summer obsession, Run Around, *on repeat*, all the way to school. John Popper's harmonica solo was stuck in my head for three whole days. *Damn you Wade!* This made the recycled teacher monologues about bold curriculums, commitments to excellence and other meaningless rhetoric more insufferable than usual. Computer Science, my one glimmer of scholastic hope for the semester, wasted the entire week re-hashing data structure concepts from last year. *l4m3!* Even lunch was a shell of what it had been last year. We sat around like a bunch of zoned out silent pandas in a tree with a bunch of half-eaten food hanging from our mouths. Angie was heads down studying for the SAT, and I was ruminating on ideas for the shop. Wade was the only one who actually tried to talk, but it was non-stop about this girl Rhonda that sat in front of him in Physics and how her hair smelled just like International Delight. *Hello, Clarice, much!?* Absolutely nothing felt right about the week and heading to the shop after school didn't make it any better.

When Wade dropped us off after school, my eyes immediately targeted the "Help Wanted" sign still hanging in the window. I timidly opened the door wondering if today was the day that Tom broke down under the stress, but to my surprise he greeted us with his normal calm smile as if everything was under control. He was just getting off with a support call but was multitasking on an unrelated computer build.

"Any interviews today?" I asked, jumping straight to the point not trying one bit to hide my genuine curiosity.

"We had one guy stop by today." Tom replied. "He was definitely a good sales guy, but he just didn't understand how to actually work with computers. He'd never been online or even opened a computer case. I asked him if that lack of hands on experience might be a problem when it came to helping customers. He said, No, so I said No." Tom was amused and chuckled at the response. "Hardest people to help are those who can't see they need it..."

That's when it hit me. *Wade!!!!* All this time, we had been searching for someone new to add to the team, but in fact, all we needed to do was train the current team manager. Ever since Wade began hanging around at the shop, I could see the knowledge and jargon rubbing off on him. I mean he is already doing scripted setups, why couldn't do more?

"What about Wade?" I blurted out.

Wade choked on his coffee, and coughed out a "Whaaaat ... *cough* ... about Wade, what?"

"You know how to troubleshoot. At least the basic stuff." My ideas were streaming out of my mouth before my brain could process them. "What if ... we documented the most common problems, and had Wade take a first pass at the customers? If it's too much for him, then he can pass it up to you or me!" I looked to Tom to gauge his reaction. He wasn't as excited as I had hoped, and then I realized that this didn't solve Tom's problem during the day when we were all at school. "OK. Maybe it's not a permanent solution, but until we find the right person, maybe it could help."

Tom's face returned to a supportive smile, "Anything is worth a shot. As long as Wade is OK with it?"

Wade was still wiping the splattered coffee off his hands, and he gave me one of those quick "Dude, what the hell?!" looks, but then settled into the reality and motioned a salute with his coffee cup to Tom with a perplexed expression.

Wade spent the remaining part of that day shadowing me and Tom on phone calls and at the service desk. Between customer interactions, I typed up a rough document about the most common support problems Wade might face and how to solve them. He was a quick study and by the next day he was already properly identifying problems via the document and pointing out the next steps for customers to take. Tom and I agreed to let him try flying solo on Friday, and it's a decision I'll never forget as long as I live.

It was a pretty normal day considering how crappy everything had been recently outside the shop. I don't think Angie spoke more than a few sentences that entire week to Wade, Tom or myself, but two of those words were "Good Luck" as she gave Wade a hug before heading to the sales counter with her dilapidated SAT study guide. There was a backlog of computers sitting at the service desk, and I told Wade that he could help me triage them until the phone rang, which lasted all of five minutes. Wade took an encouraging sip of coffee and answered the phone.

"Thank you for calling Andersson Electronics Support. This is Wade, how can I help you?"

I strained my ear trying to hear the customer on the other end of the phone, but all I could hear was muffled squawking. Wade appeared calm, as he searched through the document, and then he asked.

"Is your CAPS LOCK keyboard light on by any chance?" He paused listening to the response, "If it's on, it will have a light on underneath it. The button to turn it off and on is on the left side of the keyboard, next to the letter A." Another quick pause was then followed by, "Ok. Go ahead and turn that off and retype your username and password and try again." Wade gave me a silent thumbs up and playfully bit his lip in celebration as he hung up the phone in triumphant. He leaned back in the chair and put his feet up on the desk sipping his coffee like a Wall Street stock trader as he read through the remaining print out of miscellaneous computer problems, studying it intently. Everything looked like it was going to work out, so I put on my headphones and turned on some STP to start installing a new CD drive at the service desk. Wicked Garden had barely started when I turned to see Wade pacing around the desk, holding the phone and waving his hand dramatically in the air.

I peeled the headphones from my ears just in time to hear Wade say, "Why are you being so stupid? It's C-AAA-PS LOCK, not SCR-OOO-LLL LOCK. Are you try-yyy-ing to piss me off!?" Before he could say another word, I dropped my screwdriver and snatched the phone from his hand.

"Andersson Electronics, this is Ben, can I be of any assistance?" The whole time I was listening to the customer talk, Wade was quietly mocking her words and unleashing a visual lexicon of sign language expressions that all seemed to complement his exaggerated middle-finger gesture that he pointed at the phone. It turned out the person wasn't even a Tom-NET customer, but in fact trying to connect to CompuServe. It had nothing to do with her keyboard. After I explained the long-distance problems with CompuServe and the cost savings, I was able to sell her on a Tom-NET trial account and assured her that Wade was just having a VERY rough first day. I would soon find out from Wade that something similar happened at FlowJoe's last year when he verbally accosted a customer for defiling a cup of coffee with packets of creamer and instant oatmeal. Apparently, this was the reason he always sat in the far corner and why he was never hired to work there. I'm not sure how I never saw it before, but one of Wade's most glaring "issues" was holding back his emotions when he was frustrated. Wade apologized to Tom and me and tried to quit altogether, but Tom and I acknowledged that we rushed him into the situation, and it wasn't fair to just kick him to the curb. Truth be told, Wade was awesome at setting up computers and every bit of help mattered at this point. Besides, he was family.

Things started to return to normal a few weeks later when Angie, Wade and I finally took the SAT. It was a hectic-normal, but a close enough version of normal, nonetheless. About three hours after she left the testing room, the real Angie emerged from her cerebral cocoon. She didn't even realize she had been mentally closed off for the past month, but I was really happy to have her back. It was harder to find specialized technical help in a small town than we anticipated, so the shop stayed fairly busy throughout the week, but it was still manageable. Even though it was chaotic, Sundays were usually pretty fun because there was a predictable break in the action from 10AM to 2PM when people went to church. This was a great time to get caught up on work, or, *what usually happened*, play some Hot Shot Trivia. Tom was the trivia master this round reading questions aloud with a horrible Knights of Ni impression. As he started reading the next question, the shop door opened and a young slender bald guy wearing a Far Side t-shirt walked into the shop. *Midvale School for the Gifted. Classic!*

"Where were the 1988 Winter Olympics?" Sir Tom asked.

"Calgary," the stranger responded as he walked to the magazine rack finishing off a bag of Funyuns.

"Correct. One point for ...?" Tom prompted inquisitively.

"Patrick" he replied passively, picking up a copy of PC Shopper and thumbing through the pages not really paying much attention to anyone in the shop.

We continued to play, and Patrick was a formidable opponent, stealing two of the four remaining points in that round without even lifting his head from the massive thin-leafed compu-bible. Our game was interrupted by a customer carrying a large computer case and set in on the service desk.

"I was told you guys know how to fix computers." he said in an abrupt tone. "I have tried everything I can think of, but I can't get my computer to boot up. There's a CD stuck in the drive, and I can't eject it, but the computer keeps trying to boot from it and fails. You guys know anything about Macs?"

Tom and I looked at each other, and the answer was a resounding "No". Tom hadn't sold Apple computers in a while, and I had only used an Apple IIe at my library in Connecticut. This behemoth looked like a PC tower, but definitely had a curvier look and feel to it.

"Niiiice. Is that the new PowerMac," a voice shouted behind us. We turned to see Patrick sizing up the all-in-one computer chassis with a sultry stare. He walked around me to get a glimpse at the front, "PowerMac 6400, spiffy! What seems to be the problem?"

The customer re-explained the problem to Patrick, and all Patrick said back was, "Well, let's get that CD out then!" He took down the keyboard and mouse the customer brought with him and hooked up the service desk power cable. Patrick turned on the computer and held down the F12 key for a few seconds and the CD drive ejected the problematic CD. The customer was elated when we could hear the computer's hard disk chattering as the operating system loaded followed by a high pitch startup chime. When he reached for his wallet to pay, Tom simply told him to pay Patrick directly. Patrick passed on the money, and just wanted to geek out with the customer about his awesome computer. Tom had that look in his eye. The same look he had when we first met, and I knew that he knew we had found our next helper. After the customer left, Tom was quick to make the pitch and close the deal to bring Patrick on board.

Patrick Luft, or Patty as he preferred to be called, fit well into our shop family. He was twenty-one years old and recently moved to town after completing an RTF associate degree at a small technical college just outside Waco where he worked at the local movie theater satiating his certifiable cinema addiction. He grew up in the Dallas suburbs, but was looking for a change of pace and came to Jollyville to check out the near Austin small-town vibe. When it came to Macs, he knew practically everything worth knowing given he had been a loyal user of them ever since his dad brought home the Lisa. This depth in Mac knowledge was a great asset to our shop, but he was also proficient when it came to PCs. He just didn't like them. Not to mention, he was into all things vintage cinema, especially movie posters, props and paraphernalia, and he was obsessed with Six Degrees of Kevin Bacon. He could connect practically any actor in five connections or less, but always tried to use obscure old movies to show off. *The guy was a walking IMDb!* When combined with his laid-back optimistic attitude on the world, Patty and Tom had a special bond from the start. A few days after he started, he brought in his own Mac to teach us all about how to troubleshoot and connect Macs to the Internet. *haha, MacPPP.* This was also the first time any of us had ever seen the game Myst in action. Up to this point, all we had seen were pictures, nothing in real life. *Holy crap!* We must have lost at-least eight hours that first week just re-watching the game introduction and flipping switches on the first level. The graphics and sound were an amazing complement to the creative puzzles, and we were all hooked. The next day Tom ordered an identical Mac for the "service desk", but it was no coincidence that a fresh copy of Myst was installed even before Netscape. For all his computer knowledge and natural customer service skills, I honestly believe Patrick could have landed the job purely on his impressive Hot Shot Trivia performance and introducing Tom to Myst. He was perfect, *too perfect*.

Patrick ramped up quickly and helped Tom knock down the shop backlog of computer builds, and things began to return to normal-normal. Thoughts of him replacing me crossed my mind a few times, *OK ... every day*, so I spent some of this newfound breathing room learning a bit more about Macs. It didn't take long to come to the conclusion that I hated them!

First off, a computer that smiles at me when it starts up? *Mighty presumptive, Apple!* Second, what the hell is up with the single button mouse and Option-Click nonsense? *Intuitive my ass!* Last but not least, have you seen the price of SCSI hardware? *Just buy a new computer!* I was more than happy to let Patty be in charge of all things Mac, because they were infuriating to the core. One afternoon when Patty was off, I spent fifteen minutes trying to explain the concept of an "option-click" over the phone to a customer and nearly put my fist through the monitor. Instead, I hand sketched a frowning "X"-eyed Mac crapping its computer case and taped it dead center on the shop Mac screen. Apparently, Patty took offense to my little artistic expression and hot-glued my favorite computer mouse's buttons together while I was at school. Next to the mouse pad, was a Post-It, "Improvement. Your Welcome!". *Touché, Mac Man. It's on.*

    Despite our congenial facade in front of customers, Patty and I were constantly at war with each other to try and be the best. *At-least that is how I felt.* Whether it be computer skills, Hot Shot trivia or the ever-increasing ingenuity from our office pranks. Weeks went by without anyone conceding defeat, until our shop's Halloween party, when an unexpecting movie would unite our fractured PC and Mac worlds better than any dual booting PowerPC ever could. Hackers is a "cyber action drama" about a rag tag group of teenage miscreants that pulled computer hijinks on an interconnected society of digitally oblivious sheep with an arsenal of liberally interpreted computer technologies and hacker tactics. The first time we watched the movie, we laughed at the artistic license taken with how computers work, but there was definitely something special about this movie. We didn't know if it was the awesome soundtrack, the roller blade arcade, *Angelina Jolie's left boob* or the overall notion of kids our age being complete technology bad asses, but we knew we wanted to watch it again. A second time led to a third, fourth and fifth time until Patty and I were the only ones left awake. Tom was passed out in his recliner covered in popcorn kernels. Angie was wrapped in her puffy sleeping bag on the floor and Wade was sitting up, eyes closed, mouth agape and drooling onto his shirt. It was the most fun Halloween I'd had in quite some time!

    As sunlight peered through the window and the movie credits rolled for the final time, Patty and I had the exact same idea. We ran downstairs to the nearest computer and searched for the *Hacker Manifesto* online. We printed two copies and read it multiple times. It was captivating. Mentor sounded just like me, but with better prose. For once, it felt like this small-town Texas "island" was finally a part of the main and I started to imagine a world of limitless possibilities *and mischief*. *beep* *beep* ... *beep* *beep* *My* watch alarm went off. It was time to get ready for school. *Why did Halloween have to fall on a Thursday?* I dashed upstairs to wake Tom, Angie and Wade, and then rushed to FlowJoe's to grab everyone a caffeinated breakfast. On my way out the door, Patty jokingly yelled, "Hack the Planet!" and without breaking stride I raised my fist and replied with even louder enthusiasm and dashed out of sight.

From that day forward, Patty and I got along great. That is to say, we still pulled pranks on each other every chance we could get, but there was a newly formed comradery between the two of us. There was no more PC vs. Mac or him vs. me. A bond was created between the two of us at the intersection of technology, curiosity and mischief, and our relationship was off to a renewed start. A few solid weeks passed until Patty and I weaned ourselves from the Hacker movie, soundtrack and manifesto. I never felt so enlightened and grounded in an identity before. So was Patty. He subscribed to 2600 magazine, and we frequently lost hours browsing the latest hacker posts on Usenet. We even split the cost of a Blue Box to dabble in a little phreaking. Sadly, our town's old payphones were not as ancient as we had hoped. *Probably for the best I wasn't born 8 years earlier.*

It took another three weeks, and one pseudo intervention at the shop, for both of us to normalize our newfound obsession. My thought chemistry had been permanently altered leaving a far bolder and more curious devil on my shoulder than ever before. Even something as simple as browsing the web was no longer safe from introspection. Up to this point, if I came across a cool website, I would view the source code just to see how an animation was built and save interesting code snippets, but now when I looked, I was focused on searching for all things /cgi-bin and learning the intricacies of HTML and Perl just to see what I could break. This was when I was first fell in love with ActivePerl and started usurping shared Windows DLLs for custom projects. While learning about all things website development was intriguing, it is safe to say that the lion share of our recuperation was spearheaded when we got our copies of Warcraft II.

This was one of the first really fun games that we could both play on both PC & Mac, we splurged for both copies and set them up side by side at the shop. Our passion to play bypassed rational thought when we realized that our serial cables wouldn't work for head to head play without one of us switching computers, *not going to happen*. That didn't stop us though. We spent hours sitting next to each other listening to our simultaneously clanking computers as my humans and his orcs fought their way through the same campaigns. Patty eventually broke his one and only mouse button. *We are under attack!* Angie and Wade were happy to see my hacker bender come to a close, as it returned our lunchtime conversations back to a normal level where everyone could participate without rolling their eyes or feigning interest. Which was good, because I missed some fairly major happenings and needed to be read in.

Wade had developed a creepy habit of using his pencil eraser to flick the tips of Rhonda's long creamer-scented hair that draped behind her chair back. One week, he got his pencil clip tangled and accidentally ripped out a large lock of hair as Rhonda turned around. You would think "Sorry" would be the first words someone would utter in a situation like this, but not Wade. The believable middle ground that existed between Wade's version of events and the wildfire gossip chain across campus was that Wade extended the hair pencil to her and said, "Your hair smells great. Want to grab coffee sometime?" That was the last we ever heard about Rhonda.

Angie was dealing with her own problems. The SAT scores were due out any day and she was a nervous wreck. She just finished serving the last of her three detentions for "accidentally" smacking her flag captain in the head "three consecutive times" with her pole during practice. These incidents shortly followed the captain saying that Angie was *overreacting* about the SAT and that she should focus on improving her *inconsistent* flag handling. Stressed or not, Angie didn't take kindly to people criticizing her behavior or quality of work. I'm surprised that the captain wasn't popsicled with the nerdless roughed-up end of Angie's practice fiberglass flagpole. Some people considered her passion for perfection and her abrasive behavior, off putting, but I thought it made her awesome, and even attractive.

Needless to say, it was good to be back in a rhythm. The shop was doing well, and school was more or less uneventful, which is how I liked it. The less time I had to spend thinking about school, outside of school, the better. By the time I got home at the end of the day, it was just me, my computer and my free Tom-NET account. *Thanks Tom!* Connecting during the evening was best because it avoided a far too common scenario in our house where Mom accidentally picked up another phone receiver, which broke my internet connection and forced me to have to redial. *Mooooooommmm, Hang up. I'm online!!!* When without interruptions, I had a ten-point checklist I could execute that would have me unpacked, fed and on mIRC in under five minutes from arriving at the house. On the days I behaved responsibly, I would usually spend only one to two hours checking out the latest Undernet action, but the other 364 days of the year, I was lucky to pass out at my desk by 2AM. With so many topics to choose from, every night was a different adventure, but I spent most of my time in #warez checking out the latest updates and talking to people about software cracking. I could watch people lob half-cocked insults, cheesy pickup lines and elaborate ASCII macros at each other all night long, and in some cases, I did, but it was all over when someone tried to send me a picture. Everything came to a crawl thanks to my slow-ass modem. It was something I had been meaning to upgrade, but I was waiting to save up enough money for a complete computer overhaul. This Friday was different, though. It would stand out distinctly in my mind as the beginning of one of the happiest periods in my life.

FEATURED TRACK

Cranberries - Linger

6
Everyone Else Is Doing It

    Most nights when I came home from work there were a few norms that I grew to expect. Mom was usually at work. The house was empty. The only noise was Brisby running laps around the cage while Nicodemus did his best to ignore her, perched stoically atop his lookout platform. She was an adventurous and energetic rat, while he was more of a laid-back philosopher that mainly drug his huge rat balls around the cage. They were relatively low maintenance pets, all things considered, but offered immense entertainment when I let them run around on my desk while I surfed the web. Brisby liked to sniff at my pinky as it hovered in the air over the left side of my keyboard and gnaw at the top row keys like they were chew treats. *Who uses the Pause/Break key regularly anyway?* Even though she was absent, Mom was really good about keeping all of us hydrated and fed, including me. Whether it be a sandwich in the refrigerator, or leftovers in the microwave, there was usually something ready to eat no matter how late I got home. Last, but not least, she would place my mail for the day at the foot of the bed always making sure that any academic related items were perfectly set on top of all the junk mail such as to receive optimum attention. As hellbent as she was on me going to college, despite only having a bachelor's degree herself, you would think she had a master's degree in the art of passive aggression.

It was the week before Thanksgiving break, and I could honestly say my life would never be the same after that Friday. I walked in the door to find a massacred explosion of mail on the kitchen counter and practically no food in the kitchen. Thankfully I loaded up on Yoohoo and Oreos before heading home. *Dinner of champions.* Nico and Briz were both sound asleep snuggling in one of their hammocks, and the house was far too dark and quiet for my taste. All the lights in the house were off, which was strange because one of Mom's most infamous neuroses was leaving random lights on when she was gone to scare away burglars. Tonight, only one light was on and it was in my room. I grabbed a small metal pot from the stove and carried it with me as I made my way down the hall ready to Jackie Chan, *or Bobby Flay*, someone's ass, if needed. I peeked my head around the door frame and scanned the room for something out of the ordinary, but scatter shot clothes draped across every available surface was not it. I then noticed my mom's perfectly placed PhD dissertation laid at the foot of my bed. My SAT results had arrived.

I rolled my eyes hard and threw the pot on to my bed as I unloaded my backpack and the rest of my gear. I snatched the letter and sat down at my desk and gave the envelope a long stare. I could smell my mom's temptation all over the back of the envelope, and although the letter showed signs of obsessive handling, it's seal remained surprisingly intact. I ripped a hole down the side and slid out the results: 790 out of 800 in Math. 620 out of 800, Reading. Total Score: 1410. *Not bad, Ben.* For all the hype Angie built around this test, I was admittedly less than impressed. One thing was sure, the last thing I wanted to do was show this to Mom. It's hard enough living with a nurse that overly scrutinizes every action with the risk of death, injury or infection, *in that order*, but to live with an obsessed college guidance counselor to boot would be a nightmare. I placed the results back in the envelope and stashed them under my pillow to deal with another day. The comforter's cool touch and the long day did short work with me and I crashed instantly. No computer. Shoes on. Cuddling with my metal pot woobie.

My alarm woke me extra early that Saturday. I had to open the shop, but Wade had some errands to run that morning with his mom, so I was stuck biking it to work. Tom gave me a set of keys to the shop so I could come in without having to wake him up on the weekends. Even though I knew Tom was sleeping in his apartment in the backroom loft, I took pride in opening the shop by myself and keeping the keys safe. As I ran through the morning checklist, I decided to keep my SAT scores private to avoid unnecessary conversations about my academic future. Therefore, I consider it a great personal triumph that I stuck to my guns for an entire thirty minutes before Angie got me to spill the beans. Eleven full hours, if you count back to the exact moment, I opened the envelope the night before. *Yeah, that sounds better.*

Normally Angie arrived around nine o'clock, about an hour after we opened, but today she was running late. An hour later, the door chimes rang foreboding chaotic tones, and sure enough, it was her. The muscles in the neck instinctively spasmed and every one of my nerves was on high alert. Over the previous months, we developed a morning routine of jokes and general banter before we retreated into our corners for the day. I prepared a calm, cool and loose facade to cover my nerves; however, instead of our morning chit-chat, she simply made a straight line for her spot in the Community Corner. No glances. No words. Her head was hanging low as if to avoid any eye contact. *Something must be wrong.* I looked to Wade, who had strolled in only five minutes prior and he was observing her behavior in a similar confused state. All he did was shrug his shoulders and mimed a fake coffee cup to his lips and proceeded to use charades to inquire how many cups of coffee he should pick up. *Very helpful!* She tossed her bag onto the table and buried her face into it with a resounding thud as she sat. I didn't know what to say, so I chose to give her some space while I finished my morning tasks.

About five minutes later, I heard her muffled voice escaping from the confines of her backpack, "I want to do diiiiiiiie!"

What do you say to something like that? My instinctive response was less supportive than I would have hoped.

"Ummmmm. No?" slipped from lips, which I immediately followed with a poignant clarification, "That wasn't a question, by the way, in case you were wondering." I felt that my clarification needed a clarification, so I simply followed with, "So what's wrong?"

She raised her head from her bag itching at the zipper tab indentation now on her forehead.

"I got my SAT scores yesterday, and let's just say that I didn't do so well." Her tone was a viscous slurry of anger and frustration, but quickly transitioned into full on dejection with a dramatic pause. "I'm an idiot." *thud*. Her head re-buried itself in a mound of Jansport.

I wanted to be there for her, so I decided to wait and listen to what she had to say. *News flash: I waited too long.* She jerked her head up and gave me one of those wide-eyed "Aren't you going to correct me?" looks.

"Whatever," I replied. "You are way too smart to believe something as stupid as that." I could see a glimpse of a smile forming. *Man, she was pretty. Even with her zipper indented forehead.* "Besides, are you just upset you didn't score a perfect 2000, because you are not THAT smart," I jokingly said as I closed the distance between us. She got the joke.

"I take that back. You're the idiot. I feel better now." You could taste the salty rejoinder flying off her tongue. "The test only goes to 1600. And no, I didn't score a 2000, or even 1600. I scored a 1220." Her morose tone was followed by another long dramatic pause. I felt I should say something, but before I could talk, she started up again. "590 Math and 620 Reading. No academic distinction of any kind. Can you get any more mediocre?"

A turbulent cocktail of ego and hubris brewed in the pit of my stomach. *You did better than, Angie!? WTF!?!?!?!* My calm and cool armor eroded by the millisecond as the itch to unleash my secret surged adrenaline to my already twitching extremities.

"I studied three straight months and took three practice tests." With every word, the octave of her voice increased until she was full on yelling into the air and about to chuck her books across the shop. "If I can't handle the pressure of a simple test, how am I going to handle college when the pressure is really on?"

"I'm not sure you have to worry about added pressure. I don't think the laws of physics can quantify pressure higher than the kind you put on yourself. Trust me. ... Next time, you'll be ready. Just take a moment and try to relax. I'm sure you'll do better next year!" A subconscious smirkish smile escaped confinement and planted itself in plain sight. *Shit! She saw.*

Some people sweat when they panic, my face; however, starts to get twitchy and wide-eyed. Angie noticed that too.

"What is wrong with you? Are you having a stroke?" she asked and that is when I knew she knew. She took a deep breath, "Wait, what ... did .... YOU ... get?" *Damnit!* I backpedaled behind a table to distance myself from Angie, and then I squeaked out, "1410". She slammed her hand into the table.

"What?" she said. "Mr. I Don't Give a Rat's Ass about School gets a 1410 and didn't even study!" She lowered her head in disbelief with her white-knuckled hands firmly pressing on the table between us and sinking her head in despair. "This must be what hell's like."

Angie was a devout agnostic and hearing her say something as nonsensical as this meant things were worse than I could have imagined. I decided the bandage was best to just rip off completely at this point. "Since we're on the subject ... I might as well tell you that I scored a 790 on the Math section, so there's that, too."

In one smooth motion, Angie dropped her head and simultaneously leaned over the table and landed a straight jab on my right bicep.

"Ahhh-Ouch" I squealed. "What was that for?" I tried to rub the sting out of my frogged muscle, but I could already tell it was going to leave a bruise. *Did you really just squeal, Ben?*

"That's for letting me go on and on about my score when you knew you beat me!" She began to ramble to herself and pace in pseudo circles in bewilderment. "Great. I'm going to be stuck living in a trailer park in this podunk town for the rest of my life! Might as well start filling out Denny's applications ..."

"Whoa! Slow down," I said. "First of all, you are one of the smartest people I know. There is no way this one test is going to do anything other than make you want to try harder." Her face perked up a bit. "Not to mention you are strong ... independent ... and a complete badass. *I was on a roll.* So, what if you didn't ace the test this time? I know you. You'll learn from your mistakes, set a goal for next year and knock it out of the park. Cut yourself a little slack." I gave her shoulder a reassuring squeeze. *How did I get to this side of the table?*

Angie looked up with her signature smirk, "Why Ben, if I didn't know any better, I'd think you almost liked me."

My hand retracted as if she were hot lava, while a collision of thoughts and words in my brain rendered me a stuttering bag of hormones. She always said I was the cutest guy in the room, but that was when it was just me and Tom, a guy who is pushing 40. *Had she been flirting all this time?* My brain was overloading on possible next steps: *play it cool, deny it, chicks dig assholes*, until she broke the silence.

"I'll tell you what. Why don't we go grab some pizza tonight after your shift, and since you are cleeaarrly the genius," she said with a sarcastic chuckle. "I'll let you buy."

Gravity helped me acknowledge her offer as my frozen head nodded in agreement. My tires were spinning in a surprise rut of anxiety, but I was able to muster out a somewhat masculine "uh-huh". That was it. *I'm so lame.*

"Great. Well now that we have that settled. I've got some reading to do for Academic Decathlon, and yoouuuu," she lightly poked my chest, "have work to do!" Angie returned to her corner in a much better mood than when she arrived. I, on the other hand, was a bit terrified given my recently bruised arm and chest.

I have a Date! The biggest problem I had this morning was finding clean underwear, and now I had a date with arguably the coolest girl I could imagine. *welp* For the next ten hours, Angie was the only thing on my mind. Everywhere I looked, I thought I saw her face. Screensavers. Magazines. Blinking website text. I even mistakenly called at-least eight people Angie while on support calls that morning, but thankfully she didn't hear that as she had her headphones on. Patty arrived shortly after noon and quickly realized I was distracted. I was twenty minutes into a simple CD drive install, when he came over to point out that I had two master devices on the same IDE cable. *Rookie mistake!*

"You doing OK, man? You seem a bit off, today." he asked.

I was in the middle of planning an elaborate excuse when I heard Tripping Daisy "I Got A Girl" start playing on the radio. *Oh, come on!* I nearly lost it. I mouthed the words "follow me" to Patty and headed to the backroom. Like a ticking time bomb I unloaded four hours of pent up angst and curiosity. It felt good to get my concerns out in the open.

"So, let me get this straight," he said. "Angie asked you out, not the other way around, because you were too chicken to say something? Everyone knows you like her."

"Pretty much," I agreed. "What do you say to someone who calls you out like that, I mean really."

"It's pretty simple. You say, you want to go out?" He mocked me as I peered through the double door windows to make sure there weren't customers needing help, and that she was still wearing her headphones, but he could sense that I was really struggling for advice.

"OK. Look, I'm no expert by any means, but if you want my advice, this is what I'd do to make your first date special." He carefully studied his thoughts for a moment, and then started unloading his elaborate scheme.

"First off, before you get going, I'd make some sort of fun wager with her to make your first date a bit competitive. Like, trying to see who can correctly guess things about your past, or something like that. If you win, you get a second date. If she wins, she can choose her prize."

It was bold. More ballsy even than I could see myself being, and yet it made a bit of sense. Heck, any advice was better than nothing.

"Then, when the date is winding down, you go find an apartment complex that has a pool. You sneak in and jump in with clothes on, and she will be thoroughly impressed by your spontaneity." This was good stuff. I would have never thought to do this in a million years, *and yet it felt familiar*!

"And finally, the part that will take a bit of homework on your end. Make sure that the pool has a view of a fifty-story office building and pay the janitor to spell out *Ben n Angie* with lit office windows." *Wait, what!? Wait. Damnit!*

Patty looked me straight in the eye for a solid three seconds until he busted out laughing. The jerk was spoon feeding the plot from Dade and Kate's first date at the end of Hackers. I thought he was going to be my older and wiser wingman. *I guess not.*

"Look," he said, collecting himself, "there's nothing I can tell you, that you don't already know, that is going to make or break your first date. If you ask me, worrying about trying to be like anyone other than yourself is a horrible way to start a relationship. Unless you can find a pool and skyscrapers in downtown Jollyville. If so, you should definitely do that shit because it would be awesome!"

The sentiment of his words rang true in my head as we both returned to the shop floor. "Just be yourself!" *What a novel thought. They should put that on a poster.* Time continued to crawl. Every minute felt like five, and no amount of computer fixing, or tech support could distract my attention from the clock counting down in my head.

Angie left around 4PM, and said she would be back, which gave me less than two hours to finish up my shop tasks and freshen up. Since the date was last minute, I didn't have anything to change into that wasn't covered in sweat, computer lint or both. I dug through the random shop swag bin and found a promotional black t-shirt from one of our software vendors. It was for the game "Normality" that came out a few months prior. Right across the front of the shirt was a large indifferent yellow face, which read "Have a normal day" below it. *Yep, this was definitely me.* After dawning my refreshed gear, I cleaned my face and armpits with a combination of hand soap and individually wrapped moist towelettes that I found buried in the bathroom cabinet. *Thanks for your hot wing habit, Tom!* It was nearly six o'clock. I walked back to the front counter catching a whiff of my freshly sanitized aroma as I swung open the door. I was ready for a date, or ready to start my next job as a taxi driver.

The front door chimes rang. *Angie was right on time.* She was wearing a long brown dress with a small floral pattern I had never seen, a denim jacket and what appeared to be a new pair of black 10-eye Docs. Her normal pair were more distressed with intricate pen drawings all along the side grooves in the sole. She walked up to the counter holding back a laugh as she gave my formal wear a once over.

"Who's ready for pizza?" she said in a boisterous voice for the entire shop to hear. Patty silently raised his hand, but he was on a support call.

"Sorry Patty," she said. "I think I'll choose this completely normal and well-dressed gentleman, right here."

She grabbed my elbow, pulled me from behind the counter and started walking me to the exit. A strong wind gust surged as we opened the door and made quick work of both our hair. A friend of mine from Connecticut told me stories about his eccentric uncle who would intentionally nick the paint job of his new car in a nondescript place. From that point on, he knew his car wasn't perfect, and he wouldn't go crazy trying to keep it that way. That's how I felt about the wind and the hair. I knew my smoothness was going to be put to the test and I would make stupid mistakes along the way. Better to just get it over with so I could stop worrying about it. *It could be worse. You could be Spud and shit the bed.* The thought of that Trainspotting scene made me laugh out loud, and Angie joined in, albeit more so because the residual towelette chemicals in my hair were making the front stand straight up like it was coated in Dep. The awkward silence was broken and my brain's stranglehold on witty thought and charm was relinquished.

"You look great, by the way!" I said smashing my hair down. Maybe she thought I was being sarcastic, but I wasn't. Messed up hair or not, her laugh and smile were contagious. Conversations started to flow more naturally from that point on, and the unanimous first topic for the evening was food. We were both starving!

When it came to pizza, we didn't have too many choices in town. Mr. Gatti's and Pizza Hut were closer to the other side of town, but the best option was just across the street: Little Caesars. Tom made a deal with the store owner to get us all discounts on food in exchange for some discounted computer parts and free internet access. Needless to say, we ate there often. Angie and I both preferred their nine-piece square pizza but for different reasons. She liked the thick crispy corner crust pieces, but for some odd reason I obsessed over the edgeless center piece. It worked out perfectly! We ordered our ten-dollar deal: two medium pizzas, one pepperoni and one mushroom, two crazy sticks and two fountain drinks. As if by instinct, she gravitated towards an open table in the corner by the windows where we could see the shop.

Time flew by while we waited for our order and talked about the latest things we found online. This was one thing I *really* liked about Angie. Most kids our age, even adults, still used newspapers, local news and MTV to learn about what's going on in the world. Angie was well versed in the ways of the Internet. AltaVista. Yahoo! Lycos. You name it. She could bend them all to her will and find exactly what she needed at any time, which meant that she always had lots of new things to discuss; especially when it came to music. If she discovered a new artist or album that she liked that had been out for more than eight weeks, she took it as a challenge to figure out how it slipped through her purview so she could fine tune her process. Her latest obsession, Poe, recently initiated one of these research retrospectives, and happened to be playing over the restaurant's radio. Part way through hearing about Johnny's untimely demise at the hands of his girlfriend, I heard Angels of the Silences, and she noticed me silently mouthing the words. *Crap.*

Before I could even utter a defense, "I don't want to hear one word about Counting Crows tonight." *I was a bit of a fan.* She looked me straight in the eye, paused and wagged her finger at me to make sure her message was properly received. "You are still on probation from that August and Everything After bender from last year." Part of me knew she was only kidding, *an extremely small fractional part*, but my wiser self-decided to not test the waters and just sing along in my head.

"Well, thank you for that reminder," I said, "but it was unnecessary. For your information, I was going to impress you with a flawless performance of Amish Paradise ... a capella." I held my straw to my mouth like a distinguished gentleman with an ultra-flimsy cigarette holder that leaked soda from the end. She didn't get the joke. Instead, she gave me a deadpan expression and shifted her neck backwards, as if I had committed a heinous crime. *Who doesn't like Weird Al?* Before I could think any further on the matter, fifth period Craig tossed our paper-wrapped cardboard platter on to the table with the most congenial of salutations. *Pizza to the rescue.* We surgically popped the end staples and slid the platter out while wafting the aromatic smells of garlic, piping hot marinara and bubbling mozzarella. The cheese crusted wrapper barely had time to hit the chair seat next to me before we shamelessly devoured our food.

With our initial hunger cravings satiated, Angie kicked our conversation into an unexpected gear.

"So, what do you want to do after high school?" she said. *I think I just burned a hole through the roof of my mouth.*

"Ummm...." I exhaled bursts of hot air from my mouth, "I really haven't thought *haaaaa* about it *haa* much. *Damn that is hot!* I mean, I'm sure I'll keep my job at Tom's, but anything beyond that, I haven't really given it to much thought. Probably save the world. One line of code at a time." I puffed out my chest in a superhero-esque pose, while inconspicuously wiping marinara from the corner of my mouth. This wasn't the first time I said these words aloud, which was part of the joke. It sounds a bit catchy, but in reality, I questioned these skills every day. All I knew is that I was pretty damn good at what I did, and that most people didn't understand at all. How was I supposed to make future plans regarding skills that, up to this point, have only provided me with a highly tuned sense of curiosity, discounted tech and dirt-cheap food. All the inner dialog exhausted my forehead, which sagged in contemplation, until I resounded back, "How about you? What does the Queen of Study Hall want to do when she's done with high school?"

"The easier question might be what I do NOT want to do, but let's see." Her eyes enumerated each goal in sequential order as she mentally reviewed her list. "Ace the SAT and high school valedictorian, but you knew that. Get accepted into a prominent business school like Kellogg, Haas or Wharton and graduate Magna Cum Laude. Then Stanford Law for my Masters. Probably take a job in LA or San Francisco before heading back to school for my doctorate." She took an accomplished sip from her cup. "One thing is for sure; I want to be far away from Jollyville and that stupid trailer park! Far too many people give into the small-town life and they get stuck here like a black hole. That is not for me!"

Her answer was far superior to mine in every form. It was to be expected, as this question focused on two of her specialties: academics and planning, whereas mine were technology and video games. *I frequently look back at this moment and wonder if I had answered differently, would things have turned out differently.*

We talked for nearly an hour before our stomachs bulged with digestive remorse. Angie nibbled the last remnants of her crispy corner crust but left most of her fallen mushrooms untouched. I on the other hand suffered from, as my Mom put it, "empty plate syndrome." Simply put. If there is a plate of food, you eat it all. Especially if it's pizza. *Or Hot Pockets!* My whole pizza, plus her center slice, were eaten with exceptional efficiency on my part, followed by crazy bread chasers. I could have stayed there all night just talking and eating, but then Angie had an idea. She went to the register, came back with two rolls of pennies and pulled me from the restaurant by my shirt sleeve. "Come on. The night is not over yet." she said with determination, and we headed out the restaurant and down the street towards the courthouse. She turned on a portable radio in her bag and tuned into the only alternative rock station around. It was like finding a needle in a haystack sometimes. 101.5X was sandwiched between two local, and strong signaled, country stations, 102.1 and 100.7, which frequently played the same song at the same time making us always question the need for the other eighteen country stations. This wasn't her first radio rodeo and dialed the knob into perfect position on the first try. The tail end of Nirvana's unplugged version of Lake of Fire was just wrapping up. *Good Song!*

"For this next activity, we're going to have to use our imaginations a bit." She handed me a roll of pennies, and in prime tour director fashion began to paint the picture for the agenda. "This is our lovely courthouse. As you can see, it has five water fountains around the grounds. Our activity will be to visit each one, make a wish aloud and toss a penny into the fountain. We'll keep going until we run out of pennies, or our wishes come true. Whichever comes first ..." She paused mid-thought, focused on the radio and proclaimed, "Glycerine. Bush. Sixteen Stone. One point for me." It was obvious I was going to be learning the rules about as fast as she made them up on this excursion.

We wish-walked and talked ourselves around the courthouse for nearly two hours. If it weren't for all the trees in the hill country, the world might have run out of oxygen. We each made outlandish wishes for crazy material things, or tragic karma bestowed on persons with questionable character. One thing was clear, we both hated liars, cheaters and entitled asshats. By our third lap, we were both liberally launching fade-away three-point nothing-but-net buzzer-beater wishes. *Miller ... from long distance.* On my twentieth, or so, I shanked a penny off the top level of the largest triple-tier fountain. Per our ever-evolving rebound rules, initially devised some time on our second lap, rebound wishes counted double. We both rushed to find the penny amongst the grass and fallen leaves. Our hands met as we frantically sifted through the cracking foliage and pebbles and simultaneously arrived on the rogue wish. Her hands were smaller and colder than mine, but her skin was distinctly soft and covered with brittle specks of leaves. I brushed the dirt from the back of her hands with my thumbs. We stood with our fingers interlocked staring at each other with sheepish smiles imprinted on our faces. *She's gonna kiss me.*

She's actually gonna kiss me. Wait. Should I kiss her first? *snatch* In one swift motion, she swiped the penny with her opposite hand and hook shot it into the fountain's top tier.

"I guess that wish counts triple!" she said as she squeezed my hand leading me to the next fountain. Something told me she spent a lot of time at these fountains. I could feel my unraveled penny wrapper nearing the end, and it felt like we had covered every topic known to human existence: music, movies, politics, technology, literature, art. At one point it felt less like a date and more like I was being grilled to join her Academic Decathlon team. She dominated practically every competition that surfaced that evening, except for her impromptu "Name That Tune" on her radio. She held a commanding lead up front, but I closed the gap and tied it up thanks to staple songs by POTUS and the Bosstones. There hadn't been a rule change for quite some time, which made me believe that she was just toying with me. The next song would win the night; however, it was getting late and we seemed to be out of pennies.

A crisp evening breeze kept her cuddled into my arm as we walked back to the shop. We were both burping garlic something fierce and laughing as we personified commentary and gastric noises onto feral cats scavenging in dumpsters along the way. The shop was closed when we got back. I ran in to grab our stuff and locked up before grabbing my bike to walk Angie home. Her demeanor changed though as we drew closer to her house. I could tell she was trying to listen to the radio more intently while she talked to get a jump on the next song, because I was doing the same thing. Much to our mutual dismay, our conversation was backdropped by fluctuating radio interference, static and a never ending late-night commercial break. No song. We arrived at her home, and I opened the tiny gate to her patio-yard, but she grabbed my arm to stop me.

"Don't worry about that. It's late, and you should be on your way home." I checked my watch and it was 1AM. It felt like it should be 10PM. It indeed was late, but it felt like she was trying to ditch me. Was she embarrassed, or was she trying to escape the boredom? The cold night air sent chills down my legs and made my arm hairs stand on end, and I could see her lower lip begin to shiver.

"I want to make sure you get safely inside. Is that OK?" I said. "That's it."

"Wow." She paused as she pulled the wind-blown hair back from her eyes like one of those slow-motion shampoo commercials. *Wow!* "He's smart, chivalrous AND he can fix a computer. Ladies and gentlemen, I've hit the jackpot." She chuckled under her breath, but the look in her eyes was something different. A look that was so blatant that even a blubbering tool, such as myself, could decipher it. *Just do it, you idiot!* Without warning, or the resemblance of a plan, I closed my eyes, leaned in and kissed her. It wasn't one of those tap-tap woodpecker kisses, nor a Lloyd Christmas special, but it was some regurgitated amalgam of every Hollywood kissing scene I had ever seen.

Give me a break. Give me a break. Break me off a piece of that ... Radio commercials continued to fade in and out in the background as I stood with my hands on her shoulders and my mouth lightly pressed against hers. It wasn't romantic. It was damn awkward, and it was getting weirder by the second. *Smooth, Ben. Real Smooth!* Against my better judgement, I pulled away and cracked open my right eye to catch a glimpse of the impending fist of doom about to make contact. To my amazement, her eyes were wide open, and her lips formed that irresistible smirk, but her eyebrows were still in full on surprise mode. She placed her cold hands on my forearms and pulled herself closer. A warm cotton sensation flooded my body as we met in the middle; so warm in fact that I hardly cared I was fumbling my way through my first real kiss. A ten second eternity elapsed until she laughed under her breath and pulled away. My thoughts abruptly shifted to a crude checklist of predictable kissing mistakes, *garlic was the number one contender,* and when all internal systems checked out, I reluctantly opened my eyes to face the music. Her left eyebrow was cocked, and she had a look of confidence across her face. She leaned forward to whisper something in my ear, "Cranberries. Linger."

A slow guitar picking and humming sequence transitioned into a beautiful assorted string section backing unmistakable dulcet Irish vocals. *She had me.* I didn't have to say a word. My eyes conceded the match and any competition thereafter in that very moment. I couldn't help not to smile, grin, or let's be honest, my face felt like it was defying gravity itself. I was in uncharted territory. The subtle constellation of freckles on her face disbanded as she bit the side of her lip and grabbed my hands. She intertwined her fingers with mine and pulled me closer, our eyes locked into a mesmerizing gaze. *You know I'm such a fool for you ♪*

"Thanks for being such a good sport" she said giving my hand a squeeze. *You've got me wrapped around your finger ♪* "There's always next time." She nuzzled her head into my neck, and the tension in my body subsided and my heart radiated a warm gooey feeling that reached my toes. I held her close to shield her from the brisk night air hoping she wasn't weirded out by my heart pumping out of my chest. My concept of happiness registered new levels of existence that night that I did not yet fully comprehend. I knew this was more than just a first kiss. This was the beginning of something deeper, destiny even, and every instinct told me to never let her go. As the song faded, she pulled away from me for the last time that night.

"Now go home and get some sleep! I will see you this afternoon, Mr. Smarty Pants. "The tone of her laugh changed. She was no longer sweet and endearing, this was full on ball buster. My legs were motionless though as she entered the trailer, yet nearly gave way when she closed the door. It was like the cloud that was holding me up had abruptly vanished leaving my weakened knees to support my discombobulated body. I didn't know which room was hers, so I held for a minute to see if I could see any signs of a light or movement in the window blinds. *Would she peek?* I stumbled my way backwards out the front path, got on my bike and pedaled home. At least, I think that's what happened. The truth is that I woke up in my bed to my alarm the next morning with no recollection of how I got home and a large bruise on my shin. *What the hell!?!* I was hugging one of my misshapen pillows and there was a distinctive spot of drool near the top which helped explain the dry taste of cotton in my mouth. The past twelve hours replayed in a second, and I caught myself wondering what Angie was doing that very second. I hated the fact that she didn't have a home computer, Internet or IRC. Calling her house this early was a no-go, and she definitely didn't have a pager. All I wanted to do was send her a quick message to let her know I was thinking of her. *I need a carrier pigeon!* I felt anxious, exhausted and hungry, not to mention I was still dressed in my T-shirt and jeans from the night before. This wasn't my first rodeo sporting "formal sleepwear", but at least I remembered to kick off my shoes this time. My comforter was already sporting some gnarly dirt and mud stains, and I was getting dangerously close to having it actually bother me enough to clean it. *Crisis avoided.*

The sound of crinkling paper muffled by my pillow rattled in my head as I rolled out of bed. *SAT results.* I pulled the creased papers out and re-examined the words carefully. This time the words on the page took on different meanings. As I read them, I thought about the conversation with Angie about what to do after high school. It was one of the first times I can remember feeling a sense of personal pride about my scores, rather than my de facto reaction which revolved around one less thing to do. Maybe, Angie was right. I was completely happy working at the shop and hanging out with her, Tom, Wade and even Patty for the foreseeable future. Tom had said it before, as well, "All I had to do was apply myself" *Therein* laid the problem. I spent so much time bucking the academic institution at large, I had no formidable experience working with-in the system to plan my academic future. I was going to need some help. I reached for a pen on my desk and scribbled a quick note on the crinkled envelope. My bruised shin made for a labored hobble as I made my way to the kitchen and left the envelope on the stove for Mom. The message was short and to the point. It simply said, "Let's talk. :)"

FEATURED TRACK

Alanis Morissette - All I Really Want

7

Thank You May I Have Another

I gingerly limped to the refrigerator, dry mouthed and strained like I was dragging an iron ball shackle through the desert in search of water. Inside the door was a "freshly made" batch of frozen tropical juice. Mom dumped the concentrated iced juice blob into a pitcher of water overnight and by the time the morning rolled around it was in a prime state for a simple stir and pour. *Perfecto.* I agitated the mild pulpy contents and mainlined large gulps of the ambrosian so sweet nectar from the pour spout down my throat.

"I've told you a hundred times to stop drinking from the container!" I was so startled I shot a singeing stream of juice out my nose and choked back the remnants of burning citrus into the back of my throat. *Apparently, Mom decided not to sleep in this Sunday.* "The least you could do is not put your mouth directly on it. Let me at-least pretend I'm living with someone who cares about others in the house." She took a passing whiff and quipped "and personal hygiene".

She had a point. My clothes were especially ripe this morning. She slapped the back of my arm and rolled her eyes in jest as she started her morning coffee. That's when she noticed the sticky note.

"Talk about what?" she said as she opened the envelope. Her eyes continued to widen as she skimmed the letter. Had I not been absolutely positive that she wanted to encase the letter in glass, I could have sworn her tightly clenched hands were going to rip the paper in two. Tears filled her eyes as she gave me a massive hug. After a few seconds, she started laughing under her happy cry, "You really do smell awful this morning." She pulled away and looked me straight in the eye with her hands on my cheeks, "But, I am so very proud of you!" I'm not going to lie, it felt good to hear her praise, and see her so happy. We spent so many days merely passing in the night, hardly communicating, if at all. This was a great way to start the day, even though I was dead tired, and my shin would not ... stop ... throbbing. "So, what do you want to talk about, exactly? Coll-ege?" she asked hesitantly.

"Actually, I think so." The words tasted dirty leaving my mouth. "Two for sure." When I first opened my mind to the possibility of giving this a go, two options stood out: the best overall and the closest best. By reputation alone, MIT stood out to me as the best overall school, and it was hard not to acknowledge UT just down the road "I think I want to give MIT and UT a try." Mom stood there, atypically silent. "I mean if these tests really are all that you need to do to get into these schools, it would be dumb for me not to at-least apply, right?" The logic rattled off my tongue like a seasoned lawyer, but this was no sham. I was genuinely curious to see what would happen next, but she wasn't buying it.

"So, what brought on this sudden change?" She was naturally suspicious and scanning me for tells.

"I just did better than I thought I would, that's all." She still wasn't buying it, but she let it go to tend to her morning coffee.

"Do you mind if I call the school counselor and ask them to help you get some of the application forms?" She wasn't looking at me, only at her coffee cup as she tensely stirred it waiting for a reply. Before I could reply though, we heard a ruckus from the front yard. We cracked the kitchen blinds to see Wade's truck hopping the curb as he backed into our driveway. His rainbow "Titty Bingo" bumper sticker on his rear window was the topic of some personal mumblings for Mom, but I didn't want to re-open that conversation this morning. I quickly limped to my room and put on some new clothes. When

I pulled off my jeans, I recognized an all too familiar horizontal bruising across my shin. *Garden Hose Box.* I grabbed a fresh pair of plaid boxers and the lesser pair of wrinkled jeans draped over the back of my chair. Shirt selection was easy, *He Who Dies with the Most Toys ... Still Dies.* Not only was it on top, but it was even clean. *Bonus.* I took my mom's advice and stumbled into the bathroom for some much-needed deodorant and mouth wash. Wallet. Keys. Walkman. Backpack. *Time.* Over the years, this four-step process had become automatic, almost like calf roping. Mom was still in the kitchen drinking her coffee staring at Wade's truck clutching the results envelope in her free hand. I grabbed a Pop Tart and hobbled past her towards the door, but before I turned the corner, I answered her question, "About those application forms. Sure thing." We exchanged congenial head nods as she peered over the lip of her coffee cup. I could feel her glow and excitement radiating through the exterior walls. It was by far the happiest I had seen her in a long while. *Possibly ever.*

    Once outside the door, the evidence of my late-night arrival painted a clear picture of my final approach into the house and reaffirmed my cause for injury. It was not pretty. About ten feet from the driveway, my bike was careened on the front lawn with an obvious flat back tire. Next to it was that goddamn garden hose box. My shin pulsed fiercely as I surveyed my indented outstretched silhouette on the dew-soaked lawn. Broken blades of grass and leaves outlined my landing with a broken pair of headphones and a scrap of red paper center mass. *Penny roll?* The paper was damp, but still surprisingly crisp, which is when I noticed there was still one penny left stuck at the end of the unraveled sheath. Warm memories and feelings flushed through my body recalling every wish, joke and conversation from the night before. I tossed my headphones towards the trash can and headed to Wade's passenger door, tucking the penny sheath into my backpack for safe keeping.

    Wade was busy banging out Pepper's drum beat on his steering wheel when I tossed my bag through the open window into the seat. *That is pouring like an avalanche coming down the mountain ♪*

    "Hey man, you're here a bit early, ya think?" I asked.

    "Dude, I couldn't wait. Tom and I have been saying for months now that you two were probably going to start dating. So, how'd it go last night?" He downed a few swigs of his coffee cup, waited for me to slam the door and shot out of my driveway re-hopping the same curb on his egress.

"Well, it went ... well, I think." I replayed the evening, moment by moment, as the memories were trickling in at a much more leisurely and enjoyable pace now that I was seated and the throbbing in my leg subsided. "We just talked ... a lot. We went to Little Caesars ... walked around the fountains at the courthouse ... and then I walked her home."

Wade jumped in abruptly, "Did you guys swing by FlowJoe's?" We were only a few blocks from the shop stopped at a traffic light, and he could see their sign off in the distance. *One ... track ... mind ... much?*

"Uh ... no. Can't say we did." I replied.

Relationship small talk didn't appear to be Wade's strong suit, which is why I had no idea why I opted to divulge the next tidbits of information, except for the fact that he was the closest thing I had to a best friend and I was dying to tell someone.

"But we did kiss. Three times in fact."

I peered out the side of my eyes to see if it phased him at all, but Wade's even keeled response to this news was far from the overt spit-take jubilation I had mentally envisioned.

"That's nice." He replied. "That's better than bickering about your SAT scores all night." He rolled his eyes a bit and raised his coffee cup to salute the moment, and then followed with sager Wade wisdom. "I'd still watch your ass though, Angie seemed pretty upset about you beating her score. You never know when a flagpole might get shoved up there!" When the light turned green, he accentuated the joke by punching the accelerator and screeching the tires.

Sunday mornings were typically slow. Over half the town was in church, but there was still a lot of prep work we needed to open the shop. Wade didn't mind helping on the weekends. In fact, we co-opted the Peanut M&M ritual from Empire Records to choose the morning music. The minute Tom walked down from his apartment, Wade stopped dusting the tables and blurted out the news about my date with Angie. There was no real reason for me to say anything, Wade's steel trap recollection allowed him to repeat practically every word I uttered on the ride over.

"I'm happy for you, Ben ... even if she asked, you, out." Tom gave his reassuring smile and messed up my hair with his other hand. "You two are perfect together!"

"Thanks", I said while avoiding eye contact. It truly was shaping up to be an amazing morning. Customers called in with easy problems, and I knocked them out in short order. Expired account. Wrong phone number. Deleted dial-up networking desktop shortcut. I was on a roll, and then a few hours later, Angie arrived, and we got the morning awkwardness out of the way pretty quick. Tom gave her, what I assume to be, a similar talk and hug and now everyone at the shop knew. Technically, Patty only knew about the pre-date version, but I was sure he would pick up the remaining details on Monday when he was back in the shop.

The whole week felt surreal, in part because Angie and I were hitting it off so well, but also because it was the two-day dead week before Thanksgiving break. My favorite week of the year. It was the only holiday break that never seemed to be overly flanked by special projects, reports or tests. The non-stop series of interruptions and variable student attendance had conditioned seasoned teachers to keep fluid itineraries, or request substitutes themselves. It was sadistically satisfying watching stouthearted teachers fight against these inertial dampening forces with in-class projects or extra credit assignments and then succumb to the futility and simply watch a movie because no one gave a damn that week; especially the honors students.

Tom invited all our families to Thanksgiving at the shop. He coordinated directly with mine and Wade's mother, but Angie's parents were stuck working. At-least that is what they told Tom, but Angie was still able to attend. This would be the biggest Thanksgiving gathering I had attended by far. One slight problem arose. Mom didn't know about Angie, yet. *Crap!* When we arrived, Angie was already there helping Tom and Patty dress the tables with holiday decorations. She decided to dress "comfortably", *her words*, which consisted of her favorite Red Hot Chili Peppers t-shirt, red flannel, jeans and her regular docs. *She looked amazing.* When the door chimes rang, Angie gave me a small wave and walked towards us, while I responded with a wide-eyed frightful smile and morse code blinking eyes attempting to warn her of the impending minefield.

"Hey Ben," she said, walking to greet us. "You must be Ben's mom. I'm Angie. Nice to meet you."

"Hello there, Angie. My name is Elaine, and you must be the girl that Ben can't stop talking about." *Wait, what!?!?* My mom had a sinister grin on her face, and if I didn't know better, Angie's cheeks turned a bit red. At the time, I remember feeling upset, or betrayed even, but over time I came to realize this is where my mom excelled. She could read between the lines better than anyone, and I bet she didn't even need the door chimes to figure it out. Mom grabbed my shoulder and jostled my torso a bit to make the point, "Oh, yeah, he's gone on and on about this girl that he likes that he met. I didn't know you'd be here, but it's definitely nice to meet you, Angie."

"Yeah, we just can't get this guy to shut up, can we?" Angie gave my arm a slight slug and sent "What the Hell?" signals with her eyes. "I'm going to go finish helping Tom with the decorations. I'll let Ben give you the tour." Angie scurried off to find Tom.

Mom leaned over and whispered in my ear, "I assume this is where all your newfound interest in college is coming from?" I nodded. "Doesn't matter, she seems nice." She ruffled my hair, *Why do adults always do that!?*, and gave me a kiss on the side of the forehead. I don't think that could have gone any better, even if I had planned it. All that fuss for nothing. I gave her a quick tour of the shop from the Community Corner to the Tom-NET modem banks, and then we helped Angie and Tom finish setting the tables. Less than five minutes into napkin folding, the door chimes rang again, and this time Wade's mom barreled into the room with loud flopping paper bags draped over her arms. Her oversized sunglasses were sliding down her face exposing her hand embroidered hippie headband holding back a nest of frazzled curly bangs. Wade was still outside trying to finagle a sip of his coffee with more bags weighing down his arms.

"Happy Thanksgiving, everyone!" Wade's mom exclaimed in an odd Doubtfire-esque accent. "Sorry, we are late! I couldn't decide which table crockery to bring for today's occasion; glazed porcelain or natural stoneware. So, I decided to bring both sets. "She unloaded her bags at the support desk and pulled out a horribly malformed set of turquoise bowls with chains of sad, I presume, flowers painted along the rim. "Not my best work, but it's all I have in stock at the moment."

"Are you a sculptor?" Mom asked.

"I consider myself more of an ... earth interpreter. I listen to the clay's voice and channel it's wishes to the best of my ability." she replied while emphasizing her well-worn artist hands. In formal artistic fashion, she offered a handshake to introduce herself while clasping one of her bowls in her other arm. "I am Jackie Dennison-Bodin, also known as Wade's mother. Haha" Her fake laugh was a bit off putting, but she was quick to follow-up. "You must be Ben's mom?" When Mom reached out with her free hand, Jackie pulled her in for an awkward hug with the hideous blue ceramic pinned between their bodies.

"Yes, my name is Elaine," she exhaled in pain as the bowl wedged itself under her lowest rib, "Elaine Wilson." She backed away while rubbing her stomach. "So, what did this clay say to you?"

"Oh, that's simple enough, darling. Soup." She let out a sophisticated upbeat laugh and set the bowl on the table. "It is so nice to finally meet you, Elaine. I feel like I know all about you and Ben from the things Wade tells me about their escapades this past year." Mom was caught a bit off guard by that comment, but not as much as the following kiss on the cheek and additional embrace. The mood in the room quickly turned weird. Thankfully, Tom wheeled in some carts dressed to the nines with a delectable Boston Market feast that smelled absolutely delicious and everyone's focus turned to eating.

Before we ate, Tom stood and offered a toast. "First of all, I wanted to thank everyone for coming today. I'm sorry that everyone's family couldn't make it, but rest assured, we are all family here." Tom always had a way with words and knowing just what to say, but it was clear even he was having trouble choosing what to say next. He started off more formal than usual and recognized the record year in revenue and the inaugural anniversary of Tom-NET. The mothers in the room beamed with pride as Tom talked of the team's accomplishments. The rest of us did a poor job pretending it was no big deal, but truth be told, it felt really good to hear Tom acknowledge all our hard work. The speech quickly turned into a rambling of words for nearly ten minutes until Tom caught himself. "Ahh well, you get the idea. Thank you, everyone, for all your ideas, passion and innovative spirit. "He raised his glass. "To another successful year, and many many more!" We all raised our beverages in kind and savored the toast for one final moment before Tom exclaimed, "Let's eat!" Everyone dashed toward the food carts like they had been shot out of a cannon. *The sales floor smelled like turkey and gravy for nearly three weeks. Yum!*

Tom ordered way too much food, again. He always claimed various difficulties in ordering food for large parties, but we all knew he just really liked having leftovers. When it came to eating cold leftovers out of the employee fridge, no one could hold a candle to Tom's ninja-style grazing. He could be in and out of the fridge so fast the light wouldn't even turn on. The most indicting proof that this was no accident, and was by design, was the two-pound surplus of Mac 'n Cheese, *his favorite*, which he had already written his name on all the containers. That day, I packed away at-least three plates of turkey, mashed potatoes and dressing with gravy. My self-respect waned as I questioned my squeaking chair's structural integrity. Food comas set in around the tables while Wade talked in painstaking detail about an article he read online about the growing "coffee chemistry" industry. All the talk of hydrocarbons and alkaloids nearly sealed my overstuffed eyeballs, but then Tom came to the rescue.

"It's been a long time since I've had a fine meal with such fine company, but the day is not over, yet." He removed a cloth from an AV cart to reveal a new custom-built computer with a beautiful seventeen-inch Trinitron monitor. "I give to you, Thanksgiving Trivia Night …" he said pressing the <ENTER> key, "You Don't Know Jack edition!" All of a sudden, the voice of an obnoxious game show host blasted from the stereo speakers. If there was one thing we loved more than trivia, it was snark, and this game set the tone in the first ten seconds that it was probably going to be fun in both those aspects.

We split into teams. It was me, Wade and our moms against, Patty, Angie and Tom. The competition was fierce right out of the gate, but once the novelty of the new game wore off, we started to lose people. Wade quickly lost interest and focused his energies on trying to spice up his bland cup of shop coffee with broken pieces of miniature candy canes. So, it was pretty much me and "the moms" vs three trivia experts. It was rough. History was the only subject I could get any help from my team, *pop culture was lost on them*, but they rarely agreed. Wade surprised everyone by nailing a question on Pablo

Escobar's drug cartel before the options were even read aloud. No one thought he was even paying attention. His love for all things coffee, included learning everything about Colombia!

As time went on, the game decomposed from "team vs team" to Patty, Angie and me rapidly clicking through the game just to play the Jack Attack sequences. It was really quite enjoyable. So enjoyable, in fact, we completely missed the adults sneak away into the back room. My parents never had the "just say no" talk with me, but that might have been due to the fact that I had multiple predispositions that negated most recreational drugs: terrified of needles, hated things in my nose and mild asthma that ruled out most inhalants. The closest I ever came to doing drugs was accidentally doing a whip-it, once, but I was just trying to see if I could eat the entire bottle of whipped cream. All the more reason I was surprised when I peeked through the window and all three of the adults were chilling out around Tom's Corvette listening to the radio and passing around a cigar sized joint. To this day, Mom refuses to admit that she smoked any pot, let alone on that day in particular. Her "I didn't inhale" argument was subverted by her overly relaxed and chatty mood that evening, which proved to me that she was at-least rocking every ounce of a contact high. *Willie would be proud.*

The party officially came to a close not too long after they resurfaced from the back room. Tom was the only one who was levelheaded enough to pick up on the pot puns we were all throwing down. The moms were baked out of their minds. Wade and I collected our parents and lured them into our respective cars with bags of sour cream and onion potato chips and leftovers not claimed by Tom. I was pretty sure my learner's permit only cared that I was accompanied by a licensed driver over the age of twenty-one. Whether or not that licensed driver could tell the difference between a stop sign and a tap dancing unicorn was beside the point. I told Angie I would call her later and drove the longest twenty blocks imaginable with extreme caution. If I was pulled over, Mom's drug sobriety would be questioned instantly if she kept apologizing to the empty bag of chips on the dash for eating its friends. As weird as the day ended up, it was still the best Thanksgiving, *ever*!

Black Friday hit the shop like a ton of bricks the next morning. Tom and I opened the shop earlier than normal to prepare for the onslaught of deal hunters. Jollyville, Texas may have been small, but it was still chalk full of true American families who bonded over bouts of mass consumerism and the search for the ultimate deal. Tom promoted a combo deal in the newspaper: "Buy a new 33.6K modem on Black Friday and receive two free months of Tom-NET". We opened the shop at six, and we sold all twenty 33.6K modems by seven. By nine, every modem was gone. It was clear, people were getting two things for Christmas that year: The Internet and Tomb Raider. Everyone in town was still curious about getting online, while others were going crazy about Laura Croft and her "puzzles". One lesson I learned early on working with Tom was that everything in the computer sales world is interconnected. For example, when someone buys a computer, they usually buy Internet access to go with it. To get online, they need modems and software. If they like games, even better, because they will always need the latest OS, more RAM and larger hard drives. At the rate computers and software were changing, it was a steady revenue stream for anyone who carried all the pieces to the puzzle. Tom was well aware of this fact, and he made sure that Andersson Electronics was the best and most advertised one-stop computer shop in town. It was that reputation that ultimately delivered Anto to us a few weeks later.

FEATURED TRACK
Oasis - D'You Know What I Mean?

8
We Have Lift Off

Black Friday was a long day, but the work was well worth it. Not only did we sell every modem, we also signed up over forty new Tom-NET customers, sold ten new computers and scheduled eight in-home setups. Between the new computer sales commission and my cut from the in-home setups, I was looking at an extra two to three hundred dollars easy before Christmas. *Cha-ching!* Even better, Tom had me upgrade all the shop computers that week, and he let me keep some of the older RAM for my franken-rig at home. Getting frag drunk and knee deep in Carmack carnage with my new Pentium 200 and a free 32MB of EDO goodness was a beautiful thing. The world was moving a mile a minute. School's absurd radioactive static blurred weekdays into one another with discernible euphoric weekend blips that denoted the passage of time. About two weeks before Christmas, or six weeks after the first Christmas decoration was spotted, *whichever came first,* there was a day that stood out head and shoulder above the rest. All things being equal, it was a forgettable cold, rain soaked and slow going Saturday, until an eccentric fast-talking personality walked into the shop. Wade was conducting a cutthroat game of Hot Shot trivia, pitting Patty and me against Angie and Tom. We were tied at eight a piece, when we heard the shop chimes ring their familiar tone and a thin Hispanic girl with long neon red hair backed her way into the shop carrying a bulky wet trash bag. Her demeanor suggested she was in a rush, as she scanned the room intently with purpose until she saw our computer diagnostic station. From the moment she first spoke, we knew her stopping by was no accident.

"You guys mind if I borrow your build desk?" She sassooned her wet hair from her face, and we were all speechless, especially Patty whose lower jaw was cratered into the floor. First off, she spoke insanely fast, like Micro Machine man fast. Also, it wasn't every day that someone came in with a trash bag and such a specific and direct request. I honestly don't think it would have mattered if we told her no, or not. She walked over to the desk and set her bag on the side table before we could even say a word. "My monitor is on the fritz at home, and I need to fix a driver problem. Don't worry, this will only take a second." *Still no permission had been granted.* She unwrapped her trash bag and carefully unfolded one of those Indian blankets with tassels and revealed the most badass computer case I had ever seen. It was a sleek jet-black mid-tower with a large custom star-shaped plexiglass window on the side through which we could see multiple cooling fans, intricate venting conduits and cables routed with the precision of a surgeon. *Dayyyyyyyuum!* The opposite side of the case was adorned with a cornucopia of assorted pop culture stickers: Pulp Fiction, Star Wars, Garbage Pail Kids, radio stations and vintage fashion stickers. She sized up the service station and seamlessly had her computer connected to the power cord, monitor and peripherals in no time flat. Minus the typical grunting BIOS checks, the computer hummed along at a whisper with blue accent lights radiating from the star window cut-out, further emphasizing the cool factor. This was no ordinary compute. It was a work of art!

"You guys sure are a chatty bunch," she said in an overly sarcastic tone as she popped off her side casing and grabbed the communal bottle of canned air. Angie motioned for me to do something, but Tom beat me to it.

"That's an interesting setup you've got going on there. Mind if I take a look?" he said.

"Sure thing. Built it, myself." she replied.

Like a hungry pack of wolves on a steak, the majority of the Y-chromosomes in the room flocked to check out the hardware up close and introduce ourselves. *In that order.* The moment she started speaking our common core nerd dialect: Pentium, Socket 7, Voodoo, the more her fast paced speech seemed to slow down. It was obvious that she was smart, confident, opinionated and a bit of a rebel. In short, she fit right in.

    Her name was Antonella Vega, but she went by Anto. Her father moved the family to Jollyville to be closer to Anto's abuela just after Thanksgiving. He was a DPS officer transfer, while her mother stayed at home taking care of Anto's abuela and herding her two mischievous younger brothers at home during the rest of the school vacation. One of the coolest things about Anto was that she was eighteen but graduated a whole year early from her high school back in Miami. She spent the last five months working for a large computer shop fixing computers, which is why her rig was so tricked out. Our nerdy pow-wow lasted a solid twenty minutes. Anto pivoted from topic to topic, answering our techie questions with ease while navigating the command prompt and registry editor. I noticed a few unnecessary reboots for a simple registry key change, but I took that as a sign that she wanted to keep the pop culture and electronics conversations going. Patty suddenly developed a slight stutter and a red cheeked complexion whenever he caught Anto's eyes. If I didn't know any better, I'd say that he liked her from the get-go, and you could tell that Anto thought it was cute.

    Wade and Angie waited patiently in the Community Corner listening to the nerdfest, until Angie finally made an *eh-hmm* noise that caught everyone's attention. Anto popped her head out of the crowd and locked eyes with Angie right away.

    "Oh, my gawd ..." she busted free from the crowd, "Girl, I love what you are doing with your outfit. Where'd you get that shirt!?" Angie was wearing one of her many flannels tied at the waist with her favorite Shirley Manson undershirt. Anto sized Angie up and felt the fabric of her flannel. "You are rocking every inch of this pattern, for realz. The color matches your eyes perfectly." *She wasn't wrong.* "The name's Anto."

    "Angie." she replied and offered a handshake.

    "Bring it in, girl. I'm a hugger not a shaker." Anto grabbed Angie by the arm and pulled her in for an uncompromising hug. Angie stood confused, but smiling, nonetheless. Anto was a lot to take in for everyone, but if I had to guess, Angie was just happy to no longer be the only girl in the room!

"So, who is this, your boyfriend?" Anto motioned towards Wade. "Nice to meet you. Anto." Wade and Angie exchanged concerned looks with a hint of laughter creeping from their lips.

"Actually ... "Angie began to reply, trying not to laugh too hard, but Anto cut her off.

"Just kidding, girl. Nothing against you dude," she said, slapping the back of Wade's hand, "but the way that Angie and Bennie-boy over there have been sneaking glances at each other this past half hour, it's clear that you two are a thing." She closed her eyes and held a finger in the air for a moment taking in a few slow deep breaths. "My family spirits say that you two look good together, and that you have a strong future ahead of you. Bennie and Angie. Ha... Benji! That's what I'm calling you from two now on!" *And that's how we got our name.*

At this point, Wade was flustered. In uncomfortable social situations he would normally just fade away into the background, but Anto brought an assault of personality to his doorstep and he was more squirmy than usual.

"Seriously, dude. Sorry about that. What's your name?" she said.

"Uh... Wade." he replied.

"Well, Uh ... Wade ..." this made Wade laugh, "what is it you do around here besides stay quiet? You weren't over there drooling all over my rig like these fools. What's the matter? You don't like fine computer craftsmanship?"

I couldn't tell if she was kidding or felt truly disrespected.

"Yeah ... I'm not really a computer guy. I'm more of the coffee guy."

Anto fell forward forcing Wade to catch her and spoke into his chest. "Ay, Dios Mio! Por favor, tell me you know where to get a decent espresso in this town. If I have one more crappy cup of coffee, I'm gonna lose it!"

"You like coffee?" he asked.

"Chico, I'm from Miami. Mi familia is from Puerto Rico. Coffee is in our blood ... literally. Café Lareño, Café Rico ..."

Wade interrupted her with a sweeping bear hug that lifted her upright, "You and I are going to get along just fine." *I thought Wade was going to cry.* "I'll be right back." He slipped the tie breaking trivia card into his shirt pocket and grabbed his rain jacket. "I'm going to get you a special espresso at FlowJoe's that I know you're gonna love!" Wade vanished into the rain in a flash leaving Anto standing alone and speechless. *This didn't happen often.*

"So, all you guys work here, huh? Cool ... cool ... cool. Cool. cool." she said.

"Pretty much," I chimed in. "Tom runs the place. Patty and I do most of the tech support, build outs, and account setups. Angie handles the books and runs the floor when it's crazy. Wade ... well, Wade helps out where he can, but he is mainly here for coffee, conversation and trivia."

"Sounds like you guys have a pretty tight crew. I worked at a Computer Village back in Miami. I mainly did computer sales and tech support, but that was only because those pendejos didn't want a girl showing them the right way to build a computer." She rubbed the side of her computer with pride. "That's how I was able to afford the parts for Sierra here, so it was worth it." She chuckled as she outlined the custom side-panel cut-out with her finger at which point she noticed her computer was fixed. "But hey, "she said, shutting down her computer, "thanks for letting me borrow your table. Now I just hope mi hermanito's apple juice didn't totally kill my monitor." She did that religious cross movement thing with her hand over her chest and kissed her necklace. Tom had a familiar look in his eye, and I could tell what he was thinking.

"So, tell you what, Anto." Tom said. "Right now, we are good on headcount, but I have a feeling we are going to need some more help heading into the new year. If you're ever interested, I can start you out part time with commission. In the meantime, maybe you can stop by every now and then to see how we do things around here, and if you have the time ... maybe you can teach us all a few things about the right way to build a computer." Tom's mustache curled upward to accentuate his jovial smile. "What do you say?"

"Ayyyy!!!" Anto screamed in excitement and raised her hands above her head and Salsa-ed over to Tom for an enormous hug. "Yes yes yes Si si si!" Her words continued to rattle off her tongue even after she let Tom go. At the same time, Wade returned with a newly half emptied coffee refill in one hand and Anto's espresso in the other.

"Here you go, Anto. I call it ... the Bodin Special "

After her first sip, her knees buckled into another heartfelt Salsa to celebrate the return of good tasting coffee, a computer job and weird technical folk into her life.

Over the next few days, Anto did more than stop by every now and then, she became a live-in resident like the rest of us. She brought her latest copy of PC Shopper. It was less than a week old, and all thousand pages were already highlighted, indexed and tabbed like a grandmother's recipe book with all of Anto's favorite deals, vendors and combo specials. With only a few phone calls, she was able to hook Tom up with all the same vendors from her old job and cut the shop's costs on existing inventory by at-least ten percent. *Wow!* When she said she could do computer sales, she wasn't joking. She could sell a computer upgrade to a T-2000. Tom was thoroughly impressed and after a few days, he gave her official hours on the shop schedule. I found it interesting that things always seemed to work themselves out at just the right time when it came to the shop. Wade introduced me to the shop and Tom, where I first talked to Angie, and then we randomly found both Patty and Anto who are both extremely talented with computers. Little did we know that finding Anto in such serendipitous fashion would be the start of a new age in Andersson Electronics and Tom-NET.

The week before Christmas was hectic, but mainly because school didn't dismiss for vacation until Friday the 20th. This meant that everyone was working extra hours trying to keep ahead of the surging tech support, internet setups and computer purchases while Angie, Wade and I were held hostage to midterms. The class material was easy enough. It was just hard to carve time out to study. On one hand, I could get an A on an exam. On the other, I could get a B and probably $250 in commissions. The struggle was real, but I knew that if I let my grades slip too much, Mom would ride my ass to quit, and there was no way that was going to happen. She was pretty narrow minded when it came to stuff like that. *Wonder where I got that from?* For all her perceived faults, she tried exceptionally hard to be the best mom she could to a difficult child like me. Christmas was especially difficult since that is when she found out about the cheating. We shared a special bond around this time of the year, a mutual cynicism toward the holidays. It started with mutual coping in the absence of traditions connected to "him", but quickly evolved into the burning of his pictures and unwanted artifacts atop a crackling fireplace log. New chapters were forming in our lives and Christmas was now a holiday for us, and us alone, but we still kept one tradition that we both loved. *Gotcha.*

Gotcha was a game that pitted my parents against me to see who could outsmart the other at Christmas. Unfortunately, all my attempts to incorporate actual paintballs into the tradition were summarily denied. Gotcha was simple. Parents tried to keep their presents a secret until Christmas morning. My "job" was to find all the hiding places before Christmas and log the item and location. If I could identify at-least one present and its location on Christmas morning, I would win. If not, the parents would win. Gotcha didn't start out as a game, but Mom felt that we should embrace my over inquisitive nature rather than continue to fight it. *Smart move, Elaine.* One year, Dad took the game to the next level by setting Goonie-esque "booty" traps on Christmas Eve night to try and keep me from snooping through the loot under the Christmas tree. Trip wires, snares and alarms frequented the house each year to try and catch me in the act. Every year they got more intricate and advanced, but I'll never forget the first trap that got me. Dad strung a simple piece of red yarn across the hallway attached to an empty aluminum can filled with miscellaneous screws and soda tabs. The rattling sound erupted like a starter pistol the instant those fuzzy fibers grazed my leg. *I walked right into it.* I covered the vast distance to my room in a series of broad, fast and quiet leaps and scaled my bunk bed ladder with such grace that would make Jackie Chan envious. I pretended to sleep and made a tent over my chest with my fingers and the sheet to hide my rapid breathing in case my parents opted for a detailed fly-by. *Too close!* My heart raced and a Grinchian grin spread across my face at this exciting new development. Further investigation was required. I hummed the Mission Impossible theme music to myself as I crawled below, jumped over and practiced diffusing the trap in super spy fashion. It was the most unexpected and awesome Christmas Eve experience I could have asked for. Unfortunately, Christmas traps were a relatively short-lived Gotcha tradition. Who knew parents didn't like waking up to their traps rewired on their own bedroom door? *Not me.* Over the years, Gotcha continued in different forms, as both sides developed new strategies to jockey for superiority in the coveted present hiding/finding competition.

Sometimes I felt sorry for Mom. Buying presents for me was already difficult enough given my picky technical palette. Not to mention, there were limited local stores to purchase said gadgetry that were not our shop, but this didn't slow her down one bit. Christmas that year was one for the ages. About three weeks before Christmas, or two days after we put up our Christmas tree, I scanned the normal hiding spots for signs of presents; under the bed, back closet upper shelves and the attic. Being left at home alone most of the time had its advantages. There was no trace of any present, but in each location, I found a sliver of paper with the word "Nope" and a smiley face on it. *She was toying with me!* Another few days passed, and I continued to find antagonistic memos throughout the house. She was getting cocky; perhaps a bit too cocky. It was somewhere that she knew I couldn't find, but that she easily could. *The Gun Safe!*

We didn't have any guns, or to be more accurate, we had a few old heirloom rifles that didn't fire, and my Grandma's old BB gun. The gun safe used to be my dad's, but Mom used it to store our passports and her fancy jewelry. It had to be in there, but what was the combination? *Challenge accepted!* Mom was overly meticulous and orderly when it came to her office. So much so that when I scanned her filing cabinet, there was a folder filed under "G" labeled "Gun Safe". In it, I found the combination instructions listed on the last service order. *Boom!* I spun through the dial combination like it was my locker between classes. *34 Right.* *clank* It opened and there was the treasure trove of shopping bags stashed with their original packaging and receipts: a plaid Mossimo hat, Nike wind suit and, to my surprise, Turbo C++ 3.0. *Tom must have helped.*

This was partially new territory for me. If a wrapped present under the tree caught my attention, I would use a steak knife and slit the present at the tape seam and check out the contents. Afterwards, I would overlay a new piece of tape over the intrusion point to conceal the cut. If you looked close enough, you could tell, but I don't think they ever caught on. In this case, the presents were unwrapped, so who would notice if I slipped the disk out the bottom of the box and installed Turbo C++ on my computer right now. Besides, I'd rather spend Christmas break coding than learning my first object-oriented language. This would give me almost a week and half head start. All I needed to do now was choose how to reveal my triumph. A little of her own medicine seemed appropriate. I placed a sliver of paper inside the hat's sweatband with the phrase, "Yep! 12/09/96. Gotcha! Merry Xmas from Ben" *Perfect!* I repacked all the bags and shut the safe in triumph. Fast forward a week or so, and it was now Christmas morning and Mom was riding high on her confidence that she would take the Gotcha title. I rattled each box to establish the contents, and strategically opened the presents in order to build suspense. First the wind suit, then the Turbo C++. When I finally unwrapped the hat, I tossed it to her and said, "Merry Christmas. You can open it." When she discovered the note, she looked up at me and let out an exhaustive laugh. We convened with a ceremonial Gotcha! cup of hot cocoa, *part of our tradition,* and then I tried to explain to her what Turbo C++ was and why she did an awesome job at getting it. We sat at my computer for a solid hour, maybe even two, explaining the finer points of data types, pointers and recursion. She was so into the bonding time; I don't think she realized I never took the disks out of the box to install it.   Even if she had noticed, I'd wager she still wouldn't care.

   Both Angie and Wade left to visit their families on Christmas Eve, and wouldn't be back until New Year's Day. Wade and his mom were road tripping to Denver to spend time with his aunt in the mountains. Similarly, Angie was heading to East Texas to spend time with her uncle and cousins. It would be the longest I would go without Angie since we met. I was only a few days into my withdrawal, and it wasn't going well. I had a small fix though that evening when she called from her uncle's house in Gladewater, and we talked for a few minutes before her mother made her hang up. *Damn long-distance charges.* I called her back so we could talk a bit longer, but alas the conversations were getting expensive. *Next time, I'm buying a calling card!* She was in hell with her family and wouldn't be back for another five days. Her only salvation was that one of her cousins was a sophomore at LSU studying Botany and got a full academic scholarship. I could sense Angie's growing intrigue when we said our quick goodbyes when she mentioned grilling her cousin about SAT scores, extracurriculars and scholarship application tips.   The very real thought of Angie eventually going away to college and enduring a long-distance relationship planted itself painfully deep in the back of my mind, but for now

I was focused on counting the days to the new year when she'd be back. *6 days left.*

It was all hands-on deck the next day at the shop as the inevitable storm of post-Christmas stupidity and chaos quickly descended on the shop. Tom, Patty and Anto got to the shop extra early that morning. Unfortunately, with Wade out of town, I had to pedal my metal to the shop, so I arrived a bit stiff from the cold morning winds. Anto was wearing an oversized Santa hat, and Patty was wearing a hideous Christmas sweater. If I wasn't so cold and envious of his obvious warmth, I might have called him on it. When I opened the front door, the music in the shop was so loud I could barely hear the door chimes. The shop speakers were blasting Mariah Carey's "All I Want for Christmas" and Patty was singing right along without abandon. Anto was singing as well, but to a different tune. She was sporting a new portable CD player with headphones and was belting out her own lyrics to "What I Got" by Sublime. It was common to disagree on what music to play when opening the shop. Wade and I preferred using M&Ms, but this was the first time I had seen it settled with a sing-off. These two loved to argue about everything in extraordinary fashion.

Having the extra hands on deck paid quick dividends. We were able to tackle all the chaos Jollyville, Texas could muster in stride and even make room for some rounds of Hot Shot trivia in between. As the day came to a close, Tom pulled Patty and me aside to let us know he was leaving for Mexico that Friday for a long overdue vacation and would be back New Year's Day. Since Anto had extended family visiting her abuela's house, he wanted us to look after the shop. I couldn't help but wonder if Tom truly believed we were responsible enough to take care of everything, or if we were only the best of what was left and he said, "Ahhh, screw It!" I couldn't recall a time I had ever heard Tom talk about taking a vacation, so it was safe to say the next four days were going to be a new experience for everyone.

Patty and I spent that afternoon planning what we'd do with our newly formed vestiges of power. I suggested we turn the Community Corner into a free Quake deathmatch arcade to attract more gamers, and possibly upsell them on some games, hardware upgrades or even a Tom-NET trial account for death matching. The logistics eroded fast and the reality of playing multiplayer Quake for four days fell apart like wet toilet paper. Patty's idea on the other hand was more thoughtful. Patty spent some time learning HTML, JavaScript and CSS on the side, but he wanted a real project to put under his belt. He wanted something more reputable than his scattered portfolio of free GeoCities projects. I had become quite proficient in HTML and Perl, but casted JavaScript out as a lesser language because my perspective was tainted with simple status bar scrollers and page animations. *facepalm*

Before Tom could leave, we approached him with a proposal to redo the Tom-NET website. Patty had a rough mockup consisting of framed navigation, animated menus and a more aesthetically pleasing color palette. After all the work, Tom only had one thing to say, "Sure, knock yourself out. Just one thing, though. None of that annoying blinking crap. Damn stuff makes me feel like I'm having a stroke every time I see one." *He's kidding right?* For owning an ISP, the Tom-NET website was underwhelmingly basic and yet Tom spent the entire week before we launched putting it together. The site had a standard grey background and was filled with ramblings about the shop's history, computer basics and even a link to a site talking about flaming Pop Tarts in all different color and sizes of fonts. The fact that this information was organized into tables didn't help suppress the feeling that the "website" felt more like a dating profile than a formal business presence. The only image, a massive 480x320 JPG of the shop's distinguishable storefront, was centered at the top of the page pushing all the important information like pricing, services and our phone number off the screen. *Yikes.* Far be it from me to criticize Tom for aesthetics. I was equally, if not more, handicapped in making things look visually appeasing. The last true UI innovation I clamored over was when I discovered you could change the background and foreground colors on the DOS prompt with ANSI.SYS, and even I knew that this site was pretty bad. The moment the door slammed on Tom's taxi that Friday evening, we got to work.

Patty focused on deciphering the tidbits of relevant information for our current experience and built a design that would best accommodate them moving forward. I brushed up on my HTML and JavaScript with a little website "research" of my own. It felt awkward using shop computers to scan HTML source code from porn sites, but everyone knew that they had the coolest website tech on the Internet. Everyone, except Mom. *I'm just reading the source code!* About an hour of sifting and sketching, Patty shared a slick three paned frame concept he whipped up in Photoshop. We had our marching orders and were ready to start, there was only one thing holding us back. We had to open the shop on Saturday, and it was already ten o'clock in the evening. Mom was pulling a double shift at the hospital the next day, so we planned a caffeine and pizza fueled all-nighter at the shop to kick off the project. The next day dragged on in a most frustrating way. *Bogus!* Any hopes of squeezing in some extra dev time on the site were dashed by a steady drip of fly-by customers and asinine support calls. *If you only have one phone line, you need to hang-up with me, BEFORE you try to connect again!* The clock on the wall never looked more beautiful than when it struck five that day. We flipped over the "We are Open" sign, picked up some food and started coding.

  I fired up my extended trial of HotDog Pro, *thanks g30d00m8*, and began stubbing out a site skeleton while Patty worked on all the images. There was no questioning what music we would play in the shop that evening. It was the Hackers soundtrack for fourteen hours straight on repeat. *Good Grief!* We were both surprised the CD didn't melt in the stereo, but it worked. Patty uploaded his work to the web host, so I could download it locally onto my PC and start bringing everything together. I asked Patty to build a quick animated GIF, similar to Netscape Navigator's logo without the captain's wheel in the front, with swirling stars for the site footer that said, "built by Tom-NET Web Solutions", to accompany our makeshift CGI visit counter. It was a lame name, but every site we looked at had a similar shout out to the creators, and, let's be honest, Netscape's logo was awesome. *Best. Decision. Ever.* The final hours drug on, as Patty stood over my shoulder barking out orders, nitpicking every last detail on the screen, rather than even touch a PC keyboard or mouse. We published the site around five thirty Sunday morning; a total of about ten hours of work and subsequently about five minutes before I was ready to crack a keyboard over Patty's head, Macho Man style. For all the frustration, the site really was quite exceptional for our first joint venture. The mouse over animations and the custom Tom-NET masthead Patty designed were spot on and complete overkill for our small-town ISP, but Tom deserved the best. We both seized the opportunity to snag a quick two-hour nap before having to clean up and begrudgingly open the shop.

The new year came and went with little fanfare. The shop was damn near quiet through New Year's Day, no one visited. The server room was a different story, though. Tom-NET modems were squelching and chirping non-stop like gossiping flamingos, which made it difficult for either of us to snag some much-needed sleep. That's when things got a little tense and awkward. Patty was a practicing perfectionist, and he turned his fidgety compulsion towards the website that morning and constantly found subtle things to tweak. His obsession became my living hell. Every five minutes came yet another request to change something. It wasn't that I didn't agree with his feedback, but I had already mentally moved on to bigger better things and didn't want to be stuck in an endless loop of tech support for yet another thing. After the first five updates, I lost my patience and told him to make a list and I would take a look later. I was tired, hungry, overly caffeinated and impatient to see Angie, who was due back sometime that afternoon. I spent the rest of the day hanging in her corner, listening to California Love and fiddling with a new God's Eye animation routine in Turbo C++ when I heard the shop door chimes ring and Tom came barreling through the door nearly knocking the door chimes off the ceiling.

The old man looked relaxed, tanned and freshly limber as he finagled his body and attached luggage into the shop. He set his bags down and unstrapped two plastic wrapped sombreros from his backpack and tossed one to each of us. "You didn't burn the place down, congrats!" I tore off the plastic to try on the hat. It smelled like fresh straw tainted with the remnants of a foul-smelling odor. *Perfume?* I looked like an idiot. I had no words, so I forced a smile like I was eight years old back at Aunt Betsy's taking an Easter photo. There was a definite pep in his step, and all the clues suggested whatever went down in Mexico served him well. After a few pleasantries, Tom continued to his apartment in the back humming the distinctive tune to Margaritaville with the goofiest grin on his face. About thirty minutes later, the door chimes rang again. This time it was different. The normal clanking tones were accompanied by the squeaking of door hinges at just the right pitch that matched the slow rate in which she usually opened the door. A slight breeze cooled the back of my neck and carried an all too familiar smell of sarcasm and wit. *Angie.* I turned to face the door, yanking my tethered CD player and headphones to the floor.

Her eyes were fixed on me as she walked to her corner. I could feel her cold shivering hands wrap around my sides and onto my back. Her soft damp cheek sank into my neck and warmed my body as our embrace tightened and she whispered the most loving words, "I missed you, goofball". I responded in kind like a blubbering parent, "I missed you, more" resting my chin on her shoulder holding back the misty eyes. For some, 1997 started on January 1st at midnight. For me, it started at this very moment, right here, with Angie back in my arms.

Tom was slow to come out of vacation mode, so it took a few days for everything at the shop to return to normal. It was Friday morning and with Wade's pickup service back on schedule, my bike was relegated to the back porch and my frostbitten hands could get a much-needed reprieve. My cuticles were hard and brittle like sun damaged plastic, and no amount of pain could prevent me from picking and biting at them. It was a nasty habit, but one that was just as ingrained in my DNA as breathing. It grossed Angie out to no end, so much so that she frequently grabbed my hand with a glob of lotion in her palm and playfully massaged it into my hand while pretending it was an accident. I didn't mind as long as she used unscented ones, not any of that napalm ointment from Bath and Body Works. I walked into one of their stores once, and it took nearly two years before my singed sinuses could shake that cinnamon Crappletini smell. *Never again!* Who was I kidding? It felt great and kind of encouraged me to keep on doing it.

I heard Wade's truck rumbling outside in the driveway, so I grabbed my gear, headed out the door and locked up. I could see Wade through the rear window, slurping his coffee and beating out the bass line to his music, but there was a large odd wad of blankets and straps with a couple protruding metal hoses in the back of his truck. My thumb slowly pressed against the black latch release on the door handle. *Did I even want to know?* I was mid-thought about to open the door, when Wade rolled down the passenger window.

"She's a beaut, isn't she?" Wade said energetically across his face and holding his coffee cup in the air as if offering a toast.

"I guess ... what is it?" At this point, I had no reasonable clue on what was wrapped beneath the sheet. My mind oscillated between a small motorcycle engine or a high end party bong.

"It's a triple unit La Marzocco Linea Classic, silly. The most prolific espresso machine on the commercial market." Wade was starstruck. "And, it's all mine!" *sigh*

"That's nice, but how did you get it, and more importantly, where are you going to put this contraption? It's huge!" I replied.

I stepped into the cab and prepared myself for the series of incoherent tangents that typically accompanied Wade's stories. He proceeded to tell a tale of a seemingly lackluster Christmas break that somehow transitioned him into a book report on the life expectancy and mating habits of prairie dogs. *Wade reads encyclopedias when he's bored.* His stay in Colorado changed though when his aunt gave him a tour of her storage shed where she kept her collection of randomness amassed over the years from her small repo company. *She and Tom would have gotten along great.* A few months prior she received this espresso machine in trade for a payment extension, and she planned to sell it since she had no use for it. That is to say until Wade convinced her to give it to him as a Christmas gift. When his infatuation with coffee couldn't seal the deal, he laid on a thick layer of guilt; missed Christmases, forgotten birthdays … the works. She gave him the machine and told him to consider them square for the next twenty years. It was too bulky to keep at his house, so he made arrangements with Tom to store it in the shop's backroom. He was determined to get it working again. It had no manual, no instructions, a box of random hoses and a power cord chewed to an inch of its life. Only Wade could look at this broken mess of steel like it was the love of his life. He named it, Marge.

I helped Wade unload all two hundred pounds of Marge when we got to the shop. After we tucked the last of the blankets back in his truck, we heard a yell coming from Tom's office.

"Hot damn!", Tom was excited about something and was scribbling furiously in his notebook. I walked over to Patty and Angie to see what was going on. They were just as clueless as we were until Tom swung his door open. We could hear an answering machine beeping and cycling through messages in the background.

"Well, you guys did it!" He squared up in front of Patty and me rubbing his hands together in front of his face trying to collect his thoughts. Patty and I looked at each other recounting every questionable moment during our stay at the shop's helm. We had nothing. "Alright so when I got back, I checked out the new website. I thought it was awesome, so I shared the link to some of my BBS buddies to show it off. One of them forwarded the link to some more friends, and it seems to have taken off a bit. A lot of people like the work you two did and now my email and answering machine are bursting at the seams with people asking to speak to Tom-NET Web Solutions." *Holy crap!* "Easily thirty, maybe even forty. I've got five emails alone from Portland, and a ton more from Dallas." Just like that, Tom-NET Web Solutions was born.

Patty and I were speechless. Our late-night web development experiment was a success and was now turning into something far cooler. As if on cue, the door chimes rang and Anto joined our little party. Tom had trouble stringing together words fast enough to keep pace with his brain, as he told Anto about the news and offered her a full-time position. His hands were animated as he rambled through different ways to advertise the services and divvy up the work. Tom said he would work on selling, but would take a smaller cut of the money, as he wanted most of the money to be divided up across the team. Patty and I were still responsible for our normal shop duties, but with Anto's help we'd be able to carve out more time for web site development. Angie volunteered to set up her swim lane sticky note tracking system she used for managing schoolwork to help us keep track of our projects. She used her search skills and teamed up with Wade and Anto to do some of our browser testing and monitoring popular trends. Anto had a natural eye for cool stuff, and Wade was obsessed with curation. When the caffeinated couple got going, they were hard to stop. There was electricity in the air, *literally*, and all signs pointed towards an exciting 1997.

FEATURED TRACK

Third Eye Blind - Semi-Charmed Life

9

The Golden Age

By all accounts, business at the shop picked up in the coming weeks, including a steady stream of lagging holiday Tom-NET signups. Unfortunately, Wade and I had a looming cloud hanging over our heads; our last semester of high school. It was as if all teachers were part of a sadistic cabal hell-bent on coordinating an attack of pointless busy work, projects and exams to make these final months as painful as possible. While other Seniors had coasting final semesters, I had to deal with the ramifications of changing schools from a different state and not having all credits transfer. *Screw you and your graduation prerequisites Texas!* Even worse, the one student service period I was able to land was in the library, again. If you are a normal Senior, you can never have too many student service periods, but if you are a student known for making websites and fixing computers by practically everyone in your small town, your student service quickly devolves into indentured servitude.

My first day back in the library, I was introduced to the school district's technology director who was busy inspecting my network of Power PCs I installed last semester. After admiring my handywork, he made some passive comments about how the school district could really use a website to "make its mark" on the Internet. *Air quoting is annoying.* This put me in a bit of a pickle, since I had already made a website about the school, just not one they would like. Instead of talking about teachers and classes, I made a simple one-page write-up highlighting the distorted fiscal priorities of our wonderful school district. I got the inspiration after listening to a group of thespians eloquently rant about disproportionate budget allocations for football compared to fine art programs. The total budget for the art department, which included art, theater and music, was less than 1% of football's total budget. The site wasn't fancy, or technical. It was basically an open letter, but it did dawn my first custom built animated GIF front and center, which had the words "JollyHigh Sucks" getting sucked into a blackhole. *Thanks Patty!* It wasn't pretty, but it got the point across. The site wasn't easy to find and based on their behavior they obviously hadn't seen it.

    About two weeks later, I was called into the principal's office to talk with the school district's technology director whose disapproving frown spoke volumes. They didn't waste any time with pleasantries and quickly jumped on me about the site and asked if I had created it. Even though my name was not listed on the site, *it was signed, 0pt1mu5*, they said a student reported the site to them with concerns that I might try to tarnish the school's official site with similar rhetoric. They couldn't have painted a clearer target on the rat if they tried. *Calen.*

    Calen was a sophomore who was always pestering Tom for a job. He knew a lot about computers, but he was as annoying as those ass clowns that wrote Tubthumping. Thankfully he also annoyed the hell out of Tom, which was hard to do, which all but ensured he would never be given the job. Tom was a stickler for team chemistry. After speaking with the principal and technology director at length about the freedom of speech online, the apparent factual accuracy of the page and assurance that no content of that nature would make its way onto the school's official site, we were able to put the matter to rest. They were less clear though about the HTML comments. *Cue the descent!* As for Calen, I heard he was grounded for a month, and his mother had to change her email address, when he couldn't explain to her why her inbox was suddenly receiving hundreds of pornographic pictures and letters a day addressed to him at her address. *Hrmmm.*

Despite the school's best efforts to distract, I was able to keep my grades above warning levels and enjoy the ride. One thing that made this possible was that teachers hadn't quite yet caught on to the Internet and just how easy some of their assignments were with just the right website. My favorite time saver was my economics class where the teacher assigned students to find news articles about certain topics and bring in newspaper clippings on them. The goal of course was to get students to read the newspaper and become more aware of the world and events around them. In my case, a quick news search on chron.com and a highlighter made quick work of that assignment, while others spent hours haphazardly searching hardcopy newspapers. There were new corners to be cut popping up every day. It was a great time to be alive, except for those horrible Star Wars remakes making the rounds in the theaters. *Come on, George!*

Tom-NET Web Solutions was taking off and accounted for over a quarter of the shop revenue in the first month alone. It was like shooting fish in a barrel. Everyone wanted a website, even if they didn't need one, and we were the hottest ticket in town to deliver. After our first ten customers, we had three solid Frontpage templates that made it even easier to build sites cheaper and faster. Each of the templates had all the bells and whistles, fancy JavaScript rollovers and support for the latest CSS 1.0 styles. We couldn't copy, paste and publish fast enough, and Angie, Wade and Anto had their hands full trying to keep up with all the testing.

The week before Spring Break, I received two letters in the mail on official college letterhead: The University of Texas at Austin and MIT. I ripped open the MIT letter with cocky assurance that the words "full ride" and "welcome" would be printed in big bold letters across the top. Everything else in the world was going swimmingly, why would this be any different? Instead, the letter opened with, "we regret to inform you ...". Not only did it not say, "full ride", I wasn't even accepted. The shot to my ego was quick and damaging. If any school was going to help me to scratch my technical itch, MIT was at the top of the list. I still had the UT envelope and there was no way I was rejected from both schools. *Right?* I opened the second envelope with much more caution before peeking inside the folds to recognize the word "Congratulations". *I got in!* Upon further reading, I did get into UT; however, no scholarship was awarded. Ten thousand dollars a semester was the estimated tuition and my nuts retracted into my abdomen for protection. The thought never occurred to me that I would get accepted somewhere and not get a scholarship.

I confided in Tom about my situation, and he made some calls, as Tom does. He helped me find a more realistic, cheaper option that consisted of me deferring my acceptance and enrolling in local community colleges. When combined with my Dual high school credits, it would save a ton of money and buy time to apply for more scholarships. There were some additional benefits from this as well. First off, I didn't need to go to school full time, so I could pile on the web site work to save up money in the interim and spend more time with Angie during her senior year. Second, there was a satellite community college campus less than a mile from the shop, which was much closer than the fifteen miles by bus to the UT campus. *Tom was a genius!*

For normal kids, Spring Break was a time to get out in the sun, throw parties and road trips to nearby destinations with their gaggle of friends. I wouldn't consider myself a stick in the mud, but these activities didn't come close to cracking my top ten. For me, outdoors meant allergies, *damn Texas cedar fever*, road trips were expensive and traditional parties rarely involved computer games, trivia or even a shred of technical conversation. At the shop, Spring Break was like a holiday. It was a time we could all spend together doing the things we loved and getting paid to do it. *Win freaking win, baby!*

With the website business in full swing, the shop was hopping at all hours of the day. It was a bit of a spectacle because Patty and I did our work out in the open like well-trained performance artists. Tom arranged a pair of 8x4 tables in the opposite corner from the Community Corner and hung a sign above us that read "Get Your Website Built by Tom-NET Web Solutions". It was a good idea, at first. It generated a lot of buzz and landed us a few new website deals from foot traffic; however, it quickly devolved into a bombardment of blue hairs and website aficionados asking for help on their personal site. Rather than cut these people off completely, Patty and I juggled shifts in the Community Corner straddled by tech support calls. This allowed whoever was actively developing to remain in a zone. Furthermore, if we needed something from each other we sent messages via ICQ, as to not disrupt the flow, even when we were sitting three feet from each other. It was a solid system once we turned off the annoying *uh-oh* sound.

It was around this time that Anto convinced Tom to take a stab at selling laptops to balance out our custom desktop business in the shop. He was a tad reluctant, but Anto said that laptops were flying off the shelves in Florida, and she had a hookup who could give Tom a solid deal on some new Toshiba Satellites. From the moment they were unboxed, Tom was super critical of them, constantly comparing them to his trusted desktop. The cheaper 210cs was fairly compact and peppy but sported a dual scan display that when set side-by-side to its active matrix compatriot looked like an expensive technicolor Etch-a-Sketch. Tom's criticism was unrelenting, until he discovered one of the most obscure features in the manual, the IR COM port. Tom loved reading manuals. We came in early one morning, and Tom was hopping around like a spry young goat with an ear-to-ear smile. He had lined the laptops up across the table from each other in direct line of sight and was having a wireless conversation between the laptops. He even had his old IBM PC Jr. keyboard on the table trying to make it transmit directly to one of the laptops. *He was such a nerd.* From that day on, Tom stopped criticizing the laptops and it showed in the shop sales. Tom could sell anything he believed in.

While the shop was firing on all cylinders, graduation preparations were in full swing and my intolerance for school had reached new stratospheric levels. *Finals couldn't come fast enough.* All the ridiculous planning for the ceremony made me want to hurl myself into a trash compactor. Ordering the graduation gown. Seniors night out. Class colors!? As if there is a gnat's ass difference between Crimson/Ivory/Navy and Maroon/Egg Shell/Royal Blue. The illusion of choice was absurd, orchestrated no doubt by overbearing faculty wanting to control every aspect of the process for the students. Even when the majority of the two-hundred-and-seventy-person class are able to agree on a class song, *Going the Distance by Cake*, the song is mysteriously overruled for unknown reasons and replaced with an infuriating Savage Garden pile of crap that wasn't even on the ballot. Normally, I wouldn't have cared, but for all these silly decisions, there was an army of competing people who actually cared and were actively lobbying people for a vote. If it weren't for Angie, it is possible I would have racked up a few assault charges. Angie was the master of dissent without drawing attention to herself in the crowd, whereas I was more of a nihilist, *Burn mother fucker ... burn!*

To my surprise, the day finally came. Sitting in a chair in the middle of the football field, I looked around and observed my surroundings. I had already walked the stage, Magna Cum Laude, *Mom was happy*, but I wasn't concerned with the ceremony or the sea of faces in the bleachers in front of me, just the one: Angie. She sat directly in front of me with mine and Wade's mom and Tom. Her focus was unwavering, always ready to give me her condescending yet supportive smirk, while the moms gossiped beside her. Tom kept smiling and giving cheesy thumbs up poses trying to get me to roll my eyes. For being an adult, he sure was childish, but it suited him perfectly. To my right was the infamous Hambone cage. Behind me was where I watched Angie do her flag routines at Friday night home games. At the opposite end of the row was Wade, my friend, the one who introduced us all. This high school thing was over and while I was happy to be done, there was a part of me that was happy it happened. The mid-year move that I once cursed my mother for with every fiber of my being. The small boring Texas town where I envisioned tractor racing, water tower painting or dying at the hands of a buck-toothed buckshot toting hillbilly had far surpassed its expectations. So much in my life was absolutely perfect right now and none of it would have been possible without these unexpected twists and turns.

Tom was never one to rest when he saw an opportunity. With high school behind me and summer in front of us, he laid out an aggressive plan for everyone at the shop. He wanted to start providing his own hosting services to complement the website business and had plans to overhaul the dial-in server and finally install a LAN at the shop. It had long been on his list ever since we started playing with BNC coax and IPX/SPX back with Windows 3.1, which was overly complicated and far too rigid to justify the investment. Every time one of the T-connectors jostled loose from the coax it was a pain to troubleshoot, which made the simplicity of Ethernet and the RJ-45 jack very appealing. A perfect storm of common sense came upon us with the release of Windows NT 4.0, price drops in 100BT cards and our enhanced understanding of TCP/IP from our Tom-NET setup that it only made sense to install a TCP/IP LAN at the shop. Not only could we release the dedicated phone lines in the shop to the standard dial-in pool, but it also meant that the machines at the shop would be lightning fast online. *Sweet!*

In standard Tom fashion, he revealed this news to us via a pile of pre-purchased boxes of software and hardware and simply told us to "get to work". A bit presumptuous, but it felt like one massive technical puzzle, and we all liked puzzles. I tackled the Cisco hardware and their girthy admin manuals. Upon reading the insane performance specifications, *it was a beast*, it was clear that Tom way overshot our needs, so he must have gotten a great deal, or his vision was grander than I understood at the time. I set up the internal GNAT services and learned about how to CIDR our internal network to isolate the segments of our network, like the Community Corner, from our internal network of shop computers and servers. Wade and Patrick ran cables through conduits above the ceiling to all the computers and learned the intricacies of punching RJ45 terminals. *Hint: always leave yourself slack, especially on long runs.* Anto and Angie set up the new web hosting services and re-hosted the Tom-NET website to our fancy new servers. Tom upgraded the NICs in all the shop machines and configured them for the new LAN. After a week of reading, configuring, manual labor, pizza, and ferocious f-bombs, we cut-over Tom-NET to the new network, and as many things in the shop did so often, it just worked. Our internal workstations were wicked fast, and the dial-up customers didn't call to complain about the fifteen-minute outage. Overall, we claimed our bootstrap success with pride. *What a way to start the summer!*

Music played a pivotal role in defining that first summer of freedom, more so than any other summer to date. It was more than everyone binge listening to the new Third Eye Blind or Matchbox 20 albums, or Patty and I lobbying to lift the permanent ban on Fat of the Land and Dig Your Own Hole. That summer was the summer our team discovered the MP3. Anto was our resident digital music expert. She had mastered the art of ripping CDs to WAV and burning "mixtapes" for friends and family. It was a labor of love, which occupied excessive disk space, but it was her special way of showing how much she cared. *Nothing says love, like copyright fraud!* She kept a collection of her failed CD burns on the shop wall strung together with a bungee cord like an avant-garde installation. *We all had one.* It was a small artistic detail that went unnoticed by most customers, but if you looked closely you could count the burn tracks on the disc and see where things went awry. When Anto discovered Winamp and l3enc, her shrine to mixtape imperfection would need another bungee, *or three*.

  The door chimes rang furiously as Anto dashed into the shop and beelined for her computer, the one with the 8x CD writer. She plopped in a CD and you could tell by the reflection behind her that she was installing some sort of software. A few seconds later she cranked up her speakers and we heard the most unforgettable application start sound of all time, "Winamp. It really whips the llama's ass!" She slammed her hand against the table and bellowed out a screaming laugh as she repeatedly opened and closed the application. It was debatable which was funnier, the startup sound or Anto being brought to tears by it. Once she collected herself, she played two music files, both were the same song, and asked everyone to pick which sounded better. The two sounded practically identical. She nearly lost it when she revealed that the MP3 was one tenth the size of her traditional WAV extract. From that day forth, Anto lived and breathed MP3s and took every free moment she could to digitize her CD collection to her brand new 2.5GB Caviar drive she installed in her shop computer. She wanted to have the largest MP3 collection on the Internet, or at least in Jollyville.

  There was no question how Wade was going to spend his summer, Marge. For the past six months she had been abandoned in the back room collecting dust, and he was determined to get her running again. He reached out to the manufacturer and finagled them to send a replacement product manual, but it was going to be six to eight weeks before it would arrive. Rather than wait, he wanted to see what he could fix on his own. He unscrewed the stainless-steel backing and exposed an exploded Rorschach of coffee residue covering most of the internal plumbing and gadgetry. He meticulously wiped down the inside with a toothbrush, tightened every screw, twisted every pipe and replaced the power cable with a replacement one he picked up at Home Depot. The exterior hoses were a bit tricky. All sitting in storage and the rattling around in the box had made them stiff and brittle, but after a few trips to nearby appliance repair stores he was able to find "good enough" pieces that worked with some additional clamping. He spent nearly a month working on her before even plugging her into the new 50-amp outlet that Tom was gracious enough to install for him. We all huddled around him to watch the inaugural event, whereas I was there ready to kick Wade away from the outlet should he get electrocuted. Marge hummed, grunted and beeped in a very unladylike fashion until the ready light turned a steady green. *Success!* Now, all he had to do was figure out how to use it, but it would have to wait, because it was time for us to kick back as a group.

There were two times of day that Tom held sacred, when the shop opened and when it closed, but there was a third that held a special place in his heart: showtime. Showtime was a summer shop activity held upstairs in the breakroom that started fifteen minutes after the last customer left the shop. It was just enough time to order pizzas, pickup snacks and drinks and set the wheels in motion for whatever revelry we had planned as a group. This wasn't normally an everyday affair, but that summer we had showtime at-least three to four times a week. Patrick and Tom were on a quest to identify the all-time best movies, music and books for a given genre. They rarely agreed and the rest of the shop served as the tie-breaking committee. This resulted in an abundance of showtime movie nights that summer. Real Genius. Life of Brian. Holy Grail. Police Academy. Ghost in the Shell. All the Naked Guns. All the Hot Shots. *YESSS!!!* Ace Ventura. Dumb and Dumber. True Lies. The Crow. Goonies. Wargames. Sneakers. Citizen Kane. Top Gun. The list was long and distinguished. Every time we selected a winner, Patty would update the Top Picks section of Tom-NET's website that Tom wanted built out to share with our customers. I think Patty just enjoyed getting under Tom's skin, or simply liked watching movies as a group. Some of his arguments were pretty weak, but he had good instincts. As the movie nights became more frequent, I got tired of sitting in a folding chair, so I found a papasan on mega-clearance big enough for Angie and me to sit together. There was an art to loading and unloading while maintaining balance, which took a while to master and resulted in many inadvertent topples when we laughed too hard. *I miss her laugh.*

Showtime was a good predictable break for Angie. Her senior year was ahead of her, and she started slipping into her over preparation mode as the summer came to a close. The Community Corner was permanently stocked with ACT and SAT preparation guides, highlighters and sticky notes and her new AP English summer reading materials. When she needed to focus, she simply put on her headphones and got into her studying zone. I never understood her ability to spend four plus hours reading study guides or the full mandatory materials. I'd skim Cliff Notes of a restaurant menu if it saved me time. Before I knew it, summer was over and Angie was back at school, and I had started my classes at Community College. I can't say finding out that they set my campus username to my initials plus the last four digits of my social security number was the best first impression of sophistication, *nor was them telling me I had to read my campus email with Pine.* Despite the missteps, the more important focus was keeping Angie a part of the group while she faced JollyHigh alone. Wade and I still picked her up and dropped her off in the mornings. It never occurred to us to break tradition, even if it was a bit out of the way. She opted to fly solo for lunch since she was heads down studying in the library. Even stranger, she was the type of person that would read yet another book to decompress from reading all of her schoolbooks and study guides. Harry Potter and the Sorcerer's Stone was her go-to book that year, constantly reading and re-reading it cover to cover. I never read more than the dust jacket, but she said I reminded her of Ron. *Whatever that meant.*

    With Angie otherwise preoccupied, I found comfort in a relatively new Quake mod called Team Fortress. It was a nice twist to the standard Quake experience given that players could choose their character class and join in multiplayer online games. One day, I jumped on a random game with a bunch of players from a Quake clan and they liked my Demoman pipe bomb play, so they invited me to audition for [DS]. These guys were legit. I could barely keep up with them at first, but once it became known that I worked for an ISP, we set up a scrimmage server and I was playing every free moment I could get. *I could navigate 2Forts blindfolded!* Many of us were college aged, but there were some older tech professionals in the group, as well, but the way the personalities and skills melded in our chat room was a sight to see. The clan was stocked with creative folk who designed the clan's website, graphics and demo videos and we had more programming talent than we knew what to do with. We were good, having won the IGL title in recent years, but sadly the group didn't have a consistent stable of LPBs or dedicated players to remain competitive across the busy tournament bracket. Some of the guys were frustrated that we couldn't reclaim the title and tried branching out to other leagues. As for myself, I simply enjoyed playing the game, as much as possible, with a hilarious group of people to pass the time.

Days seemed to drag out, and when Angie finally showed up at the shop, she was an exhausted, stressed and fractured version of herself. Thankfully her next shot at the SAT was only days away, and she wouldn't be like this for too much longer. Wade and I waited outside the school that Saturday for two and a half hours with balloons and a "You did it!" banner taped to the side of Wade's truck. We had a small cooler filled with her favorite root beer in the back and a misprinted sheet cake with forks at the ready to celebrate the occasion. Angie loved sheet cakes, especially discounted ones with type-o's on them. The irony and imperfection made her laugh. *Congradulations, Pat!* When the doors finally opened, we screamed "Way to go, Angie!" and she put her head in her hands. As she walked closer, I could see tears forming in her eyes before she buried her face in my chest. I gave her my signature bear hug and told her I'm sure she did fine. All she could say was, "I'm glad that's over." *So was I.*

Everything started to return to normal shortly after. Angie received her SAT results a few months later and scored a near perfect 1580. The sense of accomplishment on her face was priceless, but you could tell she was trying to figure out which questions she missed. Patty and Tom were closing in on their final top picks, just in time for the new year. Anto discovered her new favorite website, mp3.com, and thanks to the upgraded office LAN she could download an entire album in less than ten minutes versus three hours. She started making CD backups of all her music to keep the drive from filling up. Wade got his owner's manual and started tinkering with all of Marge's settings. Every exploded espresso and ruined steamed milk experiment were followed by a typical Wade tirade of expletives, which meant he couldn't practice during business hours. My first semester at Community College was finally under my belt, an additional six hours and rocking a 4.0 without breaking a sweat. Sure, it wasn't a regular college with a full-time load, but it was a start and it made me feel that college might not be as much of a grind as I had made it out to be. *College is evil!*

1997 was an amazing year, possibly the best year I'd ever have in my life. I wasn't sure how 1998 could possibly top it, but I didn't have to wait more than a few weeks to find out. It was January 19th, and it was late in the afternoon. I was in my website corner reading the latest on Slashdot, when I saw a shiny new black Cadillac roll up in front of the shop. It wasn't uncommon for us to get fancy cars, but something about this car seemed off. The car door opened in slow motion, and a set of bright blue high heels struck the ground below the door as a mound of red hair emerged above it. The woman, who looked to be in her 50s, was wearing a matching blue skirt with a white button up shirt and extra-wide black belt. She had a pair of oversized sunglasses that appeared to prop up her massive red hair, but to be completely honest, the hair could have stood on its own. She went to the trunk of her car and pulled out a tall narrow potted palm tree and started toward the door. I pretended to not notice her and pressed random keys on my keyboard into Notepad but watched her from the side of my eye.

The door chimes rang violently as she recklessly backed her way into the door and the top of the tree clipped the chimes sending them crashing to the floor. I nearly fell out of my seat from the sudden commotion. With earphones halfcocked on my head, I made eye contact, I think, with the woman through the tree's broad fronds. She didn't seem to care that she made such a loud entrance, or that the door chimes were broken and sprawled out all over the floor. Tom popped his head from his office looking a bit flustered and waved her back. She nodded in my direction and strutted the potted plant to the back like she was on some sort of runway. I picked up the busted door chimes, whose sound I had become so accustomed to and tried to reconnect them to their string and hanger. That's how Angie was able to sneak up on me.

Angie tapped me on the shoulder and I nearly launched the chimes through the ceiling. She had the most excited look on her face. More exciting than anything I could remember. That's when she handed me the opened envelope. The letterhead read *Haas School of Business, University of California Berkeley*, and the words above the crease made me cringe, *Congratulations, you've been accepted.* Emotions ran every which way through my body, mind and heart. She tucked her head into my chest for a congratulatory bear hug, but I was still quasi-stunned. I remained speechless but embraced her, nonetheless. The day I dreaded had finally come. It was no longer a possibility. It was a reality. She was accepted into her dream school with a full scholarship, seventeen hundred miles away in California. I counted all ten million feet in my head, each one more painful than the last. As if this moment couldn't get any worse, Tom emerged from his office with his red-haired lady friend. She was now without her camo-foliage and sunglasses and had one of those overly made up faces you'd expect to see on a TV commercial. Tom's face was beet red, but he finally spit out the words. "Angie. Ben. I'd like you to meet my girlfriend ... Evelyn."

FEATURED TRACK

Eve 6 - Inside Out

10

Something Wicked Comes

*** FLASH ***

  Every muscle in my abdomen contracted, lifting my feet from the ground and my head lower into the bowl. One violent heave after another, my white knuckles finally released the back of the tank in defeat. I wasn't a religious person, but thoughts and prayers shotgunned to the usual suspects above, and below, for an end to this misery. *This was why you don't drink, idiot!* I could count the number of times I drank alcohol, of any type, since high school on one hand. *Last night was #4.* It wasn't some ultra-purity pledge, or some enlightened superiority complex, although the memory of a high school acquaintance dying in a drunk driving accident my senior year always stuck with me for some reason. *RIP, Tyson.* The broader explanation was quite simple, it had no appealing factors that it brought to the table. It didn't smell, or taste, anywhere close to the hype, and besides, the money I saved went straight to an arguably worse habit ... electronics.

  I leaned over and splashed my face with water from the sink and returned to rest my head on my forearm on the side of the toilet bowl with my eyes closed and counting each heartbeat and breath. The throbbing pain and spinning were getting better, but my body was still clinched at the ready. Frames from recently recalled memories flashed inside my head behind my eyelids like a poorly cut stop motion picture. My heart yearned for simpler times when the only things I had to worry about were wearing clean underwear and playing video games. The world was all in front of me to explore, not pinning me into submission under the weight of its mighty thumb. Tom would still be playing Minesweeper and doing "pull my finger" fart jokes, and there was no need for this insane competition to prove something I knew I couldn't do. Things were really ... really good, and then they just ... weren't.

My stomach gurgled and my ass-cheeks puckered in kind. *Get up!!!!!!* With head in hands and elbow on knees, I perched like a hawk observing the world a mighty eighteen inches from the floor. My internal organs took turns spitefully self-destructing for last night's toxic bombardment. Next victim, the bowels, and it feels like the afflicted brought the brass knuckles.

*** **FLASH** ***

Every morning since Angie's college announcement, I woke in the morning wishing it had been a dream. I arrived at the shop with a naive veil of optimistic ignorance, which repeatedly disintegrated in the harsh light of truth. It was like a depressing Groundhog's Day, over and over again. *Someone get a toaster!* Angie could see right through my facade. I was an agitated bag of happiness and sadness all wrapped into one and violently fluctuating by the minute. The mood swings alone were enough to drive anyone insane, and I knew they had to stop. This was a problem, just like any other. All I needed was a bit of technology and a computer. *I got this!*

The more she made plans for attending school far away, the more I focused on ways to bring us closer together. First and foremost was communication, as neither of us could afford enough long-distance cards to make that a viable long-term strategy. *Internet to the rescue!* I installed ICQ on her new computer, a former Community Corner machine which Tom gifted to her as an early graduation gift for getting into Berkeley, after our last mass computer rebuild. We practiced sitting twenty feet apart and pretending she was in California. There was no eye contact, or talking to each other, only sending instant messages and simple emoticons. My relationship with Angie had devolved into an IRC chat history with the main difference being I had explicit proof the person on the other end was a girl. We alternated tapping out of the exercise, usually by walking over for a much-needed hug, but I was by far the weakest. Rather than hang my hat on one solution, I kept on researching and trying new things. Anything to keep my mind occupied on solving the problem. I invested in a set of QuickCams and microphones; however, the images were super blurry and the CU-SeeMe software was a bit buggy on low bandwidth. In hindsight, the prepaid phone cards might have been more cost effective, even if I was buying everything at the shop's cost. It was hard to pretend that she was away, and it would be even harder to do this for real.

We both needed a distraction, so Angie and I walked to the movie theater and we decided on a matinee showing of Good Will Hunting. Overall, I thought the movie started out great. A badass no-nonsense genius street kid outsmarting everyone at MIT, *in my mind, I was Will*, but had some issues he needed to work through with the help of his therapist, the Genie from Aladdin. *Robin Williams is amazing!* He meets a girl, *list update: Jolie, Theron, Driver*, and they hit it off just like me and Angie. We snuggled in close and laughed, until the movie took an unexpected turn. The girl was about to graduate and planned to move back to California. My arm slowly collapsed around Angie's, holding her tight. Will's character was having trouble processing his emotions of abandonment. It was like watching an alternate reality play out in front of me with a thick Boston accent. As the movie closed with Will quitting his job and driving down the highway in his beat-up car, all I wanted to see was Skylar's face. I needed to see a simple shot of them making eye contact just one more time. Something to prove everything could in fact be okay, and not just some open ended artsy interpretive fade to black. *Damnit!* I had never cried in a movie theater before, and I wasn't about to start now. My eyes were watery puddles at the verge of spilling over and the palms of my hands were sweaty from a thunder grip on Angie's arm rest. I quickly wiped my eyes with my shoulder and turned to face Angie, who had equal remnants of emotion running down the side of her face. I wasn't ready to talk about my feelings. If I started, I might not stop. So, I blurted out, "How 'bout them apples!" in my best Bostonian accent. She laughed and interlocked her arm in mine for the walk back. *Crisis averted.*

When we got back to the shop, the door opened without a sound, which still was unsettling. I was still working on fixing the door chimes due to the number Evelyn did on the mounting bracket, but it was a bunch of small intricate strings that needed to be untangled and rethreaded. *I had bigger priorities.* Evelyn was pacing around the Community Corner looking at the merchandise on the walls, while Tom was dancing like a three-year-old who needed to go to the bathroom, or possibly already went. Tom pulled a trivia card out of his pocket and proceeded to prompt everyone on the fly. It was an older familiar card, so we dealt out the answers almost as fast as he could read off the questions but added an additional question at the end that I would not forget.

"Name the righteous dude who just registered a team for TapHouse's new trivia contest next month."

It took everyone a second to realize he was being completely serious. Answering trivia in the comfort of our own shop was one thing but flaunting our arguably useless knowledge of pop culture sounded about as pleasant as a root canal. We were already social outcasts for the most part, the only reason most people talked to us was to fix their computers or get them back online. If technology wasn't inherently prone to breaking down over time, it's feasible to assume that we'd probably go stir crazy and devolve into anti-social lemmings. Even we couldn't talk tech all day, according to Tom.

He named our team, "Hot Shots", which seemed appropriate. From the moment he told us the name, I begged everyone to recreate the movie poster for our photo, but Tom said he wasn't going to wear a tutu. The team was made up of six people, with Evelyn listed as the alternate. She didn't seem to mind much, but still showed interest because of Tom, no doubt. When she talked, she always made me feel like there was something bigger and better she could be doing with her time. *Needless to say, she didn't impress me much.* I knew she worked in real estate and was obsessed with playing golf, but I couldn't pinpoint what her actual day-to-day job entailed, as she had started frequenting the shop more and more each day, sometimes as many as four times a week.

It was hard to prepare for the tournament with Evelyn around, but given her alternate status, we were compelled to give her a shot, but herself entitled attitude sucked the fun out of the room like a black hole. Her knowledge for anything beyond real estate, fashion and old country music was severely limited. You'd think with hair as massive as hers, she would have accreted tidbits of pop culture or science knowledge in her time on this planet. *Sadly, no.* We eventually took turns concocting mundane errands for her to run just so she'd have an excuse to leave the shop. She was more than happy to oblige. A simple request to run across the street to get some more coffee, easily became a two-hour mission around town. It was this unspoken treaty that made her even remotely tolerable and kept the peace at the shop.

After a month of preparation, Hot Shots took the stage at the inaugural TapHouse Trivia Tournament to represent Andersson Electronics. Anto and Patty shined the brightest in our debut, both playing off of each other's energy and carrying the team from the beginning. Thanks to them, we didn't miss a single music, movie or history question and sailed through the early rounds, but the rest of the team was more or less distracted. Tom was busy trying to keep Evelyn's boredom at bay, while Angie and I were preoccupied with pointless arguments over which answers were correct. *Something was off.* Wade, on the other hand, didn't process new things well and sat wide-eyed, quiet and hyper-observant at the table through the first round, wired to the gills on caffeine. It was a grueling five-hour endeavor, but we made it to the finals. We faced off against the library's recruited squad of college students who returned home from Spring Break, the Dewey Decimators. Had it not been for some early missteps we would have owned them in the end. Standing front and center one on one at a podium, rather than answering as a team while seated in the comforts of our own table, was very intimidating, even for me. In the end, we came in second out of sixteen teams, a solid showing for our first trivia tournament, and everyone agreed that we were all ready to sign up for next year's event. We were all, except Evelyn, hooked!

May drew ever closer, and my mind watched the moments with Angie fleeting away like sands in an hourglass. These were the final months, weeks and days of my so-called happy life with her. It was exceedingly hard to focus, on school and on work and this made me quite apathetic and irritable. It didn't help that Netscape released an absolute turd with their new Communicator suite. All of our users blindly upgraded to the new shiny thing which led to a storm of support calls. It was dog slow, but sadly, still better than Internet Explorer. I even gave Opera a try during this stretch of browser uncertainty. It was nostalgic that the entire browser was still installable from a single floppy disk but given my trusty external Zip Drive that differentiation was quickly neutralized. BattleNet Diablo lost its luster, and I was finding it hard to give a damn about the new StarCraft, even though the word online was that it was amazing. That semester I got a 3.5. Calculus II was easy enough, but my micro-economics professor was a hard ass and gave me a B. I tried to argue for a higher-grade using sound Keynesian principles, but all he said was "A's must be in short supply this semester, I guess." *Jerk!* Despite my best efforts to keep my emotions all bottled inside, Angie could read me like one of her books. She saw through the fluctuating facade and she would squeeze my hand in support. She was scared, too. As happy as I was to be with her, I couldn't help but wonder how painful it would be the day she finally left for college.

Angie's last week in town was the week after the Fourth of July. Her family was driving her stuff to California to get things squared away in her dorm early. She was amazed her parents cared enough to take time off work to help her move but having a daughter that gets a full ride to Berkeley made Angie's mom's gossip the talk of the diner circuit for the blue hairs. How could she resist? It was too painful to watch Angie pack, so I focused on her computer to make sure it was in tip top shape and had every piece of software it could possibly need. *Microsoft lucky 7's for the win!* We had one final night in town before she left, and we just wanted to spend it alone, away from everyone and the shop. We walked to the movie theater and watched Armageddon. Angie had a soft spot in her musical repertoire for Aerosmith. Midway through the movie, both of us were flowing rivers of tears down our faces into a buttery pool of popcorn. The looming asteroid was the manifestation of my angst that summer, and the scientists proposing idiotic ideas on how to stop it reminded me of how stupid I was to try and bury my head in the sand. *I should have been more engaged, more active!*

Wade picked me up the next morning and drove me to Angie's for the long-feared goodbye. Seventeen hundred plus miles would separate us for five long months, and the only things keeping us in regular contact were a couple of Internet chat programs. We nuzzled our faces into each other's necks failing to hold back the tears. It only felt like a minute, but to others it was more like fifteen. Her dad bellowed like a stubborn mule for her to hurry up and get in the car. She gave me one last kiss and ran to the car hiding her face and waving goodbye. I walked to the curb and waved in kind as the car pulled away. I tried not to blink as to not miss a single beam of light that refracted off that navy-blue truck and trailer until it too became a speck on the horizon. The smell of her lip balm dissipated in the morning air. I stood motionless and numb to the world as if the slightest breeze could topple me at any moment.

That is when I felt Wade's hand on my shoulder and smelled the distinct fragrance of a Bodin Special. He walked me back to his truck and drove me to the lake overlook where his father used to take him. We watched the morning sun continue to rise over the tree covered hills and light-up the lake's surface. We didn't say a word the entire time we were there. We didn't need to. Our only form of interaction was through music. Wade read through album booklets and swapped CDs to try and find the perfect song to cheer me up or at least backdrop the moment. Inside Out. *Too soon.* Truly Madly Deeply. *Seriously, Wade?* Perfect Blue Buildings. *Feels about right.* For all his quirks, Wade understood me, and I understood him, which made us odder than any couple Neil Simon could imagine.

The first week after Angie left was easier than expected. Tom and the others pitched in and got me a five-hundred-minute phone card. A few days later, I surprised Angie with a phone call, and we talked for almost four hours straight. The trip out to Berkeley was rough on her too, but she spent a lot of the time reading and tuning out her parents who argued non-stop in the front seat about their own nonsensical issues. It was good to hear her voice, but it was also the beginning of a dangerous precedent that would send my emotions on a violent roller coaster for nearly a month. Each high point coinciding with a lengthy phone call, and each doldrum amplified by droughts in communication. During these valleys, I dealt with my frustration the best way I knew how, video games. While most of America was preoccupied with McGwire and Sosa's roid race to homerun immortality, Team Fortress with DS was my primary escape, until I got my hands on a cracked copy of Grand Theft Auto. The carjacking and mayhem proved to be quite cathartic for my mental state, and an outlet to survive the lamest college course of all.

Communications was by far the most boring and frustrating class of my storied college career. It was taught by a smoke ridden Vietnam glory-day buffoon that felt it was his life's mission to mold the minds of the next generation with his sage wisdom and advice. At least that was his spiel the first week. Afterwards, every class became a pre-written whiteboard list of assignments in the computer lab while watching the soles of his shoes rock side to side as he read a newspaper and tried his best to keep his chair from floating away. Any questions asked by someone with a hanging pair below, or not big enough pair up top, would be treated to an esoteric story about how he and his band of brothers had to think on their feet to survive in the jungle. Whereas, for the three, sometimes four, individuals in our class who frequently wore short skirts and low-cut tank tops, he was more than happy to have them pull up a chair and lean in to give their "work" a look. *What a pervy douche!* The only good thing about this shriveled fraction of a man was that his class was exceedingly predictable. A few cut-and-pastes from random websites and I was sitting pretty with an A without having to read any of the books. Unfortunately, I still had to sit through the insufferable class because attendance was twenty percent of the grade. *Thank god for Team Fortress!*

The computer lab where we met was connected to the school's network, and the computers were configured to keep normal college students in their stupid "integrated writing suite". They went through the trouble of hiding the "My Computer" icon from the Desktop, but still let people access the Command Prompt. *Idiots.* A few simple commands later I was browsing the myriad of connected drives on my computer just poking around to see what I could find. *My crime is that of curiosity.* I found a server with some extra space and created a hidden directory to install Quakeworld from my Zip drive. I could now play Team Fortress from any computer on campus over the LAN with a simple "net use" command, but this also meant that I had to move to the back row, so I didn't lure the eyes of other students while I practiced my sniping. This was my gift to the student body, at least for those curious enough to find it. As I closed out the plethora of folder views on my screen, one in particular caught my eye. *M:\Daedalus.* That was the name of the wannabe office tool they made everyone use on the campus computers to do writing assignments. It was a wannabe MS Works with an even crappier UI. *I couldn't NOT look.* A few clicks later my eyes narrowed in on a suspicious "USERS.DAT" file. I opened it up in Notepad and noticed a garbled structure in the data immediately. Familiar usernames were listed near the beginning of each line, and there was a bunch of gibberish rounding out the remainder. Since my Zip drive was still connected, I snagged a copy of the file to review later when I could be a bit less discrete.

A few weeks later, I was in the throes of depression laying in my room listening to Ben Folds Five's Brick and reminiscing about when Angie and I agreed it was the most wonderfully depressing song of all time. *She's feeling more alone... than she ever has before.* ♪ My eye caught a glimpse of my Zip drive hanging out of my backpack and I remembered the DAT file. I opened the file, this time in UltraEdit, and I immediately noticed a new pattern of colons breaking up the gibberish data on each line. I recorded a macro to split the lines apart, and then did a quick search for my username and the file's contents became immediately clear.

A character sequence followed my username that was eerily similar to my student password. All the l33t number substitutions were in their normal places, but the surrounding letters were different. I wrote a quick program to parse through my line in the file and realized that the letters were consistently shifted either up or down by thirteen positions on the ASCII table. Numbers and special characters were unaffected. *ROT13!* With this knowledge, I widened the net on my program and ran it against the entire file. My jaw nearly broke the keyboard after I pressed <ENTER>. Echoed on the screen were all the usernames and passwords for anyone who had ever used this piece of shit software, upwards of a few hundred users including students, faculty and even administrators. *Never reuse passwords folks.* I ran the program three or four more times. With each screen refresh, I got a stronger sense of satisfaction and more devious thoughts dangerously bubbled to the surface. I began judging people I had never met on their password choice alone, especially those poor saps who used "password" as their password. I'd wager over half of those idiots still needed to hide a reminder under their mouse pad.

They would be the first sacrificial lambs in the new connected world, no doubt. Adults always say that you have the time of your life in college, and if these chains of events were indicative of that, I had no doubt in my mind that my time in college would land me in jail. I closed my program but saved a copy of the output for posterity. *Minus my line of course.*

Halloween snuck up on me and it hit like a resounding thud in my chest. Angie and I were celebrating our second-year anniversary via instant messages and emails. Pizza and penny wishes in the fountains seemed like an eternity ago. There was a used Ford Tempo a few blocks away that had a reasonable price on it. On more than one occasion, I envisioned cashing out my savings account, buying the car and making the drive to Berkeley just like Will. The only thing stopping me was that I didn't know how to drive a standard, have a driver's license, or have insurance, but the authenticity of intent was one hundred percent real. I mentioned this idea to Angie a few times, but I couldn't gauge her reaction over instant message that well. She would always switch the subject back to schoolwork and try to draw commonalities to her college experience and mine. She lived and breathed school in one of the most renowned colleges in the country, every minute of every day. My experience was more akin to volunteering at an animal shelter, coming and going at your leisure, not a lot of homework and sometimes dealing with bodily fluids on the carpet. They were two completely different worlds with no chance of intersection, which made it difficult for us to find new things to discuss.

0pt1mu5:
How's your day?

Sm4rtyP4nt5_98:
Busy! Tons of homework. You?

0pt1mu5:
no homework here, just working on some customer websites. quick phone call? miss you =\

Sm4rtyP4nt5_98:
Can't talk right now ... study group.

*Then the long pause. 10. 9. 8. 7. 6. 5. 4. 3. 2. 1. *

Miss you, too.

For all I knew, I could have been talking to a robot. I once thought about asking her, "How many of your fellow students' passwords did you crack this week?", just to spice things up a bit, but I felt it would draw a bit more finger wagging than I'd care to deal with online. That story would have to wait for Christmas.

As if I wasn't dealing with enough mental baggage at the moment, Mom decided to step in and toss some more kindling on my emotional dumpster fire. His name was Phil. Phil liked motorcycles. Phil met Mom after crashing said motorcycle into a barricade. Mom went on dates with Phil, riding on the back of his new motorcycle. *Why she put herself in this position given his history I never understood.* These were the only facts I could remember when I first met the vacuous person known as Phil. Out of the blue, she invited me to dinner at the town's most fancy Mexican restaurant, which in and of itself was suspicious because she always worked Wednesday night shifts. About thirty minutes into our meal, the guest of honor made his appearance. He played the "what a coincidence" line at least three times, before I straight up told him to just sit down. He still had a section of gauze attached to the side of his head. I assumed that was where the doctors poked his brain back into his skull with a broom pole. To me, Phil was forgettable, until he tried to be funny. He had a sense of humor that you couldn't help but laugh at, him not the jokes. Before he delivered a punchline, he would chuckle and snort to a degree that nearly incapacitated his breathing, regardless of the joke caliber. *What did she see in him?* From that day forward, much to my obvious disgust, he called me "Buddy" and pestered me relentlessly trying to schedule bonding trips for the two of us. He felt like he was one lollipop shy of being that creepy guy at playgrounds in a trench coat. I was convinced he had lost his common sense and social IQ in the mangled construction netting that kept his low sided hog and him for sliding into a ravine. The only good thing was that he made Mom happy, and as long as that held true, I just gritted my teeth and smiled. *I need a new mouth guard.*

It was finally the last day of the semester. My Psychology class got away from me and I was barely able to scrape by with a "B". My psych professor could smell my BS a mile away, but thankfully he was easily impressed with homework assignments sporting beveled and embossed color graphics printed inline. The bar for what qualified as exceptional work was pathetically low at this place. I had one final Communications class to attend in the computer lab to get my attendance bonus for the semester, which ensured my "A" in the class, but I also wanted to leave a special parting gift for our marvelous teacher. After the "final exam", I logged into his writing suite account on another computer, *semperfi ... as if I needed my program to decipher that* and created some new material in his shared portfolio. First up, a copy of "How to: Pick Up Young Girls" and then an op-ed I found online entitled "101 Reasons I Love My Manly Merkin". Both of them were publicly shared with the entire school. *Your welcome, Professor! Oorah!* I didn't care if I got in trouble. I was done with this class, and school wasn't far behind it. Angie's flight was scheduled to land in less than twenty-four hours, and my semester of suffering was about to get a much-needed reprieve, or so I thought.

    I raced the clock that afternoon to put the final touches on my multi-search engine bar for the Tom-NET website, which had most recently added support for Google and Ask Jeeves. I hated leaving work unfinished, especially when it was so close to completion. The last thing I needed was to be thinking about source code when Angie arrived. My fingers feverishly pounded the worn keys of my trusted Microsoft natural into oblivion, *best keyboard ever*, and I finished right as the reflection of the blue truck appeared in the adjacent monitor. All the failed webcam attempts and pent up anticipation that came from extended reliance on long distance chatting flooded my nerves with adrenaline and my hands began to shake. It was simultaneously surreal and scary. This was the same truck that took her away and the thought of and it taking her back again left my throat dry and scratchy like I had swallowed dry-fallen oak leaves. Anto was ready to hit play on a mix track she made especially for Angie's arrival, while Wade, Patty and Tom lit candles on a tacky sheet cake that read, "Happy Birthday, Naoh!" The door opened with a resounding, "Surprise!" that was a bit unnecessary, given the shop's large clear front windows. Anto hit play on the stereo and was the first to tackle Angie at the door, while Four Non-Blondes' What's Up strummed in the background. Angie was wearing a Berkeley ball cap with her hair pulled back into a loosely collected ponytail. While the brim of her hat hid her eyes, I could smell her Carmex and hear her crackling voice from across the room as she tried to keep up with Anto's barrage of questions and salutations. *It sounded wonderful.*

Moments later, she turned to face me, and my heart sank into my chest. Her eyes were red and puffy, and I knew something was wrong. Anto pulled her over to the cake where Tom, Patty and Wade welcomed her back to the shop. I felt helpless like Patrick Swayze in Ghost, watching and unable to be heard or even push a silly quarter. The crowd at the table dispersed after Angie sampled the icing with her finger. According to her, this was her favorite and admittedly most trashy part of a sheet cake, but her emotions felt heavy and everyone could tell something was wrong. Her eyes locked in on me as she rubbed her arms and crossed the room. I braced myself with the back of my chair and did my best to unleash a supportive smile. I was sweating bullets and every step she took vibrated in my heart and twisted my stomach into knots with anticipation. She grabbed my trembling hand and ran her soft warm thumb over the top of it. It was like being touched by an angel that was about to tell you they just ran over your favorite cat. She took a deep breath and uttered the four fearful words I had feared since the moment she left for California ... "We need to talk."

FEATURED TRACK

Garbage - The Trick Is To Keep Breathing

11

All Good Things ...

    We left the party and sat on the bench around the side of the shop. The cool breezy air kept my arms shaking and hairs standing on end. Angie wrapped both of her hands around mine like a warm smallpox blanket.

    "So how are you, Ben?" she asked.

    "Don't do that," I said turning away to look at my feet.

    "Do what?" she replied.

    "Let's just get whatever this is over. I don't need to be treated like a child."

    "OK, then. ... I think we ... we should break up." Her hands immediately pulled away and covered her face. Her elbows dropped to her knees and she continued talking through her palms. "I don't know what it is, but this long-distance thing ... it just isn't working out. For the past five months, I've dreaded each new day, afraid that I might actually have a good day. Because if I did, it meant I would eventually talk with you and get depressed all over again. I miss you, so much."

    "Hey, I get it, OK. I miss you, too." Hearing her voice similar problems felt comforting, so I tried to wrap my arms around her shoulder, but she pivoted herself away on the bench.

"You don't get it. It ... literally ... hurts," she said poking fiercely at her sternum, "so much I can barely concentrate. We need to do this ... I ... need to do this." She said it. Her lip was quivering, while trying to look me in the eye. "I need to do this, because I don't think I can take another semester of this heartache. I must have nearly packed up and left over a dozen times and cried myself to sleep even more. The only way I could make it work was to bury myself in school and extracurriculars to the brink of exhaustion just to keep my mind from thinking about you, and that's no way for a relationship to thrive. I know this hasn't been easy for you, either. You know I'm right."

Tears streamed down the tip of my nose into a growing puddle on the sidewalk below. "No. ... I don't. Yeah ... I have my good days and bad days, but this is a problem, just like anything else. We just need to keep working at it." My brain immediately switched to a feverish Faulknerian stream of emotion and ideas, "I can buy more phone cards, we can talk less often, we can write letters every day, ..." I was at least ten ideas in until I realized Angie was bawling in her jacket.

"Don't you get it. I love you, Ben." An arrow pierced my beating heart, and my mind circled with confusion. *Where was this going?* "More than anything in the world, but all these long-distance gimmicks are killing me."

This arctic barrage of spiteful words eviscerated the final threads of my composure. In the same breath, she said she loved me, and yet insulted me by bagging on my ideas to try and save our relationship. In all the moments of my young life, this is the one time I wish my instincts would have chosen flight over fight. Instead, the most regrettable words imaginable poured from my lips without hesitation or a single drop of remorse. "You obviously don't love me as much as you love Berkeley." *Take it back!*

"That is not fair." Her eyes cleared and her tone turned from distraught girlfriend to defense attorney in an instant. "You knew it was my dream to go to a top college that wasn't here in Texas. You knew I was going almost six months before I left. If you felt this way, you should have told me. We could have responsibly ended this relationship sooner, remained friends without the stress, but in typical Ben fashion, you sat around waiting for things to fix themselves rather than risk talking about your feelings with anyone." *She wasn't wrong.* "I am not the villain in this story. Just like you, I'm trying to solve a problem, except my problem is that I cannot do this anymore. I'm the one making the hardest choice of my life. As always, you are taking the path of least resistance and letting other people do all the hard work. We're not in high school anymore. You have to grow up and take responsibility. I can't keep being the only reason you give a damn about doing something with your life."

"You're right. This isn't high school anymore, and if you think you are the only reason I give a damn about my future, then maybe you don't know me as well as you think!?" *No!!!!!!!*

Angie stood up resolutely. "Apparently not, but maybe that's a good thing. Thanks for making this much easier than I could have ever expected. Have a great life. Tell the others I'll email them." She turned to walk away but stopped short when she put her hands in her jacket pocket. "Oh … Merry Christmas …" She set a small intricately wrapped box with a bow on the bench and walked away. *Say Something!*

I held the box in my hand counting the snowflakes on the wrapping paper deliberating whether to throw, crush or protect it. I was impotent with rage, and my emotions fluctuated radically across the entire known spectrum of feelings. Anger. Sadness. Regret. Love. Pride. I sat on the cold bench for at least thirty minutes before Tom came out to check on us. The dried tear trails on my face and body posture painted a clear portrait of what had just transpired. He sat next to me and placed his hand on my shoulder.

"I was afraid something like this would happen," he said. "You two are so alike." Tom told me a story about his first real breakup when he was in high school. It wasn't a long-distance relationship thing, but something changed over a summer and the two of them drifted too far apart. He went to his twenty-year high school reunion and hoped she would be there so they could reconnect, but she had recently died. *Fuck Cancer!* As sad as the story was, ships passing in the night and all, it was quite impressive to some degree. First off, I had never mentally pictured Tom in his youth, possibly even without his mustache, let alone a dating Tom in high school. To be honest, I didn't see him as the dating type now, either. Seeing him and Evelyn together felt wrong on so many levels. Second, for all the things Tom did well, which garnered unmeasurable levels of trust and respect from me, there was one facet of his personality that was impaired: storyteller Tom. Hearing Tom tell a story was a bit like listening to twenty overlapping songs with different beats and genres all at once. With the attention span of a gnat, Tom was the king of tangential thought, which made the simplest of stories practically impossible to follow. What he lacked in coherent fluidity, he made up for in his entertaining and animated delivery that could give Billy Mays a run for his money. After fifteen minutes of random anecdotes, he realized he might have gotten off course with his life lesson.

"It's getting cold. I'm heading inside," Tom said. "Take some time and figure out what you want and then reach out to her. Angie is amazing, but she isn't perfect." Tom must have seen me perk up a bit from these comments, as he followed up quickly, "and neither are you for that matter." I caught a glimpse of his smile as he walked away. "You should think about her side of things before placing blame anywhere. It can't be easy for her, either."

Tom's words echoed in the hollowed chambers of my heart for another hour as I sat frozen in thought on the bench. He was right. She was right. I had the best of everything right at my fingertips, the shop, friends and a sense of normal, while Angie had to deal with nothing but change on every level. I couldn't even fathom. New feelings of guilt and worry joined the emotional turbulence circulating through my veins and new scenarios played out in my head. I stood up and considered running after Angie, but even if I caught her, I still had no idea what to say. *Best to collect your thoughts, like Tom said.* The tear soaked wrapping paper from her gift separated in my tightening group such that I could see the contents: a red Tamagotchi keychain. Angie had mentioned these in passing before in one of our phone calls, but they seemed silly to me. When I turned it over, I noticed an inscription on the back casing, "Benji". There was no note, but then Angie wasn't trying to be subtle. Her message was loud and clear. *So I thought.*

In that moment, my mind focused on the last quasi-polite thing Angie said to me. "Thanks for making this much easier than I could have ever expected." Right now, this was the only thing I had going for me. I had made something easier for her. So, I ran with it, resolved in my new focus, and hurting like hell on the inside. I committed to leaving Angie alone to give her time to pursue her dreams. If it was meant to be, she would know where I was and make the first move. Until then, all I had were memories, and, now, Benji. I pressed one of the front buttons and the blobby little circle beast appeared. *Hello, Benji.*

Tom must have shared the news with the others since they looked at me like a dead man walking when I came back inside. I stopped by my desk and hung Benji on the side of my monitor and then returned to the party. Healthy or not, I had become all too familiar with the art of pushing my feelings into an emotional abyss in my psyche, so a small party was going to be an easy piece of sheet cake. The evening eventually ended not too long after, since one person can only hear "everything will be alright" so many times without losing it. Wade dropped me off at my house afterwards and offered to talk for a bit if I was up for it; however, all I wanted to do was sleep. I laid in bed watching the ceiling fan blades spin and hoping I would wake up from this dystopian timeline, but with every minute that passed, the hard truth became ever more real. My nightmare was now my life, and I cried myself to sleep for the first time.

With my emotional volatility in overdrive, Mom thought it would be good for some additional male bonding, so Phil's presence became ever more prominent in the coming weeks. He and Mom were spending a lot of time together and he was trying way too hard to force a connection with me, despite my numerous rebuffs. For all his attempts, Phil was driving a wedge further and further between us, which is why it hit me so hard when he and Mom mentioned they were moving to Louisiana.

About a week before Christmas, Mom asked off of work, which rarely happened, and made a feast for the three of us at home. Phil was noticeably giggly and prancing around like he could finally remember grade school math, again. Mom was overcompensating on everything and hyper focused, which meant she was nervous. We had barely plowed through our first course, Mom's fried pickle salad, when Phil clanked his fork against his glass as if he was doing a toast at a wedding and blurted out some next level nonsense.

"I've asked your mom to move with me to Louisiana." His eyes were ping ponging between us both to gauge our reactions. "And, she said, yes!"

Mom was throwing daggers at him with her eyes as she cut him another piece of pot roast, but the idiot was too stupid to recognize. I've seen that look before. Mom joined the conversation and explained that she found a transfer opportunity and that we could live with Phil at his house just outside of Baton Rouge. We'd have to move in a couple of months. *She actually used the term, we.* The next few hours were like a poorly executed infomercial about the wonders of living in Louisiana, put on by two actors that studied two different scripts and forced to work together at the last minute. I had already made up my mind, but it was entertaining watching her constantly correct Phil. I couldn't stand to spend ten minutes with the guy, and the thought of living in a house with him, possibly walking in on him and ... *yuck*... that was all the mental imagery I needed. *No thanks!* After the entertainment portion of the meal was over, I politely stood up from the table, wiped my mouth with my napkin and said, "Thanks, but I'll figure something out." I wasn't mad at her for moving or trying to find happiness. I was disappointed that after her experience with a cheating fraction of a man, she would rebound so far down the totem pole with this screw loose moron. Besides, Louisiana didn't have Tom, the shop or any of my real family. It was time to find my own place.

  The season of change kept on delivering unexpected blows, some weird, but some long overdue. With the Angie and Phil fiascos still lingering in the back of my mind, what better time than to receive my wonderful grades from last semester in the mail. Communications. "A". Psychology. "C". *Damnit!* It looked like my final essay classifying computer illiteracy as a psychological disorder and a menace to the future of civilization didn't resonate with the professor. It was the first time I received a formal grade that was less than a "B" in my entire life. It was then that I decided to also make it the last time. *What was the point? Maybe, Angie was right. The only reason I was even interested in college was because of her. Did I really want to learn more about cognitive dissonance or economic theory?* There were new technologies springing up every day. The Internet was my classroom, not some antiquated diploma pushing institution that baited my curiosity and sharpened the snaring clutches of prison. The decision took less than a second as I crumpled the paper and tossed it in the trash. *Fuck it. I quit!*

  Even Christmas wasn't immune from the season of change. When I opened my bedroom door on Christmas morning, a table fan unleashed an explosion of glitter into my room. If there was ever a question on how to murder-death-kill a person's Christmas spirit, Phil had Scrooge beat by a mile. He popped his head out from the living room and screamed, "Gotcha!" like a smiling idiot hopped up on happy pills. I flipped him off and slammed my door. It took over an hour and two cans of air to clean out all the glitter that got sucked into my computer case. It was no surprise that this was the year the Gotcha! officially died and was replaced with a sadder and dare I say more utilitarian tradition, gift cards. Christmas became less like a holiday, and more like an annual transaction. No present hiding, wrapping or even thoughtful gifts. It was just a predictable exchange of plastic shards so we could say we went through the motions. *I'm sure that is exactly what ole J.C. and the fat man had in mind from the beginning.*

While the winds of change laid waste to my personal universe, the storm surge was busy affecting neighboring businesses around the shop. We had all just left the shop no more than four hours prior after ringing in the new year with one hellacious movie and trivia party, so it felt more like coming back from lunch than opening for the day. Tom was wide awake in his office when we arrived, so Wade peeled away to FlowJoe's to grab the morning coffee order. This too was a bit of a change over the past month, as opposed to Tom sleeping in the extra hour or inhaling his morning news radio in the backroom. I couldn't tell exactly what he was doing, but it couldn't have been that important because I could see he was working in Notepad of all things. By the time I finished booting up the last of the Community Corner computers, Wade returned with the coffee, short of breath and pale like an over caffeinated snow owl.

"FlowJoe's is closing," he said, trying to catch his breath.

"Wait, what?" I asked.

"At the end of the month. It's closing." Wade was distraught and barely coherent, but he shared the details from the conversation he had with the owner. Their building was bought out and his lease was going to double in the next two months. The same went for Little Caesars just around the corner. The rumors suggested that the building was going to be torn down and replaced with a climate controlled self-storage complex. Tom owned his land and the building out right, so he didn't have to worry about this happening to him, but it definitely cut our team where it hurt most, our caffeine and our stomachs. Random men and women started showing up in the coming weeks, asking to speak to Tom. Some of them even made it back to his office for a conversation. Eventually, it became clear that Tom was being courted to sell the shop, but despite their offers, Tom turned them away without giving it a second thought. *What a crazy way to start the new year!*

Phil and Mom were scheduled to leave in just under a month and I had procrastinated finding a place to live for far too long. With Nicodemus and Brisby passing last month, I didn't have to worry about Phil's family eating them in Louisiana, but it was just another gut punch that felt ten times harder given how things were progressing. It was now crunch time, no matter how much I didn't like it. *I had to find a place to live!* Wade drove me around to check out nearby apartments, but they were reluctant to rent to a freshly minted twenty-year-old with no credit history. I started to panic at the thought that I might need to crash on Wade's sofa for a few months, or worse, move to Louisiana. Then one night when I was closing up, Tom asked me to check something out in the backroom. I followed him up the stairs through the breakroom and towards his apartment, which was completely empty.

"What happened in here? Did you get robbed?" I asked.

Tom chuckled, "Hehe … nope. I know you are looking for a place to live, and if you'd like, I'm willing to let you stay in this apartment."

I didn't know what to say. The place was immaculate. The walls were freshly painted and the whole place smelled like chemically delicious new carpet. "What about you, where are you going to live?"

"I'm moving out, "he replied. "I'm getting too old to keep climbing up and down these steps. Besides, the modems never stop blaring. Evelyn has a house not too far from here and she and I are moving in together. I've been moving my stuff out the backdoor for the past few weeks trying to keep this a surprise. I know it's not perfect, but if you can commit to opening the shop every day on your own from here on out, then you can stay here rent free."

I expected Tom Green to jump out from the bathroom ending this elaborate Mr. Miyagi prank, but it never happened. This was really happening. It would be the world's easiest commute, and it came equipped with high-speed internet access for FREE. Most important of all, it wasn't Louisiana. *How could I say no?* I excitedly shook Tom's hand and accepted my unofficial promotion to shop manager. Tom cleaned out his office a few days later and moved his computer to Evelyn's house. He still planned to sit there from time to time but insisted that the office belonged to the shop manager and that I should use it however I deemed appropriate. I was fine letting him have it. I preferred to do my dev work at my spot on the floor. The feeling of being put on display like a sideshow attraction had grown on me, and it was a great spot to observe everything. Tom still came in every day, a bit later than usual, and immediately restarted his morning ritual in the Corvette before challenging me to a Minesweeper duel. Apparently, Evelyn wasn't a fan of the pot smell, and he was trying to figure co-habitation out. The man was nothing short of habitual, but you could tell something was different about him. He was lighter and happier, and I was happy for him, even if I didn't care for his taste in women. *Who was I to judge?*

I inventoried my personal belongings and prepared a list for the big moving day. Most of the furniture in my bedroom I could keep, but I was grossly under equipped for the rest of the apartment. I reclaimed the papasan from the breakroom to serve as my living room couch and picked up a free dining table and chairs from some of Wade's neighbors who were moving in a hurry. Tom left his kitchen appliances for me because Evelyn felt they didn't match the decor in the new place. The irony was not lost on me that I was moving into my first official bachelor pad on Valentine's day. I tried not to think about it too much, but after Wade and I unloaded my last box of crap, I immediately set up my computer to check out Angie's ICQ status. *Away. Studying.*

Instant message was a blessing and a curse. On one hand, it was a great way to communicate that was cheap and reliable. The problem was that it required a constant balance of saying all that you wanted to say, fast and clear enough to avoid ambiguity and confusion. It left so much to the imagination and interpretation. There wasn't a word, phrase, paragraph or chapter I could write that would adequately convey the full spectrum of my feelings towards Angie. Instead, I placed my finger on the monitor over the stale status message and wished her a Happy Valentine's day. I retreated to my bed and stared in silence at my lone wall decoration on a pale sea of freshly painted white canvas. It was my first Demotivator. It was fitting that I bought it with my Christmas gift card from Mom and Phil. There were so many to choose from that I had plenty queued up in the wings but this one felt perfect. *Ambition*. The agape jaws of a bear catching river salmon as they fought to swim upstream was poetic and yet so true. *Look what it gets you!*

With my new commute, I no longer needed Wade to give me a lift, and yet, there he was, every morning like clockwork just hanging around in the parking lot listening to music and waiting for me to unlock the doors. FlowJoe's closed a few weeks after I moved in and both Wade and Anto were jonesing hard to find a suitable replacement. Wade resorted to creating his own coffee creations using various packets of coffee and random spices, but nothing came close to a well-crafted cup of coffee made with real tools. Unfortunately, one of the circuit boards for Marge was fried in a milk explosion, and he was waiting for a replacement. Even when his experiments failed to please, Wade was a purist and drank every last drop. His motto was simple: "There is no bad coffee, only untapped potential for greatness." Some of the gutter brews he uncovered around town tested this resolve on many occasions. In preparation for the arrival of his replacement board, he asked me if he could move Marge from the back room and convert Tom's old office into his new brew test facility to get away from all the dust. At this point, I found myself yearning for a decent cup myself, so I had no problem with him taking it over. Besides, his shiny silver machine looked impressive through the window and nothing beat that lingering smell of freshly brewed coffee, regardless of the taste. It helped fool the senses while trying to rifle down the lesser stuff we were able to scrounge from around town.

The TapHouse trivia tournament was upon us in no time, and it was time to start preparations. Losing Angie hurt the team, a lot, and it was going to take a miracle to be able to even make it out of the elimination rounds. Evelyn was not that miracle. Contempt for her grew in everyone on the team, except Tom. It wasn't because she didn't know anything, *she was horrible*, but because she constantly blamed others for her shortcomings, even when she forgot about practices all together. No matter the situation, Evelyn plus trivia games always led to arguing. The competition was stiff again that year. There were a lot of returning teams, which made it more surprising that we made it to the semi-finals, placing fourth out of fourteen teams. I tried to give Evelyn an out by asking if the team could compete with only five people, but they insisted on six people per team to maintain equal numbers for the head-to-head challenges. Excluding the dead weight, our team was firing on all cylinders, which only made me wonder what we could have done if Angie was still here.

Murphy's Law states, "anything that can go wrong will go wrong" and that year had started off as living proof. The only thing immune seemed to be work. Tom-NET was exploding, in a good way. Everyone and their mother wanted to get online, which meant more accounts, more setups and more problems. *Truth. B.I.G.* Local businesses were throwing money at us hand over fist to connect their office networks and build their websites, and that is when the wheels started coming off the wagon. Digital cameras were on the rise and this created a surge in photo sharing through email, which inevitably clogged inboxes for practically all customers with slower internet connections when their mail programs kept timing out while downloading the attachments. The only way to fix the problem was to get a faster internet connection, such as buying a new modem, or have us delete the offending email. We kept an unused email client on the support computers that allowed us to easily change usernames and passwords and download the offending messages over our high-speed network in the office. In some cases, we would even zip all the files together and forward the emails to customers so they would at least be able to read the correspondence. That was until Pervy Joe came along.

Pervy Joe was a notoriously heavy breathing customer who signed up that Spring and frequently called tech support complaining about blocked email. I happened to be covering the phones the first day he called in, and like a creepy stalker, he kept calling back asking for me, by name, to help him. The problem with Pervy Joe wasn't that he subscribed to listservs that flooded his inbox with gay male porn. It was that he insisted on being on the phone when you opened his email to troubleshoot and always asked if we could describe or forward it regardless of how many times we all said, "No." All the while, he was breathing heavily on the phone as if he was trying to force his halitosis breath through the phone line. I pretended not to see the attachments as I gave him the all clear to try again, but I could tell he knew, I knew, he knew. This song and dance continued on and off for nearly a month, until I tried a better option. Rather than downloading the messages via the email client, I just telneted into our server and deleted the message directly with POP commands. *USER PASS LIST TOP DELE*. Once I started doing this, his support call time shrank, and his labored breathing was miraculously cured. *I should be a doctor*. It didn't matter if it was a family photo from DisneyLand or two burly dudes lathered in baby oil wearing lucha libre masks jerking each other off on the top turnbuckle, *some things you just can't forget*, my new method was faster, easier and indiscriminately treated the messages as the 1's and 0's they were. It was like looking at the Matrix in its interpreted form. *Ignorance was bliss!* Everyone in the shop saw that movie at-least five times during its opening week. The CGI was out of this world! Patty nearly broke a leg spinning around in his office chair trying to recreate Trinity's 360 kick shot! Tom wasn't as enthused by the movie, but that could have been influenced by all of us greeting him in our best Agent Smith impersonations for the following weeks. *Hello, Mr. Andersson.*

Sadly, ole Murphy wasn't done with us yet. While the Tom-NET Web solutions side of the house was humming right along, the ISP continued to fight through growing pains. Customers were referring their friends and family at a feverish pace, which forced us to increase the modem bank capacity twice in as many months, just to keep the busy signals at bay. Average online times had steadily climbed since Christmas from one to three hours per session. More and more people were surfing the web longer and an equal number leaving their modem idly connected. *I blamed BattleNet*. Making matters worse, the Melissa virus struck the Internet at large over a month prior and we were still dealing with people who hadn't fixed their infected machines. The virus continued to slam our email servers, clogging accounts and collectively screwing the tightly bound social fabric of our small-town e-Community. Complaints about sluggish internet performance kept the support lines ablaze with white hot newbie techno-fury.

Getting yelled at by people who at least get the basics is tolerable but trying to explain the differences between a slow computer, bad phone line, slow internet or even what the hell it meant when a site was in the progress of being "slashdotted" was maddening. Things got so crazy, we pulled out all the stops to try and get an advantage. We pulled Wade in to answer phones so Patty and I could get some website work done. He was under strict orders, no yelling. As a safety precaution, I installed an extra-long telephone cable so that I could yank it out of the wall if Wade strayed from any of the pre-approved scripts. We also took a bit of an unorthodox pro-active support model for some of our clingier support clients. We gave them a JPG picture of the "Hang in There" cat poster that was slipstreamed with a customized BO2K trojan. It was admittedly an ethical grey area. We did our best to explain to them what we were doing and trying to ask for consent, but their ability to grasp the concept of remote administration via a cat picture was suspect. To be on the safe side, we did change the default listening port from 31337 so our customers didn't have a flashing neon "Come Hack Me!" sign on their computer when they were online. In the end, it turned out to be an amazing tool for us to support and train our customers over the phone, and they loved us for it. *Tech support tool of the century!*

Tackling the supply vs. demand problem was easier said than done. In the end it meant that we needed to change our unlimited Internet policies, which was not popular by any means. At least twenty percent of the users threatened to leave, but we all knew they didn't have any other options since we were still the only local dial-up in town. We invited everyone to the shop for a town hall of sorts where we explained in detail the recent growth troubles and introduced our plan and new packages, many with lower prices. At least one hundred angry customers show up in person, and this is where Tom really shined. By the end of the town hall, everyone was eating out of his hand, which was a good thing, because I'm not sure I could have taken one more day of their incessant whining. Fate was throwing curve balls, but Tom kept fouling them off until he got what he wanted.

  I was never one who was afraid of normal things. I had no fear of drowning, heights or even spiders, but after a year or so of technical support, I was starting to develop a slight case of telephobia. Whenever the pager beeped, it triggered a Pavlovian grab and chuck response that claimed the lives of four pagers in the past three months out of pure frustration. The following week I fielded a support call that tested the limits of my sanity and induced nightmares that lasted nearly a month. These were not your typical nightmares about monsters or falling to your death. Instead, these were dystopian futures painted on a saturated fabric of computer illiterate "Oops ... I broke my computer's coffee cup holder" masterminds. In hindsight, my nightmares were far rosier than real life, in some regards. I covered the phones for Patty so he could take a small break, and that's when the phone receiver rang. I should have listened closer to the subtle tones of the ringer, as I'm sure it was sending morse code telling me to run.

"Thank you for calling Tom-NET tech support. This is Ben, how may I help you?" That is when I heard Ms. Waters' shrill nasal tinged voice for the first time.

"I'd like to get online please." A fair request that many of our first-time callers asked, how was I to know this call would be the near end of me. After pitching the various packages to her, I took her credit card information and set up her RADIUS account. It was now time to kick this conversation into autopilot, or so I thought. My feet went up on the desk and I fidgeted with a small desk puzzle while I quizzed her on the computer setup basics. Windows 95? Check. Modem? Check. Start button in lower-left hand corner? Check. I was mid-flight into the initial set of twenty or so steps, when she asked, "I'm sorry. I don't see that?"

"What do you mean? Did you press the start button?" I asked. That was the only thing that made any sense.

"I did ... but the screen went black," she replied. At the time I didn't notice, but an odd background noise I had been passively listening to had stopped.

"Ma'am ... I think you pressed the power button. Did you say your screen is black?"

"Yes." There was a suspicious certainty in her voice and yet it felt like she was still searching for words to complete her thoughts. I envisioned a rotating hourglass projected onto her pupils while the mental hamsters spinning the gears in her head took a break to line dance in unison. *Dibidi ba didi dou dou ... Argh. Damn that song!!!*

I was tired of waiting for further details. "Well, that's not good." My head went into my hands, "We need our computers to stay on for this to work, don't we, Ms. Waters?" I tried not to sound too obnoxious, but it was difficult to hold back the snark. I practiced flipping my pencil in the air while I waited a few minutes for her computer to reboot, and then proceeded to run through the same setup script from the top. Once again, when I mentioned the "start button" the background noises turned off. I didn't want to ask, but there was no way around it. "You turned it off, again, didn't you?"

"I'm afraid so. I'm sorry, I'm not all that good all this whole internet thing. Don't worry, I'll turn it back on again." she replied.

I didn't have the heart to explain to her that her problems were not with "the Internet". I was tempted to shut everything down at that moment, akin to a mercy killing. If she couldn't figure this out, the rest of this setup may end with me hanging myself by the RJ11 cable to my headset, but she was showing incremental signs of progress. She turned it on again by herself without instruction, and she seemed determined. I dug my heels in to give it another go and that's when I heard a brief moment of clarity in the background noise. *It was the Duke!* I wasn't a huge man of old westerns, but Tom was, and he made us all watch the entire John Wayne collection, including Rooster Cogburn. I replayed the setup conversation in my head, carefully listening for any possible misinterpretations in my directions or questions. Even though her affirmative response to the question, "Are you running Windows 95?" was as direct as anyone could get, I reluctantly asked, "Are you on your TV, Ms. Waters?"

"Yes. Is that a problem?" she replied.

"Do you have a computer?" I asked.

"I have a TV. Do I need a computer?" she innocently replied. I was speechless. This woman couldn't tell the difference between her TV and a computer. If Dante lived in modern times, he would have dedicated a special bolgia in hell for such ignorance. *Thanks college, for that sick burn.* It was at this moment that the reason for my misery was made clear when she stated, "I just saw a commercial that said I could get online using my TV? Is that not true?" *Screw you, WebTV!*

I snapped my pencil in half and proceeded to explain to Ms. Waters the subtle differences between what she saw on a commercial versus what Tom-NET offered as a service. She was embarrassed, but I told her that if she was interested to try it, that she could either order a WebTV and we could sign her up for an account, or she could come to the shop and we'd build her a custom computer and get her set up that way. It was my last-ditch effort of civil discourse before cancelling her account and faking a disconnected phone. She responded with a non-committing tone, "we'll have to see, but thank you, Jim." I didn't even bother to correct her. I simply put the headset on mute and screamed my frustration as loud as possible. Patty, Anto and Wade were laughing hysterically in the corner eating popcorn, and Tom barged out of the backroom drafting a cloud of smoke behind him. After a quick conversation with the chuckling trio, and a few handfuls of popcorn, Tom declared his allegiance with popcorn kernels in his mustache. I wasn't mad at her, for the most part. I was mad at Microsoft for making that commercial without explicit disclaimers on how their technology worked. *Goddamn marketers.*

  A month later, an older lady came into the shop and asked to speak to Jim. The sound of her voice was like fingernails on a chalk board that made my arm hairs stand on end. It was Ms. Waters. She came to buy her first computer and prepay for an annual Internet contract. Apparently, other tech support people didn't treat her as nice as we did, so she was giving Tom-NET all her business. It was a sweet commission, but to be honest, knowing I was able to help her when no other company could, or would, gave me a miniscule warm feeling inside that offered a short respite from my overall depressed and cynical mood that had become my new normal. Shortly after, my nightmares stopped, and I took that as a sign to not dwell on the past but focus on the future. No matter how painful and distant that future was from where I thought I would be only six months prior.

FEATURED TRACK

Everclear - Wonderful

12
The Spices of Life

    I would be lying if I said everything magically turned around, but some days were better than others. The turbulent free fall from my high school pentacle continued, but even though I felt like everything was inevitably crumbling under my feet, I found intermittent meaning when I helped customers with their computer problems. I wasn't some Stuart Little do-gooder always on the lookout to help everyone around me. I was more of a tragically flawed and opportunistic superhero character, like Deadpool, that stumbled into doing the right thing because he had nothing better to do at the time and then felt good about it afterwards. These investments into being a technical support superhero often paid dividends. More times than not, it involved fresh baked cookies or hand stitched doilies, but every once and a while, when the customer wasn't pushing forty, the prospect of "a date with the smart computer guy" was sometimes floated in my direction, especially since the breakup.

    One such occurrence happened when a girl named Jennifer brought her laptop in for a diagnostic and would not stop talking to me. She was an attractive tall blonde from Omaha with an accent that could pierce Kevlar and had recently dropped out of UT. Up to this point in my life, I had high standards for intelligence when it came to relationships, *the one*, but there was a certain appeal with her thumbing her nose at college that persuaded me to give it a try. She wanted to meet up to watch a movie, so I invited her up to my apartment. I offered her a wide selection of movies, but she ended up bringing her own DVD: Jawbreakers. Of all the lessons I learned that night, *and there were many,* the most important one was to always screen movie tastes before inviting someone over. There was nowhere to hide. Between the ridiculous plot and Jennifer constantly commenting on their outfits, I was ready to die. I contemplated hurling myself out of my own apartment window at-least six different times in the first twenty minutes alone.

After the movie was over, we chatted for a bit while I stopped searching for ways to kill myself and focused solely on killing the conversation. During this exchange, she let it slip out that her exodus from college was not so much voluntary as it was being forcibly removed for poor academic performance. I was not the person to judge someone on their grades, but the spark of defiance that I thought I saw in her was quickly extinguished, especially when she dismissed her parents paying for three years of parties as no big deal. As the conversation wound down, she implied that she was tired and was interested in spending the night, but I formulated an excuse about opening the shop early the next day laced with some nonsensical techno-gibberish to make it sound official. It may have been a lame move on my part, but nothing good was going to happen that night for either of us. *Not all superheroes wear capes!*

The next morning was rough. I was physically drained from all my mental leaps from my window and I was in dire need of a pick me up. Caffeine was my super juice, or my strongest vice depending on your point of view, and life without FlowJoe's was proving to be my kryptonite. Unlike Wade, I wasn't drawn to any single form of the substance, nor burdened myself with an inflated importance on quality. Any and all caffeine was welcome, except Jolt. As strange as it sounded given all the hoopla in the hacker underground, I really didn't like its overly sweet taste and how it lingered in the back of my mouth like chalky molasses. When Wade wasn't around to whip up one of his Marge coffee experiments, twenty ounce Mountain Dew or Dr. Pepper were my go-to backup beverages. Two six packs for five bucks? It was a hard deal to pass up. Normally, it would last me at-least an entire week, but whenever I saw one of those "Dude, you're getting a Dell" commercials, I was lucky to make it to Tuesday. Thoughts of bolo whipping that guy in the face with one of their crappy mice or bashing an old school IBM mechanical over his head, were not uncommon. *That guy was so damn annoying!* Dell was pushing their all-inclusive bargain basement computer deals, and since they were more or less local, we started noticing a dip in our PC sales. Our one ace in the hole that kept Dell at bay was still our local phone number for Internet, no matter how many thousand-hour AOL CDs or one-year MSN subscriptions they threw at customers. It didn't take Miss Cleo to see that this advantage was fading by the minute. If a customer just wanted "a computer", Dell's prices were hard to beat and still turn a profit. If they wanted a fast-personalized computer for a reasonable price, Dell couldn't come close to touching our team's work. Every day I checked Slashdot hoping for an ironic article about Dell getting caught packing their PCs with hand me down Packard Bell parts and going out of business. *Still waiting!*

   Holiday cheer was in the air and the small town of Jollyville was buzzing as many locals struggled navigating their first adventure into online holiday shopping. The gossip mill was filled with stories about elderly mishaps making their first e-commerce purchases. *No, Ms. Waters, I do not know anyone who needs one hundred boxes of Depends?* Much to Hasting's chagrin, Amazon was making a strong play for the sacred Christmas top three: books, music and movies, and their competitive pricing, state tax exemption and free shipping on orders over twenty-five dollars were real game changers that year, but that wasn't what kept our town in a frenzy. Y2K loomed over the entire digital world like a flock of circling well-fed pigeons, and yet nowhere in the world did it feel more meaningful, relevant or impactful than our booming fifteen thousand person town full of freshly minted cyber lemmings regurgitating unsubstantiated proclamations of the digital apocalypse they received from an "expert" on an email chain letter. *I need another Dr. Pepper!* Every day was the same question over and over again, like that damn Tubthumping sung stuck on repeat, *again!* "Is this <INSERT RANDOM HOUSEHOLD ITEM> Y2K compliant?" When it comes to computers, I can understand about checking, maybe even a pager or cell phone, but to ask if your toaster was going to stop working, as a result of Y2K, demonstrated an incomprehensible grasp of the situation that was far too common for my taste.

My biggest frustration throughout the entire Y2K ordeal was the attention it drew to the average person to perform system maintenance on their computers. It was probably for the best because I was having way too much fun bypassing Serv-U hosts with a nifty NetBIOS IPC$ trick I learned from some of my online brethren. I could feel the noose getting tighter with every "net use" command. *Moderation was never my cup of tea.* All sensationalism and frustrations aside, Y2K came and went with very little fanfare. Our traditional trivia plus pizza night new year's celebration at the shop was virtually identical to any other, except for the hour before midnight where we got the backup generators ready for the ensuing madness. All the computers in the shop were properly patched, except for the one sacrificial lamb in the Community Corner we morbidly left unprotected just to see what would happen. We watched the computer clock seconds countdown like a crystal ball descending to end all mankind. My heart and head dueled between calm logical reasoning and far out what-if scenarios, like planes dropping from the sky and swimming in piles of errantly dispensed ATM on the ground. Three. Two. One. … … Nothing. We waited another two or three minutes as if we were expecting some elaborate Rube Goldberg series of reactions to launch us into anarchy at any moment. Still nothing. We powered up the rest of the computers in the shop and double checked the servers and modem bank. All were just fine, except for Patty. The next morning, Blockbuster thought he owed over $90,000 in late charges on his Shawshank Redemption rental, it was more like $12, but thanks to Y2K, they cleared his account. Patty boasted his triumph like he got away with the crime of the century. With the great ordeal of Y2K that wasn't behind us, I ordered my annual Demotivator, *Potential*, and extended a snarky hello to the new century.

March was just around the corner, and that meant that it was trivia tournament time. The ramp up strategy was different this year, and it felt like we might be on the verge of a winning formula, working around Evelyn rather than with her. None of us felt comfortable enough to ask Tom to kick Evelyn off the team, but Anto had a brilliant idea. We all pitched in and bought her a few pop culture trivia books and suggested that since she was "so busy" that she could read these in her spare time and not worry about trying to make it to all of the practices. The red fish took the bait, which made Tom noticeably relieved. We didn't expect her to actually study the books, but we felt the team had a better chance if the rest of us were one hundred percent dialed in to make up for her shortcomings. Tom was still splitting time between home and the shop, but he added some new decks to the Hot Shot card coffers and the shop's social chemistry and quirky vibe was starting to make a comeback after a very long hiatus. I liked to think that we were somewhere in-between the eclectic rock and roll crew from Empire Records, and the music snobs from High Fidelity, *I was Rob Gordon, of course.* We were an island of misfit nerds who loved music, movies and pop culture, but were quick to complain whenever our internet speeds dropped below 128k. *We were spoiled rotten!* Nowhere was this chemistry more apparent than at the trivia tournament that year. Our core team won every match-up, and to our surprise Evelyn even won one. *Of course, she knew who shot JR!* All the success aside, she still missed the other nine of her matchups and that slipped us into third place. It was a respectable improvement from last year, and while we didn't make the finals, we were reminded of why we did this in the first place. It was fun!

    The computer marketplace was riding a welcomed wave of resurgence in first person shooter games that filled the hole left by a lackluster era of Quake II. Unreal and Half Life were going strong, but I never got into them beyond casual play. Soldier of Fortune dominated my FPS focus for a disturbing amount of time with its gruesome locational damage effects. I painted every square pixel of that first level demo with shotgun severed body parts so many times, I finally broke down and bought the game. *Headshots were the best!* As for online play, the minute Team Fortress Classic was released, our TF clan splintered. Most of the members were not fond of the sluggish game play. Thanks to Anto, we never had to worry about any of our machines ever being inadequate from a component perspective. She was a living Tom's Hardware encyclopedia of performance tuning and exceptional at orchestrating third-party peripherals into melodious harmony. Her latest experiment was to overclock a pair of cheap Celeron processors in the new dual socket Abit BP6 and see if she could outperform their Pentium III counterparts. Even with a techno-artisan like Anto at the helm to keep my rig in optimal competitive condition, I simply lost interest in the TF clan lifestyle. So, I dropped my clan tag and started flying solo in Quake 3 Arena. Video games had found a purpose again, and my collection of retail boxes grew into yet another unintended curated collection on display in my living room. I had a prime spot for my pre-ordered Diablo 2 Collector's Edition box right in the middle of the case!

It felt like Hollywood was abandoning their successful formulas from the 90s and buying script ideas from ubid1dollarscriptauctionbarn.com. They were terrible. It was rare to see a movie trailer that wasn't some half-baked sequel like Next Friday, or a rehashed story simply with 2000 tacked on at the end. We saw the trailer for Battlefield Earth, and we felt there was hope. *So, we thought.* Never before had a movie been so overhyped, underperforming and colossally stupid. Within fifteen minutes, our entire row devolved into an episode of MST3K, pointing out plot holes and disregarded principles of degradation on things like power grids, jet fuel and electronics after one thousand plus years of neglect. *Barry Pepper, how could you?* It was so bad, even Wade complained about it, which rarely happened. We were on a first-class ticket to boycotting movie theaters all together when Tom struck a trade with the local furniture store and outfitted the breakroom with a fancy new Sony WEGA Trinitron TV, THX surround sound system, popcorn machine and an assortment set of multi-color bean bags. A treat for a well-done tournament showing that year.

Minus the whole "watching movies when they came out" experience, there was no incentive to leave the comforts of our bean bag laden breakroom. We made a massive shelving system, and everyone stockpiled their personal DVDs in the breakroom. When new movies came out, we would rotate buying duties and/or all chip in money to share the cost. It was a wonderfully cosmic cinematic commune, and it was only a short stumble from my apartment door. *I'll take it!* Once the screenwriters finally dug their cookie cutter Y2K heads out of the ground, we started seeing the real wave of blockbusters land, like Gladiator and Crouching Tiger Hidden Dragon and we found ourselves watching movies day in and day out. To Tom's dismay, the Matrix was still in frequent rotation, keeping our Agent Smith quotes alive and well in the shop.

It is safe to say that the new century's first decade was all about the media. If we weren't at the movie theaters, or crashing in the breakroom watching DVDs, we were all dabbling in the MP3 revolution to some extent. Copying and sharing songs had been a thorn in the side of the music industry ever since the first cassette recorder recorded a song from the radio, but MP3s were different. Anyone with a CD drive on their computer could rip a CD to MP3 in under an hour, and household internet speeds were equally on the rise. Conceivably, a new MP3 file could travel around the world and back in under a day, and once it was out there, there was no turning back. There was no argument, in our opinion. Free access to information, that was what the internet was all about. In our idealistic minds, this included any information we could find, despite how it was obtained. This hacker backed ethos was kicked into overdrive the minute Anto downloaded Napster. She had become quite adept at scraping files from mp3.com, but Napster was a game changer, especially when she connected directly from the shop. She could scour the songs of thousands upon thousands of enthusiasts. Practically every song imaginable was downloadable, and when she was connected through the shop, each song transferred in less than a minute. *Gotta love the T1!* She burned through a 2GB hard drive almost every month, and she started organizing the drives in old 5.25" floppy disk storage trays like a massive Rolodex. With all the Cranberries, Smashed Pumpkins and KoRn, she had a literal cornucopia of music. *Seriously, Ben. Puns!?* The only problem Anto faced, minus the pending questionable legality of her MP3 collection, was her tendency to forget to turn off Napster when she was done. When connected via modem, Napster used only a limited amount of bandwidth, but when it was connected directly to the shop's T1, it was virtually unthrottled and could hog all the Tom-NET bandwidth, which slowed things down for all our customers. *I mean sloooow!* I threatened Anto with the tech support pager for a week if she kept doing it, but I never had the heart to follow through. Instead, I toyed around with the idea of hooking her computer up to an X10 outlet so I could remotely kill the power to her workstation from my apartment, but I think I was just looking for a reason to buy some of their wireless tech. We eventually did some research and changed the router config and put her in her own restricted subnet. All the missteps aside, she kept our office speakers humming with new and interesting songs from around the world. Her eclectic taste always seemed to set the right mood for the day, and customers responded with more foot traffic and better sales. Anto was something else, *and a half!*

I wasn't the only person who noticed Anto's genius. Patty and Anto had become an inseparable duo. Patty set up a Shoutcast Server to stream her music throughout the day, and they would take turns slipping in some DJ commentary throughout the day like a real radio station. Random listeners would email in their music requests, along with typical internet troll hate speech. Patty soon became self-conscious of his voice, when they said he sounded like a raspy Smurfette. Anto received similar insults, but not as harsh. Most suggested she talked too fast, but the lion's share of the commentary said she sounded "hot". It didn't take long for them to just stop reading feedback altogether, but the experiment led to the discovery that Anto was a tragically funny sound effects genius. She was like the anti-Michael Winslow. She produced some of the most hilarious, unexpected and outrageously odd and impromptu sound effects that rarely matched their intended action.

This came to light when Patty stumbled across gabocorp.com, and instantly became enamored with all things Macromedia, but in particular game design with Flash and ActionScript which needed an abundance of sound effects. Patty once asked her to make a whooshing door opening sound, like the one you hear in Star Trek. Instead, she made a noise that sounded like the slow-motion sound of a cat getting its tail slammed in a window. When Patty synced the sound with his character animation, our sides nearly split in two. It hurt to laugh that hard. He would put together new scenes and sounds every week for Anto to improvise. It was a Wednesday evening ritual for the two of them for quite some time. He would incorporate their work and demo the resulting gameplay on Friday at lunch. It was always good for a laugh. The main character was a goofy dinosaur with stubby legs, one stubby arm and one long muscular arm he carried over his head and crushed enemies with his fists like an overhead hammer. The throwbacks to DK and Yoshi were clear. He called the project, Tapper the Teleporting T-Rex. After nearly eight months of development, Patty had enough content and random material to build out a franchise for Tapper; however, it was clear from the beginning that his interest in the project was never financial. There was a creative spirit that Anto and Patty shared that mutually benefited them both. His measured and reserved nature balanced her erratic and lightning-paced personality perfectly and he liked their working chemistry.

Meanwhile, on the web services side of the business I was growing tiresome of the same old HTML, JavaScript, CSS and ASP solutions we were peddling. The lazy business side of my brain had no complaints. They were easy to sell, there was ton of demand and they paid well with little time invested, but my technical side was drowning in a quagmire of mediocrity. I recently sprung to get my first cellphone, a Motorola Razr, to accompany my most recently replaced pager. The Razr was popular because of its sleek form factor and antennaless appearance, but I was interested because it supported custom J2ME apps that I could write myself. First, I needed to learn Java. From the moment I wrote my first "Hello World", I could feel the neurons starting to wake up as they bathed in the welcoming memory of code compilation. Java took care of the most annoying parts of C++, even though they were the most powerful, such as memory and pointer management, but it was far quicker to get straight to the code to solve a problem. Thanks to sites like The Java Ranch, I was able to immerse myself quickly and even became a Sun Certified Java Developer in the less than a month. Prior to this moment, I was suspicious of anyone who flaunted their certifications like badges of honor, but when I learned that the pass rate on this exam was less than thirty percent for first timers, I can't deny that I felt a bit proud. After all that work, my dreams of writing J2ME apps for my phone became at odds with my patience for the exceeding flawed and brittle tooling for J2ME development. *The longest "Hello World" in recorded history.* In the end, my awesome blue Razr remained just a phone, until it went through the washing machine a few times, and then it was just a fancy pocket-sized electronic gadget with questionable cell reception that allowed me to play billiards at the drop of a hat. *sigh*

In an effort to salvage my newly developed skills, I dove deep into the world of Java Applets, as these were growing in popularity, but still a far cry from the user experiences available in Flash. Sadly, innovation happens at a snail's pace in small towns and the appetite was far too primitive to justify a catalog of Applet templates when even Flash was hard to sell. It was 2001, and people still asked for sites from 1998. If you tried to guide them towards using more modern designs or technologies their eyes would glaze over and point at the framed scroll happy sites of yesteryear like Neanderthals pointing at a freshly killed deer carcass. No one cared about, or wanted to pay for, Internet Explorer AND Netscape support, they just wanted it to work on their personal computer, which made me question their understanding of the business purpose for their website in the first place. If Microsoft's antitrust case had taught us anything, people would usually pick what was easiest, and the people in this town were gravitating towards stupid.

Predictability and consistency are good things, in moderation, but failing to keep them in check can rob you of precious time. The years quickly blurred with a web of monotony and produced little excitement and far less emotional or technical growth. Every new year started the same way: watching movies, playing trivia, dodging phone calls from Jennifer and purchasing my annual Demotivator. I could feel my wall's ever-growing snark laced philosophy osmosis every time I went to sleep, but when I had a rough day, those same walls helped me visualize my emotions. It was a twisted relationship, but it helped maintain my sanity. *So I thought.*

I was sitting at my desk and noticed Benji hanging on the wall. Maybe putting him next to my monitor was not such a great idea, but after all this time, it would be strange if it wasn't there. My record was thirty-four days. Lately, I was lucky if it survived the day. I watched Benji pass away in my hands many times. I could have saved him, but I just sat there as actionless as when I hover over her never changing status message. *Away (Studying).* Each time, I wondered if I could simply pull the battery and be done with it all together, but I was filled with regret and would spawn a new Benji. Over and over the cycle went, more vicious than before. The small-town grapevine revealed that she had been in town a few weeks ago to visit her father who was sick. Would of, could of and should of scenarios played through my head. I could have staged a serendipitous boombox-style rendezvous outside her dad's shop, but I was mentally tongue tied about what to say. If she just came in the shop, I'd probably curl into a ball under my desk and hide. The turbulent pool of conflicting feelings swirling throughout my head and body rendered me dumb in every meaning of the word. I yearned to see her smiling face again, but at the same time, it was my worst nightmare. The only thought that ever brought me out of my emotional tailspin was that I had committed to make it easier for her. Each time, I would revive

Benji, feed him some food and place him back on the wall. *You're a hot mess, Ben!*

    The TapHouse tournament was on hiatus that year, due to the fact the bar was under construction. Tom invited the regular teams to the shop for a friendly game of Hot Shot Trivia, but it was no contest. Even after reshuffling all the old decks and getting a neutral third-party card reader, we wiped the floor with them. In most cases, buzzing in before the question could even be read from the card. It was a win, but it wasn't the same as winning the tournament at the bar and in that environment. Tom knew that, but it didn't keep him from giving a proud smirk when he handed out the consolation prizes to the other contestants: three free months of Tom-NET. *A.B.C.* He strutted around the room handing out the gift certificates, and the old man's walk had a definite sass to it. His trash talking hips put Don King to shame. It was true, we had come a long way since our first tournament, but despite our best efforts, we were stuck in neutral until we could find a way to ditch Evelyn. Sometimes I'd hope that they would just break up, but I could tell Tom was happy and that's the only thing that kept me silent. It wasn't just the trivia though. I never felt comfortable around her. She always had an air of fakeness that filled the shop, not to mention her damn perfume that could fumigate New Zealand. It was like she really didn't care to be there, unlike the rest of us. It was a tricky situation, but we were going to have to try harder to find a solution. We all wanted our team name listed on that tournament plaque, but no one wanted it more than Tom.

    That was the year that Patty and Wade went off the deep end after we all saw the movie Fast and the Furious. As the two people in the shop who had their own cars, minus Tom, they were the most susceptible to the Pimp My Ride aftershock. Anto and I were immune. She had her grandmother's station wagon but was under strict instructions not to put a scratch on it. I was still rocking the bicycle since everything was within walking distance for me. It didn't take Patty long to install a brand-new cat back on his '94 Civic DX and covered his back window with a myriad of racing related stickers. One of which was the brand of his cat back kit, and the others were an assorted collection of red, white and yellow Asian symbols. *White people can't read this. Haha!* I was convinced he thought adding stickers would add horsepower, similar to how green

M&Ms get you home runs. By those calculations, he was sporting at-least 400 horsepower on his rear-window alone. Wade, on the other hand, didn't have the heart to change anything mechanical in his truck, but he took the excuse to get more stickers on it and ran with it. He was more interested in the drift turns from the movie, and how similar it was to the backend of his truck fish tailing out when he didn't weigh it down with bags of sand. For the next many months, I genuinely feared for my life anytime we took a hard turn in his truck. Thankfully, the fad faded in only a few months, and the traction inducing sandbags quickly returned to his truck bed, but the stickers remained in full force with razor carved sight lines in his ever-growing rear-window collage.

That was the year that Tom received an invitation to attend an ISP meetup at the Infomart, a crazy glass cathedral tech building near downtown Dallas. He asked if I wanted to go with him to double his odds of winning the $10,000 door prize. Wade overheard the conversation and offered to be our chauffeur if we could squeeze in a visit Medieval Times. Tom was fine with him coming along, but he was a stickler about driving himself and I had questions on whether Wade's truck would make it there and back, let alone if we'd all fit. Tom thought Medieval Times would be a "hoot" and booked a pair of hotel rooms and made reservations to dine with the knights and wenches on that evening. Breakfast started at 7AM, so we left the shop, coffees in hand, just after 3AM to start our journey in Tom's reliable Honda Accord. I was sitting shotgun, and Wade was sitting in the back when Tom started the car, put it into drive and exclaimed, "Excelsior!!" as he punched the gas. The car shot through the parking lot, hopping the curb as he always did when turning onto the street. *It was going to be a long day!*

The ride to Dallas was relatively smooth. We stopped at the Czech Stop to grab some kolaches for the road and made it to the parking lot just before breakfast started. The first session of the day was about to start when there was a large commotion downstairs. People were whispering and groups of people left the room heading towards the TVs in the lobby. Live footage of American Airlines Flight 11 crashed into the North Tower of the World Trade Center in New York was on all the stations. *What just happened?* Tom couldn't peel his eyes from the TV, and I didn't say a single word. We stood there stupefied for nearly twenty minutes when we saw another plane crash into the South Tower on TV. People in the crowd started to scream, panic and disperse. I looked outside over the top of the evacuating hysteria and realized that the World Trade Center in Dallas was just across the street. Tom was three steps ahead of me. He grabbed mine and Wade's hand and said, "We're leaving. Right now."

We jumped in his car and sped out of the parking lot as fast as the traffic lights would let us. To my knowledge, we never even cancelled our reservations. We only stopped for gas, checking over our shoulders and the skies above even in small remote towns like Waxahachie. The Czech Stop bounty we purchased only hours earlier to serve as our breakfast the following morning, now served as our lunch. By 2PM, we were back in Jollyville and at the shop. When Tom pulled into his parking space, we just sat there, still unsure of what we had witnessed. The ride back had been silent. Tom turned off the radio back in Dallas the minute the news started to dominate the stations.

"Are you alright, Tom?" I asked.

He contemplated his response and then replied with a heavy sigh, "I think so, Ben. I think so. You boys just head on out and make sure to see you moms, as soon as possible. OK?"

"We will, Tom," I replied, as Wade and I stepped out of the car and watched Tom drive out of the parking lot and, yet again, hop the curb. Wade headed out to see his mom, while I went back to my apartment and went down a rabbit hole of news feeds about all that had transpired that day. I felt numb from head to toe. The illusion of safety was incinerated and crumbled to the ground, just like the towers.

While the country continued to process and begin a long road of healing, two unexpected distractions were taking the nation by storm. Windows XP was launched to home users to clear up all the confusion caused by Microsoft's attempts to capitalize on all the Y2K hysteria with their nebulous marketing of Windows 2000 and Millennium Edition the previous year. *What a tech support cluster fuck!* Windows XP brought a welcomed surge of business, much like Windows 95, as it set a higher standard of computer hardware that in most cases, required users to upgrade or buy new machines all-together. For all of Microsoft's faults, they sure know how to make money. In addition to the Windows XP craze sweeping the nation and our local computer shop, the first Harry Potter movie had the entire Internet on the edge of their seat. For me, it was a spotlight on my mountain of regret, and yet I was still curious. The previews looked good enough, and let's be honest, Rollerball had already set the low bar for the year. I snuck away for an afternoon matinee by myself to avoid the peer inquisition at the shop. It wasn't the typical movie we saw together as a group, or so I thought. I walked out of the theater with a smile on my face and a few tears in my eyes. Everything Angie ever said about the book made complete sense. Part of me thought about picking up the next book in the series to find out what happened next, but that thought was ruined by Harry Potter snobs in the lobby complaining about inconsistencies in the movie with the book. I was playing Time Crisis II trying my best to drown out their whining as I fired off a hail of gunshots and vigorously slammed the metal reload pedal. *How different could they be?*

It was "New Release" Tuesday, so I stopped by Hastings on my way back to the shop to grab a copy of the book to see what all the kerfuffle was about. I was waiting in line at the book counter for Cindy, our awesome local book manager, to get me an update on a special order I placed to acquire the remaining Java O'Reilly books to complete my purple collection. In reality, I only needed a few of them; however, I felt as though I had to collect all the animals for the bookshelf at my desk. *Was it ironic that I hated Pokémon?* Unfortunately, I had another week to wait, at-least before they all came in. On my way out, I stumbled upon an end cap with a name I hadn't seen in quite some time. *Poe.* All the articles Angie had clipped over the years had conditioned my temporal lobe to the face, and I could already feel the whispers of my past creeping down the back of my neck as I read the back of her new album jacket, Haunted. That is when I heard Keith's annoying voice for the first time.

"I'd think twice about that CD, if I were you," he said.

I spun around to spot a pale wispy blonde-bearded guy with a pot belly and glasses head banging to a definitive rock beat blasting from the demo station's headphones. He had a sucker stick protruding out of his mouth that explained the gargled slur in his words. There were many signs I should have heeded that day, the most obvious being that he was listening to the new Nickelback album, but instead I made the mistake of responding.

"Didn't need to think twice, but thanks!" I replied, flipping the CD into the air by the bottom of the plastic anti-theft case like a pancake and catching the top. The train wreck I felt inside was shortly replaced with a false sense of machismo pride that was ready to spite this guy.

"Does everyone at Tom-NET listen to angry chick bands, or is it just you?" *Who the hell was this guy, and how did he know I worked at Tom-NET?* His smile exposed a missing upper tooth that allowed the stem of his sucker to bob up and down like a flip switch.

"You're Ben, right?" he asked, reaching out to shake hands with a laugh. My foot dug in and shoulder cocked back as the thought of slapping his hand away and doing a Jim Duggan style running clothesline on him grew more appealing by the millisecond.

"And, if I am?" I replied.

Something about the guy rubbed me the wrong way the moment I saw him. Needless to say, this impression didn't improve with time.

"My name is Keith. Keith Connors. I just opened up a new computer store on the other side of town near the highway. L33tRigz. You heard of it?" He pulled his card out of his shirt pocket and handed it to me.

"Sure, I've seen your ads in the paper. I just don't make it to that part of town that often." I lied. Wade and I did some recon about a month prior after seeing their ad. We thought it was a joke. It was like an out of touch marketer trying way too hard to be cool in a town that wouldn't know the difference. Sadly, it was some annoying Goomba looking dude, who appeared young enough to know better. With XBOX and PS2 holding steady, PC Gaming was emerging as a new viable option to the mainstream. Granted it was a niche I had been playing in for quite some time, but the number of specialized hardware components had skyrocketed in the past year. They even had water cooled CPU kits. *What could go wrong!?* Personalization was just as important as competitive advantage to hard core gamers. L33tR1gz not only did local computer repair services, but they also pushed having "the best gaming PCs on the Internet", which Anto took exception. I can't remember what she called them, but it was fast, fierce and filled with most of my Spanish expletive lexicon. I gritted my teeth behind my lips. *Our first real competitor.*

"Well, I'm hoping we can be friends, even though our stores have a lot in common." He paused for a moment at my reluctance to return the sentiment. "I hear you guys enter the TapHouse Trivia Tournament every year? Me and my guys back at the store are trivia folk, as well, so maybe we'll see you this year. In the meantime, if any of your guys want to join our Counter-Strike scrimmages, let me know. Happy to send the invite."

"Sounds like a plan, Keith." I replied.

He had already over drafted the balance on my patience at this point. It was time to leave. I shook his hand and left him to drown in his crappy music. It became clearer over time just how accurate my first impression of Keith and predictions of his "crew" would become. Their shop was hellbent on becoming the next AlienWare of gaming PCs, and yet everyone there was less of a computer tech and more of a wannabe pro gamer that spewed ridiculous gamer l33t speak like dollar bills on a rainy day at the strip club. It was comical at first, but quickly became annoying. I personally blame them for ruining Counter-Strike before I even got a chance to really get into it. No game was worth playing if you ended up like that. Even if he didn't know my handle, the best thing was to distance myself from the game to avoid any random offline or online conversations.

Later that evening, I sat down in my papasan and tried reading The Sorcerer's Stone. Passing out while reading was never my thing, but I also had never really read a book I enjoyed. Tech manuals and programming books, yes, but J.K.'s writing style and descriptive characterizations, even though I already knew the plot, *or so I thought*, were intoxicating. Every chapter I completed prompted assurance that there was always time for one more. I woke up at four o'clock in the morning with the book spread across my chest and a driving ambition to finish the remaining ten chapters. By seven o'clock, I could understand their outrage. *It was a scandal!* They omitted so many details, it was hard to believe the stories were even related. *What happened to Peeves!?!* I didn't want to become like them. I enjoyed my ignorant cinematic bliss and decided to wait until all the movies had been released before I even considered reading another word, despite my impatience to know what happened next. Instead, whenever I got the urge, I took a page from Angie, and read it many times over to reminisce with the plot and scour for new meaning.

The next morning, we started to get a taste of why Keith was acting so cocky. L33tR1gz announced a partnership with the local telco's new dial-up service and was pushing them hard with all their new machines. Most of our customers were extremely loyal, but it wasn't long until it felt like the telco was sabotaging our customers trying to get them to convert. Overnight, customers started reporting random disconnects, slower speeds and excessive line static. When they called the phone company to complain, they used their customer support to recruit customers under the premise that their new "digital lines" could offer the best speeds in town. It was a hair short of antitrust and unlawful business practices that made Tom lose his top on more than one occasion. We were thankful that Tom-NET Web Services was now our core source of revenue, but the foot traffic in our shop started to slow down with every account they poached. This wasn't ideal because foot traffic was the catalyst that drove shop sales, primarily because people could see us in our own element. Tom was not about to let this go without a fight and decided to double-down on the 802.11b craze and rapidly stocked up on our Linksys and Netgear merchandise. Not only did he want to be the first in the area to offer free in-store wireless internet, but he also had his eyes set on making Andersson Electronics the premiere location in Jollyville for all things WiFi. While the plan worked in terms of buzz, its efficacy was greatly hindered by the snail's pace in which technology was adopted in small towns like ours, despite how revolutionary the technology may be. I once heard Evelyn mention to Tom that he should sell the shop, while everything was still worth something, and consider selling arts and crafts on eBay. If anyone knew anything about eBay, it would be her. When she wasn't busy blabbing about herself, her next best subject was bragging about the deals she got on eBay to satiate her unhealthy fashion habit. Despite the merits of converting to an online store for parts of the shop, Tom insisted on keeping the shop open and sternly advised her to never mention it again. The man was nothing less than determined when he was pissed off, but this was definitely going to be an uphill battle for her if she persisted.

The trivia tournament was back on that year, and sure enough, L33tR1gz was there, all in official team t-shirts, ready to compete. Their team name was "J4ck4ls", an homage to their new favorite video game, Halo! As much as I hated Keith, he was right. His crew was exceptionally good, every single one. While we struggled making use of Evelyn's worthless brainpan, Keith's team sailed through to the finals effortlessly. Unlike last year's sweep on our home turf, we slid to fourth place and came up short of missing the semi-finals. It felt like a slap in the face. L33tR1gz waltzed right in and took our spot on the plaque. Tom was determined to work harder. I, on the other hand, was looking at ways to recruit someone new and push Evelyn out the door. To hell what Tom thinks. She had to go!

FEATURED TRACK

Live - The Beauty Of Gray

13
What's It All About

From that day forward, I don't recall a single interaction with Evelyn that wasn't laced with mutual disgust. It changed overnight. I didn't have to say anything. She just knew. *Did I look at her wrong?* Her fake laughs and shallow conversational pleasantries were replaced with questioning beady eye gazes and sarcastic undercutting commentary. I, of course, responded like any well-adjusted mature adult would, by amplifying all the things I knew I did to piss her off. Every time she walked in the shop, I'd yell out "Pop quiz, Hot Shot!" and pull a random question out of my ass from a category she didn't know, which was pretty much any category. *Yeah, it was petty!* I'd use my best game show host voice to incite others in the shop to play along, but she just kept walking to the back room to find Tom. The mental middle finger spotlight she blasted out of the back of that colossal clown car hairdo seemed to grow each day. It was a start. I didn't care if she kept seeing Tom, but I would be damned if I had to endure one more trivia season with her on the team. It was clear she wasn't good at it and didn't care to even try. It was like I was back in Mr. Dan's room playing chess. Only this time, I wasn't throwing the game. I was all in to win.

Tom on the other hand was preoccupied with more pressing matters than the trivia team. The dips in last year's numbers were starting to weigh on him a bit, which corresponded to the growing number of white streaks in his hair. To be honest, they weighed on all of us. Tom assured us everything was going to be fine, but he was a bit light on the details on just how that would happen. The telco was ramping up its propagandic advertising. We were hemorrhaging fair weather customers left and right, but new ones always seemed to take their place in small batches. New apartments complexes were popping up all over town, and most of the office managers and staff were loyal Tom-NET customers. Competition from Dell, and now L33tR1gz, was more prevalent than ever and we had a ton of inventory that was aging by the second that we needed to sell. When it came to service, we still had the best in town, but L33tR1gz's office was admittedly better. Their strip mall location offered them tons of foot traffic, and their neon cyber electric ambiance inside the store attracted people like insects to a bug zapper. More businesses around us were closing down or being bought out, leaving our once thriving block virtually barren, minus the self-storage facilities and a random liquor store on the opposite far corner. *Looking to get drunk and buy a PC, come on down!* These were the problems that Tom was trying to solve, and in typical Tom fashion, he never asked for help.

As high-tech as our shop might have been for the town, people would be surprised that Tom still liked to do some things old school. One of those things was reading the physical newspaper. I preferred using a web browser, but he always said there was something comforting about the texture of the paper in his hands that he didn't want to give up. He had one subscription sent to the shop and another sent to his home. Every morning I unlocked the shop's front door, grabbed his paper from the doormat and placed it in the passenger seat of his dismantled car where he liked to ceremoniously "read and chill". This day was a bit different. When I picked up the paper, I noticed a familiar face on the cover. *Angie!* I hadn't seen her face in a while or thought about her for that matter as her online status permanently changed to "Offline" a few months prior. She was wearing a cap and gown and looked more professional looking than I had imagined, but her smile was one in a million. The caption read, "Jollyville Native Graduates

Valedictorian at Berkeley". Everything was going according to her plan. She'd walk the stage, accept her diploma and head straight to her new job and then begin working on her MBA soon enough, no doubt. I brushed a small piece of debris from her picture, and I swore that I could feel strands of her hair on my fingertips. I cut the article out and placed it in my desk drawer and set the rest of the paper in Tom's car. He wouldn't mind the minor vandalism, as long as it wasn't his "sacred" comics or crossword sections. Besides, he had another paper at home.

    There are moments when a person laughs so much when they think they are going to die: truly, madly, deeply side-splitting humor. That evening, I was watching some videos I snagged off of Napster by Fensler Films that were old GI Joe cartoon PSAs with modified voice tracks. All my online friends were raving about them, and after running through all twenty of them for the first time, I could barely breathe. *I don't want to think about what could have happened if I hadn't stopped to catch my breath.* I put the videos in a repeating playlist for amusement while I played around with the SpyHunter Easter egg in Excel when I heard a crash downstairs that made me jump out of my chair. It was eleven o'clock and everything should have been locked up downstairs. *Burglar?* My sides were still in pain, and my heart was racing. I grabbed a broom and headed downstairs to see if I could see what was going on. After I cleared the breakroom, I could see the lights were on in the shop. *Why would a burglar turn on the lights?* I popped my head up to take a peek through the backroom porthole and saw a mess of papers and the media cart in the middle of the floor. It was Tom. He was on his knees holding onto the cart. I burst into the shop to see what was going on. All he said to me was, "Call 911". After rushing to the phone, I helped him onto his back and sat with him until the ambulance arrived.

    Within five minutes of showing up, they assessed the situation, diagnosed Tom and loaded him into the ambulance. They told me he was having a heart attack. Thankfully, it gave me enough time to run upstairs and grab my keys and some shoes. I jumped in the back of the ambulance with Tom, and we were off to the hospital. Never in my life had I ever gripped a person's hand so tight. Tom's handshakes were legendary. He always had a strong grip, goofy smile and the softest hardened hands you'd ever find. This was different. His grip was weak, his eyes closed and the skin on his hands felt like mush. I felt him squeezing my hand, so I did it in return. This impromptu back and forth morse code continued all the way to the hospital. I could have sworn I saw the faintest resemblance of a smile on his face. Leave it to Tom to be the one to play games during a heart attack.

When we arrived at the hospital, they wheeled Tom into the emergency room and asked that I wait in the lobby. Waiting was the hardest part of it all, not knowing if you had spent your final moments with someone special. An hour passed and I had picked away every cuticle and hangnail to the stump, when Evelyn walked through the sliding doors. She berated the front desk demanding to know where Tom was and what happened, and that's when she saw me.

"What happened? What did you do?" she said. Those were the first words out of her mouth, and then she broke it an odd sort of cry. "I'm sorry. When Tom didn't come back from the shop, I went looking for him. The shop was all locked up with the lights on and it looked like there was a fight on the floor. I didn't know what to think."

She rambled on and on for what felt like an hour. The liquor store clerk, of all people, noticed that she was pacing out front, and came to tell her about the ambulance. At some point in the monologue, she started complaining about troubles at her office and lousy clients and how new state ethics regulations were going to nickel and dime her out of business. I didn't have the heart to start a fight with her for being so selfish, not tonight. Tonight, we were both on the same team dealing with anxiety the best we could. When she finished her emotional rant, I gave her the low down on all I knew about that evening.

"The man is going to kill himself," she said. "He's been racking his brain at home trying to figure out how to deal with the telephone company and that new computer place. I've told him it's a fool's errand, and he should sell it all right now and just retire early, but he's too stubborn of a man and proud to let the store go." She dabbed her eyes with a tissue and looked as if she was struggling to find her words. Nothing she said was news to me. Tom was a competitor at heart, and I can only imagine the conversations she's had with him trying to tell him to stand down. You'd have a better chance trying to convince gravity to take a break.

"If you knew what was best for Tom," she said, taking a deep breath, "you'd tell him to sell and retire." Her eyes caught mine and for the first time, I didn't despise her. Her words hung heavy on my heart, as I contemplated the full impact of her ask. No more shop. No more apartment. In all likelihood, no more Hot Shots. Before I could respond, a nurse walked up to us in the waiting room.

"He's in stable condition now, if you'd like to go see him. He's in Room 4." the nurse said. Evelyn jumped out of her chair and followed the nurse. I decided to give them some alone time, so I propped my feet on a chair and watched muted QVC on the television. No more than three, maybe four products later, the sliding doors opened again and out walks Evelyn. She was obviously upset and walked straight to the parking lot without a single look, comment or acknowledgement of Tom's status. As if drafting in the wake of her storm, the nurse came into the room and said, "He'd like to see you now."

Tom was under a blanket wearing a hospital gown, but all I could focus on was the number of wires, lights and beeps that filled the room. His face was no longer grimaced, and he was resting with his eyes closed. I pulled up a chair next to the bed and Tom blindly reached out his hand.

"Thank you." he said. I grabbed his hand and gave his hand a few squeezes. Whether it be by morse code or telepathy, I was saying the exact same thing back to him. Tom opened his eyes.

"Is everything alright? What did the doctor say?" I asked.

"Same thing they've been telling me for the past ten years. You're pushing yourself too hard!" Tom strained to laugh at his own joke, but he could tell I was concerned. "Don't worry, Ben. It was a mild heart attack brought on by me not eating well and not taking care of myself."

"Well you should eat better!" I replied. "You know you've got a shop full of young people who can help? Maybe you should think about slowing down a bit, maybe even retiring?" Evelyn's words echoed in my head and came pouring out my mouth without a second thought, but I couldn't bring myself to suggest that he sell the shop.

"I'll retire when I'm damn good and ready, but there are things I've got to do first." he retorted. Tom took a deep breath, turned, and looked me directly in the eyes. "Do you know what my dream is Ben?" I shrugged my shoulders because I honestly had no idea. He was a master of almost everything, so the sky was literally the limit with him. "My dream is to grow the shop to a million dollar per year business. When we do that, then I'll retire."

I sat perplexed. Most people have dreams of becoming president or hiking Everest. Why did Tom, my mentor, a man with such intelligence, have such a simple capitalistic dream? I had seen the books, and even during our prime Tom-NET years, we were lucky if we hit seventy grand in a month, which would put us around eight hundred thousand, but lately, we averaged in the low to mid-sixties.

"Do you know the significance of a million dollars a year?" he asked. The continued confused look on my face was enough to answer his question. I didn't. "It is enough for me to retire on a beach and set you and the rest of the shop up with stable jobs for the next decade, at least."

"Tom that's ridiculous. We'll be fine. You shouldn't literally kill yourself on our account." I felt selfish. The words "sell sell sell" were exponentially ringing in my ears, and although it would be hard to find something more magical than the shop, I couldn't bear the guilt of knowing that Tom was doing this to himself, for us. "We all just want you to be happy!"

Tom took a moment. "Are you happy, Ben?"

"Sure ... I mean, of course, I'm happy." My instinctive deflective pause was not convincing even myself. "What's there not to be happy about? I've got a great job, great place to live, friends and you're not dead...so there's that." I laughed at my joke trying to get Tom to chuckle along.

"No, Ben. You're not happy. I've seen that emptiness in your eyes before, and that is not happy. I had the same look when my brother died."

Wait, brother!?!! How did I miss that? I stowed my bruised ego's inner dialogue after Tom implied. I was not a happy person and leaned in to listen.

"You know, when I became a bathroom fixture salesman, it wasn't what I really wanted to do. What made it tolerable was my younger brother, Michael. He was way into painting." Tom's chuckled under his breath a bit," even though he wasn't that good. After my dad died, money was tight. So, I used some of my side money to buy him art supplies. We gave him a special spot at the front of the shop by the window where he could see the trees and get lots of sunlight." *I didn't have to ask which corner. I knew!* "If you saw how focused and passionate he was about painting, you'd know what true happiness looked like." Tom took a deep breath. "When Michael was fourteen, he was hit by a drunk driver while walking home from school and died. That day I saw all happiness vanish from my mother's eyes." Tom picked at the electric cables connected to his chest and gave a saddened shrug. "She died of a heart attack, five years later." It was like Tom knew this was coming, like he read some morose tea leaves.

"When I was old enough, my grandfather and I ran the store, but I was never happy. When I say I know the look, Ben. I mean it. I know the look. I saw it in my mother's eyes, and mine, every day, in the mirror for ten years. I smiled on the outside, but I was dead and spiteful on the inside. All the people I had ever loved had been taken from me. I thought opening an electronics store would make me happy, and it did for a while ... but nothing has made me happier than these past many years, watching you kids grow into your own success. You are *all* part of my family, even Angie."

My head dropped out of sight. In part because I was hiding my misty eyes, but also because he said her name. The emotional gumbo boiling in my gut rendered me speechless and admittedly vulnerable.

"I've seen you since she left, and it's not healthy. You've got to stop dwelling on the past ... keep your eyes on the horizon ... and pursue something that makes you truly happy. For me, it ended up opening my doors to a talented misfit and giving him an environment where he could grow." I didn't know what to say. I had no words to respond to the truth he was unearthing and bringing to light. "You know, my grandfather used to believe that the door chimes would ring differently every time someone entered the store and that if you listened for it, you could tell if the person would bring you good fortune. At least that is what he would say after he made a really good sale," Tom chuckled. "I can't tell you I was ever that good at picking out the good tones from the bad ones, but I distinctly remember their sound when you first walked in the door and every day since." *I didn't have the heart to remind him that Evelyn was the one who killed his grandfather's special chimes.*

Tom squeezed my hand and shot me a labored smile. Even all wired up and the remnants of his silvery hair disheveled, I could feel the fear in my mind subside and sparks of confidence igniting in my stomach as the words "keep your eyes on the horizon" echoed in my soul. All I could do was give Tom a hug. I had hugged him before, but this wasn't a normal hug. This was my brother, my father, my friend and my family all wrapped into one type of hug. I saw a lot of myself in him and felt like I was catching a glimpse of my future, and while scary, a spark of hope was ignited. We played Hot Shot Trivia from memory well into the morning before I passed out in the most uncomfortable chair in a most uncomfortable position.

I heard the crisp baffling and popping of a newspaper. I had drool running down the side of my face and a painful crick in my neck. It was 6AM and Tom was sitting upright in his bed, newspaper in hand and giving me an unabated smile. His wires and monitors were almost completely gone, and the color had returned to his face. From behind my squinted morning crusted eyelids, his quirky smile seemed to glow and radiate an increasingly bright white light.

*** FLASH ***

I was holding Nerm's hand, literally. My right arm propped my sweating forehead up against the counter, while my stomach twisted into knots hindering my maneuver for a long overdue courtesy flush. In my left hand, I held a detached kid-size mannequin arm, while the remaining torso and attached appendages skidded in slow motion across the wall in front of me. My inadvertent Jax-esque fatality set forth a chain of actions which would soon wake the entire apartment. I ditched my forehead and haphazardly threw my arm forward in a last ditch attempt to prevent the impending crash. Given my failing state of coordination, I was more likely to break a finger, but in this rare instance, luck prevailed. My pinky finger hooked inside one of the floral leis draped around its neck and stopped the sliding. The palm of my hand rested against the wall, while my other hand tapped out gastrointestinal morse code against the side of the bowl with a distressed flesh colored shoulder joint. A mindful sense of helplessness ensued, as I closed my eyes and rested my chest on my legs. I had bought myself some breathing room, *mouth breathing only*, but the time for half measures was quickly coming to an end. These scenarios were becoming far too common for my liking, but what doesn't kill you makes you stronger, right? *Damnit, I didn't flush.*

*** FLASH ***

The doctor ordered Tom to rest at home for a week to get some stress-free time accumulated before heading back to work. In typical Tom fashion, he followed the instructions to the strictest letter of the law, which meant he found every loophole possible. He called the shop at-least three times a day, not to mention the plethora of emails. He had us measuring and counting random things like he was making a grocery list. He even forced us to play Hot Shot Trivia with him over the speaker phone. His spirit and drive were definitely renewed and when Tom returned to the shop the following week, he unloaded his plans to kickstart things into a new gear.

"The problem is simple," Tom said. "If no one comes in the shop, the shop can't sell things. They can see our #1 assets: you guys." He looked around the room into everyone's eyes letting that message sync in. "Each of you has a skill that is unique, and for the past many years, people have learned about those skills through gossip and word of mouth. I'm suggesting that we give each of you a platform to teach and help the community, and we'll do it ... right here in the shop!"

The room was dead quiet, except for Wade who was chuckling to himself thinking of the things he might teach people. Tom laid out the blueprints he had been working on at home. Our modest magazine reading nook was going to be temporarily relocated, as the wall behind it was going to be removed such that we could add roughly another twenty feet of space from the virtually endless storage warehouse attached to the back. *Now, if we could only do something about the mice.* In this new space, Tom built the Community Classroom to complement the Community Corner. It was a versatile space that held about forty to fifty people and included a projector with modular chairs and tables that could be assembled for just about any occasion. This was important because none of us knew what we were going to teach!

Tom was the first to offer his subjects into the course catalog, which were Small Electronics Repair and Plumbing 101. The rest of us married up the proposed calendar with our work schedules and divided up the time slots to create the rest of the curriculum. Anto and I teamed up for a Computers 101 class to talk about all the components of a computer, basic maintenance and how to use the Internet. Our hope was that some of our more difficult tech support customers might pop in for a class or two to try and improve that experience from another angle. I also teamed up with Patty to do a "Build Your Own Website" in HTML course, which was built around one of the first templates we designed. Wade used his better judgement and abandoned his earlier thoughts of Booger Picking 101 and decided to teach Coffee Appreciation where he would educate people on the proper ways to brew and appreciate coffee. We even rounded it out with a pop culture class every Friday evening where everyone would take turns leading a discussion about various topics followed by a few rounds of Hot-Shot Trivia. Our first topic: The fizzle of Dean Kamen's IT.

About a month before our first scheduled class, we caught wind of Tom's ingenious plan to fund this endeavor. Members of Tom-NET would get up to four free classes a month, and non-Tom-NET members could redeem their first course receipt for a free month of Tom-NET. Patty created flyers and a course catalog calendar for the website, and we posted print-outs of it on every bulletin board in town. The rumor mill started to churn and slowly but surely, foot traffic returned to our abandoned corner of town. The most popular courses were the computer and HTML programming ones by far, but overall the community loved the classes. Even Wade's coffee brewing class, which gave him an excuse to practice on Marge full-time. I started creating class module templates in PowerPoint to help structure the work and make them more repeatable, *and less work*, depending on the audience. Just as Tom predicted, shop sales increased with every person that showed up to take a class and many of them became new Tom-NET customers. We even re-signed some of our former customers who switched to the telco. Every new customer meant more tech support, and our HTML classes became a great source of revenue for Tom-NET Web Services. My lackadaisical by nature mind was struggling to juggle tech support, website development and now curriculum planning. When I felt overwhelmed, I could hear Tom's words about finding happiness resonate in the back of my mind. While I wasn't a fan of the new day-to-day chaotic pace, I did know that Tom was back, and I was busy doing so many different things that I didn't really have a spare moment to question my happiness. For now, that was good enough for me. *Distraction, my old friend.*

FEATURED TRACK

Soul Coughing - Super Bon Bon

14

What Doesn't Kill You ...

The ghostly shell of Tom that used to walk the halls of the shop was replaced with a spry, rejuvenated and engaged spirit determined to live life to the fullest. He adopted the Protein Power way of life and meticulously counted every last carb. This resulted in him having to buy new pants from losing so much weight. They weren't even khaki or beige tone. These were triple stripe Adidas athletic wear, which was a first. In only a month after the incident, he lost enough weight to force him to buy a new pair of pants, athletic ones, that were not even khaki or a beige tone, which was a first. Lunch conversations quickly turned into Sunday confessionals in front of Father Tom. *Forgive me father, for I ate a bagel.* There was a time when everyone in the shop went through different stages of sneaking sweets and baked goods in their backpacks, but eventually Tom's obsession quickly met his match: Nilla Wafers and Butterfingers. He may have been Mr. Health Genius when eviscerating our food, but he never had the willpower to forgo his two favorite snacks. You could hear him mouthing I.O.U's to himself each time he buried his hand in the bag for another treat. He could have taken up ultramarathons every day for a year and he'd still wouldn't clear the ledger. Eventually, the

Great Truce of '02 was struck after Patty helped Anto infiltrate his box of wafers and filled it with crisp Romaine lettuce. None of us had ever seen Tom that angry or disgusted, and he agreed to back off on the food criticism.

    Diet withstanding, the man was filled with energy. There was a new sense of purpose and passion that fueled his drive and it all had to do with his electronics class. When Tom cleared the backroom space behind the wall to make room for the Community Classroom, he decided to say goodbye to a small chunk of his treasure to both make room and help fund the renovation. Tom loved his antiques, even though he hardly interacted with them. Each one told a story about the history of the world, and most importantly, the deal he made to acquire it. *That was his favorite part.* He turned a fair profit on the items he sold, but Tom wasn't keeping score with money. Every time an antique left the shop, it was a story being told for the last time, and that is what hit him the most. Leave it to Tom, to channel his despair and emotions into the search for even more antiques to fill the void.

    During this age of the Andersson renaissance, Tom was compelled to orchestrate road trips to Round Top, Texas to educate us on the art of the antique deal. Anto and Patty were definitely into it more than Wade or me. Anto was a natural haggler and Patty was a sucker for any cinema paraphernalia, old or modern. An old non-functioning handheld reel camera with a missing lens and matching film? He had to have it. A tattered and water stained Night of the Living Dead poster reprint. He had to have that, too. Anto was his designated negotiator. She went as far as to hold his wallet for him because he had proven himself too weak by paying the asking price far too many times and robbing her of any chance to haggle. Wade liked old metal signs, especially signs from coffee brands, except all he ever found were rusted Folgers signs; never an Arbuckles or even a Hills Brothers. Every time he found one, he had the same joke that never seemed to get old. *To him.* His preamble was different each time, tricking us to think it was a different joke, but it always ended the same way. "Folgers would be better off scraping the rust off this sign and putting that in the filter!" The pure elation on Wade's face when he laughed afterwards was funnier than the joke itself. It may have been the reason why he kept telling it.

On the other hand, Tom and I were like birds of a feather who gravitated towards random electronics from all the generations. I was fascinated by how big everything was compared to their modern equivalents. Electronic typewriters were easily two to three times larger than the laptops we sold, and four times the weight. *Insane!* Tom enjoyed strolling down memory lane and telling war stories of how he used to fix half the junk in the room, but his main focus was looking for new projects for his electronics class to tear apart, fix and reassemble. I remember hating these trips in the beginning, but that all changed when we met Nerm.

It was some holiday, like Memorial Day or the Fourth of July, and Tom took us to this massive antique barn he frequented. The barn had these huge floors fans blowing every which direction to circulate the hot musky air around to simulate a fresh breeze. It was mighty unpleasant to shop more than an inch out of this manufactured jet stream, as the humidity and stench of dirt, dung and decaying Americana hung around your neck like a scratchy wool scarf. *So much fun!* *eyeroll* Everyone found something for Anto to haggle down, except me. Right next to the register, we spotted a well-worn gender-ambiguous child-sized mannequin with mismatched assorted clothes. It was pointing towards a sign warning parents of their liability should kids break something while shopping. Patty brought his new Canon D30 to take pictures of interesting finds he couldn't afford, but instead we filled most of his memory card with awkward poses with the mannequin decorated with additional props from the surrounding booths. We all thought it was hilarious. Tom and the owners did not, which made Anto's job negotiating the plunder that much more difficult. She was always up for a good challenge when it came to haggling. At least I thought so, until I heard the conversation turn heated.

"Fine!" She screamed. She then extended her arm and pointed in my direction like Babe Ruth calling his shot in slow motion. "If you don't want to budge from your price, then you are throwing that mannequin and that glass jar of old mouse balls in for FREE … and that's my final offer!" The owners looked to Tom, but all he could do was shrug off their glances and laugh. Anto pulled the classic "crazy misunderstood whipper snapper" move from the playbook, and it was working. Had she taken an extra half-beat to choose better words, she might have described them as a jar of *computer* mouse balls.

The way it rolled off her tongue made me think of a jar of hairy BBs and snorted a stream of snot from my nose. The jar's contents caught her eye the moment she walked into the barn, but I don't think she ever intended on paying money for it. With the rise of optical mice, we no longer needed to clean the track rollers on customer mice, something that Anto enjoyed doing for some reason. It was easier to just sell them a new mouse, which meant we would throw away the old one. She enjoyed collecting the track balls and already had a small collection going back at the shop in her desk drawer. She'd bounce them around to pass the time or bean us with them to get our attention. *Ouch!* This practice would eventually stop after we lost track of a few of them one day, and Wade slipped on one and crashed to the floor with a tray of coffee. The jar suited her, and the demand was ridiculous. That is why it worked.

"You got a deal." The owners replied. "Besides, customers complain about that mannequin too much. They think it looks creepy."

Anto slapped the cash down on the counter and we sloughed the mannequin accessories into a pile on the floor, and I walked out with a naked child mannequin under my arm. We decided to name it Nerm. It was a mix of him plus her, but also paid respects to the gender ambiguous Garfield character, Nermal.

Nerm quickly became a Where's Waldo like fixture in our shop for customers. We rotated new outfits with the seasons and random weeks throughout the year while relocating it throughout the shop in different scenarios. It was all lighthearted fun, until one of our older customers nearly had a heart attack. Nerm was dressed head to toe in blue jean denim. Patty found a ratted out blond mullet wig and cowboy hat that completed our lil' Walker Texas Ranger look-alike. We positioned Nerm with an arm leaning on top of a computer monitor in the Community Corner as if reading the screen. Our overly sensitive customer bumped into Nerm, and the mannequin fell to the floor dislodging an arm socket at the shoulder, but the blue jean jacket obfuscated the break, making it look like a free-floating appendage pointing in the opposite natural direction. Her authentic reaction would have been instant gold on America's Funniest Home Videos to anyone with a video camera, but after she calmed down it became less and less funny. She cited ADA aisle width regulations, fire safety codes and even proclaimed the disapproval of Jesus Christ himself. That was a common pattern I saw with many of the old people in our town. If they ever made a mistake, or were made to look foolish, they sought to absolve themselves and externalize the blame. Sadly, Nerm was banished to the breakroom serving as an integral fixture in every themed movie night or trivia party.

All the trips to antique barns helped Patty and Anto better appreciate the nostalgia and allure that Tom looked for in his finds. Anto started taking guided tours of Tom's curated collection, and Patty tagged along for the conversation. As messy as the backroom looked, Tom insisted there was an intricate system for finding everything. He had over two hundred feet of taped off storage bays lining the entire side of the backroom, and each was set up like a mini antique store display with items zoned by period. If I cracked the backroom door open during their tours, I could sometimes hear Tom's tour director persona as he recalled the full spectrum of detail about a specific item, how the conversation unfolded when he bought it and the leverage he used to get the deal. *Impressive!*

Over the years, Anto and Patty must have toured the backroom, top to bottom, at least twice. Anto's mind was a steel trap for this kind of information, capturing all the details and facts for each treasure's backstory, and presented with her own flare added, of course. Tom didn't have many movie themed antiques, but that didn't stop Patty from having a good time with Anto. He would pretend his hands were a camera and practice framing shots with her as the focal point and ask offscreen interview style questions to try and stump them both. Anto and Patty worked extremely well together, given how much their personalities clashed. It was fun to watch, and certainly more enjoyable than listening to Wade with his new song obsession. The irony of listening to Gotta Get Through This on infinite repeat was painfully maddening.

One of the most underrated perks of working at a computer shop is that you are rarely short on spare parts if you want to Frankenstein something together. This came in handy on more than one occasion, but in this case, I was taking my first real stab at using Linux as a primary system, and I needed some components to sacrifice to a Slackware CD I yanked from a magazine. The installation and setup went fine but getting to know the tools was a bit tricky. I had been spoiled by Windows and wanted desperately to get back to something more reminiscent of the DOS prompt where getting things done was pleasantly obscured behind typed commands. The Linux terminal was showing a lot of promise in this regard, but practically every command was different, including newline terminators which posed their own flavor of problems. *Don't get me started on the slashes!* I had plenty to learn, but that is what made it so exciting. Contrary to these goals, the computer classes regularly kept the shop full of customers with more mainstream operating systems, so finding spare time between all the chaos was a bit of a challenge. On a positive note, the level of technical discourse in the shop leveled up significantly with this new cast of customers. They were eager to learn about these topics, and many of them had already done research on their own. Spoon feeding simple factoids, support scripts or softball techno jargon wasn't always going to cut it with this new crowd. Technical monologues were more boldly interrupted with questions, and some of them were actually good ones. It was easier to find common ground with them, dare I say empathy, and gave my unchecked cynicism about the future of human intelligence, or lack thereof, a much-needed break.

    The Christmas and New Year's party was another trivia and movie filled extravaganza. It was good to see that some things were resilient to the tests of time. Evelyn went to visit friends in Dallas for an entire month, so we had Tom all to ourselves. Tom's health continued to improve. The same could be said for the shop, as well. Class attendance was at an all-time high, even Wade's coffee class started to take off. His skill with all of Marge's buttons and knobs was a perfected one-man symphony that produced world-class coffee, which in turn bolstered attendance and helped him transcend the curriculum beyond coffee basics. It was full on "Coffee Theory", as he liked to call it, and even I had to admit it had a nice ring to it. The level of detail and facts he had collected over the years were astounding. If his delivery was a bit more organized with fewer third person Bob-Dole-esque self-references, you'd think he was a legitimate college professor teaching an advanced course on coffee. His favorite source for updated news was Fresh Cup magazine, but he would mope and grumble for a few days whenever they released a tea heavy edition. He also exhausted every book at the library on coffee roasting, chemical composition, mixology and regional growing patterns from every farmer's almanac digest he could find. He was a coffee-soaked sponge filled with knowledge, and it all came flowing out in a semi-coherent narrative and great tasting coffee in his classes. The same baristas from FlowJoe's that had considered him odd and mocked him were now intently listening to his every word and taking notes. *Oh, how the tables have turned!*

The trivia tournament came and went, as expected. We put in a ton of time practicing, trying to hedge the impact of our weakest link and still placed only third. There were only six teams this time and they were all much less competitive than previous years, which made the finish sting even more. Time was running out for us to get our trophy. Despite our best intentions, TapHouse's annual tournament was shaping up more to be our masochistic Sisyphean punishment with Evelyn setting us further back every year with her increasing lack of effort. Our shop was never one to back down from a challenge, a team of quixotic fools if you will, and we were determined to push this boulder over the top of this hill, no matter what. Hopefully, when we did, her car would be parked at the bottom on the other side. *Why did Tom put up with her?*

Every now and then Hollywood strung together summer line-ups that truly impressed us. Years like 1989 and 1999 are frequently considered marquee years in cinematic history; however, if you told me that 2003, a year that lead off with the lamest Daredevil imaginable, could be considered in the same conversation, I would have called you a straight up liar. 2003 was so good that if it weren't for the periodic movie hopping at the theater, I'm sure I would have legitimately gone broke. Bruce Almighty, Matrix Reloaded, Pirates of the Caribbean, School of Rock and 2 Fast 2 Furious were all released in the first six months causing a flurry of movie nights at the local theater. If that wasn't enough, trailers for the Matrix Revolutions, Kill Bill and The Fellowship of the Rings had our eyes salivating with delight and wonder, as all of them were due out before the end of the year. It was the first time since the release of the digitally remastered Star Wars that we were able to see a follow-up sequel in the same year, let alone in under six months. Agent Smith impersonations took the shop by storm, but surprisingly enough it was Tom who started them. His health kick made him a much more chipper person, and arguably more focused because he finally was able to check off one of his more elusive goals: ninety-nine mines on Minesweeper. An act which he lorded proudly over the rest of us, as if he "kill screened" Donkey Kong on a single quarter. I had grown accustomed in my many years of game play hearing people gloat about frags, headshots, special loot or level ups, but never had I ever heard someone gloat about Minesweeper. Who was I to judge though? I took great pleasure in showcasing my skills. An almost constant need to prove to friends, even strangers, that I was the best in the room in at least some facet of the game. It took meeting an unsuspecting, gifted and quirky genius for me to see the empty meaning in all that wasted effort to impress.

*** *FLASH* ***

A slight breeze cooled my right eye from under the door as I downward-dogged my broken body on the bathroom floor. I rocked my face back and forth to distribute the fan's cooling sensation, while the shaggy floor mat dreads tickled my ear canal. The benefits from this momentary respite of full-body discomfort far-exceeded the burden of the sticky linoleum and close proximity to the dust bunnies collected near the base boards. *I really should clean more often.* My right arm and shoulder were pinned to the floor, leaving only my left hand free to crack the Da Vincian code that was the simple twisting doorknob. *Success!* A deluge of congealed grease and burger-scented air flooded the bathroom; a pleasant respite from the smell of vomit and acid shits. My right forearm and fingers were numb from the extended pronation on the floor, leaving me to crawl out of the bathroom like a wounded animal. Pins and needles surged to every nerve ending, further hindering my exit, but the fresh-*er* air felt too good to wait any longer. My arm, on the other hand, had different plans. The moment I bore weight onto its electric fingertips, it collapsed into a crumpled bag of soggy burger wrappers. Thoughts of vomiting had subsided, and I could sense the faintest hint of an appetite in-between my stomach gurgles. A tomato that smelled of hot mayonnaise was now suctioned to my face like a starfish. *Damn you, Patty!* I slid my face across the floor dislodging the parasitic stowaway as I lunged into the direct path of the oscillating breeze.

The apartment worked well for me living alone, but it didn't handle groups very well. My meager window unit already worked double overtime to combat improper second story insulation and the residual heat from the modem and computer banks below. The fans were a necessity to maintain balance if I decided to cook, or in this case, hosted chatty guests. I pulled the fan to the ground by its cord and locked the air directly onto my face. I could feel the mild onset of clarity and rational thought. At least the type of rational thought that compels people to speak nonsense words into moving fan blades just so they can hear their distorted voice. *I am your fah..therrrr.* I could see two stranded fries from the corner of my eye sticking out of the mangled take out bag. They still looked crispy, *and delicious.* The happenings that would result in any leftover fries amongst our group of friends, even the tiny broken potato nubs were most likely quite gross. *It's a trap!* I rolled off my back and attempted to stand, but the blood pounding headache quickly returned and reminded me that elevation was not my friend, yet. My hands clawed the damp sticky back of the sofa as I ascended its sheer four-foot face. Propped onto my knees like a shaky tripod, I could see everyone was still incapacitated, except Morgan, who was still on her laptop typing away, but even she was oblivious to the commotion.

    I could barely sit upright and keep my eyes open. I folded over onto the back of the couch and rested my head on the top of the backrest cushion a few feet from Patty's outstretched hairy leg. I just needed one more quick rest, and then all would be good. The right side of my face buried into the back cushion, and my left eye focused on the back of Morgan's hoodie. An unexpected sense of pride washed over me, as I started to remember meeting Morgan for the first time and how she became a part of the family.

*** FLASH ***

FEATURED TRACK

Nirvana - Come As You Are

15

Morgan Emily Books

It was October 2004, about a month before Thanksgiving Break, when Morgan Brooks first set foot into Andersson's Electronics. I was helping Tom with a soldering lesson, when a young woman walked into the back of the room and unapologetically dropped a bulging duffel bag of electronics on the table. She flashed a FREE Tom-NET course pass she clipped from the newspaper, accompanied with a stern look of indifference, and unpacked her soldering equipment. There were enough reasons to remember this moment, but the one that remains top of the list was that she was dressed head-to-toe in black; hair, eye liner, lipstick, shirt, jeans, Docs ... the works. She was a tinkering Morticia Addams that took insanely detailed notes that resembled Elven scribblings with intricate doodles in the margins. Despite her late arrival, by the end of that first class, she finished the assigned exercises before the rest of the class and had moved on to work on her bag of randomness.

Tom and I were both impressed, and we were quick to catch her at the end. He picked up one of the circuit boards on the table and observed her handy work up close.

"Your heating technique is flawless," he said, flipping the board over side to side to observe the entirety of her work, "but you still need to work on your feed. Many of these connection points will probably be too big for most modern electronics." He paused for a moment, and then handed her the board pointing to a specific component. "Except for this one. This one is practically perfect. Do more like this, and you'll be in good shape."

"Thanks," she said. Not one for small talk, she flipped back through her notes and circled what looked like a ledger entry and quickly started to pack the rest of her things.

"My name is Tom, and this is Ben. Mind telling us your name?" he asked.

"Morgan," she replied, slinging her bag over her shoulder like the anti-Santa.

"Well then, Morgan." He extended his hand to shake hers. "It was nice to meet you. Feel free to come by anytime. I have a feeling you'd get along with our cast of misfits here."

She had no response, only a perplexed look, as if we didn't line up with her preconceived notion of a misfit. Over the coming weeks, Morgan continued to attend classes, but not just Tom's. She started dropping in on all our after-school classes, and quickly became a silent, yet familiar, fixture in the room unless she had a question, which wasn't very often. She was obviously smart and came off as being extremely reserved and calculated. A few weeks later, she started saying "Hello" and "Goodbye" on a regular basis, as if her Bret Maverick social experiment was coming to an end. Breaking through to her was going to take some time, but we could tell the shop was rubbing off on her. Day by day, block by block, the iceberg sized chip on her shoulder was melting away.

On the weekends, Hot Shot Trivia reigned supreme and days would frequently blur together, as we filled, emptied and reshuffled the discard bin keeping our never-ending game running, just like the Sandlot. Anto was predictably elbow deep in a new computer, while Patty and I alternated between design and coding on a steady stream of website work. Wade blockaded himself in the office with Marge while on his quest to master latte art and drinking all his failed attempts. Tom sat in his favorite sales chair with his heels firmly propped on the back of the sales desk reading each question aloud and keeping the scoreboard up to date. The only discernible difference between these weekend days, besides the outlying chance one's shirt was different than the day before, was that Morgan would randomly appear and sit off to the side in the Community Corner and listen while typing away on her laptop or practicing her soldering by adding and removing components from her bag of boards. She normally had her bag of electronic parts, but it was clear she was more interested in watching than doing any work. She would laugh to herself whenever someone missed a question, like the time I couldn't name all of the main cast of Friends. *I had barely even seen an episode!* Out of the blue, Patty turned and put Morgan on the spot.

"So, what do you say, Morgan? Think you can name the entire cast to steal Ben's points?" he said.

She didn't even flinch or turn around. She just rattled off the names, "Ross, Rachel, Monica, Chandler, Joey and Phoebe".

Tom's ears perked at the show of confidence as he proclaimed, "Correct!", in a boisterous tone. He drew a new box on the dry erase board with Morgan's name and ceremoniously marked her first point. "Something tells me, she's a ringer. Let's move to one of the newer decks."

Morgan stopped the charade and turned off her solder station and faced the game with her full attention and was ready to compete. That was the day she let her guard down and became a part of our group. She was born in Jollyville and was a freshman in high school and a bit of a loner, but rightly so. Her parents were divorced, *same as me*, and all her computer knowledge was self-taught, *same as me*, but she took her skills to an uncanny level of depth and precision. Every aspect from the first electron out of the power outlet to the latest frame refresh on the monitor was second nature to her. Hardware. Software. Programming. She had it all. Effortless excellence and humility are the best ways to describe her personality, all bundled in a petite goth package. On a whim, she picked up ActionScript, overnight and fixed a pesky recursive rendering sequence that had been stumping Patty for over a year. It was clear that JavaScript was her language du jour. She tried to offer suggestions for our websites, but I respectfully declined. The last thing I wanted to do was get into a pissing match about who's code was better. *Her's.* This new challenger sparked a competitive spirit in me that I had been missing for quite some time. Our mutual interest in computers and hacking united us, and her direct no-nonsense attitude pushed me to be more creative. She was smart, kind and intimidating. *She reminded me of Angie.* Maybe this is what Tom saw in her as well, and why he opened the doors in the first place. Maybe she just needed to be pointed in the right direction and given an opportunity, *same as me*. The situational resemblance was undeniable, and I knew deep down that this is where she was supposed to be.

Days flew by at the shop, holidays and all. Morgan's passive observation days didn't last long and quickly became an official part time employee, often assisting Tom in his electronics classes. They became quick friends, which resulted in one hell of a birthday present for Tom that became an icon at the shop. Tom wasn't a big fan of his birthday, but we tried to make a point of celebrating it each year without rubbing his age in his face, *or bringing up his recent health scare*. Most of the time we'd scavenge the local antique spots to see if we can find any sort of antique trinket he might like. This year, we found him an enamel Corvette owner's pin to go with his smoke shack on wheels in the backroom. He rubbed his fingers over the finish, and you could see him tearing up a bit. He really liked tiny antique tchotchkes, and he really liked smoking pot in the backroom. It was the perfect gift for him. *So we thought.*

Morgan arrived late to the festivities with a resounding kick to the front door and lugged a large oblong box wrapped in black trash bags and chaotically crisscrossed "Police Line Do Not Cross" tape. The box didn't appear too heavy, because her small frame flung it around with ease, but it was difficult getting both it and Morgan through the door at the same time. With one final twist, she completed her shop entry maneuver completely unflustered by the preceding fifteen seconds of banging. She plopped the box down on the table and pulled out a handmade card from her purse. It had a tombstone on the cover that said, "You're not dead yet, Happy Birthday". The back of my throat instantly went dry, as my eyes immediately turned to the spot on the floor where I found Tom. Before I could pull focus back on this awkward situation, Tom let out a most hearty laugh.

"Well, no one is ever going to accuse you of being, subtle, now are they, Morgan?" He eyeballed the sarcophagus like packaging of his gift, and asked, "So do I open it, or do I just place it by my bed at night and wait for it to kill me?"

"I'd wager on opening it now," she paused for a moment "but I think this isn't something you want to put next to your bed. Your lady friend may have issues."

Tom unwrapped the external packaging and tore through the layers of tissue paper in between, *black ... go figure*, until his hand struck hard plastic with a thud. He felt out the object's edges and removed it from the box letting the tissue paper fall to the side. *Boobs!* Let's face it. That is what you noticed first. A prominent pair of bright white boobs with black nipples were attached to the front half of a woman's mannequin torso with a metal snake light fixture coming out the neck cavity. To be honest, I wasn't quite sure what I was looking at. The room sat quiet as Tom held it aloft examining the odd gift from all angles trying to grok what he was looking at.

"I made it myself," Morgan said.

"I can see that." He flipped the torso around to reveal its hollowed shell where a bunch of wires and random components were mounted. He flipped it back around such that the nipples were pointing directly in his face. "I think you're right. This is one-night stand light I won't be putting next to my bed." Everyone passively chuckled, but we were all still confused. Morgan's humor and gift giving personality were still unknown quantities, but she finally began the much-needed explanation after plugging it in to an extension cable.

"It's for your car ... in the passenger seat. I always see you back there, in the dark, listening to the radio. Alone. So, I thought I'd make you something out of some spare parts I had lying around." *Who has a half mannequin torso just lying around?* "I deconstructed a clock radio and desk lamp and wired them into the body of this hanging mannequin." She flipped the torso around and walked us through the components. "Down here is the core radio and AM/FM switch. I disconnected the volume controls and soldered a bridge to the other side cavity. This way you can adjust the volume by rubbing the left leg dial and adjust radio stations by rubbing the right leg dial. Not the most ideal user interface, but I thought it was funny." *Creepy, but funny!*

She continued her impassioned QVC like demo oblivious to the fact the entire room was still trying to process the totality of her pitch. "Then I ran speaker cables along the side and connected them to speakers coming out the arm stubs." The arms were amputated high on the upper arm resembling the work of a short sleeve t-shirt guillotine. Inside each sealed off stub, a speaker was flush mounted in the inner arm cavity with small perforations for sound. "But that's not all," she said, flipping the torso back around. The metallic snake neck light socket nearly hit Patty in the face in all her enthusiasm. She screwed in a light bulb that had been wrapped in tissue paper inside the box. "It's also a light," she grabbed the left nipple switch and gave it a quick twist. Everyone instinctively covered their nipples and grimaced, but low and behold the light came on as advertised. "You use the left boob for light, and the right is the on/off for the radio ... obviously. Not to mention, you can hang it on the wall, or just let it chill with you in the car ... What d'ya think?" Her question was directed at Tom, but we could see her eyes scanning the crowd for traces of feedback on her gift. The present was ludicrous, tacky and I instantly became jealous because it was by far the most perfect gift I had ever seen for Tom. We all loved it, especially Tom, and that was the first time we saw her smile.

From that day forward, Morgan officially earned her spot in the family and was a bit more vocal with everyone when she wasn't head down on her laptop. She oscillated between extreme fits of chattiness and solitude in the Community Corner, which made every day a surprise, but it was clear that her reclusive instincts were fading. Her and Anto became instant kindred spirits the moment Morgan shared her Case Logic CD binder overstuffed with burned MP3 CDs. She had a lot of goth, trance and heavy metal, genres that Anto didn't have too much depth, but it wasn't long before DJ Keoki and Sirenia slid right into the regular shop music rotation. Anto pestered Morgan relentlessly to do a My Immortal Karaoke duet with her at one of the TapHouse's Karaoke nights, but Morgan always seemed to have other plans.

If it wasn't for this distraction, we might have lost Anto down the rabbit hole that year. Due to her MtG and Pokémon obsessions, she started the shop's first "All About Blogging" and MySpace course to help people share information about their passions. As old and decrepit as many of the town elders were, it was surprising to see just how many of them were genuinely interested to learn how to blog. After looking at a couple of their first blog posts, it became clear that old people blogging was neither interesting nor something that should be encouraged to the general population. Most of their content was rarely more than a bare link, or a misshapen image and garbled text with errant anchor tags. In, sadly, not so rare cases the intended audience name(s) were listed as the blog post title. *You'd think they would have grasped the difference between email and a blog by now.*

Morgan started high school a few months prior to her visiting the shop and was still learning the ropes. Wade and I shared the ins and outs of the lunch circuit, or as we remembered it, and gave her directions to the best cedar nook this side of the circle drive. She didn't have anyone to sit with at lunch, which reminded me of my first days at Jolly High. Rather than recommend Chess club, Wade and I, and sometimes Anto, drove down to the campus to keep her company on Tuesdays and Thursdays. It had been quite a long time since I last turned that corner around the Science building. I was overcome with an unshakable sense of déjà vu. Morgan was sitting in Angie's spot, identical posture and all. She had a red flannel at her waist. It wasn't the same pattern as Angie's, but the similarities threw me off for a quick second. Wade scurried to his usual spot atop a group of forked branches and quickly screamed in dismay. His hands and shirt were smeared with sticky tree sap and pieces of flaked cedar bark, but he was most displeased with his coffee being polluted with tree debris. The scenery and memories stirred were bittersweet. I couldn't help but look at Morgan and think of Angie, and the final times we sat in this very spot. Before my mind could spiral too far, I remembered a harsh truth when I sat down. Given time, a tree will grow, and a twig in the ass hurts just as much now as it did back then. After a few visits, lunches became just that, lunch. No more awkward memories, or teachers asking what a young woman is doing eating lunch with non-students. It was only forty-five minutes, but it was clear that Morgan looked forward to those minutes each day, *same as me*. She never said so, but I recognized the look in her eyes and how they lit up when we started Hot Shot Trivia or talked about anything related to technology. She was drowning in the mediocre subjects of her day-to-day classes and every bit of stimulating conversation was savored like a fine wine.

Homecoming came and went, and so did Spring Break. If we didn't know that Morgan was actually in high school, you would hardly be able to guess. She was quite mature and calm for her age and uncannily focused, A's in all her classes and hardly breaking a sweat for studying outside school hours. College would be a piece of cake for her, if she had intentions of going. She called it the grandest waste of time and money, and who was I to disagree? Every waking moment was spent making or learning something new, an impressive sponge of knowledge and talent, which is why she dominated at trivia, but she was also observant. *Almost too observant.* Very little got by her, whether it was on a digital screen or in real life, and her no-filter demeanor in which she dealt with these anomalies tended to leave people a bit put-off, much like how some people respond to Wade.

One day in late April of 2005, Tom and Evelyn walked into the shop holding hands acting like goofy teenage love birds. Not that they don't act like a couple most of the time, but something was definitely off at the way they were *both* intrigued by the PC Shopper on the table.

"So, when are you getting married?" Morgan blurted out.

The words were spoken with such spontaneity and laser focus that they reverberated off the drab concrete walls a few times before we could hear the mulling sounds of computer fans spinning in the background, again. Evelyn's face went from happy to hostile in an instant and quickly became defensive in both her body language and her words.

"Whatever do you mean, young lady?" she replied. Her arm was now nuzzled tightly around Tom's elbow and dragging him into a shielding position between her and Morgan.

"Well, either both of you need to go to the bathroom, which is totally possible given that human bladders tend to shrink with age, or you are getting married. You're smiling and happy looking at a computer magazine, but you don't know anything about computers. And, the fact that you've been trying to hide your hand ever since you got out of your car in the parking lot ... when you think about it, the conclusion is pretty obvious."

"When you put it like that, then I guess there's no reason to hide it," she said. "Tom and I are getting married!" She sprung her hand from confinement and started flashing an overly large diamond ring like some Madonna voguing debutant. Tom just stood there with a happy, and yet disappointed, look on his face, while Evelyn kept on blabbing. "Isn't this ring amazing?!" When no one stoked her conversational fire, not even Tom, he reached into his shirt pocket and pulled out a small set of trivia cards.

"I organized these cards with questions to help us ease into the topic ... but I guess I don't need these now." He gave Morgan a wink reassuring her that everything was fine, and then we all congregated around them to get the details. Poor Anto was cornered by Evelyn talking about the ring and wedding planning, while Morgan stayed seated observing everyone from afar, but her eyes were keenly fixed on Evelyn like Jane Goodall studying her silverbacks.

  A few weeks later, I dropped off some mail in Tom's backroom "office", when I noticed the Jollyville Times Newspaper sitting in the passenger seat. It was folded to showcase the wedding announcement that Evelyn paid to have put in the paper. It was a full half page ad in the local section, and it spent more time talking about her real estate company than her or Tom. *Leave it to Evelyn to ruin love.* I flipped the article over to catch the last few sentences below the fold, and my heart sank to my stomach. I quickly checked the date on my watch, but part of me already knew what it was going to say. A recent picture of Angie holding a large bouquet of flowers was printed in the lower right-hand corner of the page under a small article entitled "Local Graduates from Stanford Graduate School of Business." *Right on schedule.* Details from my memories filled in the fidelity lost by the pixelated newspaper photo as I leaned against the car door reading and re-reading the article. I scanned for meaning in every letter, every word and every comma like the future of humanity depended on me finding a hidden encoded message. Any repressed feelings about her came bubbling to the surface, and I could feel my stomach knot up at the realization that this was what I wanted for her. I closed my eyes and held the folded newspaper visage to my forehead. *Make it easy for her.*

  News about the wedding spread through the blue-haired grapevine arguably faster than email or instant message, and the shop was once again the center of attention in Jollyville. People from all over town, some not even customers, stopped by with the sole purpose of gleaning morsels of gossip to add to the rumor mill. As disingenuous as their intentions might have been, those that showed up in person were a million times better than the ones who spent the entire day clogging up the support lines with made up computer problems trying to persuade us to spill the beans. We could have made a fortune off of all the ID10t errors we diagnosed that week. Eventually, Patty and I put up a simple wedding website with all the frequently asked questions and a congratulatory page for the happy couple. Patty made it one of the best interactive Flash websites he had done to date with all the bells and whistles. Granted, its superiority was reinforced when it stood next to the cesspool of MySpace pages most couples created for their wedding sites at the time. So many random snippets of garbage code munged together haphazardly like digital duct tape. The page counter was going berserk and Evelyn was not one to pass up any free advertising for her business. She dropped off a handwritten pad of paper with all the tweaks she requested for the site. At first the requests were simple things, like colors, backgrounds and photo cropping, but eventually it became more about logos and messaging for her real estate business. This pissed Morgan off something fierce, and we caught a small glimpse of how Morgan liked to be the change she wished to see in the world around her.

Patty had one tragic flaw when it came to his computer savvy, he rarely locked his computer, except at night. *Oh paranoia, my cherished friend.* Morgan took advantage of this predictable AFK habit to embed a surprise in our tribute to Tom and Evelyn. A few days later, we showed the page to some customers and noticed a flicker in the background image. A picture flashed into place of Tom and Evelyn holding hands at the beach where they first met, except, in this picture, Evelyn's face was replaced with an oversized velociraptor head with a poorly photoshopped bright orange curly wig. A few seconds later, the image changed back to its normal state. Morgan added a cryptic line of code that rendered a transparent layer on top of the background with the superimposed raptor head and used a simple JavaScript interval to randomly make it switch back and forth. If you weren't looking at the site for more than three minutes, you would never see it. It was a funny and well executed Easter egg, but Evelyn was not amused. She considered these the first shots in their endless feud that stemmed from Evelyn's overall shallow and petty existence. *Man, I hate that woman! Go Morgan Go!*

The eye squinting gazes between Morgan and Evelyn provided world class entertainment that made movie theaters seem a bit dull, or it could just have been another slow start for Hollywood. Anto and I had popcorn on standby whenever the two got into the same room. On the other hand, Patty was busy going down a new rabbit-hole of entertainment into the bowels of a new video sharing platform, called YouTube. He was infatuated with the concept of having a platform to share his video projects on for others to discover, so he felt compelled to start his first vlog. Sadly, it didn't take off, but that's what made him different. When I first saw the video of the guy at the zoo talking about elephants and their trunk sizes, I wasn't overcome with an avid sense of inspiration, but Patty's passion with multimedia gave him a different perspective and willingness to think outside the box. It took me replaying videos, over and over, like Star Wars Kid or the Evolution of Dance for me to understand what he saw and the potential of sharing videos in the community. *I'm so glad he did.*

  The countdown to Tom's wedding seemed to have a sixty second half-life, but one event stood out among the rest: Evelyn stepped down from the Trivia team. With four weeks to spare, she said she was too busy with wedding preparations and suggested that since Morgan was "so smart" she should take her place. All of us, including Tom, expressed our sadness in person, but were screaming with joy on the inside. Tom's time was also strapped, for his wedding was the weekend after the tournament. We all found ways to multitask to squeeze in extra time to practice. The most memorable was the day Tom carried in eight large boxes of broken Christmas lights and a bag of replacement bulbs and said, "Trivia Party?" Pizza, music and trivia was not a bad way to spend an evening with your friends, even if we were part of a tedious assembly line to test thousands of miniature light bulbs. Evelyn wasn't there and that was good enough for just about everyone.

  The day of the trivia tournament came, and I couldn't have been prouder. The team turnout was competitive once again, and despite the extra competition, Hot Shots sailed through all the way to the finals. We were head-to-head with Keith's J4ck4ls once again, but this time we had an advantage, no Evelyn. It was a rubber match for thirty straight minutes, every point countered with another. The fate of the winner was not going to be determined by intelligence, as much as Olympian level fast-firing twitch reflexes to slam the buzzer.
The box of prepared questions was running thin and the J4ck4ls were up by one when the sudden death protocol was enacted. The next one to answer the question correctly would be the champ. Morgan was facing off against Jesse, one of the more unlikeable jabronis in the bunch, and given her dominance that evening, victory felt imminent. His teammates were cheering from their table spouting their overcompensating masculine

digi-bro whooping nonsense. Morgan stood calm and was laser focused. Her eyes piercing a hole directly through his head, until the unthinkable happened.

The judge uttered only a few words from the final question when Jesse twitched his shoulder, as if going for the buzzer, and Morgan took the bait. *SLAM* Contest rules state that the judge must stop reading once the buzzer is pressed and the contestant must provide an answer without hearing any more of the question. Morgan's eyes were affixed on her hand backlit by the glowing red buzzer, while she thought. *"Category: Science Fiction. Name the captain ..."* That was all we knew about the question. Normally that would be enough when we played on our own turf, but the question was obviously handwritten. It had no preamble or leading contextual clues. There were so many angles to consider: Kirk, Piccard, Solo, Reynolds, Kelly. We needed more context. The ten second timer was counting down fast, and we all held hands, each attempting to channel our guesses telepathically as we stood helpless at our table.

"Captain Malcolm Reynolds." The words shot from Morgan's mouth with a reluctant tone. Her head was lowered, frozen in time waiting for the judge's response that would decide our fate.

The judge coldly replied, "Incorrect" and continued to read the whole question. "Category: Science Fiction. Name the captain of the underwater sea vessel that shared the name of its popular 90s TV show." All we could hope for was that Jesse missed the question and we got another chance, but he had a cocky attitude when he hit his buzzer, which made me despise him even more.

"Captain Nathan Hale Bridger of the UEO SeaQuest DSV." *Correct.* I didn't need to hear the judge's response. It was the first time I had seen Morgan lose her confidence. We all walked over to give her a supportive hug. It sucked coming so close to finally winning and falling short, but it stung even worse to know that it happened because of such a cheap trick. We packed up our gear and headed back to the shop foregoing the celebration party at TapHouse. Wade whipped up some caffeinated confections, and Tom bought ice cream for everyone to try and ease the pain. No one felt like touching trivia that evening. Instead, Morgan buried her frustration in a half gallon of Cookies N' Cream, while we all took turns finding the funniest YouTube videos to try and lift our spirits. *Thank You, Leroy Jenkins!*

With Tom's wedding just around the corner, there was nothing I wanted more for him than a win. That, and for him to be happy. For the life of me, I couldn't see what he saw in her. There were times when it felt like we were cut from the same cloth, and others where we were polar opposites. It was for this reason that I was only half shocked when Tom asked me to be his best man at the ceremony and for Wade and Patty to be his other groomsmen. Evelyn wasn't thrilled in the slightest, but she was held hostage by her innate need for order and symmetry. We each received a pair of dress slacks along with a shirt and tie to complete the outfit. We looked less like a wedding party and more like Geek Squad customer service. Anto volunteered to DJ the ceremony and reception and tried to recruit Morgan; however, she was busy dissecting a browser plugin she discovered called Firebug as a focused distraction to handle her grief. It was probably for the best.

In typical fashion, our ragtag team of procrastinators waited until the last possible moment to bring things together, but we got the job done in good-enough fashion. Every last Christmas light strand was checked and adorned on every possible surface in the outdoor reception area. Clark Griswold would have been proud of the fire hazard of extension cables, multi-plug adapters and electrical tape that hung, suspended in mid-air, from the wall outlet. Anto compiled a surprise playlist of eclectic music from around the world based on Tom's musical tendencies in the backroom for the reception. Patty designed decorative centerpieces for the tables using antique picture frames to showcase collages photos of Tom and Evelyn he digitally edited. Wade secured an array of coffee urns and filled them with his favorite brews from around the world and offered his barista services with Marge at his side. I wasn't great at writing speeches, let alone a best man's toast. So, I decided to MC a small trivia game based on what little I knew about Tom and Evelyn together and their interests. Everyone at the reception joined in and had a good time. The smile on Tom's face was unlike any I had ever seen. The man was truly happy, and it felt good to know that we helped in that moment.

FEATURED TRACK

The Cranberries - Ode To My Family

16

The Blackest of Fridays

Tom and Evelyn took an elaborate honeymoon that consisted of a collection of destinations and spanning nearly four months. It took Tom nearly two weeks to talk through all of his pictures from their adventure when they got back. They visited Machu Picchu in Peru, the shores of the Tenerife and Casablanca, the rolling hills of Scotland, the temples in Chiang Mai, the great outback in Australia and rounded it off with a weekend getaway to set foot in Antarctica to check off "setting foot on all seven continents" from his bucket list. With every story he told, he would rub his fingers on a local coin he collected to warm his memory. He had full sets of coins from at-least ten countries separated in plastic bags and no doubt countless stories to accompany each one. Leave it to Tom to start a new collection, or two or three, while on vacation. Australian customs weren't too thrilled with his assortment of sand filled glass Coca-Cola bottles from around the world, so he had to abandon that collection before entering the country. It was great having him back at the shop. Even though things operated smoothly in his absence, there was just a certain spark he brought that was not missed until it was actually gone.

Holiday buzz started to pick up as Black Friday was just around the corner. The Nintendo Wii was the coveted shopping prize that year, with people lining up five hundred deep just to have a chance to score a claim voucher at one of their favorite big box stores. At least that is how everyone else fought over them. The instant we saw the first Nintendo Revolution announcement at E3 we were all intrigued. A single machine that played the historical Nintendo catalog. It was unprecedented! We were hooked when we saw the first commercial with live action swinging and free form controls. Our inner athletes were awakened, and we convinced Tom to ask our suppliers if we could get some sent to the shop. A few phone calls later, Tom was on a waitlist that guaranteed him no less than two, but no more than eight Nintendo Wii's for their big launch. While we were not allowed to sell any of the units until Midnight of Black Friday, it didn't mean we couldn't test them out. We had a five-day head start on the rest of the town, maybe even the state, to partake in a Nintendo Wii party. In total, we received six units, and didn't sell a single one. Tom gave them all out as early holiday bonuses, keeping one for himself. We never bothered to order any more.

Hilarious videos of people accidentally chucking remotes into TV screens or giving other players black eyes flooded YouTube when it first launched in the wild. Nintendo eventually shipped replacement safety straps to early purchasers that were less prone to snapping, because apparently not all of the videos were the result of user error. Shortly thereafter, the fad that started out as full body movement, swinging and sweating exercise, devolved into zombied couch sitting with well-timed wrist flicks for most, except for Tom. He went full tilt when it came to Wii Tennis; wearing head and wristbands, broad slide side stepping, double fisted forehands and overly accentuated grunting. Game selection was fairly limited early on, but Wii Sports had our undivided attention for quite some time. It was hard to beat the satisfaction of triggering the ninety-nine pin Easter egg in bowling. *Thanks Morgan.* In addition to the games, we discovered a hack that allowed us to generate and import Miis via Bluetooth on one of the Wii controllers. It made Wii Sports a bit chaotic when selecting characters, but we customized one for each of us and then randomly generated the rest to max out the one hundred Mii count. There was this one Mii character that looked like a short, stubby toadstool with a bright red party favor sticking out its head. Naturally, we named that one Evelyn. From Thanksgiving through Christmas, our traditional trivia party nights were spent doing mashup events that consisted of Hot Shots Trivia while simultaneously competing head-to-head in a Wii Sport challenge. All signs were pointing at a New Year's party comprised of exactly the same activities, but with more Wii-based festivities.

It was the Thursday after Christmas, and Tom was out back behind the shop sitting next to the firepit amidst eerie moonlit shadow patterns from the canopy of a nearby sycamore tree. We rarely used the firepit, but if the weather was just right, nothing could beat roasting marshmallows outdoors over an open flame, assuming you had the corresponding graham crackers and chocolates. He was sitting back in one of his chairs with his sock covered feet propped up to the outer ring. It had been a long week of post-Christmas support, so we were all exhausted, but Tom was noticeably slower than usual. I stirred up a few cups of hot apple cider and went out to see how he was doing. He was so busy gazing into the fire, that he didn't even notice me until I wafted a cup in front of his nose.

"Oh hey," he said, collecting himself. His eyes were watery, possibly from fire's smoke or the crisp evening breeze. He gave them a quick wipe on his sleeve. "Is this for me, or are you double fisting cider these days?"

"If you want it." I handed him the cup. "Everything alright?" I asked.

"Yeah. It was just a good night to be outside." He looked up into the leaves that had yet to fall and appeared to be staring directly into the moon. "How about you, Ben? What brings you out here?"

"I guess I saw you out here alone and thought you might like some company …. That, and I thought you might have some marshmallows on you." I took a sip from my cup noticing the empty bag stuffed into his chair's cup holder.

Tom squeaked a sheepish grin, "Sorry, I've already eaten them all." We both laughed for a moment, and then returned to blowing on our cider. I could tell something was wrong but didn't know what to say. I felt like I was chugging my beverage and burning my tongue just to give me an excuse to not speak. Without a word, Tom pulled his feet from the fire and slipped on his Crocs. He hung in midair as he struggled to get out of his sunken position in his chair but eventually managed to playfully dismiss the incident and my offer to assist.

"I'm not that old, yet." He playfully slapped at my hand and paused next to me for a second. I could see a disturbed contemplation in his furrowed brow and a fiercely curling fog exit his mouth, as if the chaos and weight of his thoughts had sublimated into space. My hand remained outstretched just in case he needed it, but instead he rifled his hand through my hair as he always did. "You're a good kid, Ben. Don't ever forget that." He then wobble-walked back inside. I sat alone in the firelit night for a few more moments watching him through the back window. He seemed less rigid inside, perhaps it was just the cold air. Tom waved goodbye to the cavalcade of crazy playing tennis on the Wii. Anto broke away and gave him one of her giant bear hugs, *jealous*, and then he left my field of vision. Shortly after, I heard his car drive out of the parking lot in its typical curb hopping fashion onto the main street. *Some things never change*. The fire quickly faded with no maintenance, leaving me cold and coated with the distinct smell of smoke and pine ash. I poked and separated the remaining embers with a mangled marshmallow skewer until the last of their luminescence faded and then joined everyone inside.

The next morning by all accounts was the same as every morning. I woke up, showered, put on a different shirt and then headed down to meet Wade in the parking lot. He gave me the low down on our morning brew, *that day it was Koa Coffee*, while helping me straighten the floor. He recited the local farming and roasting facts that distinguished the brand as he made his way to Marge and attended to her morning wake up routine before grinding the beans for some espresso shots. Part of me believed that after all of Wade's rantings, that I could actually smell the difference each day, *it had a volcanic salty breeze*. As he started to grind the second batch of beans, *ring* the phone rang. I don't remember what drew me to answer the phone. We didn't open for another hour, but I was right next to my desk. *I guess that was it.* I sat down and cleared my throat preparing my best operator voice. *ring* I took my time and raised my chair from its low rider programming setting *ring* and cleared flakes of dead skin and hair from my keyboard. *Why is my CAPS LOCK on?* *ring* "Thank you for calling Andersson Electronics, home of Tom-NET ... the best internet in town. This is Ben, how can I help you?"

The second I heard her contempt voice on the other end, I knew I would regret picking up the phone. It was Evelyn. I stared at the tubular screensaver flooding the pixels on my monitor with randomly intertwined patterns trying to occupy the remaining ninety nine percent of my brain that didn't want to listen to her, until I heard the unmistakable words.

"It's about Tom." she said.

I leaned forward in my chair and listened attentively. She was crying. "Is everything OK? What happened to Tom?" Her gaudy bangle bracelets clanked against the handset and muffled her words as they often did, *annoying*, but no amount of distortion could drown out her next words.

"Tom died last night." I fell back in my chair in disbelief as I listened to Evelyn provide additional details. He died in his sleep from another heart attack. While waking up to a dead body next you is no doubt disturbing, I couldn't help but feel that Evelyn was already making this event more about her than Tom. Evelyn kept talking, but I had tuned her out. *Did I just hang up on her?* My mind raced. My eyes welled up. My heart pounded. An indescribable pain of sadness, fear and anxiety invaded every last nerve, while I sat in stasis in my office chair. Wade was prepping the second round of espresso shots. Oh, how I envied his ignorance. To have the ability to unring that bell and live in that world for even a millisecond more, would have meant everything. But that wasn't an option. That's not how life works. *Real life just keeps on kicking you. No matter how good or bad things go. It summarily beats you day in and day out; one relentless beating after another. Any perceived break is just your body adapting to the pain and registering the nonstop abuse as normal. Fighting back for any resemblance of happiness was futile, as it only inspired far more sinister methods. Pointless!*

"Aaaaaaaaaaaaaaaaaaaaaaaaaaaaaaaaaaaaaaaaaaaahh hhhhhhhhhhhhhhhhhhhhhhhhhhhh!" I screamed and threw the phone receiver across the room, slamming my head into the desk and banged repeatedly with my fists. Life's cruel cold blanket of despair felt heavy on my mind, while tears poured from my face and dripped onto the floor.

"You OK, dude? What happened?" Wade asked, placing his hand on my shoulder.

I couldn't bear to look him in the eye, so I just blurted it out. As cold and callous as Evelyn did to me. "Tom's dead."

"Oh god," he replied.

That was it. A few seconds later, I felt Wade's hand leave my shoulder followed by the sound of a chair rolling closer and a small ceramic mug being set on my desk. Without provocation, Wade just started talking through his emotions, calmly and methodically; one by one in a long unbroken and unsolicited monologue of raw thoughts being processed in out in the open. His hand rubbed circles on my back as he shared his experiences from the day his dad died in the car accident.

"If you are worried about that feeling of pain somewhere in here ...," he said, tapping on his chest, "it will go away in time, but I know it hurts a lot right now. Tom was a friend to me, and it hurts, but everyone knows that he was more to you ..."

Wade paused for a moment and took what felt like the longest slurp I had ever heard in my life. The anticipation for it to end distracted my runaway brain ever so slightly. He was right about the pain. It hurt a lot. When my father decided to leave us, I felt betrayal. When my mom decided to uproot and move to Louisiana, I felt anger. Neither of these were remotely close to how I was feeling at this moment. The closest I could compare was when Angie left. I didn't have the emotional fortitude to shoulder all of that baggage at once and had to drop that train of thought immediately. The spiraling thoughts in my mind needed Wade's counseling distraction to reconvene and fast.

"... I'm not going to try and tell you what you are feeling right now," he continued. "... because I'd imagine it's different for everyone. I remember endlessly pondering the what-if's of it all. How could I get just one more minute, one more word, one more memory or one more anything for that matter. It dug a deep hole that took a long time for me to crawl out of. It wasn't until I met you ... that I finally came fully out of it. So just know I'm here for you, man. Anything you need, I'm here for you, because I know this sucks a ton."

His analysis was spot on. I could already see the mental bulletin board overflowing with all my "one more" requests that all led to the same endless circling labyrinth outcome. My eyes began to dry, leaving behind a congested nose and a sore throat. I picked my head up from the desk. A paper clip dislodged itself from my forehead and fell to the floor. There was Wade with his typical goofy look. No one would have guessed by looking at him that he just gave a profoundly elegant speech; so simple, practical and yet effective. He slid me a few tissues and my second shot of espresso across the desk to me.

"Best drink it while it's hot. It'll make you feel better." he said, smiling. *He always said that about coffee.*

I blew my nose and slammed back the espresso. The liquid warmed my throat and gave my knotted stomach something to digest besides acid and lining.

"I appreciate you being here, Wade. It means a lot." I patted his shoulder but caught myself thinking about what to do next. Everything felt so meaningless and insignificant.

"If you are trying to figure out what's next," Wade interjected. "I'd recommend anything that keeps you busy. Being busy is your friend right now. Just find something to pass the time. It gets easier, but even for me, when I find myself overly dwelling in the past, I just ask myself, "What would make my dad proud?" I find the most actionable task and just do it until my mind is clear. Don't overthink it. For now, the smallest steps forward can make all the difference. Besides me, that is. Cheers." *Three shots down.*

Wade's posture straightened with a sense of accomplishment as a faint smile came across my face. It was exactly what I needed. I'm not sure how I would have done if he wasn't there. I picked up the pieces of the phone, reassembled them and started calling everyone to the shop. Patty was already scheduled to come in later that morning, but Anto and Morgan had the day off. When everyone arrived, I did my best to keep my eyes dry as I delivered the regretful news. We could hear the phones ringing and people knocking on the front door, but we left the shop closed that morning and hid in the breakroom. We all sat in the breakroom talking through our feelings and trying to figure out the next steps. Anto assaulted the heavens with her wagging finger and fast-talking Spanglish. Patty was a bit more reserved, and yet full of questions that I too wanted to know but didn't. Our therapy session consisted of a bunch of feelings and emotions, but only two known facts. Tom was dead, and it was from a heart attack. It is very likely that we would have spiraled the drain in the breakroom for days had it not been for Morgan who broke the loop with a jolting thought that I think each of us deep down wanted to ask, but didn't have the courage to say aloud.

"Do you think she killed him?" she said. Morgan had the driest eyes in the crowd, but you could tell she was not unphased. If her eyes were a gateway into her mind, then her mind was churning a million cycles a second. Her face was taught, and she was intently focused. This wasn't a "Colonel Mustard with the candlestick in the Billiard Room" hypothetical for her. It was clear that she legitimately thought it was a possibility, and while part of me wanted to believe that Evelyn was capable of something so nefarious, I just couldn't go there, *yet*. Besides, I saw Tom the night before and after re-analyzing the evening conversation a few hundred million times in my head, I think, deep down, he knew it was coming. What was important was that information was coming in very slow drips and we knew very little. It made no sense to jump to speculation.

We all had a job to do, and that's what we did. We dried our eyes and prepared ourselves for the onslaught of fly-bys and phone calls that would no doubt increase throughout the day as the gossip mill churned out the news on one of the town's most beloved citizens. Oddly enough, we did get a surge of customers, but they came to pay their respects. Over the next few days, I talked to over forty people who drove in on their own accord to share their story about how Tom had helped them, even from his days selling bathroom fixtures. It was comforting and cathartic seeing the outpouring of love the city was capable of demonstrating for one of their own, but it made me miss him even more.

It took a week for Evelyn to arrange the funeral per Tom's final wishes. It was common knowledge to us all that he wanted to throw one final celebration, for anyone who wanted to come, with his ashes and an oddball picture of him atop the drink cooler with a sign that read, "This one's on me" *Always the last laugh.* The festivities lasted for nearly four hours with even more people coming to say their peace and honor Tom one last time. Evelyn wore a black dress and hat ensemble you'd more expect to see at Seabiscuit's funeral rather than the death of a loved one. She extended the same feigned hollow gratitude and decorum she frequently used with her real estate clients when speakers left the podium. Giving them the fake Parisian kiss on the cheek and double clutched handshake. I've heard that "everyone handles grief differently", but I'm not sure slipping mourning friends business cards and talking about cashing in on rising property values, in their time of grief, is what they meant. It wasn't the classiest move we had ever seen from her, but the bar was pretty low. The fact that she even showed up to the funeral was a bit surprising, but then again, she did love being the center of attention.

There was a small lull in the flow of speakers sharing their stories at the podium when Wade suggested that I go up and say something. He cleverly slipped my drink from my hand and herded me to the stage like some border collie shaman sending me on a spirit quest.

"Trust me, man." Wade urged. "Just go up there and say the first thing that comes to your mind. In times like this, the heart and mind tend to say what needs to be said." I stumbled as I bumped into the edge of the podium riser and nearly decapitated myself on the brim of Evelyn's hat. The room was packed, standing room only, with a long line of patrons at the buffet bar at the back of the room vying for the last of the remaining chicken wings. The rest of the crowd were engaged in random conversation, some listening to the happenings on stage. I stood at the microphone for a moment taking stock of the situation and trying desperately to listen to any common ground between my mind and heart on what to say. *There was no such agreement.*

I finally eked out the words, "Pop quiz, hot shot," into the electrified steel mesh which turned most of the heads towards the front of the room. I felt naked and exposed, but I could see Wade mouthing the words for me to say something else. It was the only thing that made sense, and then, as if on cue, words just started pouring out from an unknown reservoir.

"Many of you knew Tom, but how well did you REALLY know him? If I were to ask you to name me the top three most memorable Tom moments, I'm sure we'd all have a different idea of what that might entail. ... To me, he will always be the coolest old guy I've ever met. ... He understood me in ways that I could never explain, and yet, I found something new about him practically every day. I guess that's what I ultimately liked about him, he was an open book when he wanted to be ... and there was always a new page to learn from him." My eyes started to well up and I knew my time for coherent speech was short. "I guess what I'm trying to say is ... I'm going to miss the hell out of him ..." I raised a fake glass up to the sky, and merely said, "To the best damn boss ... friend ... and mentor anyone could ask for ... To Tom!" Everyone's glasses raised and the crowd responded in unison. I jumped off the stage riser to avoid an awkward moment with Evelyn, grabbed my cup from Wade and nervously shot back the remaining punch. Wade was partially right about how it would feel. I felt incrementally better and resisted the urge to smack him up behind the head.

The next morning when I went to open the doors for Wade, I noticed that someone had placed Tom's funeral wreath with his picture in front of the shop. One might expect a gesture like this to come from a widow, or loved one, but it was clear that Morgan was responsible for this display. Her gothic exterior, while dark and mysterious, offered her a unique perspective of death that translated directly to compassion and beauty. The wreath was adorned with black ribbons, each with words written in her special calligraphy with a silver paint pen and attached to the arrangement with safety pins that had been fused together at the safety latch with a single perfect bead of solder. It was a detail most people would overlook, but we saw it as a tribute to Tom's first attempt to bring Morgan into the family. Rather than burden herself with overt acts of kindness like this, the word on the street, from our more chatty customers, was that Evelyn was looking to sell their shared home and move back into her old house that she had been renting out since they moved in together. It was all paid off, and who could blame her to not want to continue to stay in a house where your husband died ... right next to you ... and in your own bed. *Weird!*

To our knowledge, the shop was profitable and so was Tom-NET, so we all opted to keep working until someone said otherwise. Those plans lasted all of a few days until the following Wednesday when we all received a certified letter in the mail at the shop. The first sentence said it all,

> *Dear Sir or Madam, you have been invited to the reading of the last will and testament of the late Thomas Joseph Andersson this Friday afternoon at 2:00pm at the offices of John Lucas, Attorney at Law ...*

I was not ready to read the rest of the letter, and I definitely was not ready to start thinking about carving up Tom's possessions. The feelings were mixed for everyone. Flattery, guilt and remorse aerosolized and swarmed in the air with every breath until we all tucked our letters away and continued on with the day. A harsh reality quickly set in. *Where am I going to live? What's going to happen to the shop? What's going to happen to our family?* I barely knew a life in Jollyville without Tom or the shop, and the thought of it all disappearing in an instant weighed on every fear-backed breath. Emotions were running high and brewing ever more complex reactions in the shop, until Anto broke the silence with some upbeat salsa music. She grabbed Patty, a self-proclaimed poly-port-a-ped, and spun him around, getting him to loosen his hips like a rag-doll marionette until we all laughed. Even though he was a good six inches taller, and probably fifty pounds heavier, she could sling him around like a top. Pretty sure it was more voluntary than he let on. I pulled the letter from my pocket and placed it on my desk for future reading. A festering question tickled the back of my brain in a moment of clarity. *Why didn't we hear from Evelyn?* Obviously, she deserved a break after the funeral, I can only imagine what she must be going through, but I had a hard time believing that after all we had been through, good or bad, she would have at least given us a heads up on the letters, or any update at all to be honest. Her silence was deafening, but little did we know that even in death, Tom wasn't through changing our lives.

FEATURED TRACK

Poe - Haunted

17

Do You Trust Me?

The day of the reading finally came, after much anxiety. We closed the shop for a bit and piled into Anto's station wagon to head to the lawyer's office across town. When we pulled up, there was already a slew of cars in the parking lot packed in front of the building. There were at least twenty people inside, some of which I met in passing at the shop, that sat in rows of chairs gossiping with one another while waiting for the reading to begin. Each one of them dressed in their Sunday's finest, while our crew burst in looking like a nerd rock remix of the Village People. Anto and Morgan were their usual fashionable selves, leaving Wade, Patty and myself to represent every underdressed male stereotype imaginable as we sported semi decent hoodies, t-shirts and sandals. *At least I wore deodorant.* Needless to say, the experience was far less intimate and casual than I had expected.

We tried to find seats in the back and avoid making a scene, but the well-dressed lawyer, presumably John Lucas, at the front motioned for us to come forward like a teacher dealing with disruptive hooligans in class. To our surprise, his stern curling hand quickly segued into a welcoming swoop gesture as he motioned for us to occupy the front row, reserved just for us. After we seated ourselves, Mr. Lucas disappeared into a side room and came out with a large black binder, followed by Evelyn in another ridiculous outfit and hairdo straight out of an episode of Dallas. Her emotionless face, form-fitting white dress and ski goggle sunglasses made her look like a winter Bond villain, which was amplified by her complete disregard to our presence in the room. Our appearance, let alone our proximity to her, made us impossible to miss in the front row and she didn't even look in our direction. I had a sick feeling in my stomach that things were about to get very bad.

Just as he opened the binder to read the first page, a piercing bright light swept the room as we heard the rear door open in the room. I turned and pulled focus through cracks in the myriad of heads behind us and immediately recognized the face. *Angie.* I whipped my head back around and slouched down in my seat a bit. There was no need for a second glance for a decade's worth of pent up anxiety had seared a perfect high definition picture of every light particle and wave from that moment into my brain. With my eyes closed, I picked apart every pixel and every feature one by one. Minus the new fancy suit, hairstyle and approximately six new freckles on her right cheek, she was for all intents and purposes, the same. *Perfect.* When he began reading his opening statement, I figured she had found a seat in the back. The feelings of doom and anxiety re-emerged in my stomach and sweat seeped through my palms and back forcing me to unzip my hoodie for some ventilation. Murphy's law dictated this was going to take forever. *I already had sweat stains. *gulp**

One by one, Mr. Lucas called people from the back and proclaimed Tom's final wishes and issued a claim ticket to pick up their bequeathed items from the back room, until all that remained in the room was our front row, Angie, Evelyn and Mr. Lucas. Any pretense of camouflage had faded. I felt exposed yet resisted the urge to steal additional glances. He motioned for Angie to come to the front of the room. Instinctively, my head turned and took in another peek of her walking up the aisle to memory when our eyes met. *She saw me.* She sat down and settled her jacket. It was like she didn't even recognize me, like she didn't even care. My heart further sank into my stomach when she popped her head back around and shot me a quick silly cross-eyed tongue face. It startled me, but then I saw the faintest resemblance of her smirk. Weathered and broken shards of my heart resonated at a distantly familiar frequency, and for a moment, I felt a spark of something resembling joy that warmed my hollowed core of pain, regret and sadness. Mr. Lucas broke the silence with a loud throat-clearing rumble.

"There isn't much left to say here that you don't already know. A great man has passed. He spoke of each of you often and had something special in mind for you. When I call your name, I will read a brief statement from Misterrr Andersson ..." *This guy WAS Agent Smith!* "to you. ... Please remain in your seats. After I'm finished reading the statements, I will play a small video that he wanted you all to see. Once complete, you may adjourn to the back to retrieve your itemzzz."

Deep down I imagined that he was trying to show some form of emotion, but his demeanor and the way he sustained his trailing s's when he spoke made him seem more of a British humanoid automaton masquerading as a sophisticated small-town lawyer: cold, calculated and measured with a misplaced accent. I could see why Tom would want him for a lawyer. When it came to legal matters, Tom didn't like to mess around, and I doubt anyone would question this man's credibility or commitment as an executor. I felt like I was a stuffed plush doll sitting in a twisted claw machine game that always paid out, and this man was the maestro on the joystick orchestrating every win with emotionless efficiency, determined to clear the machine of every last prize.

"Ms. Angela Swanson. I leave to you our favorite 10-key calculator. Mr. Wade Bodin. I leave you an antique hand-crank coffee grinder. Mr. Patrick Luft. I leave to you this Shawshank Redemption poster signed by Tim Robbins and Morgan Freeman. Ms. Antonella Vega. I leave to you my limited-edition Employee Beanie Baby Bear. Mr. Benjamin Wilson. I leave to you my personal computer and all its data." Mr. Lucas rattled off the statements with precision, unphased at just how fast he breezed over any sentiment that might exist between the words he just read and their intended audience. "For the record," he continued, "this final item was added six months ago and was witnessed by me and a third-party notary. Ms. Morgan Brooks. Tom leaves you his soldering station and car lamp."

The room was a tearful mess. Anto went and sat by Angie and they were crying and hugging, while Patty, Wade and I did our best attempts to play it cool and ignore the waterworks leaking from our distressed eyes. *Perhaps it was better that this guy had no emotion.* Evelyn, on the other hand, seemed to be just fine. If anything, she seemed impatient as she rapped her fingers on her chair's armrest.

"Ms. Evelyn Bates-Andersson. As the sole heir, you shall inherit the sum of Mr. Andersson's estate and holdings pursuant to Texas State law."

Evelyn's smile was long, wide and almost sinister. Her sunglasses covered her eyes, but I could swear I could feel her stare piercing my chest. Every red flag was on high alert, as the fate of the shop started to become clear.

"And for our final act of business for the day," Mr. Lucas exclaimed over the rustling in the room, "... the Hot Shots Family Trust." *Wait, what?* "For the record, the Hot Shots Family Trust was formed on April 21st, 2006, by Tom, me and a third-party notary. Its holdings include all building structures, material assets, land and financial accounts that comprise Andersson Electronics and its affiliated subsidiaries including Tom-NET and Tom-NET Web Services. As the legal executor of this trust, I have been instructed to play this tape prior to announcing disbursement of these assets."

I was befuddled, but more importantly, so was Evelyn. It was an emotional street-fight inside my head where fear and anxiety had beaten hope and joy within an inch of their existence, but I knew this wasn't a coincidence. *What did you do, Tom?*

*** FADE ***

I knew the answer to my own question. My body may still be impaired, but this chaotic catharsis had my brain quickly untangling a web of scattered thoughts and mental deadlocks. Don't open your eyes, Ben! Keep playing this out. You were there. Maybe there is something you missed. You watched that video so many times, you damn near have his speech memorized. Think Ben. Think!

*** FADE ***

With sloth-like speed, the lawyer meticulously removed a DVD from his briefcase and turned on the TV prepping it for playback. When the video started, it was Tom sitting in his

Corvette's driver seat, arm up pretending to be driving and talking at the camera in his classic infomercial tone. *What a cheeseball!*

"Hey there, fellow Hot Shots! If you are watching this, then chances are that I am dead, incapacitated or have fled the country never to be heard from again." Tom had the happiest smile on his face, which made watching the video tolerable. "There's no easy way for me to say this, so I'm just going to say it. Angie, Wade, Patty, Anto, Morgan and Ben ... you have been the best family anyone could ask for, and the best damn trivia teammates I know. Speaking of which, I know our trivia tournament last month came up a bit short, but I believe we'll eventually do it. Hopefully, there's already a plaque or two hanging on the shop walls by the time you watch this tape ..." He realized he was drifting off topic and put on his best serious face. "Before Evelyn and I get married, I want to make sure that you all have a chance to do something special if I'm ever not around: a chance to keep the Hot Shots family together. If that's what you all still want."

Evelyn removed her glasses and her eyes were beaded up like a mad faced squirrel who just lost their winter nut hoard.

"I've had a dream for some time now to figure out a way to turn Andersson Electronics and Tom-NET into a million-dollar business ..." *The talk at the hospital.* "... and the Hot Shots were going to be how I did that. So, here's your chance. The challenge, whether you choose to accept it or not, starts today. Ben is the owner and operator of all things Andersson Electronics and Tom-NET. You will have one hundred days to deposit at-least $250,000 into the corporate bank account. That is one quarter of a million dollars. If you succeed, everything related to the shop will be retained by the trust with Ben as the executor. Plus, each of you will receive a $25,000 dollars bonus for a job well done. If you decide you don't want to accept this challenge, or if you fail, the trust will transfer ownership of all assets to Evelyn and each of you will still receive $25,000 as a token of my deep appreciation for all the hard work you have done for me over the years."

Leave it to Tom to make his final wishes a game. Before my mind could get too far down the road of figuring out shortcuts to his challenge, Tom continued on.

"There are a few rules though. First and foremost, you cannot sell the land or the building. You may use the land, building and the resources therein as you see fit, but at the end of one hundred days, the shop must be able to function at-least in the same capacity in which you received it. You may not take out a loan or other temporary measures to cook the books. All money must be a product of your teamwork and related to the shop." *Damn, there goes three ideas!*

Tom paused for a moment. It was clear the nature of the video was getting to him. He cleared his throat and made his final remarks.

"This is an opportunity for each of you to build something great together. I hope each of you accept the challenge with open minds and open arms, and not listen to Ben when he tries to find loopholes." Tom chuckled. "When the Hot Shots work as a team, they can accomplish anything. ... I truly believe that. ... I love you all ... Make me proud."

Tom closed the video with a tearful wink and then proceeded to fumble with the hidden camera remote to stop the recording. The lawyer turned off the TV and the gravity of the situation began its slow press on my shoulders. I could hear the whispers to my left from the rest of the crew, but to my right was nothing. Evelyn was sitting in her chair hunched over with a scowl on her face. Her eyes were dancing in their sockets as if she was slapping gnats with her retinas. *Is she, OK?*

Mr. Lucas chimed in with his monotone expression.

"Mr. Wilson. It is my duty as the executor of the Hot Shots Family Trust to ask you. Do you wish to accept Mr. Andersson's proposal?"

I looked to my friends, and then to Angie. Every one of them were staring back in wide eyed anticipation. There wasn't a doubt in my mind. Even though I had no idea what I was going to do, or how I was going to do it, I felt confident and empowered. Tom's video had hope standing firmly on two legs again, having just knocked fear and anxiety to the mat.

"I do." I replied.

"Then it is my duty to inform you that your current balance in the bank account is $24,843.19 cents. By the close of business, 100 days from now, which is April 15th, the balance of the account must be $274,843.19 or more to retain control of the trust. For the sake of this challenge, all existing operating costs for the next one hundred days will be paid for by the trust.

Good luck, Mr. Wilson." Just as emotionless as he began, he closed his binder and placed some loose papers back into his briefcase. Evelyn burst from her chair and pulled him aside, furiously whispering at him while indignantly darting her finger with rapier like precision into his chest. We couldn't hear what they said, but Evelyn was enraged. He, on the other hand, was not phased. She picked up her purse and shot me a murderous glare as she stormed out of the room slamming the door so hard that it rattled the suspended ceiling panels above. I was not looking forward to my next conversation with her. Something was definitely awry, and I wasn't the only one who noticed. Morgan looked me straight in the eye with a deadpan stare and mouthed three very clear words, "She ... killed ... him", as she pretended to stab the palm of her hand with a pencil. For now, accusations were going to have to wait. The clock was ticking, and as Tom would say, "We had work to do!"

We all collected our items from the backroom and proceeded back to the shop. Wade called shotgun in Angie's convertible Mustang rental and buckled himself in before our eyes could adjust to the sunlight. Meanwhile, Anto was stuck lugging the rest of us back with our possessions in tow. I sat in the back rear-facing seat with Tom's PC mini tower cradled in my lap. Angie drove behind us with her hair blowing in the wind. She was laughing at Wade as he stuck his hands out above the windshield screaming at the top of his lungs. *Her smile!* We pulled into the shop parking lot and unloaded our chaos. There were a few customers waiting in the parking lot, but they were mainly gossipers. Patty and Anto took care of opening the shop, while Wade started up Marge for some afternoon caffeine. Angie hung back in her car with her hands on the steering wheel and engine off.

"Aren't you going to come in?" I asked her. I recognized the conflicted expression on her face, mine was probably no different, but I knew that if we were to have any chance at pulling this off, I'd need at-least a sliver of Angie's genius, if not all of it. So, I took the first step at an olive branch.

"Come on. I bet Wade is whipping up some amazing coffee right now, and I can give you a tour of the new place. It's changed quite a bit since you were here last."

She didn't budge. I knew I was going to have to play dirty. Mr. and Mrs. Hartford were among the people in the parking lot waiting for us to open. Despite the fact that I had only ever seen them buy a single item in the past eight years, *a one-dollar clearance mousepad,* they were loyal Tom-NET customers, but most importantly, they were also the presumed epicenter of the Jollyville rumor mill. There wasn't a piece of gossip in town they didn't know or create themselves based on the slimmest margins of fact or pure speculation. A conversation with them was guaranteed to occupy your time for at least an hour as they meticulously parsed every word, breath and micro expression like seasoned intelligence operatives. Angie knew this, too.

"Mr. and Mrs. Hartford. It's good to see you." I called out. "Did you see that Angie Swanson is back in town? And look, she's driving a convertible!"

Less than four seconds later, Angie was holding the shop door open for me with a not so impressed look on her face urging me to get indoors. I set Tom's PC down at one of the Community Corner tables, and she slugged me in the side of the arm. It was just like old times, except we both had more professional attire. *If you call wrinkle-free polo shirts and shorts, professional.*

"I guess I deserved that." he said.

"You did." Angie walked in, sat in her normal spot at the Community Corner and inventoried all the changes from a familiar vantage point.

"I could give you a tour, if you'd like?" Her response was muted and indifferent like her mind was focused on something else. It looked like she was fidgeting with her hands under the table but seemed agreeable to the proposal. She then followed me to the backroom with her hands clasped behind her back, as if she was hesitant to touch anything. We picked up our coffee at Tom's old office where Wade was busy cleaning the fogged windows that him and Marge made. I opened the doors to the back room and slipped into my best "Museum of Tom" curator persona. Tom had a bunch of junk back there, most of which I helped move in, but he always placed his proudest possessions within eyeshot of the door, which made for a pretty interesting and extensive tour of randomness. His lengthy collection of Americana extended to many sub-collections of glass gas pumps, metal signs and streetlights that made it feel like we were walking down the real Route 66 under a large tin covered boardwalk. The fear of that awkward silence had me rambling non-stop facts and related stories about anything I saw, and it worked.

An hour later we completed the warehouse tour having taken a stroll down memory lane that covered the better part of the last decade. She talked about her time at Stanford a lot, and the Palo Alto culture that nearly drove her to madness, until it helped land a job at her law firm defending intellectual property rights for startups. When she talked about living her dream, I expected her to be wide-eyed and excited, but there was a hollow tone that permeated her voice. Her stories about college and her job spoke very little of friends, or even people at all. *No mention of a boyfriend.* The only people mentioned were her parents, who moved to live with her grandmother because they didn't believe in nursing homes. It was a natural segue to talk about parents up and leaving, and I told her about Mom and Phil.

"And that's when Tom let me move in here." I pointed up to Tom's old apartment.

"I was going to ask about that," she chuckled. "I noticed all the stickers on the door and wondered if Tom had turned that into a game room or something. Makes sense, now."

We continued our tour out of the backroom and showed her the Community Classroom space. Morgan was sitting at the front of the room with Tom's soldering kit staring off into space. We snuck out the back and I gave Angie the low down on Morgan, and how she, and her unique personality, made their way into the family. Hearing myself say the words out loud, I definitely had a sense of affection for Morgan. I couldn't quite label the feeling, but I knew that keeping her close was the right thing to do, especially now. Up until this moment, with Angie standing next to me, I had no idea just how strong my feelings were for both of them, and yet different in their own right. The tour around the shop ended at Patty's and my desks where all the Tom-NET Web Service magic happened.

My desk was a ransacked mess with the desk trinkets losing a righteous battle against crumpled design sketches, empty ramen cups and scattered pens and pencils. I started to show her some mockups of a site that Patty and I were working on when an alarm on my computer made a familiar *ding*. I looked at my watch and caught the time. *Time to eat.* That moment of awkward silence I spent the last hour trying to avoid arrived like a freight train, and I froze.

"Everything, okay there, Ben?" She asked perplexedly.

My mind raced on ways to explain what was about to go down. *I could ignore it. What would be the harm in missing just one meal? It wouldn't be the first time!* I ranked every possible tactic and outcome, which led me to calmly offer an explanation.

"Yeah, everything's fine. Just forgot to do something is all." I leaned over my monitor and started pointing out details of new site designs on the printouts, trying to misdirect attention away from my left hand, which was reaching around the opposite side of the monitor for the familiar wall hook. I blindly traced my fingers down the keychain and found the trio buttons pressed the sequence to feed Benji. *beep* *beepbeep* *beepbeep* *beep* *Damnit!* Angie's head quickly pivoted and noticed me hugging my monitor.

"What was that?" she asked, but she didn't need me to answer. "Is that ..."

Before she could complete her question, I picked Benji up from his hook, and cradled the digital pet in my hand to give him some fresh air

"Yep, it's Benji." I handed the little pocket monster to her. "It was time for him to eat." I tried to laugh off the moment. I didn't think I could feel more embarrassed, or stupid.

"You mean, it was time for HER to eat" she replied with a laugh. She rubbed her thumb over the case and pressed Benji's buttons to release a toy. After a bit of inspection, she raised her head with a questioning look. "97 years? The best I ever got was 31!"

I grabbed Benji from her hand and roughly cradled him in mine.

"I kept HIM alive for 97 years this time. My record is 102, but sometimes HE gets fussy."

Angie was suspicious and became extremely inquisitive.

"So, how'd you do it? You cheated somehow, I bet?" She took Benji back into her hands looked for signs of tampering.

"I don't consider what I did cheating. It was more of a long drawn-out science experiment. At first, I couldn't keep him alive for more than a few days, but when everything I thought I knew how to do wasn't working, I tried a new approach. I started trying each function on its own ... letting him die over and over and over again, until I figured out the right combination of tasks and timing. In a way, you could say I reverse engineered Benji. You might call that cheating, but I call it quality child raising, except for the repeated death part."

I realized just how insane it all sounded. How much time and over how many years had I spent caring for this nonsensical toy? It had been going on for so long, it hardly felt like work. It was as instinctive as breathing. I expected Angie to come back with a retort that would poke holes in my defense and make fun of the gesture, but instead she took a step towards me and looked at our little Benji resting in my hand. She wrapped her hands around my outstretched hand and our eyes connected for a fraction of a second, and with the warmest smile, she said "You did a great job taking care of HER, Ben." *Who was I kidding? She was right.*

In that moment, layers of permafrost melted from my abandoned heart and I forgot the negative thoughts and doubts swirling in my head about the future. An unfamiliar and distant sense of hope and warmth began to fill my body, and I knew that whatever path was in front of me, that I wanted Angie to be a part of it. My head spun with thoughts for the future untainted with cynicism and skepticism. *beepbeep* The irony of our digital progeny defecating during my first real glimpses of happiness in recent history was not lost on me. Angie pulled her hands away from mine and pretended to take a whiff.

"Awwww, I think she pooped," she said while starting to walk away. "Best wash your hands!" *Her laugh was infectious.*

I took care of Benji's sanitary needs, placed her back on the wall and proceeded to take Tom's PC from the Community Corner upstairs to the apartment. You wouldn't know it by the dingy yellowing cream-colored eyesore of a case, but every internal component had been upgraded on a regular basis. Dual SATA SSDs. 8GB of RAM. The works! I knew that if I just set it in the closet, I would forget about it in less than a week. I wasn't quite ready to lose sight of Tom just yet, and this way at-least a part of him would be there for me. I grabbed a black Sharpie and wrote "T.O.M", in my best W.O.P.R worthy font, on the blank case faceplate and claimed another step forward for the day. I was tempted to boot it up and play a game of Minesweeper, but I knew I was going to need to clean the case out before turning it on. There was already a faint smell of pot coming from the dust in the power supply, and it wouldn't mix well with my uniquely crafted scent of "single dude with questionable hygiene" that permeated my apartment walls. Besides, I needed to get downstairs, back to Angie and the business of figuring out how to raise a quarter of a million dollars in one hundred days.

FEATURED TRACK:

Republica – Out Of The Darkness

18
Trial by Fire

It had been some time since I felt such confidence to pursue a new endeavor, and yet I had absolutely no reason to justify the feeling. Ambition. Drive. Passion. These weren't aspiring goals I was used to. These were snarky posters in the making with me as the target of ridicule. My motivation laid dormant under extensive well-cultivated layers of boredom, distraction, predictability and complacency. Every emotion I felt from the moment of Tom's death; the anger, the sadness, the frustration, the love, the fear, it all eviscerated my self-induced coma and my mind was awakened. Every cerebral synapse, every nerve ending, and every rusted creative conduit resonated with energy like a neglected race car sputtering at the start line about to recklessly tear down the track without any regard for safety. With each jolting surge, flashes of my cocky arrogant younger self interwoven with less attractive visages of the harsh reality that lay before me came to bear. I was not Tom. I would never be Tom, and I would need to figure out a way to fake it until I figured things out. Thankfully, that was my specialty. *I think Tom was counting on that.*

I turned out the lights to the apartment and collected my thoughts as I headed down to the shop. *First things first, build your team.* I swung by the breakroom and grabbed the rolling

Pictionary whiteboard and lugged it clumsily down the stairs and onto the shop floor. The commotion froze all conversation, including Patty who was on a tech support call. I grabbed the red marker and wrote a simple message in the upper right-hand corner of the board in big bold letters.

100 Days Left

"OK, guys. You heard what Tom said. If we can find a way to turn the dials on the shop's revenue in the next hundred days, we'll own it out right. I know that the video says that I'll get it, but I'll make this promise to you here and now, that if we pull this off, we will all get equal shares. I don't care about the money. I just don't want Tom's legacy falling into Evelyn's hands."

At the mention of defying Evelyn, Morgan slammed her hands on her table of solitude and turned to join the rest of us. I had never seen Morgan cry before. Her usual steel-cut stare was softened by smeared eyeliner, but her bloodshot eyes radiated an aura of manic rage from obsessing over every means, motive and opportunity imaginable to pierce any alibi Evelyn could concoct. There was no convincing her otherwise, to her, Evelyn killed Tom.

"We can't focus on the past and what-if's right now," I interjected before Morgan could pivot the entire conversation into conspiracy theory theater. "Tom is dead, and it sucks. I hate saying that as much as you hate hearing it. But we have two options in front of us. We can tap out now and take the quick payday. Or, we can go big, together, and see just how far we can take Tom's dream before it's over. Whatever we do, we do it together, as a family, just as Tom wanted. What'll it be?"

Impromptu speaking was never my specialty, but this was ignited raw passion willing me and others to get on board with Tom's wishes. I was not willing to let this freshly revived spark of happiness go without a fight. It wasn't the 1980's slow clap I felt I deserved, but I saw a wave of heads nodding "Yes" as I panned over everyone looking them each in the eye. *Anto?* Yes. *Wade?* Yes. *Patty?* Yes. *Mr. and Mrs. Hartford.* Yes. *Angie? Where was Angie?* She must have just slipped away when Morgan entered the room, because she was sitting in her spot in the Community Corner with her back to the rest of us.

"Alrighty then. We need ideas. Every idea you've ever pitched to Tom, no matter how crazy, or impractical, we need to write on this board. Let's take fifteen minutes, and then we can walk through and see where we stand. Each of you take a color"

I tossed the box of markers to Wade to hand out, and then headed over to check on Angie. Her hands were folded in her lap under the table, and she was looking out her normal window.

"You OK?" I asked her. "I mean … I know that's an overloaded question right now, but just wanted to see how you were doing."

"Oh, I'm fine, I guess," she said. "I never thought in a million years Tom would be gone so soon, and so much has changed. It's just a lot to take in." She dabbed her eyes with a handkerchief but kept her back to me.

"Yeah, I know. I can only imagine how you might be feeling right now. I've at least had a week to process some of this crazy … … which brings me to the topic at hand." I knew what I needed to ask, but I was stumbling over my thoughts to spit out even a single coherent word. We had yet to discuss the elephant in the room, and here I was about to ask for an immense favor. "We need you." *I need you.* "There is no way we can do this without you. I am scared of what might happen if we don't get this right, and we need all the help we can get. You are the smartest, most capable person I know. You bring out the best in the people around you, including me. If we are going to even have a shot at pulling this off, we need …"

My mind stopped short, unable to complete the sentence. A lengthy series of rogue truths fled my hypothalamus and were being dispersed unconsciously leaving my brain in the dust trying to catch up. It felt like an egregious overshare on a first date, and my sense of preservation stepped in to regulate my remaining words.

"… the valedictorian of Berkeley."

She finally turned to face me. Her face was flushed, and I could see glassy pools welling up in her eyes and glistening tear trails down her right cheek.

"All the things you say are true. I don't think you can do this without me, but I have a job. I have a life. I can't just drop everything for three months to come out here and play shop because Tom's last wishes said so …"

My heart sank further with each syllable she uttered, but then her words started to trail off, like her brain pulled the emergency brake on her train of thought. I could see her mind grinding through something, and then she pulled out her Blackberry. Her thumbs flew as she clicked the keyboard into submission and rubbed the pearl with expert speed and precision. A few awkward minutes later, her head rose from her phone with focused dry eyes.

"I'm in." she said.

What just happened? "What about your job?"

"I just submitted an FMLA extension to my current bereavement leave. Tom's last wishes should be more than enough to justify the request, which means I've got three months to figure things out. So, let's not waste another minute."

We headed back to a group of chuckleheads who were in tears for a different reason. Angie and I looked over the rainbow collection of ideas on the board. Many of them were promising; however, it was evident when the idea pool degraded into the realm of ridiculous. Judging by the color of ink, and her inability to keep a straight face, I had Anto to thank for it.

"Alright. Not a bad first attempt. I see some good ideas worth discussing more ... does anyone have any thoughts on how to start making Teeth Whitening Suppositories or Artificial Replacement Taints?"

The room exploded in another wave of laughter as the Hartford's, who were still busy pseudo-shopping, looked on in confusion. I couldn't help but join them in the ridiculousness. After we had our long overdue laugh, we talked through the initial list and divided practical ideas into two groups to dig in deeper: Physical Improvements and Online Improvements.

At the top of the physical improvements list was Wade's idea to add coffee as an official offering. His idea was to brew large self-serve urns of coffee for regular drinkers and use Marge to craft his own specialty coffee drinks. The best part, he already had all the connections in town he needed to get going fast. Overall the idea was straight-forward and solid, but by Angie's calculations it was going to be hard to make a dent in our goal without some way to charge more. She proposed accelerating revenue by offering a pre-paid coffee membership that would give the customers one free cup of coffee per day and discounted specialty drinks for the next three months. By her calculations, once we got our food handlers permit, the business would easily pull in an extra $50,000 over the next three months, which would more than cover any new expenses. *Thankfully Tom specified revenue, and not profit. Loophole #1.* It was a start.

Foot traffic was still a concern. Quality businesses in our part of town were fading fast, leaving our shop as one of the main attractions, minus the courthouse. Unless there was a systemic plague of parking tickets about to hit our town, it was going to be hard to find something unique and universally liked enough, besides coffee, to get customers to leave the growing modern brand convenience that big box developers were building on the other end of town near the interstate. We discussed the Community Classroom model that was responsible for our last big surge in foot traffic and came to the conclusion that the model would work for our layout, as well. Morgan volunteered to MacGuyver a quick inventory system with an online store interface that customers could browse from home, or the Community Corner. All the physical products, display cases and shelving would be moved to the back room freeing up the space to make it more versatile. The idea was to recreate a mini antique mall-like feel that invited local businesses to come and fill the space with their products on a daily basis, bringing their customers and general buzz to the shop. I looked around for the Hartfords, as getting the word out about this type of thing was right up their alley, but they had already left, no doubt doing exactly what we wanted them to do.

Wade brewed up a special pot of coffee, and we took a break from brainstorming. Patty and I round-robined the support lines, which like the shop, were not seeing much action. On a normal day, someone from behind the counter would pull a card from the mega-deck dispenser and kick off a game of Hot Shot Trivia, but our focus was clear and the excitement of the unknown ahead, coupled with the caffeine from Wade's coffee, had us itching with anticipation. It was time to talk about online improvements.

Morgan's online inventory viewer was a serendipitously great start to this conversation, but we needed to drive more business. Patty and I had some new site design templates we were sitting on to start promoting for new upgrades, but the reality was that it would be hard to accelerate that business enough in only three months. We were resource constrained on our end and customers were rarely ready on time. Advertising seemed appropriate, but what to sell? What to promote? We were a small town, and with the likes of Amazon offering products online for cheaper, with no tax and free shipping, it was going to be difficult to create a compelling offer. We needed something unique. Something that couldn't be bought elsewhere, something that people wanted and wouldn't mind the inconvenience of a small business to get. My mind immediately jumped back to our previous conversations about antique malls and how we modeled the rotating layout around them. *Antiques.*

The idea felt taboo the moment it crossed my mind, but the more I thought about it, the more things fell into place. The antiques were going to be sold one way or another, why not sell them on our own terms. Hell, even Tom sold some of them to pay for the Community Classroom expansion. We just agreed to remodel everything in the image of an antique mall. Why not become one?

"What if we sell Tom's antiques?" I blurted out.

I couldn't hold the concept back any longer. Too many ideas were compounding on this one premise, and it needed to be shared. As expected, the room went quiet, unsure if I was poorly joking or being serious and insensitive.

"Hear me out, OK? Fast forward three months from now, what happens to this place if we don't succeed? Chances are it is closed down, and everything here is sold off, including the antiques. If we sell them, we have a chance at doing right by Tom in the end and the shop. Think about it. We have an antique warehouse back there. We can take pictures of everything and share them with Morgan's online store. If they want to come take a look at a piece, they'll have to come to the shop to check it out." Morgan's ears perked up at the new requirements for our online store, but so did Patty's.

"What if we did a YouTube channel? … We could do some QVC style videos for the bigger items, or feature stalls of the day and just talk about all that we find. Anto could be our on-air personality. She was really popular on our Shoutcast station. Besides, she practically remembers everything Tom has told her about all that stuff back there."

Anto didn't waste any time responding. "Oh no you don't," she said. "I see what you are doing. Trying to weasel out of being on camera. You want this to happen, you are going to have to drag your shy butt on camera with me!" Patty's intrigue quickly pivoted to dread. "You know you want to get on camera," she clarified. "Remember, the Shoutcast listeners liked you too once you loosened up." She gave his shoulders a friendly squeeze, and said "Besides, they'll be listening to me most of the time." We took Patty's face turning bright red as a sign that he was in.

This might work. The ideas all seemed to flow together. We didn't need to plan a lifelong business, just something that would last three months and hope the wheels didn't fall off in the process. Everyone stayed late that evening to celebrate Angie's prolonged return to town. We ate pizza, told stories and played Hot Shot Trivia until the card dispenser went dry. I ushered everyone out the front door and locked up. Before turning out the lights in the backroom, I took a moment to re-survey the warehouse. I felt like I was Mikey looking at One-Eyed Willie's treasure map. It wasn't only about the money. It was the sense of adventure that was just around the corner, an adventure where our outcast crew were in a unique position to win. For the first time in a long time, I nodded off to sleep in my room amused by the demotivating rhetoric plastered on my walls. Not because I bought into their jaded perception of reality, but because I could feel the winds of change slowly opening windows of opportunity, and off in the far distance was a glimmer of hope.

A mad flurry of chaos ensued the following day, as everyone was busy helping each other get their projects off the ground. It seemed that every other hour, Wade or Anto were heading off to the hardware store to pick up another thing they forgot. They were making a separate order counter for the coffee shop and a sign to put on the building roof, but you would have thought they were the A-Team constructing a makeshift RPG launching Trojan horse out of a dumpster and spare car parts. Thankfully, Tom was nothing shy of resourceful and had an entire workshop of tools in the back. They banged, clanged, zipped and whirred their own Revenge of the Nerds renovation montage that culminated in a stable countertop that fit the space perfectly. They used the sign board facia to hide their less than flush cuts and numerous failed attempts to connect the counter wall to a stubborn metal stud. Anto designed the counter sign that matched the roof design to a tee. It read, "Anderson Electronics & Coffee" with the roof sign being just an addendum "& Coffee" that was secured in place with no less than forty zip ties and some rope to the existing light board. Our addendum sign had three-dimensional style graffiti art drawn on a thick piece of plywood with small holes drilled around the lettering and we used Tom's wedding Christmas lights to accentuate it at night. *Something old, plus something new. Perfect.*

  For all the technology we sold, Tom was an ardent believer in hard copy and rarely used computers for accounting purposes. This posed a problem for Angie who was all about digital everything. She spent a few days trying to make sense of Tom's chaotic and arcane accounting practices, until she decided to just spin up a new digital system and pay someone at the end to reconcile everything. As if her adventures in hard copy land were not daunting enough, nothing could have prepared her for the application process for a food handler's permit in the city of Jollyville, not even Stanford. Dysfunctional. Repetitive, No Common Sense. Bass-Ackwards. Carbon Copy Hell. Those were the words she used to describe the ordeal. I had never seen anyone meticulously obsess more about how to improve a process, rather than just get it done and move on. To her credit, she used the disconnected chaos to her advantage, and convinced them to provide a one-off provisional thirty-day permit that would cover the shop until they got their affairs in order. The coffee shop was ready for paying customers faster than expected. Even though she triumphed, I sensed that she was questioning her decision to stay.

  Both Morgan and Patty were glued to their respective computers, while I jumped between projects and ran the day-to-day shop operations. Morgan was heads down building a quick inventory management solution that would integrate with the current Tom-NET site. This was my first exposure to AWS. Had it been Patty or myself, we would have simply added a new server and hosted the solution ourselves, but Morgan was convinced that EC2 and S3 would make for a better solution. I thought it was overkill, but I learned early on that if Morgan wants to do something, it made no sense in getting in the way, especially when it came to technology. Besides, it was nice to see her focus on something other than Evelyn conspiracy theories for a change. Patty was busy juggling the website changes for her new inventory section, designing intro music and bumpers for YouTube and updating all the site logos with the new "& Coffee" variant. They grunted and groaned when I reminded them both to take breaks for food, water and bathroom like they were two life-size Tamagotchis. I placed a set of sticky notes in the Tamagotchi button pattern on the back of their chairs just to drive home the point. Angie thought it was hilarious how Morgan and Patty played along with the theme.

Less than one week after accepting Tom's challenge, Andersson Electronics & Coffee was up and running. We held a launch party to celebrate the progress. Wade's coffee section looked top notch and his white board menu, price points and membership flyers were ready to go. Invites were sent to local businesses to share the new flexible space, and while we waited for responses, we backfilled the tables with freshly staged antiques from the warehouse. This was the backdrop used in pictures to launch the Andersson Antiques YouTube channel, which also launched that week. In the meantime, Anto and Patty were busy inventorying all the items with descriptions and pictures to load into the new website for customers to browse. It was going to be a while before they were finished, so they started with some of the easier high-profile items that would attract the most people, and which they had the most knowledge about from Tom's stories. I held off on listing Tom's Corvette on the site. A part of me still felt guilty for selling off his collection one by one; however, I wasn't ready to part with a piece that had so many integral memories tied to it. *Never.*

As we all toasted the moment with one of Wade's latest caffeinated creations, slated to be unveiled the next day, we noticed there was one extra cup. Morgan's laptop was missing, but more importantly, so was she. It wasn't like her to just up and leave unannounced. Over the years, she had become quite the over sharer, frequently exclaiming things like, "I'm heading to the bathroom!" out of the blue without any reservation, or fluctuation in tone. Just a straight-forward dead pan declaration of fact that always added comic relief to the day, and yet today, nothing. We were so busy on so many different things that I really hadn't had a chance to talk with her to see how she was holding up, but we would all find out soon enough.

FEATURED TRACK

Alice In Chains – No Excuses

19
Adding Insult to Injury

The Hartfords were consummate professionals in their craft, and word travelled fast through town without having to worry about advertising. Visitors stopped by from all parts of town to see if the rumors of Andersson Electronics adding a coffee bar and antique barn were true. Each new customer was promptly greeted by Angie or me and the changes explained at length. The Community Corner had never been so busy, or loud. Huddled masses of squinting blue haired senior citizens jockeyed for control of each mouse and keyboard. Each one confident their computer skills were superior to the others, and each one spectacularly failing in hearing, vision or aptitude, sending the group into never-ending loops of "Whaaaat?"s, "Try Right Clicking"s and "Let Me Try"s. It was madness, but it kept the shop busy and money flowing, especially at the coffee bar.

Nothing could have prepared Wade for what he was about to experience. His entire adult life had been spent experimenting with coffee, but he had never experienced the demanding pressure a barista feels when customer orders begin to pile up. He was fine the first few days, taking time to talk to each customer and educate them on some of the cool facts about their coffee. Angie came up with a three-month prepaid coffee subscription and they were an instant hit, especially with the elderly crowd, who were immediately drawn to deals that offered them any regular activity away from the house. It didn't take long for Wade to realize that they weren't physically able to appreciate his thoughtful informed coffee experience, either because they couldn't hear his explanations from across the counter or their taste buds were dead as doornails. This army of caffeine craving elderly zombies could religiously drain a full five-gallon urn in the first hour, which meant he had to brew twice as much in the morning just to get ahead. He begrudgingly decided to brew one vat of Folgers each morning, and the other was his uniquely selected pick of the week. No one seemed to notice when he switched between the two. Word was getting around that Andersson Electronics & Coffee was the happening place to be for your morning cup of joe, and things were heating up for Wade.

Meanwhile, Patty and Anto were busy filming their first pilot video for YouTube and despite all their progress to date, they were running into some struggles. They had their mini-DV camera with a small boom mic mounted on a tripod and recorded them talking in front of one of the stalls in the warehouse. Patty wrote out a loose script for them to follow that guided them around the entire stall with some key pieces of information about every item in an orderly fashion. Scripts weren't exactly Anto's specialty. She was more of a free talking energetic type and this made him uncomfortable on camera and it showed. He frequently forgot his own script, and fumbled words trying to recite facts about the various pieces. It was a tempo tug of war and Anto was dragging him through the mud pit. At one point, Patty considered giving up his on-camera presence and sticking to behind the scenes, but Anto wasn't having it. If I didn't see this on the outtakes, I would have never believed it.

"You want to know what your problem is Patty?" said Anto. "You're too stiff. You need to loosen up! Just be your normal quirky self. If you are comfortable, the audience will figure it out. Come here."

Anto pulled Patty aside by the shirt collar and gave him a quick kiss on the lips, which almost made Patty's head explode like mercury in a thermometer. Anto then spun him around and smacked him on the ass.

"Now, go put in a new tape and let's just talk like we always do. Burn that script while you are it. If you want to talk about facts, write 'em down on a card or something. No one is going to care if you don't know them off the top of your head, but everyone will stop watching if you don't pick up the energy!"

The next take started off slow but quickly became a thing of magic and the template for future videos. After they did a quick welcome blurb, they just had a conversation. They took turns retreating into the stall and bringing out different antiques and they just talked about them. They weren't antique experts. In most cases, they were just comments remembered from conversations with Tom, but Anto's genius was in her presentation. Even if she didn't know anything about the item, she found something to say, such as how Tom acquired it, what she thought it might be or even something as simple as how it made her feel. Once they got into a groove, they were very entertaining to watch playing off each other. There was no such thing as a retake, and the video editing work dropped exponentially since each video was a one-shot masterpiece. It didn't take long for the YouTube community at large to latch onto their shows. The likes started to roll in, along with the army of internet trolls in the video comments, but so did the orders. Andersson Electronics' Antique YouTube channel was off to a good start.

Foot traffic was on the rise as people continued to pour into the shop. Small businesses began to bicker with each other over days of the week to be a part of the new Andersson Electronics & Coffee shopping experience. The insurgence of a more diverse crowd had a profound impact on Wade's coffee stand and Marge was getting a steady workout. What started as mainly pre-brewed coffee sales quickly turned into over fifty percent specialty drinks, which meant that Wade needed to manage the queue of orders. He had seen it done for years at other coffee shops, so he started writing names and orders on the cups and setting them inline. After two or three he would stop taking new orders and start making the drinks. As the traffic continued to increase, Wade's concentration for anything but coffee began to fade. He started not being able to read his own handwriting and orders started to get mixed up. Non-caff lattes and double shot espressos with extra foam packaged in similar cups were transposed and had to be remade, which only slowed the lines down further. Only people who had truly unique orders, such as Wade's favorite tongue twister customer who always ordered a medium half half caff, half half and half half caff cap, could rest assured that they wouldn't get their drinks mixed up. Angie tried to step in and help organize things, but Wade's organization started and stopped with him. He didn't work well in other people's systems, and the outlook for his coffee endeavor was not looking great. Until one day when, instead of asking them for their name, he simply assigned them a code word off the top of his head, such as: "Beaver", "StarScream", "Rocky Road" and "Clydesdale". What started out as people taking small offense to their code word, became a gimmick for people to come back and see how their code word would change across visits. Some people even tried altering their attire to influence a name, but Wade rarely picked the same code word for a person, and he never divulged his secret for selecting them. The moment he started his new system, everything fell back into place just in time for Keith to go and screw things up.

It was the late afternoon on February 1st, when Keith strutted into the shop dragging his imitation machismo like wet toilet paper stuck to the bottom of his faux leather boot. His presence on this side of town was uncommon in part to an unwritten rule that this was Andersson Electronics territory. He would have been less inciteful if he was clanking glass bottles in his hand chanting "Hot Shots, come out and play." He circumnavigated the sales floor with indiscriminate curiosity browsing the local wares and fumbling with some of the Community Classroom flyers until he made his way all the way around to the Community Corner, where Angie and I were chatting with some customers about antiques.

"Like what you've done with the place," he mocked in a condescending tone. "I see that you are finely acknowledging that your computers are antiques. Very down to earth ... very ... small town. It will be a shame when we run you out of business."

"In your dreams, Keith." I responded. "Andersson Electronics is the digital pulse in this town, there is no way they'd let it go for a sleaze ball hack like you." *Contrary to my words, customers said he was quite nice and personable, but that didn't matter, right now.* "Besides, if you haven't noticed ... business is booming." It was true, the shop was packed with people, more so than any other time in the past month.

"Yeah, I can see that. How many of these people are paying Tom-NET customers? Or asking for a website? Or even asking you to buy a computer? From what I can tell, Andersson Electronics has turned itself into a coffee and antique shop." At this point it was obvious he was intentionally projecting his voice like this was his pulpit. "So, when you run out of antiques and people realize they can get a better computer and freshly brewed Keurig at L33tRigz, that is just as good as anything they can get here ...."

BAM ... *CRASH* ... *ra-ra-rat-rat-t-t-tl-tl-tl-tle*

Over at the coffee counter, a coffee pot broke and a small serving tray hit the ground and rattled its way flat on the ground. Wade was holding the handle of the broken coffee pot and pointed the jagged glass pot handle towards Keith, and in no uncertain tone exclaimed, "You shut that dirty Keurig drinking mouth of yours before I shove a tamper down your throat."

His eyes were fixed on Keith while his other hand was noticeably searching the counter in front of him, probably for the closest tamper. I had rarely seen him that angry before, but he had a special place of hatred for Keurig drinkers and this Keurig drinker insulted his coffee. *Double whammy!* Keith's life was saved in that moment no doubt to the fact that Wade's coffee counter was too tall for him to hurdle.

"Ouch .... OK ... OK ... Such hostilityyyyy." Keith started to retreat a bit. Physical violence was apparently not his thing but hitting on women definitely was and that's when he first spotted Angie. She was standing up and bent over helping a customer on the computer and wearing her Andersson name tag. He eyed her body up and down and leaned on the computer monitor next to her.

"Except for you little lady. Angie, is it? You seem all kinds of fiiiine." *I threw up in my mouth a little.* "Name's Keith. I'm the owner of L33tR1gz across town. If you want a job at a real computer company, you should give me a call." He handed her his business card and a cheesy grin. *I envisioned slitting his throat with the broken coffee pot.*

Angie took the card and inspected it quickly and without batting an eye and with the sharpest of tongues responded, "Seems like that money would be better spent on hiring a designer who can make you a company logo that doesn't look like a conga line of neon colored scrotums." *Savage.*

Once she said it, I could not see their logo any other way, and by the look on Keith's face when he took his card back, neither could he. Everyone was laughing or trying not to laugh. He put on his sunglasses and headed for the door, but before he left, he said,

"Just one thing, I wanted to let you know ... no hard feelings for the billboard."

"What billboard?" I asked in a snarky retort.

"You'll see." He looked over his shoulder towards the south end of the parking lot, got on his motorcycle and sped off.

There had been a billboard there ever since I first moved to town, but it was always for the local State Farm agent on both sides. I grabbed my jacket and we walked out to the end of the parking lot to check out the opposite side, and sure enough, there was the L33tR1gz neon logo in all its ball sagging glory. It said, "For the best computers in Jollyville, we're #1" and included a small map on how to take cut over streets to locate their store. This was the last straw. It was one thing to be smug. It was one thing to hit on my former girlfriend. It was something altogether different to come to our side of town and so egregiously try to poach our customers. I was committed to strike back at anything to deflate his ego, and the first thing that came to mind was the TapHouse trivia competition next month.

We all walked back inside fuming from the new billboard. Anto and Patty were plotting a way to counterattack them via YouTube, when we noticed that Morgan was talking to Wade at the coffee counter. She had been acting a bit off lately and spending less and less time at the shop that usual. This morning was the first shift she missed and didn't even bother to give us a heads up or reason. She dropped her change in Wade's tip jar and asked me and Angie to talk with her in the empty Community Classroom. It was odd that she specifically asked for Angie, given that she had barely said ten words the past few weeks to her, but nonetheless, we went into the room and shut the door.

She sipped her coffee with both hands and was shaking a bit like she was cold, nervous or maybe even anxious. Before she spoke, she pivoted more towards me as if she wasn't quite sure how to engage Angie.

"So, I've got some things to tell you that are a bit far out there, and before I tell you, I need you to understand that my intentions for these past few weeks have been nothing but honorable."

"OK, Morgan. I'm a bit scared, now." I replied in a joking manner. "What's going on?"

"It's about Evelyn and Tom." she said.

My eyes rolled with exasperation. *Not this again.*

"Hear me out, please. I know it sounds crazy, but everything I'm about to tell you is one hundred percent true and verified." She took a deep breath. "While I don't have any proof that Evelyn killed Tom, yet, I do have proof that she is up to something with the shop. She's been trying to sell the shop for some time, and I believe behind Tom's back."

I didn't disagree with the statement. Evelyn worked in real estate, and I've heard her broach the subject in the past, but why was Morgan so confident now?

"A few weeks ago," she continued, "I MAY have gone over to her office and tampered with their phone lines to cause an internet outage."

It was clear at this point, why Angie was in the room. Morgan was confessing to some not so above-board behavior and wanted a friendly lawyer present.

"I then showed up at their office a few hours later telling them that I was there to fix their computers. I MAY have hypothetically ... installed a keylogger and Firefox plugin on each of their machines and MAY have told their anti-virus to ignore them. I MAY ... now be able see every key they press and control the speed of their browsers at any time."

My attention was torn between legal culpability and how cool this story had become. She straight up Mitnick'd her way into the lion's den.

"On my way out, I was repairing the phone lines to restore the internet, when Evelyn noticed me in the parking lot. She recognized me and asked me what I was doing there. I told her that I was fixing her office's Internet, and then she tried to recruit me."

"Recruit you?" I asked. "To be a real estate agent?"

"No, she tried to recruit me to be a spy. She wants to know everything that we are doing here in the shop."

Here we go with the conspiracy theories again.

"She offered me another ten thousand dollars if I would give me a heads up on anything we are trying to do that would earn a lot of money. She tried to frame it like some sort of twisted scholarship to send me away from this small town. I told her I would think about it. My gut says that she is up to no good, but with the keylogger installed, I'd be able to find out for sure. When I built the inventory system on AWS, I also installed a simple Linux service to capture the output from the keylogger through the browser plugin. I've been sifting through the output on S3 the last few days and I've stumbled upon some very interesting details."

Bribery? Espionage? Hacking? This had all the hallmark makings of a blockbuster movie, and we didn't even know how it would end yet. What language did she write her keylogger in? How did the browser plugin work with it? What tools was she using? Could I get a copy of her code? The anticipation was killing me!

"Long story short, I got Evelyn's email password and was able to review all her sent emails for the past year. Keep in mind, this isn't her Tom-NET email account, this is her Yahoo personal account. She's been talking with this commercial real-estate company in Dallas on and off for the past three years, specifically about the shop. Apparently, they have some sort of large apartment project in the works, and had been making Tom numerous offers, but he kept turning them down. *The letters.* But they can't proceed until they buy this land, because it is in the middle of everything. They are the ones who own all the self-storage and empty lots around here, and they are offering her a massive bonus if she can get him to sell."

Morgan took a moment to let all of the information sink in. I mentally graphed out all the interconnected lots around us that were now vacant. FlowJoe's, Little Caesars. All gone, because some jackhole wants to build some mega apartments. The footprint for this apartment project was going to be massive, and all of a sudden, Evelyn's appearance in Tom's life made sense. Their happenstance meeting in Mexico. One of her best friends runs the travel agency. Her overall fake demeanor and lack of interest in anything genuine from Tom's life. It was all a ruse to gain Tom's trust. The conspiracy theory was starting to take shape. *That bitch!*

My ears were steaming with rage, when Morgan interjected. "I have until tomorrow to get back with her about the offer. I wanted to talk with you to see what you want me to do."

I looked at Morgan and then to Angie who was sitting flummoxed having learned of something so scandalous happening in small town Jollyville. I didn't need legal advice at the moment, I needed Tom's calming voice of reason. If it were him, he would simply let things go and move on in different directions, but Evelyn was standing in the crossroads with every possible direction covered. She had the legacy reputation in town that would be hard to refute, especially with illegally obtained evidence. I wasn't a lawyer, but I knew that anything we learned from Morgan's investigation would not hold up in court. I closed my eyes and tried to breathe, but all I could see was Evelyn's evil smile as she stabbed Tom in the back. *Forgive me, Tom, but she is going to pay.*

"Hold that thought. I'll be right back."

I walked out of the room and announced to everyone in the shop that we needed to close the shop for a few hours to do some emergency maintenance, but that we would be back up and running tomorrow morning, as usual. I asked Wade to finish up his coffee orders and get us a round of drinks before locking up and motioned for the rest of the crew to join Angie and Morgan in the Community Classroom. There was lots to discuss and we were on the clock. It was a win or go home type moment, and I knew that given Evelyn's history screwing us all over for these many years, everyone would be on board to see it through.

FEATURED TRACK

Prodigy - One Love

20

Best Served Cold

Morgan, Angie and I brought everyone up to speed, and as expected, tempers flared, mainly for deceiving Tom, but also for all the crap they had to endure over the years from Evelyn. A new surge of ideas started flying faster than we could transcribe them to the whiteboard, and soon the room was louder than a trade floor. Brainstorming went well into the evening, as we hatched a plan to make Evelyn's life hell and score one for Tom. The added benefit, besides the catharsis that comes with primal revenge was that if we did it right, she'd be too distracted to focus any of her energy on us. We focused our ideas into two main categories: Personal and Business. As the ideas flew, Patty and I couldn't help spotting the similarities to Agent Richard Gill and did our best to refrain from slipping back into some bad habits.

On the Personal front, we had a ton of ideas, but needed to stay within some reasonable legal parameters for obvious reasons. After a bit of digging in the key logger files for her computer, we discovered that she used the same username, email and password, *divalady1? Please!*, for practically everything and thanks to Morgan's browser plugin, we had a complete list of her most frequented websites. The stage was set to have a little fun. We reported two of her credit cards stolen, forcing her numbers to be locked and new cards sent via mail. Of all the websites, eBay was the one she visited the most, so we decided to give her buyer rating a bit of an adjustment by registering complaints and requesting refunds / exchanges / returns on all her purchases from the past ninety days, which was roughly forty different sellers. This coupled with a bunch of nonsensical high dollar bids on random objects like a four-foot solid ball of duct tape and a three-gallon bag of guinea pig poop, should have her buyer feedback score plummeting in no time flat.

  Money seemed to be the only thing she cared about, which meant reciprocating her attempts to sabotage our efforts would be fitting karmic justice. As my old friend Calen could testify, nothing is more awkward than having floods of random emails show up in your inbox out of nowhere, but our goal was to top it if we could. We registered every one of her employee addresses, especially their "Contact Us" address, to a lengthy list of chatty listservs, marketing mail lists and the new trolling cesspool that was /r/nsfw. Anywhere we saw the option to send alerts to text messages, we religiously checked the box. By our estimates, they should have been getting upwards of fifty emails per hour per employee inbox. Our only customer who even came close to this volume was Pervy Joe, but we upgrade his mail storage every now and then just to keep him from calling support. *Ick!*

  With email more or less incapacitated, we pivoted to her company's phones, which were far more impactful to her old school way of doing business and a bit harder to affect. They had a local PBX and voicemail system that wasn't connected to the Internet, email or any sort of text message gateway. Instead, we simply copy and pasted the number into a bunch of random public phantom profiles we created on Farmers Only, Mullet Passions, Tall Friends and Trek Passions dating websites with some very specific interests that were sure to generate some curious callers. To be honest, we could have just checked the "Female" and "Single" boxes and we would have probably generated just as much interest. This was a straight up play from Hackers, but sometimes it's the simplest ideas that yield the best results. In this case, we had it on good authority that the mood at her office was borderline PTSD inducing, with all her agents afraid to pick up the next phone call. *Welcome to tech support!*

Even if they all figured out how to create email inbox rules, which we knew they wouldn't, and if they figured out how to block all the unwanted callers, very unlikely, we still had one more ace up our sleeves: Morgan's browser plugin. She designed the plugin to call home to a server every hour to pick up new information to control how it behaved until its next check in. She was able to configure the payload to launch a background HTTP request to download a simple file that she hosted on AWS every few minutes. Given that their office was still using a shared 128K ISDN connection, all it took to slow the entire network down was one or two people downloading a 5MB attachment. Which is why we set up a cron on that EC2 instance to clear caches and oscillate the plugin's target file between 1K, 5MB and 25MB throughout the day. The result was an intermittent Internet connection with frequent timeouts and slow page loads that would be difficult to pinpoint a root cause by anyone in town that didn't already work at Tom-NET.

All it took were some pizzas, a few all-nighters, such that any registration email confirmations could be removed from her inbox before she woke up, and a few new boxes of trivia cards to have our spiteful army of technophiles do their thing. *It's scary when you think how simple everything came together.* A celebratory toast was held in Morgan's honor, for her impressive work to uncover Evelyn's plan and creative revenge tactics. *Farmers Only was her idea.* Anto pulled a brand new long-haired blue wig from her backpack and dubbed Morgan the new "Queen of the Shop". Morgan tried to give her a small hug of appreciation, but Anto pulled in her tight, picked her up and spun her around. When the electric blue hair cleared Morgan's face, an uncharacteristic smile could be seen, and she looked genuinely happy. *Who knew electric blue was her color?*

It was almost March, and minus some Hot Shot Trivia every now and then, our team had yet to properly prepare to take on Keith and his band of bros. With Angie on our team, we felt invincible. If anyone was going to fill Tom's spot and give us a chance to win, it would be her. We loaded the card dispenser with a freshly shuffled deck of trivia cards, old and new, and commenced in the longest game of Hot Shots Trivia of all time; every day, before, after work and during between calls and customers. We yelled out questions and practiced slamming our hands on the nearest horizontal surface to finally tune our reaction times and prepare for inevitable fake outs that were coming our way. Angie wasn't there to witness the head fake that robbed us of the trophy the previous year, so she thought we might be taking it a bit too seriously. Over the course of that week, the lead changed numerous times with Patty, Angie and me each jockeying for supremacy. Wade was too busy with his coffee duties to remain consistently competitive, and Morgan was preoccupied teaching a new JavaScript class and reviewing payloads from her keystroke logger for new recon. In the end, it was Patty with his knowledge of world geography and history that reigned supreme. Anto recycled an antique golf trophy from one of the stalls in the backroom and made a makeshift Hot Shots Trivia grand champion award and wrote his name on the cup with a black Sharpie. I wasn't sure if Patty was more excited about the actual trophy, or that Anto took the time to make it for him. Either way, he had bragging rights, until next time.

By the day before the tournament, everyone at the shop hit a brick wall when it came to practice. Everyone was burning candles at both ends and the card stacks had been cycled through so many times that their edges and overall texture had been worn smooth. There was little more we could do to prepare. It was time for a break. Anto and Patty's YouTube channel was starting to get quite the following, and sales were picking up as a result. Since the challenge started, they had pulled in over seventy thousand dollars in extra revenue for the shop and there were still plenty of awesome pieces buried in the warehouse stalls. Wade hustled every day in a caffeinated frenzy, but his unique coffee selection and Angie's pre-paid discount program earned him some solid money towards our goal; nearly an extra twenty thousand dollars to date. The rest of us were pulling double-duty trying to keep Andersson Electronics and Tom-NET from slipping from its forty grand a month clip to keep us within spitting distance. When Anto wasn't filming, she was cold calling customers asking if they would like to come in for a free cleaning and PC health check. Patty often designed graphics while he was on long boring tech support calls. Morgan's new JavaScript class was popular, but if we were facing facts, the four or five people that came in to listen to her were not going to make the type of impact we needed, but anything that helped foot traffic was a step in the right direction. This left me and Angie rotating around where we were needed to try and keep our makeshift business model from falling apart.

Later that morning, Angie received a call, which she took outside as our visiting small business vendors were having an Elvis Presley exhibition for the blue hairs in the shop to demonstrate the musical versatility of their custom-built cedar plank guitars and drums. I glanced outside every so often to check in on her, and her body language seemed to radically fluctuate between excitement and something far less enjoyable until finally, she disappeared. I broadened my search pattern and casually scanned the shop and surrounding rooms. *Nothing.* That sixth sense that tells you to follow your gut in blind faith because something just isn't right was on high alert. I grabbed a few coffees from the counter and headed out for an expedition.

After circling the building and not finding anything, I went to the only remaining place around that she would recognize, since everything else had been turned into self-storage and vacant lots and she wasn't a day drinker. *The fountains.*

When I turned the corner towards the courthouse, I could see her sitting on the edge of the triple-tier fountain staring into the water. The flickering sparks in my heart, that restarted a few months prior, ignited a bonfire of memories and repressed thoughts that traced back to the first time I was here with Angie. *The penny!* I set the coffee cups down on the top of a mailbox and reached for my overstuffed wallet. It may have just been a simple black bifold leather wallet, but it was so stuffed to the gills with receipts and membership cards from over the years that it looked like a partially-flattened baseball. There was only one spot I needed to check, because it was the only reserved spot in my wallet. I slipped my fingers into the right pocket behind the credit card sleeve and pulled out a business card covered in scotch tape. It was a lazy person's laminating effort, but it was effective. Attached to the card were the remnants of the penny roll wrapper and the unused penny from my first date with Angie. If ever there was a time to use it, now seemed better than any. I secured the card between my fingers, grabbed the coffee cups and headed over to the fountain.

"Penny for your thoughts?" I asked from her blind side. She jumped a bit, and I could see that she was still clutching her phone in her hand.

"GEEEEEZUS ..." she replied, turning to identify the name of her auditory assailant. "Ben ... A little warning next time."

"Sorry. Subtlety was never my thing, remember." I handed her a coffee with the card clasped between my outstretched fingers on the same hand. Her instincts to drink her coffee were overruled by her curiosity to examine the card leaving her cup stranded midair inches from her mouth.

"What is this ...? "She looked up at me for an explanation, but it only took seconds for her to realize. *She knew.*

My delivery of the, hands down, most smooth, most romantic, most John Hughes worthy line in my life was quickly faltering on my brain's inability to string together even a single set of remotely coherent syllables. I pointed at the card, shrugged my shoulders and grunted a string of sounds that started me off into an explanation.

"If you were going to say my roll of pennies from our first date, then you would be correct." I tried to laugh away a creepy feeling that associated me with stalkers and hair doll collectors, but the humor just made things more awkward.

"You kept it? All this time? "she asked.

"It kind of made its way to my desk the morning after our date, and I found it sandwiched inside one of my old disk caddies when I moved into Tom's apartment. Things weren't going all that great back then, and it reminded me of something good. So ... I put in my wallet for safe keeping. I've pulled it out every now and then when I needed a little pick-me-up."

Her eyes glistened in the afternoon light and a smile eventually emerged from her obviously distressed face. With each sniff, I could hear the questions queuing up in her head, and I was ready to start rattling off answers. All she had to do was ask.

"So, what was your favorite part about that day?" she asked, rubbing the card between her fingers.

"Besides the pizza, you mean?" I finally got a laugh out of her. "I don't know. Maybe just the talking. I think, besides Wade, that was the first time I really opened up to anyone about anything real since the move. We had a lot in common back then, and it was great to just talk with someone that gets you. What about you? Any positive thoughts come to your mind?"

"I remember beating you at just about everything that night. That is a pretty positive thought."

"Only because you kept making up new rules."

"Hehe ... I did, didn't I," she said. "... I remember looking through the slats in the living room blinds after you dropped me off and thinking I was going to burn that ridiculous t-shirt you were wearing." *So that's where it went.* She wiped a small tear from her eye and turned her head away from me to face the fountain. "I also remember thinking you were really nice ... quirky ... but nice."

I couldn't see her face, but the inflection in her voice was undoubtedly positive, until her entire body let out a long sigh.

"And then, I remember the whole long-distance thing ... and how much it sucked and ..."

"I know." Interrupting her was never a good idea. She hated it. I was tempting fate just being within arm's reach of her when I did it, but in that absurd moment, it felt like fate was giving me a second chance to say the things I always wished I had said. "It did suck, but not just for me. I had a long time to think about how things went down, and you definitely got the worst end of the deal on everything and I'm sorry for that. ... New town. New college. Trying to make new friends. I can only imagine how stressful for you that must have been, and then there's this guy who keeps pinging you to chat over ICQ that thinks he can solve all that with a webcam and a computer..." *Self-deprecation never felt so good.*

"Why didn't you ever say anything?" she asked.

"What? Do you think I was this introspective back then?" I laughed at my younger self's immaturity. "It took me years of talks with Tom to figure this stuff out. I mean, I thought about reaching out. I must have cancelled over a hundred messages to you on ICQ the year after we broke up, but nothing ever sounded right out loud ... besides ... I was doing my best to help make things easier for you."

"Easier? What does that mean?" she asked.

"I figured ... drama wasn't what you needed. You needed the clean break. I'm not saying I went into our last conversation as a couple with the intention of breaking up. Once it happened, though, it didn't take long for me to realize that it really was the best thing I could do for you at the moment. I mean ... come on ... you were actually chasing your dream. All I was doing was holding you back."

At this point, Angie's eyes were gushing with tears but she narrowly blinked. It was a lot to unpack all at once, but she was definitely ready for the conversation.

"You are the nicest ... and dumbest, smart guy I know, Ben Wilson. I didn't need you to cut me out of your life. I wanted you to stop trying to solve the problem like it was one of your programs and just listen to me. We could have found a way to make it work, but every time I told you a problem, you immediately tried to get me some new gizmo or app to install. I spent years leaving ICQ open ... just hovering over your name or typing out half-baked messages that I'd eventually erase ... " *I was a fool!*

Thoughts of Tom's high school romance rolled through my head. *Had we waited too long? Was one of us going to die?*

"... and then almost ten years go by and you finally get it. Do you know why I gave you Benji?"

She pulled Benji from her pocket and held it up for me to see. She was dead.

"Because, it was the only way I thought I could help you understand that relationships take work, not just logic and gimmicks. And, here you go and keep this little bugger alive for longer than I thought was possible because you figured out a way to game the system ... Don't get me wrong, I think it is all very cute, but you did exactly what I didn't want you to do. Solve it and take the shortcut no less. Sometimes you have to put in the full amount of effort, because that is just what is needed, regardless of how glamourous the deed." *It was no easy way out, it took months to ... Zip it, Ben!*

"Hey, I get it. Believe me, I've done a lot of growing up these past years. I wasn't perfect then, nor am I now. I couldn't even bring myself to read your favorite Harry Potter book back then, even though it's amazing."

A suspicious look adorned her face as her left eyebrow rose like a hydrogen balloon about to explode into a fully-fledged lawyer caliber inquisition.

"You actually read Harry Potter?" she asked.

"Yep," I nodded, "but just the first book though." This unleashed a two-way flurry of poignant questions, grilling each other on the nuances between the movie and the book. We sat on the fountain edge, leaning in towards each other to lobby Potter trivia back and forth in the hopes of stumping the other person, *just like our first date*, but every question was met with an equally passionate and correct response. In her defense, it was fair for her to assume I took an easy way out, but she was surprised at just how much I knew about the first book. My guess was that she was expecting me to try and fake my way through it, which is why I immediately disclosed my reluctance to read any more of the books until the movies were complete. By the time we started to rehash previous questions, we knew it was a draw.

"You are just full of surprises now, aren't you Ben Wilson?" she said looking into my eyes. There were no more tears. Her face was still tense from the competition, but her forehead and cheeks were relaxed. My heart was racing, and coupled with the mid-day Texas heat, I was sweating through my Polo. This was the closest I had been to Angie since we broke up, and my instincts were on auto pilot. I slowly inched my head closer, and I could have sworn I saw her do the same when …. *BRRRRRRRRING* *BRRRRRRRRING* *Damn cell phone!*

It was someone from Angie's work. Unlike some people who say they don't eavesdrop on people's cell phone calls; I wholeheartedly admit it. I am curious by nature, especially when the call disrupts a moment like this one. Angie began pacing around the fountain, and I could only pick up pieces of the conversation. Some ruling for a case she worked on finally came back, and it was good news. The more they talked the faster she walked, and the brighter her smile grew. She continued her slow-paced orbit around the fountain adding random hops, skips and jumps intermittently as the conversation appeared to turn favorable until she abruptly stopped dead in her tracks. Her hand was still covering her mouth from her last excited screech, when she turned her back to me on the other side of the fountain and adopted a more secretive posture. Whatever she was saying, she was not pleased. She eventually hung up the phone and took a moment to collect herself and then came back to the other side of the fountain, where her reluctant eye contact was not a good sign.

"If I had to guess who you were talking to by your mood swings on that call, I would have guessed me … but since I'm here …." *A little bit more self-deprecation to lighten the mood.* This time, all I got was a half-breathed grin. "What's going on?" I asked.

"A lot, actually," she replied, "a bit of good news and a bit of bad."

I didn't have anywhere else I wanted to be, so I just took a sip of my coffee and waited for her to spill the beans.

"A case I was working on almost a year ago was finally settled and our client won a ton of money. My firm wants to make me a senior partner and have me run a new tech IP division..."

"Ok, so I'm pretty sure that's the good news?" I jokingly replied, still fishing for some sort of laugh, smile or dent in her malaise. *No dice.*

"Yeah, the bad news is that they want me to fly back tonight to sign some paperwork and then get started right away. If I can't make it back, they are going to give the job to this sleazy fifth year named Greg. I've been pushing myself hard to get this opportunity ever since I joined, and now that it's here, it couldn't have come at a worse time. I don't know what to do."

Her head fell to her hands as she pulled the hair from her eyes. I didn't know what to say. Asking her to stay would definitely be seen as selfish, but just letting her leave sucked as well. My mouth fell agape, hoping a word, or two, would succumb to gravity and fall off my tongue into this circling drain of a conversation.

"Is there no way to ask for an extension? I mean, technically you ..." Before I could finish my thought, she interrupted me, and I could tell she was frustrated.

"Look Ben, I know what you are going to say, but right now it's not what I need. Would you mind if I stayed here for a bit ... alone ... and I'll sync back with you later?"

With reluctance in my heart, I agreed, but not before trying to crack off a few more jokes to lighten the mood. According to Angie's reaction, the mood was already locked in for a bit. I returned to the shop just in time to experience the worst adaptation of Heartbreak Hotel I had ever experienced in my life. Patty and Anto's facial expressions said it all, *"Run!!!"* but I stuck it out to wait for Angie. An hour passed, and then two, but still no sign of her. I tried sending her a text message, but she didn't reply. Even though the live music session had stopped, their conversational voices played in the background like some eye twitching elevator muzak derivative. As if I didn't feel enough displeasure at the moment, my stomach joined the soiree with the warm sour churning of anxiety, and I took the opportunity to head to my apartment to desensitize.

After depositing a portion of angst to the bowels of the Jollyville wastewater processing facility, I washed my hands and sat on the couch to collect my thoughts and that's when I received a text message from an unknown number.

As each letter in the message unfolded into syllables, the reality of who the sender was and their meaning became clear and, brick by brick, the recent garden of positivity and happiness began to crumble. My heart fought off the signals my eyes and mind were sending like a shotgun wielding grandma in a rocking chair protecting her lawn from would be miscreants. Alas, the shotgun only had two shots and the invaders of truth overwhelmed the yard's lush greenery turning it into a dirty, muddy and broken quagmire of letter pressed puddles and despair.

I'm heading back tonight. I'm sorry. Please don't hate me.

A mature course of action is acceptance and dealing with the situation, but I chose denial. I sank into my squishy sticky pleather couch like Artax into the swamp of sadness, until I had a passing thought. *What would Tom do?* The question ran laps in my head coming back into focus every few minutes, and the same answer always snapped into focus and eventually gave me a slight chuckle. *He'd get high and play Minesweeper.* Weed really wasn't my thing, but Minesweeper was a mere minute away with Tom's computer nearly hooked up on my desk. Call it a purpose, or a convenient distraction, I peeled myself from the couch and grabbed some canned air to finish clearing the power supply of its intoxicating debris. Unexpected bonus, there was a fifty-fifty chance I might get a contact high.

With every cable and plug connected, I continued my audible inner dialog as I processed the situation. *Why come back in the first place? Was it some sort of revenge? That isn't who she is! Maybe?* For as ugly as the computer was on the outside, Tom definitely took care of what mattered on the inside. The computer booted in seconds as it expelled the last remnants of the dust from the power supply fan. I held my breath, just in case. *I really didn't know how drugs worked.* To say Tom was a creature of habit would be an understatement. His desktop was ultra-bare with only a few icons, but before I could read them, he apparently had Minesweeper in the startup folder, and it launched a fresh level ninety-nine game. I poked around in frustration for about an hour, always exploding ten to fifteen moves in without any resemblance of progressive learning or strategy. My mind just wasn't in it. *How could he sit and play this game for so long?*

The clock read five o'clock and that meant our resident cover band collective would be on their way out shortly and I would have to break the news to the team about Angie and the tournament. With only five members on the team, we would need to find a last-minute sub or just go ahead and accept the loss. We could make it to the quarter finals with only five, but when it came to head-to-head matchups, we would automatically forfeit one out of every six, which would be difficult to overcome. I wrapped up my last game with another equally resounding failure, closed Minesweeper and instinctively activated the shutdown sequence. Before the screen could flicker off, I noticed one of the folders on his desktop that was hidden behind the Minesweeper window … *Diary*. As fast as it booted up, the computer shutdown and the screen went black. My curiosity was scratched, and every nerve begged me to push the smeared creamy power button again. It would only take another minute or two to boot back up, but I knew deep down it was, at least at this moment, a distraction and I needed to brief the team and come up with a plan. The diary would just have to wait, *for now*.

FEATURED TRACK

Stone Temple Pilots - Trippin' On A Hole In A Paper Heart

21

Trivia Fever: Part One

I walked downstairs to the sounds of Anto and Patty still talking with our ensemble of minstrels. The last thing I wanted to do was fan the smoldering conversation and ignite a new topic that would delay their departure further. I hung back in the warehouse and peeped through the porthole window to observe the situation. The shop was clear, except the remaining players who were standing in the swing path of the front door. Anto had a thunder-grip on the side of the door, and her fingers were fidgeting with the dead bolt in anticipation of its imminent closure, but the talkative group of hippie blue hairs had other plans. Patty was not directly engaged in the discussion, but I could hear him interjecting conversational pleasantries like, "Have a good evening" and "See you next time" as he made clear attempts to draw their attention to the closed sign that he just flipped over and was actively dusting with his bare hands. There was a loud noise that came from the coffee bar that froze the moment. I shifted to the other door's porthole, and I saw Wade cowering on the floor biting his knuckled hand and feverishly swiping at his pants. He was definitely hiding from the conversation, and apparently spilled a pot of coffee on himself. Unintended as it may have been, Anto took the distraction and feigned an emergency which gave her justifiable cause to shut the door and lock it in place. Patty and her waved goodbye through the glass and then turned inward toward the coffee counter with exasperated looks of frustration and relief. *The coast was clear.*

As they walked back, her hands made large sweeping motions from her forehead to the sky. She rattled off some other words, but I couldn't quite catch them over the door hinge squeaking on my way out from the warehouse. When she caught me smiling at her, she squinted her eyes at me and wagged a fierce finger in my direction.

"NUNCA! Nunca, nunca. Never again!!!" she exclaimed.

Patty fiercely double-tapped on the coffee bar as Wade lined up rows of coffee shots and Advil, while Anto proceeded straight to the shop stereo to prepare an auditory palate cleanse for the shop. She inhaled her music's crescendo like pure oxygen and then burned some sage incense in the corner. She joined Patty and Wade at the bar and threw back two quick shots of espresso. Morgan was hiding in the farthest corner in the Community Classroom. The door was shut, she was about-faced, and her headphones were pinching her hoodie on top of her head. Her ability to zone out and be productive in the face of absolute chaos was admirable, but she was unapologetically terse when she was dialed in like that. I approached the counter, motioning for Wade the barkeep to pour me a shot, when Anto decided to set the tone for our conversation.

"No more trivia, Ben. My head hurts too much right now.", she said while grabbing her temple and humming the beat to her song in the background.

Patty was a dead-eyed, hollowed-out husk of himself. He looked like Doc Brown stunned and stupefied at the bar, mumbling things like, "Music has been ruined for me."

"That wasn't music", Anto interrupted. "If there was a sound ... that a Chupacabra made when it ate your bones, while you were still alive, that would be it. ... But that's not possible, because the Chupacabra eats your headfirst to silence the screams." She threw back another shot of coffee and danced whimsically back through the sage cloud to select some new music.

The awkward silence was broken when Wade chimed in with his typical left field commentary, "I kinda liked the Ukuleles."

"Then you go THERE and buy one!" Anto yelled sternly, while skipping to a new track. "Besides, not only was their music horrible, they drove away pretty much every customer. Not exactly the outcome we were going for." *She was right.*

Wade swiftly poured her another shot of coffee, which Anto returned and acknowledged with a smile, but also a no nonsense look that screamed, *"I'm Serious!"*

"Guys we need to talk about tomorrow," I said. "There's a bit of a problem. Angie isn't going to make it."

"What?" "What???" "¿Que?" Each of them responded nearly in unison. I explained the chain of events, as I knew them and reluctantly showed them the text message. The room went into a new phase of quiet as Anto's office music eerily rotated to a somber track right as I finished the story. They exchanged concerning looks, considering what to say next.

"You doing OK, Ben? Anto finally asked, skipping over the lengthy list of tangential impacts I itemized in my explanation.

"Yeah. ... I'm happy for her. ... It's been her dream for a long time, but we need to focus on tomorrow." The words tasted bitter as the repressed acidic frustration bubbled in my stomach. *Who was I kidding?* Wade's solemn look was all I needed to see to know that I wasn't hiding anything. Everyone knew I was hurting, but we needed to figure out how to solve this bigger problem, so my personal feelings were going to have to find a way to fit their bloated selves back into the tiny dark box in my mind for another time.

We brainstormed for at-least three hours, citing every possible person around town who might be able to complete our team roster. After the first hour, we abandoned all hope of finding anyone with even half a brain, until Wade pointed out that we played with Evelyn for so many years that we could probably be fine getting by with just five, given that she had no brains whatsoever. It was a well-timed and much needed respite for the conversation, but one that ended with the sad reality that competing with only five was the right thing to do. Even if we got bounced in the quarter finals, this was Tom's team and bringing in an outsider that didn't believe in what we were doing just didn't feel right. We all agreed to abandon the search for a sixth, and with that everyone turned in for the night. I locked up the shop for the night and headed upstairs with the hope of getting some sleep.

I fell onto my bed staring at the ceiling fan blades spinning around in circles. It had been a few months since I consulted the walls of wisdom that lined my bedroom. For better or worse, these pictorial prophets offered me a sense of comfort that helped me through some pretty dark days. My eyes cycled through each of their teachings in search of inspiration.

Procrastination. Lazy feels good right about now. **Ambition**. I'm screwed just like the salmon. **Indifference**. I didn't know what my face was doing. **Potential**. Damnit, now I'm hungry. **Stupidity**. Why even go tomorrow? **Idiocy**. Those damn musicians. **Irresponsibility**. Oh, I know where the blame will fall. **Cluelessness**. I wish I never knew happiness.

Like a broad-spectrum emotional antibiotic, all productive and positive thoughts were dispelled from my mind, leaving me immobilized under a frigid block of ice dripping melting thoughts of despair and failure. The sparks of hope lit only a few months prior by the resurgence of Angie and the opportunity to carry forward a legacy were all but reduced to fading futuristic embers. At some point in the middle of this mental maelstrom, I closed my eyes and succumbed to the sleep I most desperately desired to escape the crashing perils of the present.

*** FADE ***

I sniffed my nose while I wiped the tears from my face with the rough back of my hand. The memories were ever more lucid and detailed tugging at my emotional strings like an unrelenting puppeteer. As I leaned forward, I could see Morgan still at the table across the room, typing away at her computer as if her headphones had shielded her from this entire introspective journey. I could only see faint colors of her screen over her shoulder but based on the way her leg was bouncing and the terminal-like nature of her background, I could tell she was programming and was in a zone. She reached back and scratched the back of her head, and as her hand retreated, the layers of her hair fell in slow motion conjuring a disturbing faint memory into focus. *Something was different about her hair.*

There was no denying it. It was significant. Rarely in my life did I experience tunnel vision outside the boundaries of programming, but this was one of those moments. I felt as if I could smell the memory, but neither see, nor hear it. Every time I tried to pivot my thoughts to something different, my mind snapped back into focus on her hair. *What is it?* The answer was on the tip of my tongue like a pesky stray hair that you just can't find. Her hair was always long and black, why obsess over it now? I put my head in my hands and massaged my scalp trying to nurture any recollection out of hibernation. My hands drifted down the sides of my neck until I found a tender spot just above my shoulder. As my fingers ran over the affected area, a series of tactile immersive imagery pulled into focus as if I had deployed eyes at the ends of my fingers. *Did we?* I quickly closed my eyes and leaned back into the couch, hoping my mind would resume its turbulent tale to solve this new, uncomfortable and mysterious development.

*** *FADE* ***

I woke the next morning around six in the morning to loud banging coming from the front of the shop. Even with all of our business model adjustments in full swing, Sundays were still extremely slow, sometimes almost completely void of foot traffic. I blamed religion mainly, *for this and many other things*, not to mention all the Sunday sales in the newspaper at the big box stores near the highway that tilted the city on its axis leaving our side of town elevated to a proverbial ghost town. I headed down the stairs and peaked through the backroom door. Wade, Anto, Patty and Morgan were each standing outside the front of the doors, wearing matching Hot Shots t-shirts that screamed "Anto art project". Matching was a loose term, given that most uniforms look identical, whereas these shirts were all different colors, patterns and eras, *someone went thrift shopping*, but had the same white letters stenciled across the chest, "Hot Shots". The array of shirt colors made them look like some low-end Teletubby or Wiggles knock offs. At least this early wake-up call was catered. I could see indications of donuts, breakfast taquitos and coffee in their hands.

I unlocked the front door, allowing the technicolored chaos into the shop. Wade handed me a cup of coffee, while Anto tossed a dark purple t-shirt in my face whilst berating my decision to wear the same clothes from the day before. Patty finished off a small box of donut holes and headed straight for his desk. The man could stress eat like no one's business, and he was obviously nervous. The breakfast buffet was spread out across the coffee counter, while Wade poured everyone cups of a special "memory improving" coffee blend that he read about online. He couldn't find any actual "science" to back up their claims, but it tasted good enough, and if he had to pick a day to try and get an advantage, today would be it. Anto wasted no time in setting the mood for the day with her proclaimed Stone Temple Pilots mega-mix. *Trippin' On a Hole In a Paper Heart ...* ♪ *Nice!* I took a few sips of Wade's coffee and visualized the caffeine activating dormant neurons in my head, but all I felt was the increasing urge to take a leak. The tournament check-in was still another six hours away, so we spent the time reviewing our most troublesome pile of Hot Shot Trivia cards, a curated collection of cards that frequently stumped our memories in some form or fashion.

By the time lunch rolled around, we had shaved milliseconds from our response times and assimilated the decks into our collective hive mind. To celebrate the moment, I ordered a six-foot party sub; one foot for each of us and an extra foot with bologna for Tom. It was so large and cumbersome to carry, the delivery guy had to tilt it on its side to fit it through the door and all the loose toppings made paper popping sounds as they tumbled into the lower end of the bag. *thwap* We went around the table, toasting Tom and each other for being a part of Hot Shots over the years. We reminisced about all the close calls, and times where despite Evelyn's indifference, we were at the top of our game. There was no reason we couldn't be that or better this time. Anto asked for a moment of silence during her turn, so she could pay respects to her family spirits for being watching over her and invite Tom to kick it with them if he was feeling lonely.

The sandwiches were thick, hearty and coma inducing. The world slowed to a crawl for a few minutes, giving me time to come to terms with what was about to happen. *Tom was dead. Angie left. We were one person short, and Keith's team was in all likelihood going to win. He would rub it in our faces until the shop eventually closed, and ....* I caught myself spiraling down a doomsday narrative that I wasn't ready to believe. *One step at a time.* It was almost one o'clock and it was time to clean the shredded lettuce explosion that covered Wade's coffee bar like confetti. As we left the shop, we gathered by the door and put our hands into a circle. This was the moment that Tom would normally say something inspiring and uplifting. Sadly, it fell to me to fill this void and all I could muster was some butchered Coach Bombay material, *sans the quacking*. "No matter what happens ... This is for Tom." *1, 2, 3 .... Hot Shots!*

The crew piled into Anto's station wagon along with the framed photo of Tom from the funeral soiree for good measure. We arrived at the pub just after one and the parking lot was virtually empty, which was good. Our sideshow clown car was one of the first to arrive. We trickled out sans the hurdy gurdy theme music and everyone headed for the bar. I held back for a moment with Tom's picture and closed my eyes waiting for words of wisdom to come, but my mind was pulling up blanks. The fright of me freezing up like this during a face-off, assuming we made it that far, entered my mind and triggered a small panic. So, I simply pointed to the sky, snapped my fingers and headed toward the large wooden door to face destiny head on. I could hear a loud conversation going on inside and prepared my best happy crowd face. It was dark inside the bar, and my eyes took a moment to adjust from the blinding sunlight outside. When they pulled focus, I could see the team staring back at me with joyous smiles on their faces. One by one, I sifted through the shadowy figures trying to comprehend what on earth was responsible for their drastic change in demeanor. Anto. Wade. Patty. Morgan. *Angie!?* She was standing next to the registration table with her hair disheveled and wearing the same clothes from the day before. Anto had apparently brought her team shirt and had given it to her, because she was clutching a colorfully loud wad of fabric in her hands. In my mind, I raced over to her and gave her a huge hug, but my feet were ladened in emotional concrete. Instead she walked to me and pulled me to a corner bench.

"What are you doing here?" I asked.

"It's a bit of a long story ..." Angie replied.

"We have time." My interjection was sharp and wicked, but not fully baked. Part of me loved that she was back, but the newly resuscitated cynicism in me had its doubts and had already erected a heavily fortified mental barricade.

"Well," she continued. "My layover in Phoenix was delayed, and I had a bit of an epiphany." She grabbed my hands and placed them on her knee with hers over mine. Her hands were dry, but warm, and radiated a crackling electricity that pulsed with the beat of my heart. Each shockwave surged throughout my body, waking up all things dormant and broken.

"What's that." I said in a more calm and measured tone. I couldn't look her in the eye, in part because I was transfixed on the way her thumb was rubbing the back of my hand.

"My dream. ... Every decision I've made since I was twelve has been in pursuit of this grandiose plan to have the perfect life. And, even though my goal is there for the taking, I couldn't help but feel as if none of it would have happened without Tom. He gave me a place to study, when my parents forgot to pay the electric bill. He gave me friendship when I needed it the most, and he led me to you."

She squeezed my hand, and like a mighty battering ram, my barricade started to shake.

"And this got me thinking," she continued. "I want to do this for Tom, and help you cross the finish line. So, what if it takes a little longer? So, I cancelled my flight and booked a return trip and got here about thirty minutes ago and ... well ... here I am."

"Yes, I can see that," I acknowledged dismissively. It all still felt like a dream.

" So ... Are we good? Or, ... ," she probed.

"Of course, we're good ... ," I cut her off quick. I had no interest in hearing how that sentence might have ended. " ... Part of me knew you were going to come back. I know how much you like to make an entrance, but I have to admit, you had me worried." I was joking and smiling on the outside, but my hand clutched her knee, not wanting to let go.

One of the perks of getting to the pub early was that we had our choice of tables. This was one of Tom's passionate traditions, and frequently complained that our generation didn't understand the value of punctuality. We picked Tom's favorite table. It was the one off to the side of the stage, not too close to the bathrooms, but also not too far from the bar. There was a raised banister wall for the mezzanine level behind us which gave us a great spot to lean our chairs against, and a large framed Barbarella poster above our heads on the back wall. Tom used to joke that Andy Dufresne would crawl out from behind the poster one day and deliver us the trophy. All we had to do now was wait for things to start.

Teams started to pile in, one after another. A few of the regulars arrived, and then a whole slew of new teams showed up shortly after. Apparently, word got out in the Austin circuit about our tournament, and some of their local teams decided to slum it in the suburbs for some trivia fun. By the time two o'clock rolled around, the bar was packed with twenty-three teams. New tables were brought in from the back and a piece of plywood laid on top of the pool table to squeeze in the last two. It was the largest tournament I had ever seen, and across the room was the team to beat, Keith and the J4ck4l5. *They were going down.*

After the emcee was situated and the first round of drinks and food were taken, he came to the podium and announced that they were ready to begin. Volunteers passed out the packets of answer sheets to each team. Each packet had ten sheets with ten empty spaces. Categories were selected at random, and then ten questions were asked in each category. Points were tallied at the end, and top teams were selected to go to the head-to-head challenge. In previous years, this was only the top two teams, but given the large number of teams, they opted for the top four teams to make it a bit more competitive.

Hot Shots was one of only three teams that scored more than 90% in the opening round, which meant that there was most likely only one other real contender, besides us and the J4ck4l5. The organizers took an hour break to allow everyone to restock their food and beverages, and then shared the head-to-head bracket via a projector. To get to Keith, we would have to go through the other contender, Tequila Mockingbirds. Keith and his team dismantled their competition, icing them out twenty to zero. The nauseating musk of overcompensating masculinity billowed from the stage like a dank fog of aerosolized Red Bull and Drakkar, as the J4ck4l5 returned to their table, flexing and pumping their arms like idiots. It was now time for Hot Shots to do what they do best, trivia.

Our quarter-final round started, and the score was neck and neck. The judges ripped cards almost verbatim from Trivia Pursuit Millennium Edition and the Greatest Hits, both staples in our training repertoire, but it looked like the Tequila Mockingbirds knew that too. Timing for the buzzers came down to microseconds with no one able to pull away, no mistakes by anyone. Our break came late in the match when we were up twenty-five to twenty-four, and Angie's opponent beat her by a hair on the buzzer. The question was simple enough, "The

United States' government is a shining example of a <BLANK>", but the guy responded "democracy". The judges said his answer was correct and tried to move on; however, Angie slammed her hand down on the buzzer and took over the room.

"Point of order!" She said, fiercely and repeatedly tapping her buzzer like she was playing Ikari Warriors. "I would like to challenge his answer. The correct answer is a republic."

The room was taken aback. No one had ever challenged anything before, and I wasn't even sure if you could do it. When the judges tried to correct Angie in a condescending tone, I saw Angie's smirk emerge and her right eyebrow shot up like a signal flare. *He was toast.* Angie started to walk the stage like a courtroom and put everyone in their place. All I could do was watch intently as I ate the salty stale popcorn that was left on our table.

"Ladies and gentlemen, truth is not limited to words on the back of some card. Truth is knowledge, and knowledge that is not factual is nothing short of deception. I argue that the United States is not a democracy, but rather a shining example of a democratic republic. I know this not just because I graduated top of my class at Stanford Law, but if you go online to any credible information source, you will see that I'm right. Ask John Adams, he'll tell you! ... I urge each of you to challenge your perceptions of following the status quo and seek the truth, no matter where it lies. Furthermore ... "

"OK. You don't need to continue ..." One of the judges had already pulled out his laptop and found a reference on Wikipedia. "It appears that she is right. With that, we accept the challenge and award the point to Hot Shots, which ends this round with a final score of twenty-six to twenty-four ... Hot Shots advances to the final round, which will begin in fifteen minutes. Ready your teams."

Angie turned and raised her hands in the air with excitement. It was unclear if she was reacting to winning her "case", or moving on to the final round, but she was undeniably and unequivocally happy. The team rushed to the podium for a massive group hug, while I kept Tom's picture company at the table. All I could do was admire her from afar, at the fear of breaking down and crying. The air of confidence and joy she radiated was infectious. It made me crave the feelings even more, and fear of losing her again spun helplessly in the back of my head. The saturated embers in my heart were drying out, now well crisped and ready for reignition. The next hour would be a pivotal moment that could make or break the future of our tight-knit family. We had practiced so hard, and come so far, and yet, if we failed to beat Keith and his cronies this time, who knows if we would get another shot. *Would we all still be together? What about Angie? What are her plans?*

I shrugged off the unthinkable, slammed back a glass of water and joined the team, with Tom held aloft in hand during the celebration. Every attempt to live in this moment was being made, and not to think too far into the future, but our team was on a collision course with destiny. Next up, the J4cK4l5.

FEATURED TRACK

Veruca Salt – Volcano Girls

22

Trivia Fever: Part Two

The celebration was quick, but it was time to get down to business. Everyone took turns rubbing Angie's hair for good luck before heading off to empty their bladders and fill their glasses with more drinks. As for myself, I simply offered a high five. We had less than ten minutes until the next round began, and I knew that if I touched her hair I would inevitably slip into a hug, probably never let go and turn into a blubbering mess. I could already see Keith talking up his team in the corner. For all his chest pounding, you would think he had just mainlined a full thirty-two ounce Monster and was about to play in the Super Bowl. The bell rang signaling everyone to take their seats. *Welcome to another edition of Thunder Dome!*

Tensions were high. A blended slurry of animosity, fear and sweat seeped through my pores. It was win or go home, and we planned on going home with the trophy for Tom. When it was time to send someone to the podium, I put my drink down and headed up to face Marco, the ultra-bro. The podium wood still felt warm from Angie's hand in the last round. After only a few words into the first question, I unleashed a massive shoulder fake that sent Marco's hand flying for the buzzer before even a whiff of the question topic was known. He looked at Keith frantically, but there was no avoiding it. The first missed question was in the books. I calmly let the judge read the entire question and did the easy trivia lay-up to claim first blood. On my way back to the table, I gave my best two-finger Jack Byrnes gesture, *I'm watching you*, to the L33tR1gz table, and slid passed Morgan in line and whispered, "That one's for you!" Little did I know that Morgan had her own plans for payback in mind, and no one was ready for it.

A few questions later, it was Morgan's' turn. Before heading up to the podium, she reached into her bag and pulled out her blue wig. She skipped to the podium with a deranged look in her eyes like Harley Quinn about to unleash some chaos. It was clear that it was no coincidence that her opponent was Jesse. She stood with one hand behind her back, rocking on her heels back and forth waiting for the question. As soon as Jesse motioned his arm for the buzzer, she spontaneously uncorked the loudest and highest pitched scream I had ever heard. The scream lasted for at-least ten seconds, but it could very well have been longer. Jesse was startled and forgot to actually press the buzzer, allowing Morgan time to swoop in and snag the question. As soon as she pressed her button, her scream dissipated, and she quickly cleared her throat and followed with her answer. The judge could only look at her with confusion as he nodded in the affirmative, and Morgan skipped her way back to the table with her long blue wig flowing behind her. As she passed me, she whispered back to me, "That one's for myself!" All of sudden my chivalrous act seemed patently unnecessary.

*** FADE ***

Wait. Blue hair! A mental image of my disturbed bed sheets popped into my head with perfect clarity. The same wig that Anto gave to Morgan only a few months ago; the same wig that Morgan wore at the Trivia finals last night, was the same wig laying at the foot of my bed this morning. My hands returned to the tender spot on my neck, which despite being out of practice, started to feel more and more like a hickey. *We couldn't have!* I closed my eyes tight again, rocking back and forth, trying to fast forward my memory as fast as it would go.

*** FADE ***

It was a rubber match. Despite a relatively quick lead out the gate, Keith and his team kept the game interesting. Every time we would pull ahead, they would rattle off a pair and take the lead once again. The score was 36-35, J4ck4l5, and we were well into overtime. Wade and Patty scored two sci-fi questions, their specialty, in a row which put us in another chance to win it all. Anto was next, and she was flipping out like no one's business. Her opponent, Cody, was easily a foot taller than her and his burly untamed red beard made him look like a high-tech Scottish lumberjack. The category was "Movies", which wasn't her forte.

"In this iconic scene with Patrick Swayze and Demi Moore in the movie Ghost, what ..."

BUZZZZZZZ!

They jumped the question. Cody's hand had crushed the buzzer. Part of me thought I could hear a small digital whimper all the way from my table. The first words out of his mouth sounded odd, like he was stuck in between two answers but had to recover midway through.

"Making ... Pottery". He held his breath waiting for confirmation, but it never came. *He was wrong!*

"Incorrect. For the chance to win, we will read the entire question ... In this iconic scene with Patrick Swayze and Demi Moore in the movie Ghost, what famous song was playing when they were spinning pottery in the basement?"

A music question!?!?! This was Anto's bread and butter. I could hear the song in my head, but the name of the song was eluding me. Her eyes were closed, and she was rocking her head around in circles and holding her necklaces like she was in a deep trance. She immediately raised her outstretched arms above her head and slowly returned her hands to the podium rails with a long exhale and focus. Her eyes opened with a blank stare.

"Unchained Melody by the Righteous Brothers," she said in a calm and collected tone.

There was an uneasy pause after she responded, as if we were destined to spin our tires in the mud with these guys until someone dropped dead from exhaustion. Then the judge chimed in.

"That is correct!" the judge exclaimed, "We have a new champion ... Hot Shots!"

I slammed my hands down on the table instinctively and pointed to the sky as my eyes overflowed with joy. We rushed to the podium to congratulate Anto, but she was still a bit frozen in place, like she was a drowsy narcoleptic coming out of an episode. Her eyelids fluttered the moment we touched her, like she was waking up from a dream. She couldn't remember the question that was asked or providing a response, but she was doubly sure her family spirits were responsible because her tia "loved her some Patrick Swayze". There were times that I simply laughed Anto's strange beliefs and rituals off as quirky personality traits, but with Tom gone and the miraculous feat I just witnessed, I felt compelled to believe that the warm feeling on my shoulder was Tom's hand as we triumphantly hoisted the relatively undersized tournament trophy cup above our heads in victory.

Not too long later, the after party started at the bar with half priced drinks and appetizers. We never really stayed to partake in the festivities before, for obvious reasons, but today, we aimed to savor every last second. We kept ordering round after round of drinks and food, but the food was being consumed before the baskets or napkins could hit the table. Most of the regular tournament teams stopped by our table to pay their condolences and congratulate us on breaking the streak. The fact that we were giving out fried pickles and hot wings like Halloween candy may have had something to do with their overt sportsmanship, as well.

At some point during these fly-by conversations, I noticed that I was alone at the table. Angie, Anto and Morgan snuck off to the jukebox and were pumping it full of quarters, while Wade and Patty ordered another round of apps and drinks for the table. A loud scream followed by inebriated laughs drew my attention back to the jukebox, where Anto had given Morgan a drink of her Rum and Coke. She had never had rum before, and the subsequent spit take that coated the glass of the jukebox suggested she might not be trying it again any time soon. Out of the corner of my eye, I noticed someone heading to the table. *Keith?*

"Congratulations," he said with his tongue literally in his cheek. His tone, demeanor and wandering eye contact suggested that he was three sheets to the wind drunk. I had trouble fathoming how his tell-tale arrogance would be impacted by alcohol, but to my surprise, he was quite the congenial drinker.

"For what it's worth, I'm sorry if I've been such an asshole to you guys this past year." *Just this year?!* Shock didn't even begin to cover it. It would have been less jarring to see the four horsemen riding in with a mushroom cap cloud backdrop. I grabbed the nearest glass, *I hope this is mine*, and took a swig to prevent the concentrated snark pinging in my head from leaving my lips. *Vodka spritzer ... it burns! *squint**

"Truth is, business hasn't been doing so great this past year. We were working closely with a few of the Dell product managers to prove to them that we could be their next big acquisition target. They had all but assured us that the deal was going to happen, so we pumped a ton of money into custom form factors and new vendors to ensure that our products would be more compatible with Dell support. Then, out of the blue, we found out that Dell had acquired Alienware, and it all went downhill from there."

He tossed back the remaining third of his pint, while I squirmed in my seat looking for a social out to the conversation because I couldn't bear to take another sip of the glass in my hand and I had already chewed up all the ice cubes trying to suppress conversation. I nodded my head in agreement, that definitely was a crappy situation, but no crappier than an annoying competitor buying up a billboard right across the street from our shop. At one point in the conversation, I thought that Keith might have been delirious, because he just kept on talking. Most of the time it made sense, but his transitions between topics was a tad chaotic.

"And now, my asshole landlords are raising our rent, again, because all the new stores are opening up in a few months. Rumor has it that they are in talks with Best Buy to fill one of the new buildings they just broke ground on. If I wasn't so desperate, I wouldn't have accepted that lady's offer to put up the billboard."

It was like he had just read my mind, *wait ... what?!* "What do you mean lady?" I asked.

"You know, Evelyn, that real estate lady," he replied. "Tom's wife. Err ex-wife, I guess? She said that you guys did something that pissed her off, so she wanted to teach you a lesson. She paid for the billboard through the end of April and told me to keep it on the down low. I thought it was a bit weird, but that billboard has helped keep the lights on. Every penny counts! Am I right?"

That woman was pure evil! Keith raised his empty beer glass in the air searching for someone that would get him a refill. In a few short minutes, my perspective of Keith and his store changed completely. Nothing could forgive their disgusting frat boy "bro-culture"; however, hearing about him struggling like we were, painted things into perspective for me. Our clock of borrowed time wasn't just running out for Andersson Electronics, but perhaps Jollyville as a whole. As more of the big businesses moved into the popular big box complexes and strip malls, the harder it would be for all of us to compete. We were in the same hole ridden boat just trying to keep things afloat. When Keith's beer arrived, I grabbed a glass and raised it in the air.

"To the J4ck4l5 ... it was an impressive run, but today Hot Shots reigned supreme," I said.

"Thanks man, Cheers!" he replied.

I half expected him to reciprocate the complement with some sort of acknowledgement, but the part of his brain that manages human decency was probably floating in a putrid lake of sudsy pilsner. Instead, he responded with a slurred belching shout-out to his boys in the pub, which sounded more like William Wallace screaming "Jack-*belch*-holes...."

The nine o'clock hour was upon us, and the discounted drinks and apps were coming to a close, yet the party was still raging between the two computer crews. It was time to settle our bill and take this celebration on the road. Three hundred dollars later, the two crews loaded up into their respective vehicles, *thanks for being the DD Morgan*, and headed to the What-a-Burger across the street. We huddled in the parking lot, fearing that we might be a tad too loud, and opted to walk through the empty drive thru and pretend we were in the world's longest stretch limousine. *Forty cheeseburgers, eight small fries and one small Diet Coke, please.* Burgers were eaten as fast as they could come out the drive-thru window. Packets of ketchup and napkins fumbled between ill-coordinated hands, until the carnage ceased and only a few dozen bags of burgers and condiments were left and ready for transport back to the shop.

We all parked in the back and entered through the warehouse heading straight up to my apartment for some after-party videogames and music! We brought some extra controllers in from the breakroom and cleared the area in front of my TV to see who could get the farthest on the Wii Tennis wall mini game. Morgan and Angie tossed handfuls of Cheerios, *there goes breakfast* and shot silly string at people as they struggled to beat the high score from last year; set by a motivated tracksuit-wearing Tom. Connor, Cody's twin brother on the team, offered in-depth color commentary pretending to use my small dumbbell doorstop he found in the corner as a microphone. This prompted Anto to launch into full DJ mode and turn my stereo into a game show boombox. She literally had every type of music in her collection! In no time flat, the party had successfully transplanted itself to new grounds and turned itself up to a thunderous eleven thanks to one of Wade's super caffeinated creations. Everyone was having a blast, except Patty. He was not a fan of how Connor and Anto were becoming quick friends. That is when the dust covered alcohol cabinet filled with left-over liquor from past holiday parties opened up and the bottles made their way to the kitchen table with a large sleeve of blue Solo cups. Patty grabbed the half empty bottle of Crown Royal and poured a hefty shot into one of the cups and tossed it back. He wasn't much of a drinker, so this was going to be interesting.

    One by one, Keith and his team began to fade and retired for the night, which was fine with me. Jesse abandoned the celebrations at the bar, but Marco hung with us for a few hours, eating a disproportionate number of our hamburgers before he tapped out for the evening when my window unit crapped out. The dial was cratered at sixty degrees, but apparently it was never rated to handle ten plus people simultaneously talking, yelling, laughing and breathing in less than six hundred square feet. Patty was doing all he knew how to, *which wasn't much,* to draw Anto's attention in his direction. In part, this meant challenging people to a ton of random challenges and over the top speaking so that he could be heard over the crowd until people got tired of the Wii and vacated the gaming arena for another round of hamburgers. Seeing the break in play, Patty seized his moment and hurdled the back of the couch and dialed in the AV switch combination to switch to the PS2 for some Crash Nitro Kart.

    "Time to show Crash Bandicoot who's boss ...," he said. "Upside down, that is!"

He fought the clinging sofa to flip around and dangle his feet off the back of the couch, as he poked around in the configuration menus to undo all my preferred button mappings. *Ya jerk!* Wade joined him, upside down on the couch. Personally, I think he just liked having the excuse to flail his legs around in the air like a maniac. Every time Patty failed to complete the level, Wade deposited a piece of popcorn in Patty's mouth like he was an arcade cabinet. Eventually Patty's little stunt worked and everyone, Anto, Angie, Cody, Connor and Morgan, surrounded the couch cheering him on.

I was never much of a drinker, which is why it was even weirder that I would use over twenty percent of my apartment's storage space to store it, but ever since I started antiquing with Tom, I had a thing for collecting interesting bottles. Fact is, I was more inclined to admit that I was an alcoholic than admit to being a hoarder. When other people drink, they get relaxed, overly emotional and sometimes non-stop giggly; however, when I drink, I just get tired. It's like all of my energy is zapped from my body. That night was different. I had a few drinks at the pub, and I had taken at-least nine shots in the past hour as Patty's upside-down racing had turned into a sadistic drinking game that somehow ended up with me wearing Morgan's blue wig. My innards felt nice and toasty, and I was just glad that I wasn't asleep on the floor covered in silly string. *New Year's 2002.* Patty was working on a new world track, which meant others were drinking heavily with every crash and failed turn. I could sense that I was ready to start turning it in, so I opted for one final shot for the evening. A shot to share with someone special. I poured myself some tequila, Tom's favorite alcohol, and headed to my desk.

His computer sat on the edge of my desk, still plugged in and tempting me to boot it up to read the mysterious Desktop folder. The trivia tournament win was the brightest light in an otherwise lackluster, albeit fun, string of ideas that appeared to fall short of their intended financial outcome. This is why people drink. They drink to forget. They drink to escape. I wanted both. I wanted to forget that Tom was gone, and I wanted to escape the responsibilities he so recklessly left me. I made a final salute with my glass, but before I could sling it back, I felt a jabbing pain in my side and a voice from behind me.

"You're not going to drink that alone, are you?"

Angie was laughing and retracting her arm. Her fingers got me directly between my top two ribs and pierced some funky muscle that sent my shoulder into spasms. We had been keeping a passive distance between each other the entire evening, as she was having a great time hanging with Anto. Every time I walked into the conversation, she seemed to find a reason to leave, but here she was smiling in my face, assaulting me and ... *geezus, that hurt!*

"You know a tap on the shoulder would be a nice change of pace," I said rotating my arm and shoulder trying to find a stretch that would help. "I think you might have punctured a lung that time."

"My apologies, oh wise and frail one. I just saw you over here by your lonesome and figured you could use some company. Cheers." She tapped her cup against mine. "What are we drinking to?"

"To Tom." I motioned toward the computer.

"Wow. I can't believe he still had this. Does it still work?"

"Yep. He upgraded everything on the inside, probably ten times over, and custom-made mounts for at-least six different motherboards, but he could never bring himself to buy a new case." I stared at the faded white mini tower laughing to myself. "Now spending a thousand dollars on an antique gas station dispenser, that was a different story." We both laughed at the irony.

"Wasn't this the computer case guys bought that summer when you rebuilt all the Community Corner computers? It looks like the one that he gave me when I went to college."

She was right. Tom and I got a sweetheart deal on these cases, except we had to be eight or more to get the price. I also had this exact case from that same order, but that was countless upgrades ago. *Was that why he kept it?* I stared off into space traversing familiar rabbit holes of contemplation about what could have been when a strand of the blue hair fell in front of my face. I tried and failed a few times to blow it out of my eyes, and then Angie snatched the wig from my head.

"Seriously, Ben. Just take the wig off." She nestled the wig on her fist and held her hand up to let the blue hair lay flat and all without spilling a drop from her cup.

"To be honest, I kinda liked it." *If I was being really honest, I forgot I had it on and had yet to question why my hair was suddenly long, blue or hanging in my face.*

She tilted her hand into a sock puppet like head and started ventriloquizing in a heavy European accent.

"So tellz me, Ben. What eez your obsessiooon with blue hair? Do you want to make ouut veet a Smurf? Perhapz zyou have a ting for Violet from Villy Vonka. No?"

"Seriously? You haven't spoken to me almost all day, and now when you have the chance ... this is what you want to say?" *Who was I kidding, I loved it!* There was a prolonged uncomfortable silence, but our eyes were locked. "But, for the record. Negative on the Smurf and negative on Violet."

"You had me there for a second. I thought you were legitimately upset," she replied.

"I wouldn't count it out just yet." I slurred. "I'm not quite sure what I'm feeling right now. It's complicated ... and I'm pretty sure I'm drunk." I searched for words in my stockpile of useless filler to unload into the conversation, but they were only coming out in drips due to an alcoholic obstruction. *To hell with it.* "If I didn't know any better, I'd say you were hitting on me."

"Well you are right about one thing. You don't know any better. Of course, I'm hitting on you. That's how it works in this relationship, remember. I hit on you, then you pretend to not notice and then I have to do all the work."

"What's that supposed to mean?" Part of me had taken offense to her commentary, but I also knew she wasn't completely wrong, and I was about to get an ear full.

"Let's see. After we first met, I gave you one week at school and the shop to muster up the courage to strike up a conversation. I had a guy I tutored in Math that worked in the office write down your schedule and made sure that we would see each other between classes whenever possible. I wrote little notes that I slipped into your locker to say hello, but I at the time, I didn't realize the extent of the dumpster fire you had going on in there, which would explain why you never wrote back. *I had never seen any notes.* So, I decided to take action. I purposefully left my book behind at the shop that day. I purposefully walked slower than normal to give you a chance to catch up. Tom already spoke to me about your personality by then. He even asked me if I had a crush on you, and I told him that I didn't know yet."

"What are you telling me this for? Aren't you just going to head back afterwards?" I asked.

"If I do, it will only be to go back and get my things. ... I quit," she replied.

"You quit? As in staying in Jollyville kinda quit?" I was pleasantly confused. *Sort of.*

"I don't have another definition of quit at the moment," she smirked.

My ears couldn't believe what she was saying, but my eyes couldn't have painted a more honest and clearer portrait of my happiness.

She raised her glass to salute the computer.

"To Tom," she said, with all of us echoing.

We took our final shots of the evening in honor of a great man. She placed the blue wig on her head, pulled Benji from her pocket and placed her, *err him*, in my hand. Across the display, I could see a piece of tape with a message that read, "*All I need is you. Love Angie*". Angie grabbed me by the bottom of my shirt and pulled me into the doorway of my room and pushed my back against the door jamb leaving her hand firmly on my chest.

"What are you doing?" I asked stupidly. Nothing could have been worse than to assume at this point.

"Doing what I do best. Taking control." she said.

I was not ready for what happened next. She leaned in and gave me the most impassioned kiss of my life. Years of pent up pining and endless wonder rushed through my veins and arteries sending my heart pumping into overdrive. Every emotional kindling, no matter how damp, fractured or displaced it may have been, ignited in an instant. I dropped my cup sending my arms around her waist pulling her closer. Her hands ran through my hair, and mine through hers until the wig got tangled and slid off her head. I tossed it onto the bed and tried to kick the door shut with my other foot, *I missed*, which sent us tumbling to the floor in a drunken giggly mess. *Smooth, Ben. Real smooth.* On our way down, her hand reached to the wall for something to grab and ended up tearing large pieces from two of my posters in the process: **Procrastination** and **Ambition**. *Something told me, I wouldn't miss them.*

*** ***FADE*** ***

FEATURED TRACK

Matchbox Twenty - Bent

23

No Day Like the Present

    Reality faded into focus as the feeling of imprinted palm ridges retracted from my tingling forehead and temple, followed by an overwhelming sense of ease. I looked up to spot Morgan, who was still bouncing her leg and pounding away at her laptop keyboard listening to music. Had she known the various alleys my mind explored, it might have made things awkward, but crisis averted. My eyes scanned the room, and for the first time this morning I could draw some meaning at the extraordinary level in which my apartment had been destroyed. Every ill-placed aluminum can, every hamburger wrapper and every pile of carpet cereal crush'ns now had a faded memory associated to help make sense of it all, but there was only one memory I wanted to relive.

    I peeled my legs from the couch and headed towards my bedroom pausing at the door frame to reconjure visages of last night. On the floor, the empty vessels from our final drinks last night laid on the floor; trampled by overzealous feet, no doubt. My eyes worked their way up from the floor, following the contour in the left door frame which had been most noticeable when being pressed against the opposite side. The bedroom door was ajar, and I could see the scattered mess of clothes and crumpled torn poster scraps on the ground. I walked in like a crime scene inspector analyzing the still warm carpet tracks which outlined our frolicking on our way to the bed. The bed showed evidence of multiple sleepers with one slight depressed region and another cavernous valley on the other side. *I need a new mattress.* On the opposite side of the bed, I now noticed a note on the pillow. When I sat down to read it, *the pillow still smelled like her hair,* the perfect handwriting and crispness of the paper edges was the final telltale evidence that eliminated any last shred of doubt about the veracity of my memories from last night. The note read:

Will be back later for breakfast. Love Angie! xoxo

I couldn't help but smile as I rubbed the paper stock between my fingers and then re-folded it on the crease. With the door open, a pale light flooded in from the living room that illuminated the minefield that was my bedroom floor allowing me to tiptoe with minimal problem. *Coordination still needed some work.*

All things come at a price, including clarity, and while my victory lap around the bedroom was nearing completion, the cost of that clarity reared its head on the large whiteboard by my computer desk.

7 Days Left

The reminder of this impending deadline induced a panic familiar to the tendril like nerves in my skin and my ailing abdominal muscles. The naive internal voices of excitement that bolstered my confidence into accepting this fool's quest were now completely drowned out by the even stronger voices of pragmatism that were quick to emphasize the looming seven-day deadline and the large gap still to close. The surging tidal wave of ideas that spearheaded our initial successes had dissipated into a subdued leaking kiddie pool, syphoning confidence and office morale by the boatload. It was just a matter of scale and time, while we tried to figure out where Evelyn was going to strike next. Ever since Morgan turned down her offer, the chances of us getting any more physical recon was limited, as the digital trail left little to be gleaned due to her and her employee's habitually boring browsing tendencies. If I knew

Evelyn half as well as I thought I did, she would have something in store for us this final week. *The Evil Wench!*

I could speculate doomsday scenarios all day if I let myself, but I had more immediate problems to address. The lone operational oscillating fan in the apartment was working hard to cool everything down, but all it was successful in doing was smearing a stale viscous sheet of beef farts, alcohol and sweat around the living room. *And yet, I've smelled worse.* Picking up the trash wasn't going to be hard, a little air freshener and the place would be in tip top shape, but Anto and Patty showed zero signs of life. I overly crinkled and smashed the dispersed burger wrappers into one of the larger to-go bags, which was enough to trigger movement in the papasan. Not too much long later, Patty snorted and fidgeted until he shot up off the couch in a disoriented jolt, scaring me half to death. He mumbled a few words that sounded like "Bandicoot" and then collapsed back onto the couch grabbing his head. Words continued to pour from his mouth, but his face was buried in the cracks of the cushions. Meanwhile Anto started to unearth herself from her Cheerio encrusted cocoon and started to fold her beach towel coverings in suspect curiosity.

"Hey Patty," she said to him as his head was still buried in the couch, "If you're placing an order for tacos, get me one."

Her playful banter aside, it looked like Patty was going to be out of commission for the day, but I think hearing how composed Anto responded, it compelled him to toughen up. His response was heard through the cracks in the sofa cushions. "For your information, they are all out of tacos. All they have are crumbs, pocket lint and a few quarters."

"Before we get any tacos, we've got to straighten this place up." I interjected. "Which means we all need to help a bit."

"And we need to open a window in here, pronto! It smells like someone was cooked menudo up in here." *A savory bowl of her grandma's menudo actually sounded really good at the moment.* "I didn't mean that as a compliment, Ben."

Morgan turned around at the commotion. "Glad you guys finally got up. I couldn't sleep, so I just crashed here and worked on some things. Hope you don't mind, Ben."

Patty opened the window in the kitchen and the change was noticeable in a matter of minutes. The cool morning air billowed in with a faint smell of "dirt lot" that seemed to cut right through the stinky shroud in the room. It wasn't long before we were able to discern the aroma of coffee coming from downstairs, which meant that Wade was already busy getting ready for the day. Anto, Patty and Morgan headed down to grab a few cups of go juice, while I hung back and tidied up a bit. By that I mean, reattaching Nerm's arm in the bathroom and detoxing my apartment with god's gift to lazy people, Febreze. There was no avoiding it this morning, a shower was imperative, unless I planned to work outside the rest of the day. A quick rinse did the body good, and after I put on a fresh shirt, I headed downstairs to join the others for coffee and open the shop. *So, I thought.*

In the distance, I could hear a loud banging coming from the shop floor. At first, I assumed it was Wade cleaning Marge for another big day, but as I got closer to the warehouse door, it was clear the sound was coming from the front glass door. Our customers were fanatics, but this was a first for them to assault the front door for some coffee. On my way through the warehouse doors, I bumped into Wade who was apparently on his way to come get me.

"Hey man, this guy out there is looking pretty serious," Wade said.

"Serious how so?" I hadn't yet turned the corner, so I was able to peer through the door porthole to get a reflection. The man was dressed in his finest khakis and button up polo shirt.

"He says he's representing the state health board and that we have to close, or at least I think that is what he is saying. It is hard to hear him through the door."

"Waaaaaa-de. Why didn't you let him in?"

"Because we weren't open yet. Besides, he was being very rude."

At this point, I was dreading to even take a step outside, and that's when I heard a commotion outside. We peered around the porthole and saw Angie standing out front, holding some brown paper sacks in one hand and a small drink tray in the other. She had her rigid forward-leaning attack lawyer stance in full affect, waving the drinks around in dramatic fashion.

"Wait. Just wait. Right here." She told the man, and then screamed, "WADE!!!! Let me in NOW! ... please."

The spine snapping "do it now before I get really mad" tone in her voice was all too familiar to both of us, which sent

Wade darting for the door. I met them at the counter, where she unloaded her goodies.

"I bought doughnuts and kolaches for you guys today and a couple glasses of orange juice. Too bad I'm going to have mine to-go ... According to Mr. Genius out there, we never filed for a permanent food handler's permit for Wade's coffee stand, which is false, and they are closing us down until we get things resolved. I told him I'd go with him right now to get it squared away, but until I get back, you can't sell any coffee. I'm serious, under NO circumstances are you to sell ANY coffee today, otherwise we may lose it outright. Okay?" She jettisoned her kolaches and drinks on the counter and immediately marched back out the door in a manner that left little doubt that she would take care of it or kill someone in the process. My gut told me that Evelyn was involved here but would need to wait to hear back from Angie before jumping to conclusions.

"OK, well that just blows." I said.

"No kidding, I've got four urns of coffee made. What are we supposed to do, drink it all? If you keep heating and reheating it, it's going to lose all its flavor. I hate wasting coffee like this." Wade was pretty upset, but I think it had more to do with his coffee store closing than the wasted product. *Maybe it didn't have to go to waste?*

"Let's go ahead and open the doors. What's ten minutes early for some of our most loyal customers?" Wade had a confused look on his face, when I went to unlock the front door.

"Good morning, everyone. Due to a small snafu, we are not going to be able to sell you any coffee this morning." The early morning groans started to rumble. "But, while I cannot SELL you coffee this morning, I can sell you one of these beautiful Tom-NET mousepads for one dollar, and with it, we will throw in a free cup of coffee. If you are interested in one of Wade's specialty drinks, we have some small USB flash drives over there in various sizes that should do the trick. Let me know if you have any questions."

There were no questions. Few things get in between coffee-folk and their morning brew, and I wasn't about to deliberate the point further. They understood the subtext. I brought the stack of computer accessories over to the coffee counter, and then waited for the early wave to finish their ritual socialization and clear the shop. The moment the shop cleared, everyone collapsed in their nearest chair to rest. It had been an eventful morning, and we all needed an extra beat, or four, to get started. Patty plopped down at his desk, put on his sunglasses and just sat in front of his computer with his hands resting on his keyboard and mouse. *I think he fell asleep.* Anto retreated to her desk, sitting backwards in her swivel chair and was intently texting Connor on her phone. Morgan was straightening the Community Classroom for her next class, while trying to cycle the stale meat and sweat smell that permeated the walls from my apartment. I returned to my desk with the intentions to try to build something, but my mind was deadlocked and could do little more than unlock and relock my workstation.

    Press a letter, backspace a letter. Tab to one program, and Alt-Tab back. My command prompt cursor taunted me with every blink, bragging that it was ready to do whatever I asked, but it needed me to decide. Clarity and decisions were coming in short supply this morning, minus the coffee giveaway idea, but I consider that more poking holes in rules, which has been ingrained in my DNA since birth. After nearly an hour of impotent clicking and internet surfing, I called it. Morgan's JavaScript class had started, and the entirety of the shop's constituency was confined into a single room. Her star pupil over the past few weeks was sitting in front, leaning forward intently and actively raising his hand every opportunity he could. She spoke of him a few times, specifically about how he dressed. The first time he showed up, he looked like any normal computer bum, but he started dressing in more khaki slacks and button-down shirts as classes progressed. Today, he looked like he was birthed directly from the Banana Republic catalog. Between his odd dress, and his asking of non-trivial JavaScript questions, Morgan was convinced he was trying to hit on her.

    If I was going to sit at a computer and just stare at it, I figured I might as well do something productive. *Tom's diary.* I asked Wade to cover the floor. Normally, this responsibility would fall to Anto or Patty, but given both of their preoccupations, and Wade's open availability, it was worth a shot.

    The apartment was still airing out, and a bit in shambles, but Tom's computer stood out like a clear beacon of purpose amidst all the disaster. It held its place on my desk like a mausoleum, unweathered by time, waiting for visitors to arrive. *I'm here, Tom.*

While the computer was booting up, I questioned whether reading the diary was an invasion of privacy. Was this responsible, or was I simply being nosey? When the folder appeared on the screen, my doubt and responsibility succumbed to curiosity and I double-clicked. A flood of .txt files filled the explorer window and the scrollbar kept building out, becoming smaller and smaller. A cursory look at the status bar showed over just over three thousand files with no folder structure, just files with an obvious YYYYMMDD prefix to keep them organized. The earliest files were from the early 1990's, I guess Tom had been doing this for a while and just carried the files over. The first big block of files was all from 1992, and relatively short. My favorite though was one of the firsts.

> *Doctor's suggestion to write down what I eat and feel each day is starting to get annoying. I had steak and eggs for breakfast. You like that doc?!?! I feel fine!*

It was short, to the point and totally Tom. Perhaps I hadn't stumbled onto something worthwhile after all, but as I kept scrolling, I noticed that the file sizes and frequency started increasing in 1993. I clicked on a few, and you could see Tom getting familiar with his near daily routine and opening up about loneliness and regret. At some point in my life, I knew I would sit down and read every last one of these entries, but I needed a way to cut through it all and look for clues or some sign that I was supposed to be here. I sorted the files by file-size and then by filename, which revealed about a hundred .txt files that were 50KB or larger. *That's a ton of text.*

I started to see a pattern emerge as I stepped through the first set of files in this reduced set that aligned with big moments in Tom's life that compelled him to write it all down. Conversations from his fellow BBS folk when he decided to launch his BBS. Happenings from when he first caught Angie saving her schoolwork to the Community Corner computers. Memories from the day when he offered me a job. The week we launched our ISP, and nearly two weeks straight were dedicated to chronicling and cursing the Planetarium level in Myst alone. He was all over the page, sometimes. It was as if my morning's mental journey was a precursor designed by fate to prepare me for this endeavor. Perspective was everything, and I had no idea just how many emotions Tom felt because he rarely talked about them when it counted. Every year on August 11th, there was a large entry where Tom wrote a letter to his deceased brother, Michael, as if he was still alive. *I had no idea he was so lonely.*

The recorded moments continued to pile onto my freshly minted memories, but then the file sizes started increasing even more around the time when Angie first went away to college.

> *Talked with Angie again, tonight. She's nervous about coming home for Christmas, and I can't blame her. Asking me to help her break up with Ben is the hardest thing I've had to do in a while. I am thinking about staying neutral, in case things go sideways, but we'll see what happens. If only he would listen to someone. I see him going to a dark place, and I'm worried for him. As long as Ben has Wade, he'll be fine. I would have given anything to have had a friend like that when I was his age.*

As if Tom learning about my breakup before me or having secret phone calls with Angie wasn't enough, she apparently made a regular habit of seeing him when she came to town over the years. They always met across town though, since they knew I never ventured that far. The next notable block of larger posts started when my Mom left town and Tom moved into Evelyn's place. At first the posts seemed to be focused on me a bit, but then the tone shifted, and his writing became more upbeat. I knew what was coming soon enough. *The bitch.* It wouldn't be too long in this timeline until Tom went on his trip to Mexico. Every sentence I read from here on out would need a safety valve cut-off in case Tom let some romantic details slip out. That was the last mental image I needed, and it was best not to know what went on between the two of them behind closed doors.

I had only scanned less than thirty of these longer posts, when I came upon a block of oversized files that I instantly knew what they were about without having to look at a calendar. They were all posted the week after his first heart attack, a date that I will never ever forget. A new version of the same debate emerged: to read, or not to read. *That is the question.* Did I really want to read about these moments, when living through them the first time was so rough and knowing how they would ultimately play out? Despite my mind's preoccupation with sorting through the minutiae of the decision, my finger forged its own rogue path and instinctively pulled the window into focus with a mouse click. The words poured into my reluctant brain, doing its best job to deflect, denounce and discombobulate the barrage of imagery, until one section cut through my defenses.

> *So that just happened. Tom, let me be the first one to tell you that heart attacks are lame. First off, your chest hurts so bad you shit yourself, and then everyone looks at you differently. You can't go to the grocery store, without someone offering to pick things up for you. Wouldn't want you to strain yourself and die right here in the bread aisle! I'm not sure how much more of this I can take. If it wasn't for the shop, I'd probably already be dead. How does the saying go? Get Busy Living, or Get Busy Dying, right?*
>
> *Ben is a good kid. I just wish he didn't have to see me like that. He's been through a ton already. I don't want to be a burden. And then there's Evelyn, who hasn't stopped suggesting that I hang it all up and sell the shop. Sometimes I just don't think she listens. The shop is more than just money to me. It's a family. My family. I have to say that Evelyn's Dallas contact made a compelling offer yesterday. They screwed over everyone else in the neighborhood, but apparently, I'm the only one who actually owns their land, so I'm holding all the cards. Who knew that I had it in me to turn down two and a half million dollars for an old bath and bidet store? Grandpa would be so ticked with me!*
>
> *Part of me thinks I should sell though. Just to shake things up. It doesn't mean things have to stop. With that type of money, we could move anywhere in the city. It is just that Ben has been so frustrated and angry lately. I think he's getting complacent. Dropping out of college is one thing, but I think he has lost his way. Even though he's not my son, I can't imagine having one any better. The longer I allow him to coast on auto-pilot, the worse it will get. One day, I'll figure out a way to challenge him ... to make him realize that life is more than a series of rinse and repeat actions ... its more than money ... more than Jollyville ...*

and no matter how much fun we have ... it's also way more than just the shop.

It felt like he was writing to me, *or his brother*, this whole time, even before we met. Maybe, this is why he left me the computer. Knowing I'd boot it up, see his folder and be too curious not to look. Never in a thousand years, would I have thought I would find such succinct answers to the questions swirling in my head these past months. Questions I had since written off as things I would never get a real father figures perspective on, and yet Tom was so open and candid in his writing it was like he was right in front of me giving me one of his lectures. I can't lie. If I owned the shop, I can't say that I would pass up millions of dollars for nostalgia and family, but if the last few months had taught me anything, it was that the shop was not near as profitable as Tom made it out to be. If recent accounting was any indication, the amount of charity Tom infused into the shop's books to keep things afloat was not insignificant. As each paragraph rolled into the next, I could hear an echo of Tom's voice growing louder and gnawing at my subconscious telling me in no uncertain terms that this challenge was designed for me to make a simple choice: *Get busy living ... or get busy dying!*

Spiteful images of Evelyn rolling around on a mountain of money covering Tom's lifeless body flashed in my head, and I knew I had already made my decision. This realization snapped the strap tethering me to my predictable low-effort safety nets and finally opened the doors to a new dimension of ideas and thought that was unbound by these artificially self-imposed constraints. For the first time, thoughts of an actual future with Angie came into focus. A house. Kids. A farm with loads of animals. A dedicated fiber optic internet pipe. White picket fences. The whole shebang. Then there was Wade. Slinging coffee at the coffee bar with a smile on his face, absolutely crushing life. Despite his dad, despite social awkwardness, despite everyone discounting his ability to contribute, he was always there for me as a friend. Tom was right. I was lucky. He was my rock, and I was embarrassed to have lost sight of that fact. What would happen to him if this all goes south? As quickly as the thoughts flowed in, new ideas began to congeal, and a new vision of the shop started to take shape.

I grabbed a pencil and some scratch paper and started to sketch them out as quick as they surfaced. Every flick of the pencil seemed to spring me into a new direction and expand things even further. A quick search online for the commercial real estate firm and a few terms listed in Tom's diary confirmed my suspicions of why they wanted all this land, which added even more harmonious fuel to the frenzied bonfire inside my head. A small ding went off alerting me to the fact that it was almost time for Morgan's class to end. *Had three hours passed already?* I could feel the zoned-in focus fading as day-to-day responsibilities supplanted themselves into my active concentration, while the OCD part of me wanted to shed responsibility and keep on drawing. I peered down at the mad scribblings on the paper in front of me and one section's sketch leapt out from the page. The longer I stared at it, the more the lines seemed to converge into an interconnected idea that was recalled with absolute clarity. All we had to do was beat Tom's challenge, and this might be the answer.

Before heading down, I clicked on the Contact Us form on the real-estate company's website and left a shot in the dark message as a backup plan, just in case.

> *Interested in finally acquiring Andersson's Electronics in Jollyville? Come to the shop on April 15th at 4PM and let's discuss. You can call me at any time for more details. I live there. -- Ben*

After sending the message, I headed down just in time to see the last of a large crowd from Morgan's class walking out the front door, but her creepy stalker friend was still in the room grilling her with questions. She didn't seem to mind. The rest of the shop floor was sadly empty, minus the gathering waiting at the coffee bar with newly purchased thumb drives. Angie came back in time to see the last of the customers leave with their coffee in hand.

"Ben, I told you to not sell coffee! Do you realize how much crap I had to go through to get this straightened out today?" she said.

"Hey hey hey ..., slow down. We didn't sell them coffee." A confused bullshit calling look immediately knocked me back. "We sold them some mousepads and thumb drives that came with a free coffee."

Her eyes rolled hard and slammed the signed extension on the counter.

"Fine, but you are playing on a fine line. I've got a seventy-two hour order that allows us to resume food and beverage sales to re-open until Thursday, but these guys are not trying to make it easy. If I had to guess, Evelyn is behind this somehow. I would expect this type of treatment if we were a company one hundred times this size, but for a small town like this to go after a local business with so little leeway, it is unheard of. Something is off. It's just a good thing that I'm that much better." Her smirk may have been playful, but her eyes were all business, and still pissed at me for my rogue interpretation of her instructions.

"OK. Got it." Angie turned to Wade. "Wade. Looks like they are going to be extra curious this week, so let's make sure to double check all the health code stuff. Don't give them anything easy to find." He responded with a military salute and immediately got to work.

Maybe it was the fact that we had recently watched the recent Miracle movie, but I felt compelled to rally the team like we were playing the Russians in the final period. "Now, I don't need to tell you what is at stake here. We have a lot of money still to raise this week, or Evelyn gets the shop and you can be rest assured that she is going to sell it in a hot minute. This means that we are going to have to lean heavily on Anto and Patty this week, as that is where most of the extra money is coming from. We have a ton of stuff back there; we just need to get it sold. Do you think you guys can make some more videos and get them posted throughout the week?"

Patty nodded in affirmation, but Anto had a suggestion.

"I was kinda thinking that we should move things around a bit. You know, change the video format to be more of an interactive talk show tour rather than just an inventory video like we've been doing. It might give people something different to watch, and I could get Connor to come over and shoot the video for us."

Patty was still reeling from Anto's infatuation with Connor the night before and was visibly not pleased with the proposal. He rarely proposed new ideas once Anto had said her peace, but he was suddenly feeling feisty. "I had a similar thought, but I was thinking we could try shooting in the style of The Office. Maybe not as many cutaways, or whatnot, but have them actively engaged in the video quick panning as we talk, etc...."

"Sounds good," I replied. "Just get as many new videos up this week as you can. Focus on the bigger ticket items and let's move more of the smaller items out here into the front area since we don't have any more vendors coming in this week. Live tours might not be a bad idea when we are not shooting videos, and we probably have enough stuff to do some buy one get something free type promotions to people who come in person. If we are going to close the gap in any significant way, we are going to need to sell a ton."

Anto and Patty headed off to work on their videos with Anto's first stop being the phone to give Connor a call. Meanwhile, Morgan and her prize pupil were wrapping up their lengthy discussion. He hurried out of the room frantically trying to graffiti notes into his Palm Pilot, nearly running face first into the door frame. When he got to his car in the parking lot, he stood for another two or three minutes nodding his head as he feverishly kept scribbling and trying to fish his keys from his pocket with his elbows. He eventually made his way into his car and left, but not before Morgan came out of the room counting a large stack of cash.

"I swear." Morgan state. "That guy is going to save the shop all on this own."

"Who is that guy? Where'd you get all that cash?" I asked.

"Oh, him? ... That's Tim. ... A lot of college students have been crashing my course asking me to do their homework for them and answer questions. I told them for twenty dollars I'd fix any JavaScript problem they had, figuring that would weed out all the questions. Instead, word got out last week and now I've got students from the community college and even UT paying to ask me questions. Even the professor at the community college has reached out asking me to help her create her curriculum, which makes it even easier, since I create the problems I get paid to help solve." Morgan laughed trying to keep count as she thumbed through the bills."

"That's awesome. How much did you get today?" I asked.

In a low voice Morgan tried to finish counting, "forty ... sixty ... eighty ... nine ... twenty ... forty ... forty-five ... fifty ... fifty-two. Nine hundred fifty-two dollars and ... fifty-four cents. That's twenty people paying for the class and just over an hour or so digging through all the questions. I cut some kid a break since he didn't have all the money, and his question was simple enough. Hehe"

She handed Angie the stack of cash and the loose change in her palm. I have never been a party to a drug deal, but the nonchalant way in which Morgan plopped the stack down had me suspiciously checking the windows and blind spots for spotters, just to be sure.

"That guy Tim is at-least three hundred of that alone. He keeps coming in here with these detailed questions and scenarios, asking me what I'd do and how I'd approach things. At first it was kinda cool to have someone bringing in interesting questions, but now it just feels like I'm just coding by proxy. As far as I can tell, he's working on some sort of browser plugin, but hey, he has the money, so there's that."

"Morgan this is great. Do you think you have enough ideas to do two of these classes a day for the rest of the week?"

"I guess. I mean I just kinda stand up there and walk through the syntax and show some sample code. I could probably do three a day if you needed." she replied.

"Okay, then work with Angie to get the word out to UT and the rest of the community college with the times. If we can pull in money like this for each of those sessions that could really help us out."

I turned to Wade who had waited patiently for additional direction, which had only been unblocked in the past half hour.

"As for you Wade, you just keep being you. Give our customers a reason to stop by, making the best damn coffee you can, and the rest will be up to me and Angie to get the word out. If you have any special brewing lessons you'd like to throw on the schedule, just be sure to work with Morgan, or have the lessons out here at the coffee bar." I took a deep breath. "Sound good, everyone?"

Wade and Morgan nodded in the affirmative and then slipped away leaving Angie and me to discuss further in private.

"You know," she said, "we are going to need a miracle to pull this off this week. By my rough calculations, we still have at-least forty to fifty thousand dollars to raise and not a lot of time to do it in. I think it's admirable you've made it this far, but I'm worried about what will happen if it doesn't pan out. Not just to the shop, or to everyone else, but you. Are you going to be OK?"

I gave Angie a large reassuring hug, and then rubbed the back of her hand with my thumb. I contemplated sharing my plans with her, but I was certain that she would want to pick them apart and I hadn't fully formed them yet. Deep down in my gut, I knew this was going to work, *it had to*, even though this concept of planning for the future was still foreign to me.

"I'll be fine. I promise," I reassured her. It will be what it will be, but we're not going down without a fight. That much I knew for sure."

300

FEATURED TRACK

Lifehouse – Somewhere In Between

24

Get Busy Living, or Get Busy …

After Angie fell asleep that evening, I snuck out of bed and returned to my desk to continue percolating ideas. My notebook was safely hidden in the side drawer of my desk under an avalanche of forgotten desk toys and computer game paraphernalia from over the years. An anthropologist would have a field day cataloging my trans-period collection of used Battle.net gift cards. *I'm still a sucker for Blizzard art!* Every expedition into the drawer was an adventure, as the cards were excellent camouflage; sometimes revealing lost treasures when they shifted. Much like a leap of faith, I submerged my hand further into the abyss and retracted the notebook letting years of plastic pop culture roll off the cover into a freshly churned pile. *Oh look, a Nod soldier!*

The ideas were just as fresh in my head since the last time I saw the annotated sketch. When I opened the notebook to the bookmarked page, I remembered every insignificant detail as if the pencil strokes had stenciled themselves onto my brain, and yet, still an intense wave of uncertainty washed over me. The cynical voices returned in full force and reminded me that this was far larger than anything I had ever attempted in my life, or accomplished, and with far more consequences should I get it wrong. If reading Tom's diary had taught me anything, it was that life was about taking chances. Something I had always been reluctant to do. If I were ever to change my ways, there was no time better than the present because the probability of failure was universally significant across every realistic timeline I could imagine.

Over the last week, each day operated much like the next. Wade showed up bright and early with the back of his truck filled to the brim with plastic crates, bags and supplies from an early morning run to the grocery store. The one-day hiatus lit a fire beneath him. It was clear his world was much more complete when he was at the helm of his own coffee empire, which only further drove his creativity and manic attention to detail. He easily brought forty pounds of various coffee packages from his private collection and unloaded double-fisted pairs of whole milk gallon jugs each day. The older customers, even the dark coffee drinkers, had become accustomed to his frothy milk toppings and we were burning through milk faster than he could pour.

Anto and Patty would arrive not too long after Wade, and they would be dressed in what were known as their de facto outfits for their channel. It started out by accident, when Patty wore the same shirt on three consecutive videos. His polo shirt and shorts look was a stark contrast to Anto's eclectic apparel, which now included homemade techno-jewelry made from bright colored RJ-45 patch cables with analog mouse trackball pendants from her jar. That was Anto. Always bringing the creativity. She got the idea from one of our visiting merchants that was making a killing selling simple beaded jewelry by the handful. Once the Internet started commenting on their odd relationship, and disparities in wardrobe, Anto worked it into their sign-off phrase.

"Will see you next time, and who knows, maybe Patty will finally change his shirt."

They would grab a cup of coffee at the bar and start shuttling smaller items to the front to fill up the dedicated browsing space. Connor volunteered himself and his brother Cody to help Anto shoot their videos; however, they consistently showed up later than she preferred. On Monday, it was only fifteen minutes, but by the third day they were clocking nearly a full hour late. Anyone who knew Anto, knew that punctuality, by her clock, was expected for all things from funerals, weddings to game nights. Eventually, the morning routine consisted of her asking them to present themselves for a slap upside the back of their head, but that too was ineffective. By Thursday, her expectations were as low as she could get them, and her tone was full of condescension.

"Today is very simple. It's the same as yesterday." Anto stopped for a moment to make sure the laggards were paying attention. "We are recording, everything. Follow us through the warehouse and just make sure to keep rolling. No cuts. No edits. No matter how much you think we need to! Nada! We'll shoot for 5-10 minutes, and then switch out tapes and upload videos like we have been doing ALL week. Think you can handle that!?" She snapped her fingers and waved her arm towards the warehouse. "Vamos!" There was never a question who was in charge, as all three of them jumped and followed her instantly on command.

Anto's on-camera voice was as loud as her personality. We could hear her voice echo off the walls in the warehouse and through the doors. While they recorded, Angie would sit at my computer and field questions found in the piles of Internet Troll filth on YouTube. Frankly, I wish she didn't read them, because it always put her into a sour mood; however, despite all our attempts to ask people to email, call in or use Morgan's website to request more information, YouTube comments seemed to be the most popular source of actionable leads and interest. Sadly, some of our older fanbase were unable to discern the difference between an email client and YouTube comments, despite navigating the YouTube registration process. This led to some to some comedic gold at their expense and resulted in many of the videos going viral. *#OldPeopleVsTechnology*

The additional attention helped one of our videos about Tom's antique board game collection get featured on YouTube's homepage, and drove our channel subscribers past five thousand in only a few hours. Online selling was already having a massive impact on our daily lives, even here in small town Texas. All we needed was one or two more sparks to make this week really count.

After every recording, Patty would pop out from the warehouse with a MiniDV cassette in hand and head for his computer to copy, convert and upload to YouTube. On that Thursday, while Patty waited for the tape copy to finish playing through, we could hear an elevating conversation approaching from the backroom. Anto didn't sound happy.

Connor came out of the backroom pleading his case. Cody was peeking through the door porthole trying to keep his distance.

"All I'm saying is that maybe you should slow down when you talk so people can understand everything you're saying," he said.

"And, all I'm saying," Anto argued inches from his face, "is, people understand me just fine. If they want me to talk slower, they can listen faster. Isn't that right, Patty?"

"Yep." Patty replied refraining from making eye contact.

"How's it looking over there, Patty? You almost done?" she asked.

"Almost done copying. Shot wise, it looks like we got the footage we needed." Patty tried to diffuse the tension with some positive notes, but Anto wasn't having it.

"Not what I asked, Patty. How did my voice sound? Did I talk too fast? Could you understand me, clear enough?" Her eyes rolled daggers at Connor as she asked the question.

"To be fair, I haven't heard any of the audio yet, just watching the video." Patty had a concerned look on his face, as he contemplated what to say next. He was obviously trying to play Switzerland in the dispute, despite his feelings for Anto.

"If it were me ... I would just be myself. Some wise person once told me that if you just be yourself and be comfortable, the audience will figure it out."

He smiled at Anto and then quickly turned back to his machine to finish up the video extraction.

"Exactly," she said, clapping her hands loudly and pointing her hands at Patty, "that is what it's all about ... the viewers. I'm going to go with my partner on this one, OK." She patted the side of Connor's face with her hand; her ethernet bracelets spun around like muted bangles on her forearm. "From now on, please just stick to doing what you do best, which appears to be working the camera."

"Sorry to interrupt this tender moment," I interjected timidly, "but did you happen to remember to mention the buy one get one offer and start with the big-ticket items?"

I strategically was maintaining my distance from Anto, just in case she decided to take a swing. Before she could answer, Patty stood up and said, "it's uploaded!"

"I guess you'll have to watch the video ... to find out." she replied.

Her eyes squinted at me in a most devious way, before sticking her tongue out at me, but then a silly grin emerged on her face as she turned around to head back to the shop. She snapped her fingers and yelled, "Vamos!" to which Patty and Connor leapt to action and Cody darted away from the door.

As for myself, I was covering Patty for tech support and I was nearing the end of any conceivable website work I would be able to complete before our looming deadline. With Patty busy shooting videos, all I had were the digital assets he was able to build last week. We were running a special on our templated site packages, which drummed up some more business; however, all of the packages required people to send us details about their business, including photos that we could use to make it more personal. Unfortunately, most people, not just in Jollyville, didn't understand the concept of resolution and sent us these super low-resolution photos as if they expected CSI photo enhancement to pull pixels out of thin air. This is why we normally went onsite and took photos with our own equipment whenever we could; however, given the time constraints it just wasn't feasible. *Sigh. Idiots suck.*

Everything that morning felt recycled for the first few hours. Customers would walk in, order some coffee, browse the shop while waiting and then take their coffee and leave. Every twenty minutes or so, Patty emerged from the warehouse and did his routine to copy, process and upload new videos to YouTube. Reset. Rinse. Repeat. My nerves were on edge. There was no way we would make our goal if this kept up, and then the phone rang, and everything changed.

"Thank you for calling Andersson Electronics, home of Tom-NET. This is Angie, how can I help you?"

Angie's face sublimated from boredom directly to excitement when she realized it was a call about the latest video. As she talked with the person on the phone, her computer started *ding* incessantly. Emails started to pile up in the inbox, all interested in getting more information about some of the recently featured antiques. I jumped on the computer and checked YouTube and our most recent video already had over a thousand likes and a hundred comments. Angie hung up the phone and scribbled a few more notes down on a piece of paper, and then snapped her head up with her charismatic smirk.

"Guess who has two thumbs and just sold two of those glass gas pumps for three thousand dollars? This gaaaaall!" she said.

"Are you serious?" I asked.

"Yep. Their son saw the video online and sent them the link. Apparently, they are avid collectors of these things." She pulled two red sold tags out and scribbled some notes and hurried back to place on the items before the next recording started.

Patty, Anto, Connor and Cody came back in from the warehouse just in time to hear the news. They had knocked out three videos and were even more energized to keep on filming. Meanwhile, Morgan showed up for her late morning class sporting her Andersson Electronic polo, but this time she was also carrying a computer tower into the shop for a middle-aged woman. She set the tower down on the counter, unaware of all that just happened.

"Hey Ben," she yelled across the room, "this lady is looking for you. I've got to get ready for my class, do you mind helping her out?"

I walked over to greet her and quickly realized that this was a L33tR1gz computer. Their debossed side panel was a dead giveaway. All it needed was some knockoff Photoshop solar flare and drop-shadow action for their logo to be complete cliché, at-least it wasn't yet another swoosh. *Sagging scrotums is WAY better, hehe!* Either way, their stuff paled in comparison to Anto's work.

"Hello, I'm Ben. How can I help you?" I asked the woman.

"The other computer store across town told me they were slammed this week, and that I should bring my computer here to get it worked on. He wrote down some notes for you."

She pulled the taped envelope from her purse and handed it to me to read. It was short and to the point.

Figured you could use the help this week. Good luck, Keith.

Now I really felt bad. It was going to be really hard to hate him again after this. I folded the letter and put it in my back pocket and continued to discuss her problems with the customer. All she needed was a quick OS tune-up, defrag and a registry cleaning, but she was so happy we were able to fix it the same day that she opted to throw in a RAM upgrade, as well. It gave me something tangible to focus on for a bit, which I didn't mind.

More customers started to trickle in. The older crowd browsed the antiques in the front, while most of the younger crowd headed to Morgan's JavaScript class. I could see her title slide emblazoned on the projector screen on the far wall, "Dissecting jQuery", just over the heads of the late arrivals who had to stand at the back. jQuery was a pretty slick tool. It helped me simplify a common rat's nest of JavaScript code I created to help our sites be browser agnostic; something I had been craving for years. It was fast, lightweight, convenient and most importantly, something people wanted to learn more about and were willing to pay for that knowledge. Morgan was going to make a pretty penny this week, on tuition alone, not to mention her extracurricular scholastic revenue source. A special part of me recognized the irony that the shop, a company that I more or less owned, was profiting from doing student's homework for them, something I would have paid for in a heartbeat in high school had the option been available to me. It wasn't a black or white situation; it was firmly in a comfortable shade of gray that we both were willing to accept.

The feedback and general buzz coming out of her morning class was exceptional, which made me want to squat in on the afternoon class just to see the master at work. Watching her naturally command the attention in the room and explain the technology in such relatable ways, it was hard to think this was the same Morgan that timidly came into the shop all those years ago. In four years, she had matured to a whole new level beyond the shop, and part of me felt that I had known this for quite some time. When I first got to know Morgan, I remembered thinking she was in need of direction and that Tom and the shop could help. *The same that it did for me.* Seeing her grow, stumble and continue to pick herself back up on her own left a lasting impression. She was not the hurt little animal I once thought she was, nor was she in need of saving. If anything, she had quietly emerged as a leader amongst our ranks in these past few months. Sneaking into Evelyn's office and putting L33tR1gz in their place at the trivia tournament were only the highlights of a lengthy resume. Morgan was going to be fine; she had the entire computer science community in and around Jollyville, listening to her every word, even the community college professor who was in the front row taking notes. Deep down, I knew she had a great future waiting for her, and that her time at the shop was coming to a close.

After the class was over, I watched the hordes of people line up to get some extra instruction from the lady of the hour. One by one, she tore through their questions and the pile of cash on the front table comically overflowed like an eighties stop motion montage. Her obsessive friend waited at the back of the line, and he had his notebook in hand and based on the stack of bills he had in his hand, he was going to be there for a while. *Cha-ching!*

I stepped out of the room, to find a bustling shop floor with an overwhelming familiar fragrance. Someone ordered a significant number of pizzas, and customers were plowing through the food as a tower of empty boxes started to form in the corner next to the coffee bar. The line to order drinks was wrapped around the shop floor, each person in line holding onto their slices of pizza. Wade was slinging brew behind the corner like a pro, multitasking orders in a calm collected fashion. All his personality quirks were working for him to make the unique and informative coffee drinking experience special for everyone. I remembered how bummed he was when he didn't get the job at FlowJoe's, and how far he had come doing things his way.
Everywhere I seemed to turn, I saw yet another way this shop, run by an eccentric old man, consistently attracted talented quirky people and helped them realize their potential. Of all the people I worried about with regards to losing the shop, Wade was always number one. Over the years, the shop was a safe space that allowed his true self to shine and most coffee chains would never be able to make him happy.

People hung around the shop quite a bit that night. They found our Tribes 2 server installation on the Community Corner computers and were launching a makeshift tournament using the shop's backbone. Anto and Patty finished their last video and made it out in time for one of the last pizza boxes, while Morgan was stuck in the Community Classroom getting grilled by her favorite friend. Judging by the stack of the remaining dollars in his hands, they had ten to fifty minutes, tops, remaining. Meanwhile the providence of this mystery pizza buffet had yet to be confirmed, but I had my suspicions. *Angie*.

As if reading my mind, she appeared behind me with a pizza box in hand.

"Want to go for a walk, Mr. Manager?" She floated the cracked pizza box in front of my nose and accompanied the banter with her irresistible smirk. *How could I say no?*

"Sure, it looks like we are winding down in a "winding up" sort of way. Why not?!" I signaled Anto and Patty to keep an eye on the shop, while Angie and I went to get some fresh air in our lungs. We walked for a solid hour, just randomly turning corners, crossing streets and eating pizza, but it was the conversation that I enjoyed the most. *It has always been the conversation.*

It's odd how your mind can subconsciously revert to known patterns and learned behavior. Angie and I never discussed where we were going, or what we were doing, but we instinctively ended up at the courthouse fountains. The fountain lights weren't on yet, but the sun was sliding faster towards the horizon and it wouldn't be long. We sat at the edge of our infamous triple decker fountain listening to the sound of the water trickling down and finishing the last morsels of crust from the box.

"So how are you feeling about tomorrow?" she asked.

"It will be what it will be, I guess. When we get back, we'll have to see what is left to cover. I'm not expecting it to be a pretty number." Optimism was in short supply. We had been squeezing water from our stony town for a month already, and it wasn't wise to be overly bullish.

"Yeah, me neither" said Angie. "But Tom would be proud of you for how you pulled everyone together and gave it a go. I mean seriously, I can't think of a worst time to try and grow a business in this town. From what I could tell in the courthouse, it seems that commercial real estate developers are gobbling up all the available land. The competition is going to get even worse when more of the big companies move in. To be honest, Ben, part of me thinks you should sell while you can. If anything, these past few months have shown how saturated it is here in Jollyville for computers and internet services. Even with so few options, there just aren't enough people in this town to go around, anymore."

"Yeah, I get that. Which is why I have a plan forming that should help." My tone was not that of confidence, but of concern and it showed. Earlier that day, I had received a reply from the real estate company, and they said they would meet me at the shop at the proposed time. It was a bit of a gamble, but worst case, all I would do is waste their evening and some gas money.

"Does your plan involve robbing a bank, or blackmailing Evelyn? As your most likely lawyer, client confidentiality notwithstanding, I'd prefer not to know about anything illicit and premeditated."

"Well in that case, I'll just keep it to myself then." I tried to keep a straight face; however, she knew me too well. "But don't worry. Neither of those options are on the table ... for now." *think*

"In that case, then there is just one thing left to do here." She reached into her bag and pulled out her wallet. She popped open the coin pouch snaps and retrieved the laminated penny wrapper and proceeded to unpeel the layers of tape to free the encased penny.

"One wish for all the marbles," she said.

She set the penny in the palm of my hand and closed my fist around it. The look in her eyes could calm a hurricane, and the warmth in her hands sent my heart fluttering.

If you had asked me about fate and destiny only three months prior, you would have gotten some witty half-cocked rhetoric summarily rejecting the notion of its existence; however, since Tom's passing, I wasn't so sure. Even here and now, did we end up at the fountains by chance, or was some other force at play. In my hand, I held a powerful symbol that proved without a shadow of doubt that fate finds a way. In my head, a decade of reanimated stories, memories and experiences that would be inherently improbable to a random person, revolved conspicuously around a notion of fate relative to one man, Tom. By throwing this penny into the fountain, I was effectively throwing this last remaining artifact of my former self, an immature and childish adolescent who was unsure of his feelings for a girl, and fully accepting the world in front of me. Yes, a world without Tom, but a world with a chosen family. With Angie ... and that was enough.

I rocked my fist and slung the penny with conviction towards the top tier fountain. As the penny sailed, I closed my eyes and visualized a life that would make Tom proud, like Wade told me. A life with Angie that would make me truly happy. The clean plopping sound of the penny as it plunged into the high waters in the algae-covered concrete basin triggered a deep sigh that released a lifetime of repressed baggage in one fell swoop.

"I guess, now we just have to wait to see if it works." I grabbed Angie's hand and pulled it to my lips to kiss the top of her knuckles.

We took a long way back to the shop, savoring a loving moment of calm together. During our sauntering escapade, nearly all the customers left, except for Morgan's stalker friend who was still talking her ear off. Thankfully, she had migrated to the coffee bar where Wade was able to keep an extra eye. *Something was off about that guy.* Anto and Patty were sitting on the hood of her station wagon, going over notes for tomorrow's "everything must go" video and responding to YouTube comments from her laptop.

Angie and I headed back to the what was left of the office where we were able to get a full tally of the daily sales on the computer. Someone had tucked both Wade and Morgan's earnings into an envelope underneath the keyboard with the details jotted down on a napkin. Over twenty-four hundred dollars in her last class alone, and Wade pulled in just over a thousand as well. Angie charted our latest progress and shared the details in her best, "we're probably screwed" tone.

"Ok, so good news. We made nearly double the money we made last week to date; however, we are still going to be about twenty-three thousand dollars short of our goal starting tomorrow."

There were still significant items in the warehouse that we could easily sell, if we could only find a buyer. Tomorrow was going to be different. *It had to be.* The pit of my stomach felt raw and worn. My newfound beliefs in fate were being tested with a very real, foreboding and yet, simple number challenge: twenty-three thousand. It would need to be the best-selling day of the shop's illustrious history no doubt, and if we failed, I had no doubt the shop would be destroyed. My heart sank in my chest and I could feel a waves of panic shoot through my arms. There was too much to process at the moment, and I was admittedly tired. Besides, I noticed Angie slip out and head for the apartment. Whatever tomorrow would bring, I knew I wanted to spend this last night of suspended disbelief and hope with her in my arms, counting the seconds until tomorrow finally revealed our fate.

FEATURED TRACK
Bush - Comedown

25
Twenty Fifth Hour

*** BUZ- ***

My hand was at the ready on the stand to stop the alarm in its tracks, as my head laid on the pillow staring at the glowing red digits. *5:30*. A mere three hours and twelve minutes had passed with me counting the rhythmic blinking colon and watching the changing digital bars usher new minutes into existence, drawing me closer to this moment of absolution I was reluctant to face. The only thing making these final days bearable was curled up beside me with her head resting on my opposite shoulder, a pleasant change I was growing more used to with every blink. Nothing good comes without sacrifice, though, and that cost was my enhanced awareness of hygiene, which threw a wrinkle in my normal morning routine of putting on clean-*ish* clothes and slapping on some deodorant. I would have never considered this before, *whiff*, but I questioned how Angie could sleep so soundly that close to my armpit. The remnant stench of day old sweat and body odor filled my nasal cavity and triggered a newly refined response to clean myself. I slid my arm out from under her neck, kissed her forehead and headed for the bathroom.

Long showers were not a common occurrence in my apartment. Over the past three years, the aging water heater seemed to know the exact minimum amount of hot water to produce to keep me from figuring out how to replace it. That morning though, the water from the spigot was pleasantly hot, compelling me to take extra care and shave the bearded stubble from my face and even wash *and condition* my hair. *It was Angie's conditioner.* I washed and re-washed every part of my body, half expecting cold water to signal the end of my aquatic distraction, but it was the loofa rubbing my forearm raw that beat it to the punch. The stubble on my face was mostly gone, shaving blindly in the shower with leftover shampoo and no mirror had its limits, but a quick wipe of the fogged mirror pane in front of the sink was all that was needed to finish things off. When I was done, a strange respectable adult-like figure was left staring back at me. The puzzled look on his face portrayed a concerned confidence that nodded in unison with my own visage and I knew that no matter what happened we had both done our best.

Shower vapor billowed out of the bathroom when I opened the door, and I could feel the cooling air from the oscillating fan blowing my body like a kite towards the now infamous whiteboard where the dry-erase markers waited for me to commence with the official ceremony.

4 0 Days Left

It was 6AM and I could sense that the crew was downstairs waiting for me. I cut my air-drying session short, put on my Andersson's best, grabbed my sketchbook and headed downstairs to meet fate's rugged early morning self, head on. As expected, Wade was impatiently waiting at the door with his two-wheel dolly loaded six feet high with stacked grocery crates from his morning shop. His truck was backed up with the tailgate down where Morgan was sitting and swinging her feet to the music in her headphones and typing away at her laptop. Anto and Patty were sitting in similar positions as the night before, on Anto's station wagon hood; however, they had the sense to change clothes and surprise their audience on their final day of filming. As I unlocked the door and helped Wade carry his crates inside, a cool breeze stirred the morning air and the resonating worrisome thoughts on everyone's minds. No one could look me in the eyes, except Wade, who was more focused on me holding the door for him, so he didn't spill any of his coffee urns. Everyone else had migrated to their corners of the shop, intently focused and ready to give the day their all.

A few hours later, we got a double dose of help for YouTube filming, when both Cody and Connor finally showed up. I'm sure that Anto would figure out a better way to deal with tardiness than constant beratement, but today was not that day and surprisingly Anto was quite convincing to help them decide to stay. Connor jumped back on camera duty, while Cody followed them around the warehouse stalls with a small boom mic as they continued to record videos about what was left in Tom's treasure chest. Anto and Patty already consolidated most of the remaining items into stalls containing large cumbersome items, but there were still seven storage bays that had barely received any attention online. Tom had a ton of stuff, *a certifiable hoarder*, and there just wasn't enough time to give thoughtful attention to everything, especially when shooting such short segments. Whatever they were doing, though, was working, as their YouTube subscribership had grown to over seven thousand members in these past few months. I had no doubt that if we were going to meet our lofty goal for the day, that we would need some big movement from the people in that online crowd.

Meanwhile, Angie was busy keeping conversations with interested buyers flowing via phone and email. Ever since their subscribers started to spike, there was a deluge of inbound messages asking for more information about specific items. Sadly, many people inquired about things they saw in older videos that had already been sold, and we had to keep explaining to them that the items with a red tag on them were already purchased. *You would think they'd never been to an antique store!?* The system wasn't perfect, but it was good enough to get us through this last day, as long as Angie didn't try to actually package and ship any items. That was an entirely different time-suck altogether, especially when the phone lines started to ring after the West Coast viewers finally woke up and saw the new videos. Angie and I looked like traders on Wall Street using hand signals and mouthing words to each other to make sure we were telling people the same most up-to-date information. Morgan was doing her best to answer customer questions about the front antiques, but she was also trying to prepare for her class and kept pushing them off to buy more coffee. The day had only started and the insanely complicated art of being an all-purpose gopher had already turned up the crazy.

Morgan's first class started early and was packed, *again*. Word had made its way through backchannels to all the neighboring Austin suburbs about a local *woman* JavaScript expert and students, practitioners and enthusiasts alike were jumping at the chance to see if the rumors were true, like she was some sort of arctic fox living in the desert. Their reactions when they realized that she was a gothed up teenager in a hoodie, and not the stereotypical basement dwelling programmer dude was quite entertaining. Pockets of guys often gossiped outside the Community Classroom, debating whether to go in, feeling as if this was all part of some sort of con to sell timeshares, but when Morgan started to talk, she set them straight right away. When she finished her prepared topics for the day, a seismic pulse shuttered the floor as everyone in the room shot their hands up to be the first to ask a question. I could overhear most of their inquiries and JavaScript's asynchronous event-based execution was a concept that most of them struggled to fully grasp coming from traditional object-oriented programming backgrounds. *I used to be one of them.* Thankfully, for them, Morgan was an exceptionally gifted teacher and had a nuanced understanding of JavaScript's intricate event driven underbelly. She methodically answered their questions one at a time in exquisite detail like she was extinguishing church candles with one of those long snuffer stick things; smoke billowing from their ears from having their mind blown. Her class was scheduled for only an hour but based on the number of hands in the air, it would run well past lunch, which presented another opportunity to make a little extra money: food.

Most of us at the shop were pizza'd out, having eaten pizza six times in the past four day, so I placed a call to one of Tom's favorite local Mexican restaurants to order an assortment of tacos for about a hundred people. The man who picked up the phone, Carlos, was the owner, *typical small-town Texas.* It became clear that he knew Tom very well and a conversation that started with a lunch order quickly turned into him sharing stories about how he used to go fishing with Tom and often invited him to his house for dinner to eat their freshly caught bounty.

"And that reminds me," Carlos said, "when my granddaughter came back from college last year, Tom helped fix her computer and wouldn't accept a dime. Please allow me to return the favor and consider this order on the house."

I wasn't one to pass up free food, especially when it felt like something that was meant to be. *Destiny?* One hour later, four banker boxes filled to the brim with tacos including a full spread of sides and condiments arrived at the shop. The mouthwatering smell of refried borracha beans and grilled fajitas flooded the shop with an aroma that would bring a vegan hunger strike to its knees. One by one, the attendees started to peel out from the back of Morgan's class and happily doled out three dollars per taco and grazed the buffet for assorted sides and toppings. With every unwrapped foil taco, the majestic aromatic bouquet intensified, beckoning would-be stomachs to seek sustenance. Even Anto, a person who frequently criticized practically every Mexican cuisine in Texas as queso infested garbage, was drawn in by the smell from the warehouse and couldn't stop eating the handmade corn tortillas.

Four hours had passed on our last day and Angie and I collected the tallies from around the shop while everyone ate their lunches. Anto and Patty's videos were starting to generate a ton of new questions, but very few actual sales that morning, which meant that Morgan and Wade were neck and neck for the highest contributor of the day. It was a bit hard to compare them evenly, because Wade never stopped moving behind the counter. He had become a master in all aspects of his craft, excelling even more when the pressure was on. Unfortunately, regardless of how much he worked or how long Morgan taught, the facts were becoming clear that we were going to be at-least sixteen thousand dollars, if not more, short of our goal. That is when we saw Mr. Lucas' car park in front followed by an all too familiar black Cadillac. *They're early.*

Mr. Lucas spent a few minutes in his car collecting his things, and eventually made his way through the taco bro barricade standing outside the front doors. The antichrist remained in her idling car, leaking distilled evil onto our parking lot with every drip from her condenser. Judging by his reddened face and shortness of breath, Mr. Lucas wasn't keen on the crop-dusted smells that now clung to him like a wet poncho. He reached into his breast pocket and pulled out a handkerchief and dabbed sweat from his brow.

"Good afternoon, Mr. Wilson." *I hated being called that.* "If you do not mind, where might I set up my things. I'd like to get a head start on verifying your last few months of records?"

"You can take Tom's old office if you'd like." I motioned for him to move towards the office behind the counter. "It's not perfect, but it's the best place we have. Angie can go over all the numbers with you in just a moment."

I closed the door behind me, knowing all too well that the office was not soundproof by any means, but keeping him out of the way and out of mind was the best thing to help everyone focus. Between the crowd, the lawyer and Evelyn's car, there was already plenty of distraction, not to mention Cody and Connor sneaking out during the lunch intermission. Anto claimed that they had creative differences, *Patty smartly remained quiet*, but they at-least finished their last video. Nine videos in total were recorded, all already uploaded to YouTube and generating buzz on the YouTube channel. With Angie now tending to Mr. Lucas, Anto and Patty took over answering phones and responding to the comments from their following. When word got out that the hosts of the videos were answering calls themselves, the call volume rocketed to a whole new level along with comments and likes on the videos by the hundreds. *These last few hours might get interesting after-all.*

Meanwhile, Morgan found her way back into the training room with her favorite pupil nipping at her heels, but this time he was flanked by two taller guys wearing business slacks, dress shirts and ties. They were having a pretty intense conversation about one of her diagrams on the whiteboard. Judging by the look on Morgan's face, they probably tried to tell her she was wrong and were minutes away from getting a dump truck of humility dropped on their heads. The remaining crowd in the shop, which was more than seventy percent of the last class, curiously looked on from afar trying to decipher the vigorous topic from their diagrams on the wall. They'd get their chance to ask their questions in the next twenty minutes during Morgan's last session of the day. *Possibly last ever.*

My expectations were tempered, but I couldn't help feeling as if things were heading in the right direction. As if by clockwork to dampen all hope, the door to Evelyn's demon chariot opened and a gaudy bright blue high-heel extended below to the pavement. When she stood up, her ridiculously large bug-eyed sunglasses peeped above the door frame. If the goal was to cover her entire face, then she was winning admirably; however, long seeded resentment planted deep in the furrows of her brow could not be contained, hidden or obfuscated by any amount of polarized plastic. *I wonder if she knew we knew?* She paced back and forth in the parking lot screaming into her cell phone for a bit, which compelled me to check my phone. *No calls. No texts. They said they would be here by lunch?* To keep from going insane, I helped Anto and Patty gopher things from the back to the sales floor, while keeping an eye on the yelling devil in heels in the parking lot. *She was up to no good.*

Around an hour and a half passed and the shop was still bustling with activity. People were swinging by to check out the remaining antiques and meet the surging local celebrities of YouTube. *A novel idea I wished I had capitalized on sooner.* People visiting the shop and trying to see if they could sneak themselves onto camera had become a thing to do in town, and most of the things they ended up buying were in the less than ten-dollar variety. Evelyn must have used the chaos to sneak inside during one of my errands, because she was now sequestered in the office with Mr. Lucas and Angie, who was busy reconciling her spreadsheets with Mr. Lucas' format. Angie body language made clear that she was not pleased by Evelyn's lack of social etiquette, constantly yapping on her cellphone as if she owned the place. *Not yet.* Time was running out, and while we were busy, it was hard to say how much progress we were making. We didn't have anything in the way of real-time information, it was more like an aggregation of periodic finger counting. Morgan's session let out only fifteen minutes late this time with very few follow-up questions. I didn't track all of the attendees in the room, but most of them were either a familiar face or had taco stains on their shirt. The room shed small waves of people until all that was left were Morgan, 'Stalker Guy', 'Ralph' and 'Lauren', *at least that's what I called them.* Their conversation was much more amicable this time, and Morgan looked like she might even be smiling. Just then the office door opened and out walked Mr. Lucas, who was being shooed by Evelyn to move faster. Angie looked worried.

"Mr. Wilson. It is nearly 5:00PM and I must inform you that as of 2:00PM today your ledger shows that you are approximately nineteen thousand three hundred forty-two dollars short of the required funds for Mr. Andersson's challenge. Does this sound about right to you?"

The ambient noise in the shop instantly stopped and ears from every fame seeking opportunist perked up to listen in to the reality TV moment unfolding in front of them.

"I'll need to talk to my team really quick, I guess, just a moment."

I motioned for them to meet me on the far side of the room for a quick conversation. I'm not sure what I planned to accomplish, besides buying time and making room for wisdom.

"I take it that since you didn't raise your hand and volunteer any information, that we are more or less where we were around lunch time?" I asked them.

"Not that bad," Anto said, "but not that good either. We still have a ton of people interested, but actual sales have been around fifteen hundred dollars since lunch."

There was no need for advanced mathematics, even if we doubled Wade's best day, we would still be significantly short. *I hate quiet rooms.* The silence was wearing on me, and I felt compelled to seek a manner of explanation that felt less like failure, but more so just to hear the sound of something. Thankfully, my train of thought was interrupted by Morgan emerging from the training room with a huge smile on her face.

"OK, why am I the only one in this place smiling?" She asked.

"Unless you made a killing this afternoon, we are probably going to come up short." I replied heavy handedly.

"Oh." Morgan didn't have a retort. Her smile faded back to neutral posture, but Anto was curious.

"So did *Stalker Guy* propose or something?" Anto asked.

Stalker Guy puffed his chest a bit, and then responded. "For your information, I'm happily married with a four-year-old at home."

"Does your wife know you hang around teenage women way too often?" She replied.

Before he could reply, Ralph chimed in. "Hey Anto, how's it going?"

"You stalkers like to travel in packs or something?" Anto was not okay with some random Abercrombie knowing her business. "How do you know my name?"

"Actually, I've been following your videos on YouTube the last few weeks. I was hoping to run into you guys. Great stuff!"

"Then why are you here?" Anto asked.

"Simple. For her. He boldly pointed to Morgan. "I'm VP of R&D at Symantec, and Stalker Guy, as you like to call him, works for us. He has been raving about this young lady for over a month now as some sort of JavaScript wizard and we wanted to come down and see for ourselves."

Forget Morgan's stalker conundrum, Anto's demeanor changed instantly when she realized she was talking with a fan. She walked up and shook his hand, so did Patty, and commenced with typical celebrity small talk.

"So random question, I noticed on your video this morning you have an old Stingray back there. Is that here, or somewhere else? I'd love to take a look at it. I'm an avid muscle car collector."

Anto's eyes immediately locked on mine. When we first started selling the antiques, there wasn't a conceivable reality where Tom's lounge car was up for sale; however, things were different now. Very soon, a harsh reality would start to take hold. One where I was twenty-five thousand dollars richer, but without the shop and possibly losing my family.

I gave one of those cheesy cinematic head nods to Anto, and she took him back to see the car. In the meantime, I wanted to dig in a bit more with the *Stalker Guy* and what exactly they wanted from Morgan.

"So, we know you didn't come all this way to just look at old cars. How'd the meeting go with Morgan? Saw you drawing up some intense flow diagrams in there?" I asked.

"Finally!! Where to start?" Morgan had been patiently waiting to spill her news, and had no problems claiming her time. "They want to give me a four-year paid internship, while I go to school. Apparently, they are working on some new browser tech and want me to come and consult on their team of engineers."

"Wait … what? School? What happened to school is just a waste of time?" I asked.

"My problem was never with schools. All my applications were accepted," Morgan explained. "The problem was that I didn't get a single scholarship that covered anything more than twenty percent of the out of state tuition fees. If I had taken

Satan's offer," she scowled at Evelyn, "I would have had almost a full year paid, but out of state tuition is expensive. Now that I've got this internship where I can work during school, I'm pretty sure I'm going to give MIT a shot and work out of their Boston office!"

"Well then. That is some news. I guess." The parallel to my own high school exodus was too eerie to ignore. The ill-fated whimsy to attend MIT I once possessed and the realization that it was a person like Morgan, not me, who would truly flourish there. If my short stint in community college had taught me anything, it was that work for work sake was not for me, but Morgan had the focus, the drive and the skill to do great things and I knew she was going to be just fine.

Angie jumped for Morgan and gave her a huge hug. Morgan was reluctant, as she wasn't the hugging kind, but gave in to Angie's excitement. We continued to discuss Morgan's opportunity, and deconstruct the past few weeks with regards to Stalker Guy's behavior. He really didn't like it when we called him that aloud, but even after we were able to explain most of his behavior ... the name had already been set. Stalker Guy was official. *S.G. for short.*

Anto and Ralph emerged from the backroom and it was obvious the guy was a bit giddy, like a kid leaving a candy store all hopped up on sugar.

"That is quite the collector piece you have back there. It's disassembled, but did you know that you have a 427 with air conditioning back there with matching tank sticker? That's pretty rare for a car that old. How much do you want for it?" Ralph asked.

"I did know that. *bluff* Why do you think I didn't want to sell it?"

Anto was standing behind Ralph and Lauren and her eyebrows were gesturing toward the ceiling.

"But given that we are trying to wrap up a few things today, I'll let it go for thirty-two five." *I had no idea what it was worth. I was just quoting a price I saw in a Grand Cherokee ad.*

"Ouch ....," he replied. "I didn't say I wanted to marry it. There's still a ton of work to invest to get it in one piece, let alone operational. I was thinking something more like ten ...."

"Twenty-five," I retorted back before he could finish his thought. "And remember, this car belonged to the shop owner before he died. It's a piece of history in this shop. Sentimental and all."

"The best I can do is twenty thousand ...," he replied.

"You've got a deal." He didn't need to finish the sentence. I knew with the close of this deal, we would clear the mark and could send Evelyn packing in fury. I had already committed myself to sell the car, so no need to jeopardize the transaction by bickering over a few meaningless dollars I wouldn't miss.

I turned to Mr. Lucas, and proudly announced, "It looks like we have just one more sale to report, and I think it puts us over the top."

The team erupted in celebration, even Morgan let out her own awkward "woo-hoo".

"No. no. no. no. no. no. noooooooooo." Evelyn's face and hair were a seamless continuous spectrum of red and fire. "You can't do this. That last sale should count. It was after 5PM. It was after the close of business."

"You want to talk about fair Evelyn?" My knuckles shattered beneath my clenched fists. *This woman dares to utter the word fair in this building* "Let's talk about fair, shall we? How's pretending to love someone just so you can inherit their property just so you can sell it to your Dallas real estate friends? Is that fair? Or how about sabotaging us every step of the way these past three months, despite what we were doing was something your former husband ... OUR FRIEND ... wanted us to do. We know about your deal with L33tR1gz, and you trying to bribe Morgan to turn on us, you influencing the health inspector to jack with our food permit. When it comes to you, Evelyn, things are never fair. So why should it start now?" *I wasn't sure about the food permit, but I wasn't concerned at this point.*

"I loooooved .... Tom," she cried. Her crocodile tears and mannerisms fueled a homicidal rage I struggled to contain. "How can you say such things?"

"Because they're true, and we all know it." Tears of anger, frustration and sadness welled in my eyes as the words came lashing out of my mouth. Years of repressed criticism boiled over like carbonated spitfire and I was erupting lethal spears of truth. "Never once ... did I ever ... ever ... feel that you loved Tom. Maybe you liked him at first, but you never loved him. Not in any way he deserved. All you saw was an opportunity for a quick payday. He was a kind and giving human being that was alone for far too long in his life. He built this place and this family. A closer family than I have ever known, and one that tried to let you in, but you were too busy stabbing us in the back. You didn't deserve him, and he deserved a whole hell of a lot more than you. ... To be honest, I don't care if we win the challenge and get the shop, or not, it was worth every penny just to say this to your face, right here and now."

"About that," Mr. Lucas interrupted, "while the 5PM deadline won't be a problem, I'm afraid a verbal commitment doesn't constitute a payment. For this to count, we are going to need proof of payment."

All eyes turned to Ralph who had long since stepped aside to let the drama unfold. Lauren poked him in the ribs to switch him out of observation mode.

"Right," he said. "I have an Amex Black Card, sooooo ... if we are good on the price, let's just get this done." *Of course, he has a Black Card.* All things being equal, on other days, I would have found reasons to make fun of good 'ole Ralph, but today, he earned himself a pass. He could have called me "brah" and done a chest bump while slamming a six pack of Zima, and I would have nothing but love for the guy. *But just today.*

"AaaaaaaaaaaRRRrrra!!!!" *crash* Evelyn pushed a large CRT computer monitor off the table sending shards of plastic and glass all over the floor and stormed out of the shop. Her tires screeched as she backed up her car and peeled out of the driveway just like Cruella Deville.

Mr. Lucas verified the transaction from Ralph's card, and then reviewed the trust documents one final time.

"By the power vested in me, by the Hot Shots Family Trust, I hereby award sole ownership of Andersson Electronics, including this building, resources, land and all operational bank accounts associated with it and its sub-entities, including Tom-NET, to the Hot Shots Family Trust and appoint Mr. Benjamin Wilson as its executor."

He pulled a pen from his breast pocket and directed me to sign and date the form while he notarized the signature.

"Congratulations, Mr. Wilson. I wish you and your family good luck on all your future endeavors. I know Tom would be proud of all of you." *Did he say, Tom?*

He packed up his briefcase and exited the shop through the crowd of people who had stuck around for the live action telenovela. The team circled up around Angie for a large group hug. Tears were streaming down my face. I couldn't believe it. Wade's chin was awkwardly on my shoulder and more arms continued to pull the group closer together. The Hot Shots crew pulled off another tremendous upset victory. *We might wait a week or two for the celebration!*

"Excuse me." An unfamiliar male voice called out from an uncomfortably close distance. "You're Ben Wilson, correct?"

He was wearing fancy jeans with a vintage AC/DC t-shirt and a pair of massaging sole sport sandals. *Two points for sandals. One for the shirt. Negative one million for everything else.*

"Uhhhh, yeah, weren't you paying attention?" My snark defenses were still a tad elevated from dealing with Evelyn.

"And how. My name's Duke from the Hartford Real Estate in Dallas, did you get my voicemail? Sorry, I'm late. Traffic was hell in Waco."

I rapidly tapped out on a variety of shoulders and squirted out of the huddle like a footie in a rugby scrum.

"Hey man. Nice to meet you. Glad to see you came down. Sorry you had to see all that." I said.

"Sure thing, and no worries. Almost made it worth the drive," he said jokingly. *Thank you?* "You know, we've been trying to buy this property for quite some time now, but just to be clear, we didn't know that Evelyn was doing anything behind Tom's back. She reached out to us with the opportunity to buy, but that's all we knew. We have talked to Tom many times in the past few years, as well. Seemed like a good guy."

"Yeah, I know." I replied.

"Look, I'm not going to lie to you. Our project on the other side of town is wrapping up soon, and I'm ready to sink my teeth into this one. Is there ANY chance we can settle this today and make a deal?" he asked.

"That all depends," I said, taking a deep breath. I looked at Angie and the rest of the team who were perplexed as to why I was even entertaining the conversation. "You see, I have this idea that I've been working on, inspired in part by words of wisdom from Tom and things we've learned during our little exercise these past three months. If you like what you hear, then I think there is a strong chance you can return to Dallas with an agreement."

Duke clapped his hands and rubbed them together and simply said, "Let's do this." Everyone else looked at me with confusion.

FEATURED TRACK

The Pogues – Love You 'Till The End

26
What Kind of Day Has It Been?

      My sweaty palms were shaking as I spoke. I knew I hadn't shared the idea with the team, but what was the point if we didn't actually win. Not to mention that I wasn't quite sure how they would react to me even inviting the guy down from Dallas, but as more time passed and the idea took on a clearer form. There was no question in my mind that this was the right decision and Tom would definitely approve. Now, all I had to do was sell it.

      "Look, I'm not up here trying to sound like a sellout, but I do ask that everyone listen to the idea all the way through before everyone starts chiming in." My eyes focused straight on Anto, who was sitting next to Angie probably plotting a coup. "Fact of the matter is that these guys probably own over half of Jollyville right now and have been courting Tom for quite some time trying to get him to sell. Not only do they own the new shopping complex on the other side of town, they also bought FlowJoe's, Little Caesars and every commercial piece of land within four blocks of here, except the corner liquor store for whatever reason. Them buying this land is not a question of "if", but "when" … All I've been able to put together is that they are trying to build one of their large mixed multi-use apartment communities. According to their website, they have completed three of these in the past two years. When you think about how empty this side of town is right now, I can see why they'd be interested ..."

"You are absolutely right," Duke interjected. "Our firm is looking to bring Jollyville into the 21st century, and this project will hopefully be a one of a kind project."

"By one of a kind," I cut him off, "he means that they will take the same thing they did in Dallas, Houston and Scottsdale and hope they can turn the same type of profit." My look to Duke was not malicious, just trying to cleanse the energy in the room and keep everyone honest, which persuaded Duke to lean back in his chair. "The only reason that Tom was holding out was because of us, I think ... As much as it pains me to say it, Andersson Electronics was a dying business, and I think Tom knew it. Angie and I have been tracking all the money from these past few months and while we have accomplished a lot, our ability to repeat this level of success day in and day out is not sustainable. Tom knew this, and I have just recently discovered that he has been sinking good chunks of his own money into the shop just to keep it afloat, but I'm not sure for how long. Everything has been getting more competitive with the Telco and L33tr1gz ... Just look at what we had to do to win this competition these past three months. We had to open a coffee bar, resell antiques like hucksters and sell Morgan's brain for money."

As quiet as the room had been, it was nice to get a chuckle. The portrait I was painting was not abstract. It didn't have much room for interpretation, for it was based on the sheer facts and reality in front of us. I think they got it.

"None of those things are core to what we do here, or what this place was built to be. I remember talking to Tom a long time ago about when this place used to be Andersson Bath & Bidet, and how hard it was for him to let go of the old and make room for something new. When he turned this place into Andersson Electronics, he had to let a bunch of things go, but he built his vision around the things that made him happy. For me, the thing that makes me the happiest is this family, right here, and what I'm about to propose is designed to keep that family together for as long as possible."

I paused for a moment to make sure that everyone realized the sincerity of my previous comments. My imagination couldn't fathom the person I would be today had my mother not moved us to Jollyville, had I not met Wade, had he not introduced me to Tom and then Angie. ... and then Patty ... and Anto ... and Morgan.

"... When Tom left me his computer, I'm pretty sure he was leaving me his diary from the past ten years. I found it on his Desktop, of all places, in a folder full of text files. *It felt odd saying that part aloud, but I knew they'd get the irony.* I've read a lot of his entries, and I feel as though I've gotten to know a whole different side to the man that I consider to be the closest thing to a father I've ever had ... So, I decided to do what I think Tom would do, and figure out a way to let go of the old and make room for something new, which is why I suggest we sell the shop, but not in the way you might think."

I opened my notebook and turned to the illustrated pages which held all my scribblings and ideas from the past month that had trickled from my brain onto paper. Admittedly, the drawings looked better when viewed with tired eyes and under the late-night sheen of an LED desk lamp with forgiving shadows, but I was hopeful that they would be able to connect the dots.

"Each one of their mixed multi-use projects looks almost identical, for the most part, but one of the biggest common factors is that there are four stories with businesses on the bottom and apartments above. If we lay out the footprint of all the abandoned buildings and sold businesses around us, you can get a sense for how their plan would lay out. We are smack in the middle, where one of the central four-story parking structures would go."

Thus far, Duke had yet to interrupt me, and I wasn't the only one who noticed. In hindsight, the idea was so capitalistic and straightforward, I'm not sure how I didn't catch on when all the business started to close down. People's eyes started to wander, so I dove right in to keep the conversation moving along.

"If you make me wait any longer," said Anto, "I'm going to slap you. VAMOS!"

"Okay, okay." She could be really pushy sometimes. "I'm proposing that we sell the shop and the land in exchange for a new building to be put back in its place that is connected to this central parking structure and this building will be exclusively leased by the Hot Shots Family Trust for a nominal locked-in fee.

Each floor will have a specific business that services the residents and will be a focal social point for the immediate community. On the first floor, we will have our very own coffee and Internet bar. Not a coffee counter, or some hole in the wall, but a place for people to come and get the best damn cup of coffee around by our very own Wade Bodin. Should he be so bold, he will be the general manager of the coffee shop and run the day-to-day business, answering to no one but himself on how to provide the best coffee experience in Jollyville, much like what he has done so well here at the shop, except with more help and far more equipment. Our location will all but guarantee a corner on the coffee market for this side of town, especially since I ask that no other coffee shop business lease be signed into the community for the first three years or so."

I toasted Wade with my best Tony Soprano impression. *Salud!* The look in his eyes was pure joy. I knew how much it meant to him to continue to do what he loved, and had I not been so focused on thinking that Morgan needed my help, I could have been there more for him, better supporting his dreams the way he and Tom were always there for me.

"Next, I proposed that we move Andersson Electronics to the second floor and become the resident technology center for the community. Since Telco will probably look to lock up everyone with high speed internet in this new construction, I think we should just strike a deal with them and agree to stop our Tom-NET internet service. We can still keep the BBS running for enthusiasts and those that want to keep their email addresses, but let's face it. Dial-up internet is basically dead, the Telco is much better equipped to support our aging customers, and this will allow Patty and I to focus on the Tom-NET Web Services side of the business, which if we are being honest, has been the main source of business these past many years." *And no more Pervy Joe!*

So far so good. I could tell the change was uncomfortable, but the message was being received well enough and inquisitive gazes were propagating.

"On the third floor, and this is where there is a lot of room for creativity. I think it makes sense to have a flexible space where we can continue to host the Community Classroom classes, but anyone in the community can rent the space for special functions, as well. There is definitely appetite for this type of service here in Jollyville; however, it doesn't need to be limited to just technology. By separating this out, we can have a more open class catalog and provide a community spot for people to come together, play games, or whatever floats their boat. In the end, keeping this space flexible and accessible to the community as an extension of the coffee or computer shop is my main suggestion. And, last but not least, on the fourth floor, there should be space for four large apartments that will be price controlled for as long as we lease the building. If any of us, or our families," I gave Anto a sincere look because I knew her family wanted to move her abuela closer to town, "want to live there, they can, or we can simply sublet it to some lucky people. The idea is that all of these businesses will be part of the Hot Shots Family Trust and we can do profit sharing as equal partners despite being in separate buildings. So that's my idea. Sell the shop, to build a new version of the shop."

Pause for effect.

Angie looked impressed, *I think*, or perhaps surprised that all that came from a page of scribblings from my own head. It was exhilarating to see each piece of the puzzle fit together, say them aloud and be received with such relative acceptance. I think Wade was already packing things up. He was definitely excited. Anto was holding Patty's hand with an obvious tear of joy running down her cheek. Patty just sat there with a smile; his face redder than a fire hydrant.

"Well," said Duke, interrupting my mental moment of triumph, "this all sounds great, but how much is this all going to cost?"

I looked to Angie and shrugged. All I had were the previous numbers they offered Tom. Selling the car disregarding a few hundred dollars was one thing, but possibly losing thousands, or millions, of dollars was something altogether different.

"Rather than address a final number right now," Angie interjected, "if we both agree to be flexible within twenty-five percent of fair market value on both the purchase and leasing terms, I can work with our attorney, Mr. Lucas over there, to send you a proposal this week." She extended her hand to Duke, and said, "We have a deal?"

"Give me one second, I've got to make a call". Duke tucked himself into a corner plugging his ear while conversing with someone from his team. He was only gone a few minutes before he returned and mightily shook Angie's hand. "You've got a deal. Here's my card, let me know when you want to set up the meeting. Now, if you don't mind, I've got a long drive ahead of me. This surely has been one of the strangest business meetings I've had in my entire life, but hey ... Keep Austin Weird, am I right?"

Our team's eyes rolled in unison, but we all mustered the minimal level of cordiality on his way out the front door. Upon his departure we realized that most of the telenovela in-studio audience had already left, including both Ralph and Lauren, which meant we were all alone with a massively looming question. *What's Next?*

Over the next few weeks, the lawyers hammered out the details, and Angie was able to negotiate a bonus stipend into the contract to assist us with the transition from the old shop while the new building was being built. We all took a vacation to Mexico to celebrate the closing of the deal and commemorate Tom's life, *his picture was in tow*. Angie was able to convince the high school to excuse Morgan's absences on the ground of bereavement, as long as she turned in all her work when they got back. While she wasn't a family relative, nor was Tom, Angie may have hinted at reprising her role of animal liberator extraordinaire at next year's opening football game if they weren't willing to be flexible. Needless to say, we didn't invite Evelyn, but before we left, she was in our thoughts, as we decided to re-enact operation slow Internet on her whole office before heading out of town and out of reach of cellular service.

By the time we got back in mid-May, Angie and I were officially engaged, *underwater scuba proposal for the win*, and we needed to start packing up our belongings to prepare for the shop's demolition. To minimize the downtime, our building would be built first as a standalone entity and the rest of the complex would trickle in over twelve to fourteen months. We contacted some of Tom's favorite antique dealers and told them they could swing by the warehouse and pick-up whatever they wanted. All they had to do was make an offer and it wouldn't be refused. In two days, the warehouse that took Tom a lifetime to fill had been emptied into a barren wasteland of musky air. All of his remaining antiques were dispersed to collector friends in his circle, free to create new stories for the next would-be collector.

Not one for packing, I handled my apartment much the same way I handled my office desk, which meant dumping drawers full of clothes, toys and crap into boxes with the sole intention of re-dumping the contents back into said drawers once it was time to unpack. To come full circle, Wade helped me move all my apartment furniture, *sans my computer desk and Nerm*, to the curb and we posted them on the Craigslist free stuff board. My eclectic decor eroded with every trip to the back gate, as memories of my past were literally kicked to the curb making room for new tastes that prioritized a sense of "we" over "me". After three hours, there was nothing left, not even the broken fans. It was like a plague of locusts devoured it all to smithereens. I did manage to keep one of my Demotivators, though. **Stupidity**, *my favorite*. We loaded up Marge into the back of Wade's truck and sent her to storage with the rest of the shop items, including the Andersson Electronics illuminated roof sign. In less than a week, we gutted the building, rerouted web servers and sold our dial-up services to the Telco with a non-compete clause for a hefty penny. We were finally ready to say goodbye.

On the day of the demolition, we all met at the shop one last time. Angie brought a bottle of champagne to share a final toast of our most memorable moments from the shop and the tears flowed steady, hard and heavy for everyone.

Angie went first.

"My favorite memory had to be when Tom tried to convince me that Ben was worth the time of day. He was so sure that we would hit it off, but I just didn't see it. The man wise beyond his years. ... To Tom."

Then, Wade.

"My most memorable moment had to be when Ben and Angie got in their first big argument that led to their first date."

"Aaaaawwww," Angie said, touching the techno-jeweled necklace Anto made her. "That's so sweet, Wade."

"Yeah, seeing how angry you were at Ben for beating you with a 1410 on the SAT, I was scared out of my mind that you might find out I scored a 1530. It's very possible that it is the most terrified I've been in my entire life. To Tom!"

Hahaahahahaha. Wait, what?!!!? Angie's face is priceless. Crap, she saw me smiling.

"Let's see," I posited with my glass of water held aloft, "my most memorable moment would have to be when we first launched Tom-NET. Angie, Wade, Tom and I were working around the clock getting that setup. Until then, I didn't understand what true hustle meant. Thanks, Tom!"

Next up was Patty.

"Trying to teach Tom all things Mac in five minutes so he could play Myst. Final answer." Judging by Patty's laugh, there was more to this story, but it looked like he was keeping those details for himself. He continued, "Oh, and that time I made your PC mouse a uni-button. Heh heh. Low and behold, I guess I get to claim victory there ... Mr. OS X".

"Yeah yeah yeah," I replied jokingly. *He was right.* I had been running Ubuntu for a few years as my primary setup, until I saw Patty running OS X and that is all she wrote. Apple's new smartphone was on the horizon, and I was quickly downing the Kool-Aid as fast as they could serve it. *iNerd!*

Anto didn't like being the last at things, so she jumped out of order.

"Easy. The first day I came into the shop, carrying my rig in a blanket. You all looked at me like I was crazy, but the minute I unwrapped it you were all little starry-eyed nerds. The rest is history ... well, except the starry-eyed nerd stuff, Patty still does that."

Patty coughed and spit out his drink, and Anto laughed at him. Since the trip, it was obvious to everyone by their change in behavior that they were more or less dating. The only person left who didn't know ... was Patty.

"Por Tom, ¡Salud!" she cheered.

Morgan was the last to toast her memory. She had been quieter than usual that day, as she was about to leave for early admission to MIT later that evening. Her eyes were uncharacteristically misted as they searched for something to share.

"To be honest, I don't think I can pick just one. So much has happened these past four years. But, if I had to choose, I think it would be when Tom gave me my practice solder board. That's the moment I became determined to learn more about you guys, and I'm glad I did." Morgan held up her glass of apple juice. "To Tom!"

"Speaking of which," I said, slightly interrupting the tail end of her toast, "We are glad you gave us a chance, and we wanted to give you a little something before you headed off tonight. I remember when Angie left for Berkeley, staying connected was painful." Angie raised her glass in agreement.

"Thankfully, it's easier and faster now, but we wanted to give you something to take with you to always keep a part of the family with you. We are all super proud and excited for you. If there is ever ANYTHING you need ... we are here to help."

I handed her a small padding envelope, which she promptly opened and slid out a hand-sized board of silicon. After unwrapping the last layer of bubble wrap, she read aloud the plaque that was soldered in the middle of the board.

"Keep Your Eyes on the Horizon," she said.

"The board is from one of your first soldering classes here. Tom had this stashed away in a box from your first day in case you never came back. Pardon, but my soldering skills were never fully refined like yours, but they were good enough to clear a flat surface for that plaque plate. Tom frequently told me that phrase when I was first learning the ropes. Things might get tough and be frustrating, but stay focused on what you want to achieve, and don't let all the distractions drag you down."

I raised my glass and said, "To Morgan."

Morgan's authentic smile seemed more deranged, like Harley Quinn, than happy when juxtaposed with her running black make-up, but the group hug she solicited made it clear that she genuinely appreciated the sentiment.

We headed out to the parking lot and gave the signal to the wrecking crew to commence with the demolition. We took a before picture for posterity, as the wrecking ball made quick work of the exterior walls. Our shop was reduced to a pile of rubble in no time at all. Now, we just had to wait for the new building to be built.

The construction crews worked lightning fast and had our building open for occupancy in just under ten months, but a lot had already changed in that time. Morgan was crushing it at both school and Symantec and was quickly making a name for herself in information security circles. Her product was leading the competitions with the fastest internet malware detection and remediation on the market. *She was where she was meant to be.* In addition, not only did Patty finally muster the courage to ask Anto out on an official date, *she said Yes*, but they also received an offer from A&E to host a new antique TV show where they travelled the nation interviewing collectors about their antiques. Their fame on YouTube was spilling over and creating new opportunities for them, left and right, and unfortunately, they would not be able to help keep things running. We reached out to Keith at L33tR1gz and asked if he was interested in moving, and thanks to some negotiation on Angie's part, she was able to get Keith's lease agreement transferred to our building at a much-discounted rate. Keith and his team would run the Andersson Electronics shop as their own but would continue to sell their L33tR1gz branded computers. It was a win for everyone.

As for Angie, she passed the bar in Texas and opened her own IP consultancy for law firms helping them prepare cases and, in some instances, testifying as an expert witness. Never in my life, would I have ever imagined things turning out this amazing. I was effectively a millionaire before the age of forty. I married the woman of my dreams. I'm still friends with my best friend, and I'm rubbing elbows with TV celebrity personalities and one of the Internet's most formidable female hackers. The weight of the world was no longer resting on my shoulders but was firmly beneath my feet. All the weeks of hopelessness and distress seemed insignificant in the long run. I spend my time building iOS apps and continue to help convert local businesses to a more digital existence; something that I knew would make Tom proud. *I still haven't beat level 99 on Minesweeper. =*

Angie and I moved into one of the top floor apartments when they first opened. We decided to convert one of our three bedrooms into an office for her, while I worked out of a small office in the new shop a few floors down. I dumped the contents of my packed boxes into their respective drawers trying to make room my new monitors on top of the table. *cling* *cling* *cling* That is when I heard the faintest high pitch sound of metal being bombarded with miscellaneous trinkets. *Tom's door chimes.* I remembered the day that Evelyn knocked them down with the door. It was sad that I never got around to fixing them and putting them back up, but there was only one logical place for these chimes to go, and it was not in my home.

When Wade received his final permits, he was allowed to open his internet and coffee bar: Hot Shots Coffee. *Nice!* The day before the grand opening, Angie and I were helping him with the final preparations, when I handed him a neatly wrapped business opening gift in a small bag with tissue paper. *Thanks Angie.* He knew what they were right away, but he didn't know their backstory. I proceeded to tell him about their legendary good fortune while he let them sway and collide against his finger producing their familiar tones. As was tradition, we hung them above his main entrance and finished prepping the grand opening.

The next morning, Hot Shots Coffee was bustling from the moment it opened, but Wade was taking it all in stride. He trained his employees to incorporate all his crowd control tactics and unique customer naming norms into their daily routine, while he would help and provide the coffee trivia of the day to round out the experience. Customers enjoyed the personal touch nearly as much as they enjoyed the free WiFi. I was waiting in line for my coffee and a hot tea for Angie, when I heard a distinct set of tones from the door chimes. I turned around, fully expecting to see Angie, but instead there was a woman with mousy brown hair who walked up to the counter to place an order. She was wearing a yellow beret, yellow t-shirt, a tattered jean jacket covered with patches with matching jean skirt and a worn-out pair of yellow high-top Chuck Taylors. If a picture was worth a thousand words, the dissertation in front of us screamed "Save the Planet", "Equal Rights" and "The Truth is Out There!". When she passed me to head to the register, I could see Wade's attention shift, and I couldn't help but listen in.

"I heard you have the best coffee in town?" She said. "Do you happen to have any farm direct coffee beans, dark roast perhaps? If so, which ones?"

Wade didn't respond. He simply stood there for a second with his mouth agape and measuring her up to see if she was for real or a figment of his imagination.

"Err … ummmm … Well, yes. … Yes, I do, in fact. I collect direct roasts from all over the world, but if you want something very unique, I'd recommend a special blend I personally use. It never fails to hit the spot."

"Sounds interesting," she said while reading his name tag. "Wade, is it?"

"Yep," he replied. "That's me. I'll call you … Phoenix."

Wade had already begun writing the name, when she reached out and touched his hand.

"You can call me, Maggie, if you'd like." The upbeat way she ended her comment caught my ear, as well as Wade's.

"Ok Marg-, err I mean Maggie. You got it. You know what. Consider this one on the house. If you don't like it, I'll let you buy the next one. In the meantime, why don't you go find a seat and we'll get this coffee out to you as soon as possible."

He scratched out the "Phoe-" and tried correcting it with "Mar-" before having to scratch that out and finally correctly writing "Maggie" on her cup. As she left the counter, I made some faces at him to try and get him to loosen up. *He was freaking out on the inside!* It was clear she was flirting with him, and he was into her, as well. His eyes followed her like a hawk all the way to a booth near the same corner where Angie and Tom's brother once sat. Chimes. Coffee. Booth. I could sense there was something special brewing in the air when Wade took off his apron and headed over to the booth to have a chat. He had come a long way since Rhonda, but thankfully he never lost that quirky Wade charm. Unfortunately, I couldn't hang back and be his silent wingman, I needed to get back upstairs for my own something special. Angie and I were six months pregnant with our first daughter, and she just texted me for a foot rub.

<< EOF

Afterword

There are times in life when we all ask ourselves questions that make absolutely no sense coming out of our own mouths. For me, in 2018, one such question was, "Why not write a full-length fiction novel?" I enjoy having a hyperactive and creative mind, and one of the few places it gets to run free without compromise is through writing. At no point during this consideration did I fully comprehend the time, commitment and patience that it would take to actually see this through to the end. When I first came up with the idea for this story, I originally thought it would be best served as a screenplay, something like an Empire Records tribute for the unsung nerd heroes of the nineties, but as the words came to paper, I found that my writing style worked best as a novel. Was it the right decision? I can't be sure, but I immensely enjoyed the memories it surfaced. Below are a few snapshots of inspiration from my life I used in the plot. I hope you enjoyed the story!

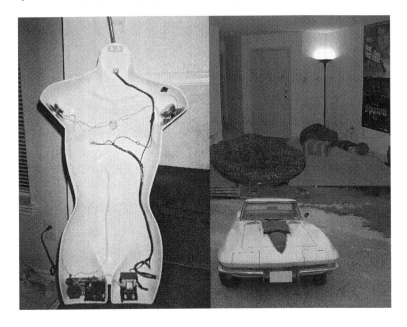

Thanks for reading,
RR

P.S. Don't fall for the #l4m3345t3r3gg ;)

fork this life

Volume One

An Internet revolution tech tribute

by: ryan rutan

https://www.forkthislife.com

Made in the USA
Middletown, DE
24 September 2022

10936549R00210